ALSO BY J.B. RIVARD

Handful of Air
Illusions of Magic: Love and Intrigue in 1933 Chicago
Illusions of Magic: The Movie (with Anya Carlson)
Low on Gas – High on Sky: Nick Mamer's 1929 Venture
Dangerous Parallel

DEAD
HEAT
to
DESTINY

THREE LIVES
AND A SPY

J.B. RIVARD

ISBN: 978-0-9968363-6-4 (Paperback)
ISBN: 978-0-9968363-7-1 (eBook)
Library of Congress Control Number: 2022918887

For information, write
Impressit Press
1452 S. Ellsworth Rd #3017
Mesa AZ 85209
U.S.A.

Design by Books Fluent, New Orleans LA 70117

For Anya

AUTHOR'S NOTE

In writing this book, I intended to supply the reader with a highly-realistic picture of the 1903-1917 time period. Thus many hours were consumed on historical research over the more than 500 days it took to complete the manuscript.

During that mostly WWI period, the navy of Germany was known as the Imperial German Navy (*Kaiserliche Marine*). Its officers were ranked by the titles in the Table below.[1]

IMPERIAL GERMAN NAVY	UNITED STATES NAVY
Admiral	Admiral
Vizeadmiral	Vice Admiral
Kontreadmiral	Rear Admiral
Kommodore	———
Kapitän zur See	Captain
Fregattenkapitän	———
Korvettenkapitän	Commander
Kapitänleutnant	Lt. Commander
Oberleutnant zur See	Lieutenant
———	Lieutenant, j.g. (junior grade)
Leutnant zur See	Ensign

from Messimer, Dwight R., *The Baltimore Sabotage Cell*, Naval Institute Press, Annapolis, MD, 2015, p.xiii

Referring to these ranks in the novel proved to be a serious dilemma, for several reasons:

1 Although the table compares ranks between navies, the comparison does not necessarily imply similar levels of responsibility.

First, the German titles are long and, in three ranks, include three words. Second, the relative ranking of the titles is not obvious from the names—it's not apparent that a Fregattenkapitän outranks a Korvettenkapitän.

Comparison with officer ranks in the U.S. Navy is not feasible because two German ranks, Fregattenkapitän and Kommodore, have no equivalents in the U.S. Navy.

Finally, translating the titles directly from German to English (Leutnant zur See = Lieutenant at Sea) provides no useful distinction.

To deal with this dilemma I chose to employ the German designations, often deleting the "zur See" as too confusing. As unsatisfactory as it is, I ask readers to avoid censuring me for employing this shortcut.

THE CHARACTERS

Lt. Pritchen *Canal Zone Police*
Gustave Bachmann *Admiral, Chief of Staff, German Navy*
Ludwig Geighoffer *Kapitän zur See, Admiral Bachmann's staff*
Hans Techel *U-boat designer*
Captain B. D. Foulois *commander, 1st Aero Squadron, U.S. Army*
Grover A. Magnin *president, I. Magnin Co.*
James Oakley *Master Signal Electrician, U.S. Army*
Heinrich von Kupwurzer *Kapitän zur See*
Max Krauss *Oberleutnant*
Ernestine *German citizen*
Emile Ligier *French soldier*
José Mendez Dias *Portuguese guide*
Kellog "Cog" McCrorie *U.S. Congressman*

1903

COLÓN, PANAMA

Rain pounded on the roof of the second-story room behind Avenida Herrera. Its windows were covered by shades. It was almost eight o'clock at night. A single flickering kerosene lamp dimly lit the fifteen men and their speaker.

Over the voice of the speaker, Bruno Ackermann heard the thump of boots on the outside stairs. He turned in his chair toward the door.

The standing guard, pistol in hand, cracked the door, peered down, shut it. "Not a threat. It is Fuentes—from the Railroad."

Fuentes stomped the mud from his boots before entering. He tossed his soaked jacket aside and swept water from his hair.

The speaker paused and said, "Perhaps Fuentes brings good news."

Fuentes smiled as he went to the front. "General Tobar and General Amaya are jailed."

Bruno joined the others in subdued chants of "Bravo" over the capture of the Columbians by the revolutionaries in Panama City.

"Their vessel—Cartagena—escaped home without saying 'adios.'"

The men laughed.

"Colonel Eliseo Torres is left charge of the five hundred sharpshooters. Torres threatened on the station, where the Americans stood for defense. But he accepted four hundred pieces of American twenty-dollar gold to leave on the Royal Mail Steam Packet *Orinoco*." He paused and squinted at the group. "They are now gone."

Bruno and the other men applauded.

Fuentes enjoyed the attention. "And now, an American gunboat has landed a squad of well-armed Marines."

Most of the men clapped.

The speaker said, "Thank you, Manuel, for your report. I believe it is now time for the Group Sixteen to disband. The provisional government of the Republic of the Isthmus, composed of José Augustin Arango, Federico Boyd, and Tomas Arias, is now installed in the city of Panama." He raised his hand. "All members in favor of disbanding the Sixteen Committee for a Free Panama, raise your hands."

Only Bruno Ackermann and a man called Rudolfo failed to raise their hands.

•   •   •

One at a time, the men slipped out the door, descended the stairs, and walked away. Only three carried rifles. Bruno Ackermann, unarmed, waited beneath the stairs until Rodolfo emerged.

Bruno addressed him in Spanish. "Rodolfo—I saw that you withheld your vote."

Rodolfo hunched against the rain and nodded.

Bruno walked beside him. "My objection convinced you?"

Rodolfo slowed and stopped near a puddle. "You speak with an accent."

Bruno smiled. "Yes. I came from Germany to work—at that time the French digging the canal needed mechanics. When the French quit digging the canal, I stayed, working the trains."

Despite the rain, Bruno saw Rodolfo's frown deepen as he spoke. "Our views are not popular."

"Yes. But our view is a matter of conscience."

"Will you continue working as a mechanic?"

Bruno shrugged. "I have bought a boat."

A slight smile crossed Rodolfo's face. "So you will leave."

"No, I will stay. Perhaps I will run a water taxi out of the harbor."

Rodolfo pursed his lips and began walking again. "The American military is here now." He spread his hands in a submissive gesture. "They are the price of our independence."

"No," Bruno said, raising his voice. "The isthmus must not be given to the Americans. An isthmus divided by an American canal is not an independent country."

"What can you do?"

Bruno clenched his fist within Rodolfo's view. "I am not certain how, but I will fight."

Rodolfo kicked a wet palm frond and turned toward Calle 5. "You will find yourself alone."

Bruno shook his head. "There must be others that feel as we do."

"Who?"

Bruno stopped. "I will find them."

Rodolfo continued on Calle 5, turning his head toward Bruno. "Good evening. I wish you a good result."

OSTENDE, BELGIUM

T he big open-wheeled race car roared by. A cloud of dust lingered, then settled to the road. The crowd on the roadside screamed in excitement. Marie Boudreau was so excited she failed to realize her frilly dress obscured the boy's view.

"Doggone!" Will Marra exclaimed in French, "I missed it!"

Mademoiselle Boudreau glanced at the ten-year-old. "I am sorry," she replied, "very sorry."

American Harlan Marra saw the disappointment on his son's face—disappointment after the long train ride from Paris to Ostende, Belgium to witness the event. In English, Harlan said to him, "I'll make it up to you, son." He grasped Marie's hand and said to Will, "Follow us." The adults turned away from the road. Harlan said, "Excuse me, excuse me," as he led the way through the crowd.

Will followed in the hollow behind his father, despite the attendees who seemed as unyielding as the trees. When they'd gained a few yards behind the road, the crowd thinned. Harlan turned to parallel the road and strode toward the end of the course. Will and Marie, clutching her dress, hurried to stay with him. Harlan spoke French to Marie. "This is not planned, but I must do it. We shall see if the French officials will honor my competency."

Marie said, "Please do as you think. I am sorry about—Will."

They approached an enclave fenced with temporary barriers. A mounted sign said "ACF - Automobile Club de France—Official Committee." Behind the sign, a half-dozen or more officials crowded around a table. They compared notes and talked to each other in excited tones.

Harlan spoke to the nearest man with a badge on his coat. "I am Harlan Marra. I've come here to Ostende with my son from Paris, to interview driver Arthur Duray."

The official touched his derby hat to Marie and frowned. "Monsieur Marra—I'm not aware . . ." He turned and gestured. "You can see that we are very busy here. The Committee—"

"I am well aware of the meritorious work of the Automobile Club of France. I assure you, my presence will offer no hindrance to the committee's work. I see Monsieur Duray, there behind the racing car, and it would be most felicitous of you—"

"This is most awkward." The official frowned. "I believe we have not received an official request—"

"Perhaps you've not seen my reports." Harlan handed the official a card. "Here is a credential. It is out of date, of course. I publish not only on sports, but on major news events, such as this attempt to break the international record. Please allow—"

Cheers and cries from the officials interrupted. "A miracle!" shouted an official. "It's a 1903 record—134 kilometers per hour!" The official in the derby turned to his colleague. "It is difficult to believe—it is beautiful." When he turned back to Harlan, he squinted at the card. "I'm unsure." He studied the card. "This says *Chicago Morning News*. That would be an American newspaper, am I correct?"

"Yes. My work is widely published, here in Belgium, in Britain and . . . although I now work independently from Paris. Surely it would be important for Mr. Duray to speak to me on the occasion of such a meritorious record for the ACF."

The official gave Harlan a serious look and returned the card. "It is indeed a grand achievement for the ACF. I suppose an interview would be appropriate—please wait here while I speak to Monsieur Duray."

When the official returned, he moved one of the wooden barriers aside. Marie stood aside as Harlan went to where Duray, a young man in wool sweater and cap, stood. Will followed his father, but lingered behind, near the leather-belted hood over the big car's engine compartment.

"Hello," Harlan said, speaking English. "I understand you are from the States. Am I right?"

Arthur Duray nodded. "Right. New York City."

"How would you describe your run?"

"The main thing is to get it into fourth gear."

As Harlan continued the interview, Will examined the rear of the car. "Father!" he said. "Look here!"

Harlan stepped toward his son, but continued to speak to Duray. "The machine—it's especially adjusted for speed?"

Arthur nodded. "It's the Gobron-Brillié racer."

Will pointed at the drive sprocket protruding from the side, and the chain that connected it with the sprocket on the car's rear axle. "Look, Father. This—this is just like my bicycle."

Harlan nodded at his son. "Somewhat more sturdy, I believe." He turned back to Duray. "A Gobron—what did you say?"

"I said it's a damn Gobron-Brillié racer."

Harlan smiled at Duray. "Now, Mr. Duray—" He glanced at Will, whose hand gripped an iron lever on the side of the car. "Don't touch the machine, son."

Will spoke to Duray, "What's this?"

Duray started to reply, "That's the gear-change—"

"Mr. Duray," Harlan said, "the official said you broke the record—130-some kilometers per hour. How fast would that be in miles per hour?"

"I—I'm not sure." Arthur frowned. "Better than eighty, I bet."

"It took a long distance to build the necessary speed for the flying kilometer. How far would you say that was?"

"The main thing is to get it into fourth gear. That's really it. You—"

"And you are—how old are you?"

"Twenty-one."

"Thank you, Mr. Duray, it's a pleasure to meet you. Perhaps we will see you in Paris, soon?"

"Yeah, sure. Who knows?"

CUXHAVEN, GERMANY

H elmuth flung his Flotilla hat to the settee and settled into his upholstered chair. He had heard quite enough on mines and the process for loading them.

"A busy day?" his wife Catherine said.

"Yes." He gazed around at the cramped interior before his eyes settled on Gregor. "Must he play so loud?"

"It is as written. In the Sonata, it is *fortissimo*. What was the subject today?"

"Hertz horns. Working to avoid the acid."

Catherine gazed at Gregor, hunched over the piano. "It's Beethoven—so beautiful." She reversed Helmuth's jumper and took the iron from the stove. As she pressed the arm of the uniform opposite the embroidery marking his rank, she smiled.

Helmuth knew it was Beethoven. *Loud* Beethoven. Like that intense man had played at the concert hall, what was his name? And for what? Gregor, now nearly sixteen, should be studying, not pounding the piano at maximum volume. "What about the tests?"

Catherine pressed on the iron. "The examinations?" A hiss rose from the damp cloth. Catherine lifted the iron. "They are still scheduled for July."

"You do not realize. They are invented to produce failure by the applicants. The Imperial Naval Academy prefers—"

Gregor stopped playing. "Father." He turned to face Helmuth. "Did I hear you say the Imperial Naval Academy?"

Gregor's mother held the hot iron in the air. "Now Gregor. We've discussed this. Your father wants a secure career for you. As an officer in the—"

"But Mother, we have talked about Martinus Sieveking . . ."

Helmuth held up his index finger. "Gregor, I paid a good price for those notes. You should be studying them. They will help pass the tests. Then, you can join the Academy and—"

"But Father, I would rather study with Herr Sieveking. He—"

"Helmuth . . ." Catherine set the iron on the stove. "Before Martinus Sieveking performed at the Hall, he consented to hear the best of Madame Combritte's students. Herr Sieveking says Gregor is exceptionally talented, and that he would consider tutoring him."

So it was Sieveking whose name he could not recall. Helmuth nodded to Catherine. "Herr Sieveking would exact a fee for each lesson, of course."

"Yes, though I did not inquire of the amount."

Helmuth noticed a smudge on one of his highly-polished boots. "Which I suppose would be justified by the fees Gregor's future performances in concert halls would earn."

Catherine crossed her arms. "That was not discussed."

"That is the analysis we should perform." Helmuth used his thumb to remove the smudge from his boot. "Meanwhile, it is important that Gregor gain as much advantage as possible in the upcoming examinations. Yes?"

Catherine nodded and returned to ironing Helmuth's uniform.

"Gregor, you should inquire, but I suspect there are pianos in the Academy halls which you might play." He glanced at his boot to ascertain the smudge was gone. "In any event, Kiel is a short train ride from Cuxhaven. You can visit whenever you are eligible for leave."

CHARLEROI, BELGIUM

Fifteen-year-old Adrienne Boch leaned into the tall window that fronted Boulevard Defontaine. Her breath formed a fogged patch on the cool glass. With the nail of an index finger, she instinctively drew a small image in the condensate—a curly-headed girl's face with tiny circles for eyes.

She laughed, then turned her attention to the street, three stories below, where she knew her father's cab would soon appear.

At the sound of a horse's hooves, she was eager with anticipation. The cab passed on. Where is he? She turned quickly and dashed to the rear room, where her mother was seated, reading. "Is it not time, Mother?"

Dominique Boch consulted her watch and nodded. "Perhaps there was a delay. Sometimes there is a clog—a snarl near the bank."

"Oh, I am so anxious. Papa promised he would bring me the latest—oh, *there*!" Adrienne rushed back to the window from which again came the sounds of a horse. She was in time to see her father step from a cab onto Rue Tumelaire. He strode past Maison Dorée toward the Boulevard entrance to their apartment and disappeared from sight. She turned and loped down the stairs as her mother called behind her, "Adrienne! Slow down, you'll—"

"Papa!" Adrienne cried, as Jean Boch set his valise upon the entrance bench. The maid closed the entrance door, excused herself, and left.

Adrienne smiled at her father. "I can't wait!"

"Yes, yes, I know, Daughter. It's not for the loved one, or the father, you can't wait." He removed his hat. "It is for the magazine." He smiled, tossed the straps of the valise aside, and withdrew a magazine. He held it over his head—too high for Adrienne to reach it. "What is the proper saying, Adrienne?"

"Thank you, Papa. I love you."

"That's better," he said, as his light coat slid off his shoulder. He handed Adrienne the May issue of Les Modes, and folded the coat over his arm. "Your mother, she's upstairs?"

"Oh look, Papa, at this gown! It is—" She glanced from the cover of Les Modes to her father. "Yes, Mother is upstairs—on the third."

Adrienne's father frowned at the cover. "That is extreme, don't you think?"

"The colors—aren't they glorious? This deep blue, accented by the dark flowers . . . and the light green."

"Oh, the colors. I was remarking on the rendering of the woman— her exaggerated . . ."

"That is the style, now, Papa. The latest trend."

"Mmm. You are so observant of the colors. Reminds me of your Aunt Anna."

"The painter. Yes. But I like to draw and color the fashions. And to sew, too."

"You have the Boch eye. I did not inherit any of the Boch artistic talent. My only talent is in the dreary business of banking. It is humbling. But Anna, she has a following—she is well-regarded."

"Aunt Anna favors the 'fevered' palette, like that Van Gogh painting she bought—La Vigne Rouge. I prefer the soft colors—like that sketch I showed you yesterday. Do you remember?"

Her father raised his eyebrows. "The lady's face and hat. Yes, that was beautifully done."

"Do you think, Papa, that when I finish school, I can attend art classes? I want to learn to draw these ladies, like this man deFeure. In Brussels, there is—"

"We shall see. Right now, I must see your mother." Jean Boch excused himself and headed toward the stairs.

Adrienne hurried to her favored pillowed bench in the corner of the library, where she quickly became lost in the pages of Les Modes.

1905

PARIS

Will Marra lingered, in cap and knickers, near Rue Cuvier & Quai Saint-Bernard.

Professor Jozef Gedlowski tapped his cane on the curb. "Come, come," he said in French. "I have been patient. It's time we resume your lessons."

Will turned from the iron railing and fixed his gaze on the sidewalk. He said in English, "But I am not prepared."

Jozef continued in English. "It is nevertheless essential. We shall today review." He began walking toward the cab stand. "You do remember adding and subtracting fractions—as you practiced the day before yesterday?"

Will pulled up his calf stocking and began walking next to Jozef. "The common denominator—yes, I remember."

"And how do we arrive at the common denominator?"

"Oh, I don't—it's about the common multiple—but I forget."

Jozef frowned at the eleven-year-old. "You are distracted today. What is the cause?"

"It might be the Zoo."

"I think not." Jozef slowed and stared at Will. "You will tell me."

"Yesterday, what a mess. I don't know why it happened."

Jozef stopped and nodded. "You know, precisely. What happened was a ceremony at your apartment. It was a ceremony during which your father was married to Mademoiselle Marie Boudreau. Why do you say it was 'a mess'?"

"Because. That's what it was."

"As I have stressed to you in elocution, Will, you must explain what you mean. Do not substitute a tautology. Explain what is in your mind."

"It was not, well, I don't see—Mademoiselle Boudreau is all right, but . . ."

"Go on," said Jozef.

"I can't explain. Everything is turning upside-down . . ."

"Perhaps . . ." Jozef resumed walking with Will at his side. "Perhaps I see what the problem is."

Later, as Will and the professor alighted from the cab near the flat, Jozef said, "Do you remember, in our literature studies, poems by the American, Henry Wadsworth Longfellow?"

"Yes, I remember the name Longfellow."

As they climbed the stairs, Jozef said, "I will find the volume. The poem begins, 'The day is cold, and dark, and dreary'—do you recall it?"

Will shook his head. "No."

When they entered the tutor's flat, Jozef went to the bookcase opposite the heavy sofa. Returning with a book he'd selected, he searched it. He sat down behind his desk and placed the open book on top. "Your father has told me about what happened before you came to Paris. You were in America, in Iowa. Your mother became very sick and died. That was approximately three years ago, if I am correct."

"Yes," Will said. "I was eight. I don't remember much, except we were all very sad. Me and my father. We were very sad."

"Your father loved your mother. As you did, too, I am sure."

Will nodded. "Uh-huh."

"And that has something to do with yesterday's event being a 'mess.' Am I correct?"

Will nodded, quickly stopped, but said nothing.

Jozef handed the volume to Will and said, "Read the last two lines of the poem."

"'Into each life some rain must fall—Some days must be dark and dreary.'"

"Now read the line before that."

Will glanced at Jozef, then read, "'Thy fate is the common fate of all.'"

Jozef took the book from Will's hands. "Longfellow tells us that sadness—even death—are our lot in life. That's the 'rain' he speaks of." He paused. "But you must also realize, as Longfellow says earlier in the poem, 'Behind the clouds is the sun, still shining.'"

Jozef Gedlowski smiled and looked kindly at Will. "Your father is trying to view the sun." He closed the book, rose from his desk, and returned the book to its bookcase. "And so must you."

KIEL, GERMANY

G regor stared at the envelope. Its address, in blue ink, was full of graceful scrolls, yet neatly ordered: "Midshipman Gregor Steiner, Kaiserliche Marine."

He plunged to his bunk and tore the envelope open. Inside were two sheets of thin paper. The letter was handwritten in French:

Dearest Cousin Gregor,

This morning Papa told me that you have now become a Midshipman in the German Navy. After only one year—that seems exceptional to me. After all, it is only a few years since you pushed my head under the Sea of the North. Do you remember at Ostende? It was summer. We stayed at Grandmother Anne Boch's, playing on the beach. I hope you remember, I was very angry. I coughed water and my hair was all in knots!

I am now fifteen. I am sewing all my own clothes. I have drawn a plan of my own. I cut the fabric and made a frock, what you call a Kittel. At Ostende this summer I will wear it, but you will not attend. You will also not see I am better at swimming. You will also miss that I am good at design and can sew accurately.

On Saturday last, our family attended a concert given by two men. The two men played two pianos at the same time. Mother said what they played is new music composed by the French composer

Claude Debussy. The music was called Prelude to the Afternoon of a Faun.

One man explained it as how Monsieur Debussy interpreted a poem by Stéphane Mallarmé. It is full of the most exotic sounds I have ever heard! It is not like Bach or those with which we are familiar. About halfway, the two pianos were playing two different compositions—so I thought.

I remember you play the piano very well. I hope you continue your studies. You may know this Prelude by Debussy, is that right?

When you sail in the Navy, will you be assigned to the sea for a long time?

I also write of sad news. I have learned that the master artist, Constantin Meunier, died this year in Ixelles. He was seventy-four. The paintings by Meunier are excellent. I saw his painting of Ophelia in Brussels. It is a dark painting, about one meter wide, with a heavy, clouded sky. This tragic woman from Shakespeare was very poignant to me. She is painted dead, drowned in a shallow bay, yet the fingers of her right hand curl in the exact portrait of agony!

Because of her age, Grandmother Anne Boch will not continue at Ostende. She says she must soon move to Brussels. It is thus probable you and I will not meet in Ostende again.

Please reply to my letter. I promise to answer your correspondence. I wish you an excellent career in the German Navy.

Your Cousin,
Adrienne Boch

CHARLEROI, BELGIUM

Less than two weeks after Adrienne posted her letter to Gregor, she received a reply. It came in a manila envelope with a Kaiserliche Marine label. Gregor's handwritten reply was in French:

Dear Cousin Adrienne,

Thank you for your post. I'm writing in French because I know you speak only a little German. My French is not excellent, although I will make a true effort. Please forgive any mistakes.

Yes, it is a long time since our days at the beach in Ostende. You have grown into a youthful lady, and I will turn eighteen after the end of the year. I share your sorrow that Grandmother Anne Boch is to stay no longer at Ostende. She radiated such a love that warmed us all. We owe to her for the wonderful memories of our childhood days.

My duties here at the Academy more than fill a day. There is much studying to pass the tests on science, seamanship, and gunnery. Learning the language of sea-going is also required. Team efforts are constant. There are daily gymnastics and drilling and marching and many rules to obey. We also swim, but not like at Ostende. Our superiors are experienced officers of the line. They are punctual to the minute, strict, but masterful. I am sure that what I am learning will contribute to my military career.

Your description of the two men playing two pianos took my interest. I have attended several piano recitals at home, but not witnessed this type (two pianos). My teacher had a folio for Prelude to the Afternoon of a Faun by Claude Debussy, but I understood it is a composition for orchestra. The piano is poorly suited to the reproduction of the sounds of an orchestra. After all, inside the piano there are only stretched metal strings being struck by hammers! This may explain why you did not respond to the latter half of the Prelude. I could show you on my piano in Cuxhaven, although I am seldom at home.

In the dank of evening with the wind-driven fog, I sometimes feel as an exile. It is then I miss the piano. Before I entered the Academy, I performed for Martinus Sieveking, a concert pianist. He said I was suited to the study of becoming a concert pianist, but this now seems impossible. Although my mother favored it, my father is correct, it might have been only a dead end.

There is a piano in the assembly room of the Academy here, but I do not have permission to use it. An old upright piano in the lobby here is poorly tuned, so I have only played it once. Also, my fellow midshipmen are not interested in serious music. They only know the common tunes.

You asked about my assignment to the sea. This past summer I served on board a torpedo boat in the Baltic for eight weeks. Although it was different, I realize I have much to learn before becoming an officer on a ship. These are complicated machines.

Your tale of the death of a master artist was news. I cannot draw anything, but I saw from drawings you made at Ostende that you have this ability. I did not know you were also skilled in sewing clothing. I know nothing about that, so you will need to tell me more about it.

You did not mention how your parents are in Charleroi. They have treated me very well; I recall receiving games and other objects at Christmas from Uncle Jean Boch and Aunt Dominique Boch.

It is very good receiving letters here at the Academy. In the future I am happy to receive more from you.

Your Cousin,
Gregor Steiner

1906

COLÓN, PANAMA

Bruno Ackermann made his way down Calle 7 to the wharf. Once over the timber rail and onto the pier, he threw an arm around a piling and slipped into the boat's stern. It was early, but he was already sweating.

Would the diesel start? He'd had some trouble, but thought he had it repaired. He set the controls, bent to his knees, and grasped the handle. He began cranking, first slowly, then faster. With the flywheel now spinning, he popped the lever. A loud thump sounded, black exhaust shot from the stack, and the small motor began a steady pom-pom-pom. He stood and grinned. He threw off the ropes from bow and stern and pushed the twenty-two-foot boat away from the dock.

It was ten minutes to nine when he arrived at the merchant ship anchored in Limon Bay. A seaman appeared at the rail, saw him, and disappeared from view. Bruno steadied the boat alongside the hull, from which a rope ladder hung.

Hand over hand, a man in a straw hat slowly descended the rope ladder. When his foot touched the wood, Bruno grasped the man's arm to help his transition to the tippy deck of Bruno's boat.

"Thank you," said the man in Spanish, regaining his balance and letting his hands droop. He had a straw beard, wore long trousers and a long-sleeved shirt with a tie. A valise with a long leather strap hung from his shoulder.

Bruno regarded the straw beard and small dark eyes. He urged his passenger to sit out of the sun under the rusted metal awning. As he pushed the boat away from the steel hull, Bruno asked in Spanish, "Where shall I take you?"

The passenger struggled to reply in Spanish. "Where is—what is the Spanish for it—ah, commerce?"

"Commerce?" Bruno recognized the man's accent. He grinned. "You speak German!"

The passenger's eyes went wide. He laughed, and Bruno laughed with him.

The passenger switched from Spanish to German. "I did not expect to speak my native language."

"You will find it rare. I came here while the French were still digging their canal. I spoke decent French. Gradually, I learned to speak adequate Spanish." Bruno shook his head. "Now, my German grows stale and awkward."

"Well!" The passenger smiled and offered his hand. "I am Herr Lindoch, from Berlin."

"I am Bruno Ackermann." The men shook hands. "Call me Bruno."

"Excellent," Lindoch said. "I wish to meet with the people who build the Canal."

"You will need to talk to the Americans. Colón is Panama," Bruno said. "I will take you to Cristóbal, which they now name 'Canal Zone.'"

Herr Lindoch sat on the bench in the deep shadow of the overhead metal. "I represent many companies, many businesses. I came here to the Republic to offer help to the engineers."

Bruno put the diesel motor in gear. "What kind?" The small motor chugged and the boat edged away from the side of the ship.

"Apparatus and machines. Steam shovels and rail wagons. Instruments for surveying. Also harnesses, cameras, and tools for machinists."

"I think I understand," Bruno said. "People in the Canal offices at Cristóbal will guide you." He turned the helm wheel and the boat rotated south. "I will stay at the dock until you return."

"What about the fee?" He placed his valise on his lap. "I may be busy for awhile."

"The fee is the same. I do not charge for time, only for distance traveled."

Lindoch appeared initially troubled by Bruno's reply. However, he cheerfully asked, "You are acquainted with some of the people in Cristóbal?"

"No. The French built Cristóbal on spoil. Now the Americans run it. Chief Engineer Wallace has left. His replacement is called John Frank Stevens. A certain William Gorgas issues sanitation rules. I do not know any of these men."

Herr Lindoch's eyes narrowed. He opened his valise and went through the papers inside until the boat arrived at the Cristóbal dock.

Bruno arrested the boat's progress and steadied it so Lindoch could alight. The German shook hands again with Bruno and said, "Farewell, until I see you again," before striding off toward one of the larger buildings. Bruno ducked under the metal roof and sat down.

When Herr Lindoch returned to the dock an hour and a half later, sweat stains marred his long-sleeved shirt. As he approached, he loosened his tie.

Bruno greeted him. "I trust you made suitable contacts there." He squinted at the sky. "I believe it will rain soon."

Herr Lindoch wiped his brow with a linen handkerchief. "Yes. It was useful. I think the Americans believe they have superior machinery and equipment. They perhaps do not realize the excellence of German machines or the superior quality of German instruments and optics."

Bruno clutched Lindoch's arm to aid his entry into the boat. "They believe in the superiority of all things American. It is not only their machinery. It is their methods, their rules, their ideas."

Herr Lindoch nodded. "I sensed that. They appeared not fully engaged in my presentations." He grinned. "Obviously, my English language is not perfect."

Bruno cranked the motor again. When it caught, he released the lines and cast the boat off. As he guided the boat toward the Bay, he saw that Lindoch was studying him.

Finally, Herr Lindoch spoke. "Has your experience with the Americans been satisfactory?"

"Cristóbal is always busy," Bruno said, giving the motor more throttle. "The factory producing coffins is very busy. They seldom keep to the demand."

"I have heard it is a sickness—yellow fever, is that correct?"

"That is but one of many, Herr Lindoch."

"What else—about Cristóbal?"

"I was young and enthusiastic—I thought working on the French canal would make a good life." As he guided the boat out into the Bay, Bruno shook his head. "But then the French left and there was no work. The ditches in Colón still ran with waste. No one cared—the stench was terrible. The men—those hired by the French and then let go—they turned to drink, they quarreled, they fought. Many people died as did their horses and other animals. Now there is work and the Americans run everything."

"The Americans are making improvements, are they not? They told me they are fighting the pests. They plan sewer projects and a supply of safe drinking water."

Bruno turned the wheel to correct its path to Lindoch's ship. "Yes, there are plans. Many poor laborers died awaiting their plans."

"You are not happy with the Americans." Herr Lindoch frowned. "Am I correct?"

"Herr Lindoch, the people for Panama Independence were dedicated. Many of us believed in a continuous Panama, a single country without interruption. I was one with them. The Americans brought their military, which prevented Columbia from halting the independence movement. The result is the Republic of Panama, divided in the middle by the Zone where only America rules."

"Your disillusion is with a divided Panama?"

Bruno nodded. "Panama is now second-class. As poor as ever."

"Your attitude is understandable. What would you say to working with me in the Etappendienst? It serves our country rather than

America, and I believe you would be an excellent man here in Panama. It could pay well. What do you think of that possibility?"

As the boat approached the ship, Bruno took it out of gear. "The Etappendienst? I have not heard of it. What is it exactly?"

"It is an arm of the government, although we do not acknowledge that. I serve the German Navy. We try to make certain that, regardless of where the ships of the High Fleet are in the world, they are assured of supplies, fuel, recreation—that their needs are met. Does this interest you?"

The boat bumped against the hull of the ship, and Bruno grasped one of the hanging ropes. "Perhaps. It interests me, but I would need to learn more—about the duties, and other things."

Herr Lindoch smiled. "Why don't you come aboard. You and I can sit together in my stateroom, perhaps enjoy a beer, and discuss the topic."

Bruno nodded in agreement. He secured the boat to the vessel and both men climbed the rope ladder.

1908

WILHELMSHAVEN, GERMANY

Although *Torpedoboot T.127* was in port, Gregor sat in the ward room reading his mail. The brown envelope was addressed to Fähnrich zur See Gregor Steiner at Naval Academy Kiel. The address had been crossed out. Inside was a letter from cousin Adrienne, hand-written in French. It bore the date 4 March 1908, although the present day was more than a month later.

Dearest Cousin Gregor,

It is uncertain this letter will reach you because I believe you are now assigned to a ship. It is certain Postbriefs are not delivered onto the sea!

I cannot write a long letter because I have classes today. I graduated secondary level in the autumn and I am living now in Brussels, where I attend the Académie Royale des Beaux-Arts. This prepares for my career in couture.

I study art. In the moment it is exclusively drawing. Many difficult hours are spent drawing with charcoal in the attempt to convey onto paper the proportions and form of statues made from plaster of Paris. The instructor is exacting, requiring extreme fidelity in the rendering. Pray that I become practiced enough to pass the examinations that will later allow me to advance to drawing from live models—real people!

I have here only a single room. In it is a small stove, a chair, a very small table, my bed, and one window.

It is cramped, but I have sewn by hand a nice curtain over the window, which improves the appearance.

Papa said you are now an officer. I have copied the rank as he wrote it, but I am unsure what it means. Can you tell me? Papa could not tell me the type of ship upon which you serve. Only that it is a vessel upon which you journey into the North Sea. I will anticipate more information from you about your duties and adventures.

When I have the leisure, I make sketches of dresses that I should like to see. If you could see them, you might understand my ideas. Today there is a new freedom to fashion called "Modernism." In particular, I view the designs by Paul Poiret of Paris as upsetting the old ways. The bright colors, clean lines, and simple shapes suggest a different future for dressmaking. Some of my friends at the Académie agree, although different ideas are not approved by Staff.

Last Tuesday I visited Grandmother Anne Boch at her small apartment here in Brussels. She sends along her best wishes to you in your Naval endeavors. I regret to say she does not move about without pain, but she says her doctor tells her it is not serious.

We now see a few of the new horseless carriages on the streets of Brussels. They emit loud noises and appear incompatible with normal taxis. How strange!

Your Cousin,
Adrienne Boch

PARIS

Following their visit to Marie's sister in Orleans, Harlan, Will, and Marie Marra left the great hall of the train station. Harlan, ahead of the porter carrying their luggage, strode toward the nearest hackney carriage.

"Look, Father!" Will said, pointing at the motorized taxi, its exhaust sputtering. "We can ride a taxi without a horse."

"Ah," Harlan said, glimpsing the strange, four-wheeled vehicle. He glanced at Marie, who was fanning against the August heat. She returned his glance absent a smile.

Harlan faced Will. "Perhaps we had better—"

Will grinned. "Please, Father."

"Yes, all right," Harlan said, altering his path. He began to speak English to Marie, caught himself, and said in French, "It *is* 1908, you know."

From his seat, the cabbie pointed, indicating to the porter where to stow the bags. Harlan tipped the porter, who hastened back inside Gare d'Orsay. The cabbie alighted beside his jittering machine and opened the door of the gleaming cabin.

Marie, with raised eyebrow, said, "There is room for three?"

"Yes, Madam." The cabbie gestured. "Three. You are all so svelte." He smiled and offered his gloved hand to assist her.

Marie smiled. Grasping the cabbie's hand, she lifted her long skirt a few inches, stepped onto the running board and into the cabin where she sank into the seat. Harlan followed.

Will stood, straining to glimpse the radiator emblem without touching the car. "It is a Richard," he exclaimed in French.

The cabbie, still holding the open door, said, "No. It is a Unic."

Harlan leaned out. "Come, Will, get in."

Will edged closer to the radiator. "Oh, I see now. But there is 'Georges Richard' 'round the top."

"He is the man who designed it," the cabbie said.

Harlan leaned farther out. "Will."

Will moved slowly to the cabin and climbed inside. As he passed the driver, he said, "Someone left a newspaper. What shall I—"

"One moment, Will," Harlan said. "The driver needs our destination." He spoke a number on Boulevard Montmartre.

The cabbie swung the door toward closure. "The paper is yours," he said to Will. He latched the door and seated himself behind the controls on the exposed front of the vehicle.

They began moving. Will said, "I wonder how fast this machine will go."

They turned at the Quai and Marie said, "It is very warm. The apartment will be uncomfortable."

Harlan nodded. "Yes. When we arrive, we must open windows and exhaust the heat."

Will unfurled the rolled newspaper and studied it. Abruptly, he thrust it toward his father. "Look! This is all about Wilbur Wright at Le Mans—!"

Harlan glanced at the picture of what looked to be two big wings and an astride man within a structure of sticks in the sky. He scanned a few sentences. "One minute forty-five seconds," he said, returning the paper to Will, "that will disconcert some of the skeptics."

"What news!" Will said, returning to read the report.

They crossed the Seine. Marie turned from looking through the window. "What is it all about?"

Harlan chuckled. "The American, Wilbur Wright, has demonstrated his flying machine for the French. His flight at Le Mans on the eighth was unexpectedly spectacular."

"Listen to this!" Will said, reading, "Ernest Archdeacon, founder of

Aéro-Club de France, who had attacked the Wright brothers' design, admitted, 'They are today hallowed in France.'"

Avoiding a slow carriage, the driver swerved to the left. The unexpected move flung Harlan against Marie. She uttered, "My God!"

Harlan smiled. "Pardon. We have a very vigorous navigator!"

Will continued reading.

At Place de l'Opéra, Marie pointed. "See the sign?"

"What?" Harlan said, "I am sorry, I missed it. What did—"

"It is the tenor. The tenor I told you about. A sign promoting his appearance."

"Yes, I recall." He scanned the path taken by the cabbie. "We must inquire about tickets."

When the taxi halted outside the apartment building, Will hopped to the sidewalk and stood by the shiny machine, admiring its appearance.

Harlan alighted and said to the cabbie, "I'm grateful you did not collide with that carriage." He withdrew money and paid the cabbie. "You may wish to reconsider your velocity until we Parisians—and the horses—become more accustomed to the speed of these vehicles."

Will grinned at the cabbie. "What is the power of the motor?"

The cabbie smiled. "Fourteen. Fourteen horsepower."

"Father and I witnessed the setting of the world speed record in—"

"Will," Harlan said, "please remove our luggage from the taxi. You can watch over it while Marie and I take the lift."

"Sure," Will said. He began transferring bags to the sidewalk.

The cabbie thanked Harlan for the tip, climbed onto his perch and, when Will had finished with the bags, drove away. Will stared after the machine until it was lost in the traffic.

Upstairs, Marie and Harlan entered the apartment. "Not bad," Harlan said.

Marie nodded. "Perhaps the maid aired it, knowing we were returning."

"Indeed," Harlan said as he turned toward the study. "And I can return to my work."

Will arrived carrying one of their bags. He deposited it on the floor and approached his parents near the doorway to the study. "I have been thinking, Father. Wilbur Wright is continuing to fly at Le Mans. He may stay there throughout the month of August. We could catch the train and—"

"You are perhaps forget, Will," Marie began in English, "your father faces a—" She looked from Will to Harlan. "How you say it?"

Harlan said, "Deadline." He paused and continued, "I realize you are keen to see the Wright Flyer, Will. But my publisher is also keen to receive my corrected galleys on the Offenbach biography in time for the Christmas releases."

"Maybe I could go alone . . ."

"No, no. That would not do," Harlan said. "I will not have a fourteen-year-old—"

"I'll be fifteen in a few months."

Harlan stroked his chin. "Let us see what develops. If my progress is good, we'll take a few days off and go to Le Mans."

•   •   •

Beads of sweat on a pink rim of flesh became visible as Jozef Gedlowski removed and refitted his straw hat to better block the sun. He consulted his watch. "The train from Paris arrived a half-hour after noon. It is now a quarter-hour past three. We have expended almost three hours in Le Mans waiting. The Members' Platform affords excellent viewing of the horse racing track, the surrounding trees, the four-legged tower. Have you become satiated?"

Will Marra frowned at his tutor. He replied in French, "What do you mean?"

"Are you yet regretting the journey, the heat, the unrelenting wait?"

Will squinted at the shed at the edge of the grass that supposedly housed Wilbur Wright. "No, but I do not understand the reason for it. What would cause so large a delay?"

Jozef gestured to his right, toward a spectator. "The gentleman over there in the white jacket and straw hat said yesterday's wait was four hours. With no reason forthcoming."

"There are hundreds of people waiting. They must know something. I don't want to give up our places."

Jozef nodded. "Very well. But I suspect we are the victims of an American sham. I fail to understand your zeal to view such a display. We French have aviators—Henri Farman, Louis Blériot . . ."

"It is Wilbur Wright, the American, demonstrating the Wright brothers' machine! The newspaper says it is spec—look! A man has appeared."

In the infield, a portly man in a suit with knickers and leggings spoke over the public speakers. "Ladies and gentlemen . . ." he began. The shouts and applause from the grandstand rendered his announcement inaudible.

A tall, thin man in a gray suit, wearing a stiff collar and tie, emerged from the shed. He wore a cap with a bill. He strode to the four-legged tower where he directed the crew. They hoisted its heavy weight to the top. When the weight was secured, the tall, thin man oversaw the attachment of the catapult's rope to the aeroplane.

After walking beside and inspecting the long, slim rail on the ground in front of the aeroplane, the tall man in the cap examined the two chain-driven propellers behind the aeroplane's wings. Afterward, he circled to the front, where he climbed between its wings. He sat on a thin pad, fingered the control levers, and positioned his feet astride the transverse bar, seemingly oblivious to the exuberant expectation of the spectators.

He turned the bill of his cap backward and adjusted something on the motor at his side. Satisfied that it was ready, he gestured to two men who stood behind the spindly craft. Each man went forward and grasped the outer half of a propeller with both hands. Coordinating their timing, the men spun the two propellers in opposite directions as vigorously as their arm strength allowed. After two tries, the motor roared to life, emitting a puff of blue smoke. The propellers spun rapidly and the starting men backed away.

A few shouts of encouragement echoed from youngsters who had climbed into the branches of the trees at the rear of the track.

The pilot waited a few seconds to allow the crew to scramble aside. With hands ready to grasp the control levers, he released the catapult restraint. The weight inside the four-legged tower plummeted down and thudded to earth, thrusting the aeroplane to quickly accelerate. Well before the aeroplane reached the end of the rail, it rose into the air.

"Look at that," cried Will. "It is instantly in the air—and gaining height!"

Wilbur Wright manipulated the aeroplane's controls. The craft tilted into a gentle left turn.

The crowd stomped, screamed, and shouted its approval.

Will Marra did a lighthearted jump. "Oh wow!" he said in English. "He's turning—it is going to pass directly over us!"

The aeroplane straightened about thirty feet in the air and swept directly above the grandstand, causing the spectators to stare skyward and gasp in complete wonder.

Will's eyes followed the craft as it tilted to the right. "He's going to turn back! He is returning!"

The aircraft completed a second half-circle, straightened, and began a slow descent.

"It's passing overhead!" Will said. "I can even see the pilot's face!"

The craft flew by with a steady drone, dropped lower, and glided to a halt on the infield grass, not far from where it had taken off. With a joyous roar, the crowd on the Members' Platform waved their hats, bonnets, and caps.

Wilbur Wright's entire flight, a figure eight in the air, took less than two minutes.

"Wonderful," cried Will Marra, squinting at his tutor to see his reaction. Jozef Gedlowski did not respond. He simply gazed at the infield, his face expressionless.

Wilbur Wright turned off the aeroplane's motor and rose from the machine. He did not look toward the crowd or the boys in the trees, despite their clamor. He grasped the bill of his cap and swung it to the front. He thrust his hands into his jacket pockets, sauntered to the shed, and went inside.

BRUSSELS, BELGIUM

I nvolved with her studies at the Académie in Brussels and convinced that her letter to Gregor was lost, Adrienne was surprised
to receive the post. It came in a manila envelope from Wilhelmshaven
and was dated nearly two months after she'd written to him.

> Dear Cousin Adrienne,
>
> Thank you for your post. It was delayed by my
> relocation and sea duty. I finally received it yesterday
> when we returned to port.
>
> Your Aunt Catherine wrote me of your move
> to Brussels to study at the Académie. I salute your
> achievement at the secondary level and your matric-
> ulation into such a distinguished institution.
>
> It must seem strange to be alone in the city of
> Brussels, although you are a very capable person
> and should be successful there in your studies. Your
> description of the difficulties in conveying the form
> of statuary on paper was compelling. I should never
> master that! And to accomplish it with charcoal must
> be impossible.
>
> You asked about my rank, Fähnrich zur See, which
> I believe to be similar to Ensign of the Vessel in the
> Belgian Navy. It is the most junior of officers. I am
> assigned to torpedo boat T.127, a two-funnel ship
> with about sixty men aboard. We port and coal out
> of Wilhelmshaven on Jade Bight. The port is close

to home (Cuxhaven), but lack of a long leave means I have had only a single visit. Mostly we are granted half-day or day-long leave of insufficient duration for travel home and return.

Orienting myself to a seaborne life has been without major difficulty. We venture at regular intervals onto the North Sea for training sorties. Head gales that sweep in from the west cause big waves and discomfort, yet I do not suffer the fate of several others (seasickness).

I am learning much about navigation, gunnery, and torpedoes as well as the routine of staying alert on watch for many hours.

Last month there was an inspection during the visit to port of Admiral Alfred Tirpitz. He spoke of our seagoing fleet as Risikoflotte—deterring attack—but also as earning respect for the Fatherland during peaceful times. He is a great man.

You write of fashions. I know nothing of Paul Poiret or the "Modernism" you describe, yet I agree that simple dresses are more appealing. It is unfortunate that staff at the Académie do not approve of your thinking.

Thank you for telling of Grandmother Boch, and her wishes for me. I too am sorry she suffers from the aches. These appear to be the trials of life!

Please continue to write to me. Not many friends can continue with me, due to the erratic postal service for the High Fleet—I hope you will try.

Your Cousin,
Gregor Steiner

COLÓN, PANAMA

H einrich Ackermann mounted the steps, paused to catch his breath, rapped his knuckles on the door.

It opened and Bruno Ackermann exclaimed in Spanish, "Father! I did not expect you." The son embraced his father.

Heinrich, with a grin, spoke German, "I came as soon as I could. There is a problem . . ."

"Please, Father," Bruno replied in German, "we must not—"

"But you do not understand—"

Bruno grasped his father's arm. In German, he said, "Father— come with me."

"What?"

Silently, with his father's arm firmly in his grip, Bruno guided the elder man down the steps to Calle 7 and across to Parque Sucre. With his father finally seated on one of the benches, he smiled. "You must understand. We do not speak German near my apartment." He gestured. "Out here, no one listens."

"I understand." Squinting at Bruno to shield his eyes from the sunshine, Heinrich said, "I forgot. It was the moment."

"Do not mind. It is forgiven."

Heinrich smiled at his son, wiped sweat from his brow. "You have grown chin whiskers, Bruno."

Bruno sat down beside his father. "It seems my mustache was lonely."

Heinrich chuckled. "It has been months since I have seen you. What is new?"

"There is much." Bruno glanced up at the sky. "Free Panama is no more. Cristóbal is now the Canal Zone. Construction of the Canal has brought so many workers, yet there are not enough houses. It is terrible."

"Yes. I hear the same in Paraíso." Heinrich stared at his son. "But I am curious about you."

Bruno laughed. "I am fine. I have a new boat. I am busier than ever."

"A new boat! You own it?"

Bruno raised his eyebrows. "Yes. I am grateful to Herr Lindoch. The position with Etappendienst is a big help."

Heinrich smiled. "They pay well?"

"Herr Lindoch says the Imperial Navy affirms my aid in assuring its Caribbean traffic of berths and coaling."

"Very good." Heinrich peered up and down Calle 7. "This is a nice neighborhood. The smell is not bad. A little run down, perhaps. Your apartment—it is comfortable?"

"It is comfortable. The rent is too high, but I am very lucky to have it."

"I understand," Heinrich said with dismay. "But I came to tell you—"

"And how is Mother?"

"Your mother is good. Growing older, I fear, like all of us."

"And what of the Telefunken utility?"

"The iron towers we installed near that abandoned French shanty are excellent. We send and receive wireless messages. Perhaps the Telefunken sound intensifier will help." Heinrich's face turned solemn. "But I must tell you why I came." He fumbled at his shirt pocket and withdrew a slip of paper. "Our operator, Jules, gave me this."

Bruno grinned. "Yes. I know Jules, the operator."

Heinrich lowered his voice and read from the paper. "The message says, 'Butterfly seeks fish at 13.33-87.85.' You know Butterfly."

"Yes," Bruno said, nodding. "It concerns our Butterfly—Fritz Joubert."

Heinrich handed the paper to his son. "It must have come from Nauen. I thought I should bring it to you at once."

"Thank you, Father."

"There is trouble, is there?"

"Before I get to that, you should know I received a letter from Fritz. It came just yesterday, by post. The postal service is so slow."

"I know."

"Fritz is accused of killing a man."

"But it is false, no?"

"I must tell you, Father. The agent position can be dangerous."

"You are always careful, are you not?"

"Certainly. Now I will tell you of Fritz's letter. He is in El Salvador, there among the campesinos. They work those big coffee farms around San Miguel. That is where he was charged."

Heinrich nodded.

"The dead man—his name is Estrada—was the landowners' proxy. Estrada was employed to keep order among the workers. He quelled their protests, using threats and abuse. Fritz says Estrada was a mean man. The campesinos hated him. An opportunity arose, and the campesinos knifed him."

"So why is Fritz accused?"

"Because he—" Bruno stared at a passing mule-drawn cart. Its driver stared at the two men. Bruno waved at the man, naked above the waist except for a large straw hat. "It seems," Bruno said, continuing, "Fritz was in a crowded bar where the knifing occurred. Following the knifing, the crowd scattered. Fritz lingered to summon medical help. But before help arrived Estrada died. The rural police came and Fritz became identified as the person responsible for the death."

"So Fritz is now in jail?"

Bruno smiled. "No, no. Not our Fritz. He gave the rural police—they call themselves part of the Army—the slip. Fritz's post said he was on his way to La Union, where a friend has a safe house." Bruno chuckled. "According to Fritz, the police are still searching for him around San Miguel."

"He is very clever, Fritz."

"Yes. But he is more than clever. I have not told you this before, but if I remember properly, in the early 1890s, Fritz's Boer father ran a trading house. While he was away on business his Dutch mother was engaged in bartering with a Zulu customer. When she would not meet the Zulu's asking price for goods the Zulu wanted to sell, he attacked her. Fritz grabbed the Zulu's spear and ran it through his stomach. He was at that time twelve years old."

Heinrich said, "So brave, for a mere boy." He pointed to the paper in Bruno's hand. "So what does this wireless message mean?"

Bruno paused as three children ran across Calle 7 and passed by them. "I think the message means he needs a rescue."

Heinrich frowned.

"The message means His Majesty's Etappendienst supports his rescue from latitude 13.33 North, longitude 87.85 West. I'll look those up, but those numbers likely identify the town of La Union in El Salvador."

"What will you do?"

"I will prepare a coded message for Jules to transmit. You can take it with you when you return. It will instruct our contact in Nicaragua to hire a boat to meet Fritz and ferry him across the Gulf of Fonseca to safety."

1910

BRUSSELS, BELGIUM

Having arrived in Brussels on the early train from Paris, Will Marra inquired of a fellow passenger who seemed to Will quite old. The man informed him where to catch the Exposition tram. "You will be viewing the locomotive at the Expo, of course," he said to the teen. "It is quite spectacular."

Will smiled. "Without question. I am breathless awaiting. And thank you for your helpful directions."

The 'old' man tipped his hat to the youngster and strode off.

A knot of enthused people was gathered at the junction. The trams, bright green with yellow striping, were aligned neatly along the track as people boarded. Will purchased a second-class ticket and boarded the compact No. 983 trolley. Within moments, the driver behind his glass signaled, and they were away, sparks buzzing from the overhead wire. They bumped across intersecting rails and curved along city streets as cabs darted, avoiding a collision.

At the grounds of the giant Exposition, the tram halted at the station on Avenue Émile De Mot. Will alighted and glanced up at the expansive terrace with its crowd of visitors. Beyond was the ornate Grand Palais, its whiteness seeming to stretch for half a mile. As he strode up the wide walkway to the terrace, he studied his foldout map.

On the terrace, he entered the tall archway on the left, which led to a long walk through the English Section and onto a long portal, open on one side. From there, he found his way into the Railways Equipment shed, lit by openings high in its steel-trussed roof. Below, gleaming on its own rails with its own tender, was the new steam locomotive.

Will consulted the description on the signboard. It said the designer of this 104-ton behemoth was Jean-Baptiste Flamme. The locomotive's power derived from its four cylinders driving six huge iron wheels. The sign claimed it "the most powerful locomotive in the world." Will wished somehow the motionless machine might have fire in its boiler, the hiss of steam from its steam dome, and grind forward, its cylinders pushing the great levers on its giant wheels round and round! He could almost feel cinders raining from its smoke! What exciting thoughts!

After saturating his mind with the mechanical details of the Flamme locomotive, he refreshed himself at one of the concessionaires' cafés. He then began retracing his arrival to the railways shed, lingering often to gaze at the latest designs of motorcars, lorries, and motorcycles.

In the Belgian Section, he was diverted by the sight of a young woman dressed in a puffed blouse and a fluted skirt. Such a narrow waist! She stood alone, her head held high, behind a surround. The surround featured scenes of the Académie Royale des Beaux-Arts,'École supérieure des Arts de la Ville de Bruxelles,' with messages extolling its virtues.

Will approached and gestured at the signs. "Mademoiselle. Are you an artist?"

"I am here to answer inquiries about the Académie."

Will saw that her dark curls danced lightly as she spoke. "So you are an employee?"

"No." Her eyes flashed a little. "At what level are you in your schooling?"

Will tried not to stare at the suppleness of her body. "I live in Paris where I have been tutored by Professor Jozef Gedlowski."

"If you were to apply at the Académie Royale des Beaux-Arts, you would have first to complete your secondary education. After that, you—and your family—would need to relocate to Brussels."

"I have surpassed all tests at the secondary level. I am presently undergoing examinations for entry into École Polytechnique—in Paris."

"I have heard of that," she said, smiling and cocking her arm with a hand on her hip. "And how old are you?"

Will smiled. "I am sixteen."

She raised an eyebrow. "That is very young for completing secondary level."

"My name is Will Marra. I study well. If you please, Mademoiselle, may I inquire your name?"

Adrienne lowered her eyebrows, uncocked her arm, and turned to face him. "You are quite audacious for a person of sixteen years."

Will smiled while swinging his hand and arm in a wide arc. "This is a beautiful fair. The exhibits are of the highest quality. But I should not want to return to Paris without the name of the Exposition's most charming attraction."

Adrienne's eyes widened. "You are . . . most kind." She turned her side toward Will and dropped her gaze. "My name is Adrienne." After returning her focus to him, she said, "Adrienne Boch."

Will nodded. "And you are neither an artist nor an employee." He gestured at the signage on the surround. "Yet you represent the Académie Royale des Beaux-Arts . . . ?"

"I am a second-year student at the Académie."

"But you deny being an artist." Will frowned. "I will admit, that has me confused."

Adrienne laughed. She laughed more heartily when Will joined in the laughter. "There is reason," she said, "it is too difficult to explain."

Will raised both hands with open palms. "If you please, Mademoiselle Boch . . ."

A young man with a dark goatee approached and nodded to Adrienne.

Adrienne said to Will, "It would take much too much time to explain."

The goateed man said to Adrienne, "I am Louis Perrot."

"Oh," Adrienne said, swinging open the gate in the surround, "very well." She stepped out of the surround and Louis Perrot stepped in.

Will came toward Adrienne. "Aha! Your replacement is here, so now you have time to explain."

Adrienne looked beyond Will and began walking toward the entrance to the Exposition. "No. I must catch the tram."

"Please, Mademoiselle." Will strode quickly to her side. "I want to understand . . ."

Adrienne frowned. "If you must." She slowed a little. "My studies at the Académie have taught me how to render the human body. But my dedication is to couture."

"Couture," Will said. "What is that . . . garments? Fashions?"

"In the autumn I will join a house of haute couture—the house of Latir." She resumed her quick pace, her fluted skirt swaying gracefully.

Will matched her pace. "You will draw for this fashion house—this Maison Latir?"

Adrienne chuckled. "No, no. Not to start. As an apprentice, I will likely sew."

"Fascinating." Will glanced ahead at the archway that led to the terrace. "Unless you have an engagement, please join me at one of the concessionaires. You can then tell me about—"

"You are indeed audacious, Monsieur Marra. You should bestow your boldness upon someone your own age."

"But how else shall I learn of haute couture, of Maison Latir, and—"

"Please," Adrienne said, as they passed under the archway into the flooding sunshine, "you must excuse me. I must catch my tram."

"All right." Will slowed and called after her. "But where is Maison Latir?"

As Adrienne swept across the terrace toward the tram station, she smiled and replied over her shoulder. "In Paris, of course."

1911

ON BOARD SMS BERLIN

On June 27, 1911, Leutnant zur See[1] Gregor Steiner returned to the SMS Berlin, docked at Emden. He carried a brown envelope. After climbing the gangway and checking with the deck officer, he made his way forward and up a deck. He knocked on the Kapitän's cabin door and identified himself. Cleared, he entered and saluted.

Fregattenkapitän Heinrich Lohlein was seated at his desk. He stuck a finger onto the page of the book he was reading. "What is it, Herr Steiner?"

"Orders, my Kapitän. They come from the dispatch office."

Lohlein placed the open pages face down and took the envelope from Steiner. "Hmm," he said as he fingered the crown in the wax seal. He broke the seal and read the communique. "Very well, Herr Steiner. Berlin has spoken. Return to your station."

Gregor saluted and retreated. As he headed aft, the harsh din of coal being dumped into the ship's bunkers engulfed him. Why were the orders he'd delivered sealed with wax? The light cruiser SMS Berlin had yesterday returned from training exercises in the North Sea, and he knew of no threat or urgency. If the orders were to leave Emden, the wax seal indicated something more serious than a training sortie.

He entered the wireless room, receiving section. The duty petty officer lifted the earpieces of his bulky headset from his head and saluted.

"Never mind, Lindner. Where are we on coaling? Have you heard?"

"Shy two hundred tons," Lindner said. "That's what Hermann told me an hour ago. Would be less now."

"Looks like that racket will continue into the night. Any messages?"

1 See Author's Note

"Nothing for us. Lots of overlap on the six-hundred-meter wave. Nauen comes in loud and clear here, but there is no—"

A loud announcement from the speaker interrupted. "Attention! These are Kapitän's orders. All leaves are cancelled. All officers and enlisted ashore are ordered to the ship. Navigation, report to the Kapitän. All hands prepare to weigh at six o'clock tomorrow morning. That is all."

"Bah," Lindner said, wrinkling his nose and returning the earpieces to his ears. "We got no leave at all."

This reminded Gregor of something. "Mind your watch, Lindner. I will return." He went to the quarterdeck, spoke to the deck officer, then bounded off the ship and headed down the harborside road.

At Die Kiste on the street Nesserlander, he found Enders. "Bad news," he said with a smile.

"No," said his friend Karl Enders, sitting at a table with two civilians. "We are barely in port."

"Perhaps it is something . . ." Gregor said with a sly smile.

"Really?"

"I delivered an envelope to the commander. It was sealed with official wax."

Karl grinned. "Oh! You have me there. I'll be along as soon as I finish this beer."

•   •   •

Gregor watched wisps of low fog slip by as the 3,200-ton cruiser advanced slowly toward the sea on the River Ems. Despite the noise of coaling into the night, he had completed four or five hours of sleep before the early morning start.

He glanced up and saw Enders leaning against one of the forecastle gun turrets. Gregor grinned. Enders saw Gregor and shook his head soberly. The previous night they had endlessly discussed the possible destination of SMS Berlin. "The Mediterranean, to flash the Kaiser's ensign," Gregor said. "Southwest Africa, to visit the colonies," Karl said. Each man felt sure he would win the wager.

The ship turned southwest and around midnight passed through the Straits of Dover.

Forty-eight hours later the Berlin passed the winking lights of Lisbon.

The next morning, as the two leutnants drank coffee in the wardroom, Karl Enders said to Gregor, "We passed Lisbon last night and did not turn toward Gibraltar. Daylight reveals what has to be Morocco off the port bow." He smiled. "You may as well pay up."

Gregor squinted through the porthole glass. "It's difficult for me to understand why Commander Lohlein does not announce our destination."

"Perhaps the sealed orders you delivered in Emden require him to keep the destination secret."

Gregor nodded. "That is probable. Although any secret is assuredly secure out here, many kilometers from any coast."

Karl chuckled. "Exactly!" The two men sipped more of the hot brew. Karl said, "It seems we are steaming southwest. In a few more days, we'll clear the bulge of West Africa. Most likely we will then turn toward the colonies. I think I have the better of you."

"It doesn't look good," Gregor said. "But suppose we don't go that far. Suppose we stop at the Canary Islands. What then?"

"Why should we go to the Canaries? I believe it is a colony of Spain. And we have many tons of coal remaining."

The next morning, with most of the ship's officers at breakfast at the officer's mess, the commander spoke: "Gentlemen. I know you are curious regarding our mission and destination. Unfortunately, I cannot advise you on the mission." He glanced around, fingering his mustache. "Berlin has simply directed us to Agadir, Morocco, to join SMS Panther . . ."

The navigation officer said, "Please excuse, Kapitän, but Panther?"

Several of the dozen officers present murmured quizzically.

"SMS Panther is an Imperial Navy gunboat," Lohlein said. "It is quite a small ship, lightly armed, and already stationed in the harbor at Agadir."

Another officer spoke. "Sir, I do not know Agadir, Morocco. It is a coastal town?"

"Yes," Lohlein said. "It is almost the southernmost port on the coast of Morocco." He nodded to the navigation officer. "What else, Herr Weissmann?"

The navigation officer chuckled. "I cannot say much, except the harbor at Agadir is fine. Plenty of depth, and naturally sheltered. Tidal range, about two meters. Wave action should be minimal, though there is no jetty. Port facilities are most likely primitive."

"Thank you, Weissmann. Other questions?" No one spoke, so Lohlein continued. "Herr Steiner, I have prepared a message for Berlin seeking information on the mission. Obtain, if possible, a relay to Nauen."

Gregor nodded. "Aye, sir. Maybe I can locate a merchant ship in the Mediterranean with Telefunken capability."

Weissmann said, "Why is a merchant ship needed, Herr Steiner?"

"Our daytime range will not reach Germany." Gregor paused. "And wireless stations in France refuse to relay German messages."

Weissmann frowned. "How corrupt."

In a low voice, someone said, "Damned Frenchmen!"

"Otherwise, gentlemen," Lohlein said, "we will post watches for maximum security during our approach and anchoring. That is all."

•   •   •

Lindner removed his headset. "There are many messages," he said, "but no replies."

Gregor plopped into the extra chair. "Our request for a relay was broadcast on . . . ?"

"The six-hundred-meter wave, at 1100 hours—as soon as we were anchored."

"We have not reached any possible relay source?"

"Many of the messages I hear are foreign—French or Darija—probably coming from only a few hundred kilometers' distance."

Wrinkles forming on his forehead, Gregor gazed at the overhead. "Your evaluation is that our signal is short of the Mediterranean?"

"Yes. When the sun sets we may gain more distance."

Gregor bounced to his feet. "We need more power. But there is little we can do right now. Keep listening." After Lindner clamped his headset back on, Gregor left and joined Karl Enders outside at the rail.

Gregor looked off toward the docked gunboat. "Panther is not especially tidy."

Karl looked at Gregor. "You refer, I surmise, to the laundry drying on its rail."

"At least that."

"Agadir is not precisely scenic, either," Karl said, peering now at the shore. "Unpainted buildings with few windows facing narrow passages. Ancient wooden boats chained to rotting wharfs. Black men with white head coverings in loose gowns and sandals moving slowly, if at all."

"That's a good summary," Gregor said.

"Not a single woman in sight."

"You are very observant."

"Gunnery is my expertise, not reporting. What in heaven's name are we doing here?"

●   ●   ●

Gregor stood at attention in the Kapitän's cabin.

"Be at ease," the commander said. "I hope you bring good news."

"The Berlin's wireless crew was successful during the night. Our signal reached the Mediterranean. We were fortunate that the ship receiving our messages could serve as a relay." Gregor handed Lohlein a folded paper. "Here is the reply to your message, received only minutes ago, relayed by that ship."

Lohlein unfolded the paper and held it between his hands. "This is the complete message?"

"Yes, sir."

Lohlein frowned, placed the paper on his desk, and smoothed it. He glanced at the ship's clock on the bulkhead, then back at the paper. "You believe this is Berlin's reply to my message?"

"I believe it to be the true reply because it was relayed by our own SMS Schwalbe!"

"The Schwalbe. Ahh, that is a familiar vessel, but . . ." He reached for something on the bookshelf to his left.

Gregor hurried to display his knowledge. "SMS Schwalbe is the fleet's wireless training ship. It has the most dependable Telefunken apparatus available. And you doubtless are aware of the staff's expertise."

"Yes, yes. There is little doubt," Lohlein said, withdrawing his hand. "But this message . . . 'Standby' . . . One word is hardly the description of a mission."

"I understand, sir. However, I personally verified that all cipher authentications were present with the message."

Lohlein shook his head in dismay. He glanced at Gregor. "Good work, Steiner . . ."

Gregor smiled. "If I may, sir."

"Go on."

"I took account of several other messages that were passed on by the telegrapher on Schwalbe."

"Go on."

"Berlin reported France has dispatched twenty thousand soldiers to Morocco. The government of France claimed this was to protect foreign residents in Morocco from attack by rebels opposed to Morocco's Sultan, Moulai Hafid."

Lohlein nodded.

"In response to this French action, our foreign minister sent SMS Panther to Agadir with the mission to rescue a German mining engineer named Hermann Wilberg—"

Lohlein picked up his pen and wrote the surname, "Wilberg," on his blotter.

"—and the minister also sent the Berlin to support the Panther."

Lohlein nodded. "I see. A reasonable follow-on."

"But in answer to my direct question, the telegrapher said the German mining engineer Wilberg is not here—in Morocco."

"What?"

"Berlin has reported that, due to unfortunate travel delays, Herr Wilberg has not yet arrived in Morocco."

"So the Imperial Navy is sent to rescue a man who is not here?"

Gregor paused. "Most likely that is why Berlin's order reads: 'Standby.'"

PARIS

It was dusk, the second time Will Marra had observed workers leaving the Maison. The unsuccessful first time, he had arrived in the 9th Arrondissement as the employees were dispersing. This time he was earlier by a quarter-hour.

He hoped to remain unnoticed, so he lingered on the pavement of Rue Taitbout, avoiding traffic but maintaining a careful watch. He stared at each person as they exited Maison Latir, thinking he would have no difficulty in recognition, despite the failing light.

When a well-dressed brunette fitting a wide-brimmed hat to her head appeared, he approached and tipped his hat. "I hope this will be all right," he began. "I think you . . ." Only then did he realize the woman was not Adrienne Boch.

The brunette gave him a quizzical look and halted next to the streetlamp. "You have taken me for someone else."

"Indeed I have. I apologize." He thought he might be blushing. "But perhaps you could help me . . ."

She smiled. "That is impossible . . ." She began walking south. "I must meet my uncle."

"It's not that, at all." Will gestured toward the doorway from which she had exited. "I know someone here. Her name is Adrienne Boch. Do you—"

"Really?" She stopped. "You are mistaken. Adrienne is no longer at Maison Latir."

"Oh, no." Will's heart sank. "Do you know where she is?"

"I am not sure. I believe it is one of the houses on Rue de la Paix."

"Thank you, Mademoiselle." Will tipped his hat again. "I apologize for any delay I have caused."

He halted while the brunette continued on toward Boulevard Haussmann. When she was some distance ahead, he followed without urgency to the Boulevard, his eyes downcast.

The next day he appeared earlier still, this time on Rue de la Paix. No boulevard trees here, the narrow pavement looking narrower for its jam of people, cabs, and creaking carriages.

He remembered when he was fifteen, his father had squired him to a glossy shop here on Rue de la Paix for a suit, all itchy of worsted wool, when there were no more than a few dozen people present. Now you had to pick your way to avoid bumping noses to shoulders. Were Adrienne Boch here, he'd need more than luck to find her.

Treat this, he told himself, as a problem in logic, exactly as taught by his professor at École Polytechnique: Clients leaving a house of haute couture were likely to exit wearing hats, whereas workers leaving employment would exit without hats. To increase the probability of sighting Adrienne, he should disregard the hatted crowds and scan only for streams of hatless heads entering the sidewalk.

He told himself Rue number 7 provided a test. He had gained a place on the curb less than ten yards from Maison Worth's double doors.

One of the doors swung open and workers poured out. Will scanned the stream of bobbing heads, mostly women with hair piled high, but could identify no brunette as Adrienne.

A short time later, the doors of Rue number 3 opened. With even less distance to the doors of Maison Paquin, Will quickly identified Adrienne as the third person passing out the opening. She carried a bag and her hat, which she quickly donned.

Will made his way to her. "Mademoiselle Boch—I hope this is all right, I came to see you."

Adrienne's eyes went wide. She slowed while scanning Will's face. "What? I don't—"

"Please—will you pause for a minute?" A warm feeling surged

within him.

"Oh," she said, without smiling. "It's *you*." She nodded to the woman next to her, who returned her nod. Adrienne went to the curb and halted. "You are that fellow in Brussels—"

"Yes," Will said, smiling. "We chatted in Brussels, at the Exposition. May I walk with you?"

Adrienne took a step and stopped. She raised her hand, palm toward Will. Her eyes blazed. "Wait. How did you find me?"

"My inquiries led from Maison Latir to this location." He stared at the slender face framed in dark curls as a starving man gapes at bread leaving an oven.

Adrienne began walking. "I do not approve."

The smile left Will's face. "You are married, are . . . ?"

"No." She looked at him without expression, but continued walking. "Nevertheless, I disapprove."

Walking alongside her, Will said, "A great philosopher said avoiding disapproval is easy—say nothing, do nothing, be nothing." He smiled at her. "But that is not me."

"You are a very strange person." She increased her pace. "I do not understand you."

"Maybe, if you allow me to continue with you, you will discover the basis for your disapproval."

Adrienne laughed. Will grinned.

Silently, the two of them weaved around a kiosk, she with her gaze directed forward, he with his eyes on her. After a short time, she glanced at Will. "I don't remember—what is your name?"

He told her. She said, "Oh, yes, now I remember. You completed your secondary education—at age sixteen. With a tutor . . ."

"Yes. Professor Gedlowski, of the University. But please tell me why you are no longer at Maison Latir."

"Why?"

Will grinned. "Because I want to know more about you—and about couture."

They came to Place Vendôme and she slowed. "I must catch a taxi-cab here," she said.

Will faced her. "If you leave now, how will I contact you?"

"If I fail to give you a means, that will discourage you."

He smiled, but shook his head indicating "no."

"Why must you pursue me? I am very busy at Paquin."

"Your fidelity is it, exactly. I seek to hear—about you, Latir, couture. And now, Paquin."

Adrienne glanced about for an unengaged cab. "You are . . . oh, I don't know!"

"I'll hail you a cab." He dashed to a nearby slow-moving carriage and accosted the driver. "Are you engaged?" The driver reined in the horse. Will beckoned to Adrienne and she scurried to the cab. As she boarded, she smiled. "Thank you, Monsieur Marra. That was very nice."

"You are most welcome. How will I—"

She settled into the seat. "Goodbye," she said, and called up to the driver. "Drive on, please." The driver urged the carriage on, toward the river.

●   ●   ●

Adrienne strode smartly toward Place Vendôme. "Monsieur Marra. You simply 'happened by Maison Paquin.' Is that what you wish me to think?"

Will stepped quickly to her side to maintain the pace. "Not at all. I came at midday planning for the possibility of lunch. What is your destination?"

"My intent is to walk. No lunch will be taken." She stepped from the curb of Rue de la Paix, wary of passing cabs and horses. After regaining the sidewalk opposite, she frowned at Will. "Why do you pursue me on this street of commerce?"

"As I said previously, because I want to know more about you—and about couture." He followed as she aimed for the east side of Place Vendôme. "You have not said why you left the employ of Maison Latir . . ."

"It was unsatisfactory."

"Of course." Will smiled at Adrienne. "But your métier there was very short."

"My design was stolen."

At Rue St. Honoré, Will slowed. "That is a serious charge."

Adrienne continued on to St. Honoré. "M. Latir was designing a walking suit. The suit jacket was pleasing and hung well. But he could not decide the sleeve."

Will hurried to Adrienne's side. "I don't understand. Do you mean—"

"Termination of the sleeve is exceedingly important, how to end it. The sleeve leads to the hands, the second-most expressive feature of the feminine body."

"Oh. And the first . . . ?"

Adrienne stared wide-eyed at Will and laughed. "The face, of course. The eyes, the expression . . ."

They came to the Seine, and crossed on Pont Royal.

"The face, of course," Will said. "And yours is so beautiful."

Adrienne did not acknowledge, but kept walking.

They walked off the bridge entering the Left Bank. Will said, "So what happened?"

"I knew exactly how to end it, in a tapered slit with the decorative fabric slightly exposed."

"I'm sorry. I do not understand."

"You will not understand because it is couture, it is visual. If you were there at that moment, you would have seen me folding the suit fabric in—oh, it is useless to explain." Adrienne led onto Rue du Bac and across Boulevard St. Germain. "I do not know why I am telling you this. It is not your business."

Will said, "When we met in Brussels a year ago, you said to me, 'My dedication is to couture.' That makes it important."

Adrienne glanced at him. Her face softened. "You have a good memory."

"As I see it," Will continued, "you left Maison Latir because of the sleeve—is that right? The—the 'termination,' as you put it?"

Adrienne pursed her lips and said not another word as she guided herself skillfully between carts, carriages, and omnibuses across several more streets. They came to the building named Le Bon Marché, and Adrienne entered. Awkwardly, Will followed her through the aisles of goods until they came to women's fashions. Adrienne slowed, glanced around, and approached a manikin in a blue serge suit priced at 165 francs.

Adrienne grasped its sleeve. "This is ready-to-wear, but it will demonstrate what I mean. Instead of this simple braided trim here, my design was of a multiple, angled slit, exposing at the same time less than two centimeters"—she placed two fingers across the braid—"of contrasting fabric, the same fabric as is featured on the front of the jacket. It was unique and it was stunning. Everyone present exclaimed, 'Oh là là.'"

Adrienne dropped the sleeve. "M. Latir went on to produce the walking suit, with that exact sleeve. Each sold for ten times this price and more." She began to walk away. "But nothing was said. M. Latir did not acknowledge me, my contribution."

"That was rudely unfair," Will said. "Did you complain?"

"Oh, Will Marra! You are too fresh. You will never understand." With eyes glistening, Adrienne turned and swept from the aisle and after, from the store. Will followed.

For several blocks on the return toward Rue de la Paix, Will walked by Adrienne's side. Neither spoke.

At last Adrienne paused and said, "What is your plan, Will Marra? What will you do with your life?"

"That's easy," he said, in a light spirit. "I will fly."

She squinted at him. "Fly? You mean—"

"Yes. Fly like a bird. Once my studies at École Polytechnique are complete."

She stared forward, as if seeking her way on a darkened street. "Aviation? That is madness. You will be killed."

Will grinned at her. "The brothers Wright are still alive. After hundreds of flights—"

"But why would you—"

"Three years ago . . ." he began as they halted for the traffic at Boulevard St. Germain. "In nought-eight I was at Le Mans, west of here. Wilbur Wright—the inventor—flew a perfect figure eight over my head in an amazing aeroplane. It flew like a bird—so smooth, so glorious. It was the most—"

"Madness, I say."

"Your dedication to couture is not madness."

"It does not risk my life."

Will's face turned grim. "Only that your creation was stolen from you."

Adrienne went silent as they entered Pont Royal. She slowed, then strolled to the parapet and stopped. Will joined her at the parapet.

Gazing at the flow of the Seine with her hands caressing the stones, Adrienne said, "You are so much younger than I, yet you do not give way. What causes you to be so persistent?"

"Why is our age important?" Will placed his right hand softly on her left hand. "Over the past half-hour we shared thoughts—and life—and walked together. Was it all meaningless?"

"No. It was not meaningless." She withdrew her hand from under his. "But I must now return to Maison Paquin."

As they exited the bridge, Will said, "In the future, you would find it less awkward if I could find you on a street less public than the one fronting Maison Paquin."

Adrienne chuckled. "You *are* persistent."

Will grinned at her. "What do you say?"

"I do not wish to encourage you, Monsieur Marra. But I will think of some sort of accommodation."

1912

WILHELMSHAVEN, GERMANY

G regor entered the building, then the office of the commander. He saluted.

"Be at ease, Herr Steiner."

Gregor relaxed slightly, but remained standing.

"I came as quickly as I was able," Gregor said, glancing at the clock. It registered quarter-past-nine.

"I have good news, Steiner."

Gregor breathed easier. "Thank you, sir." He noticed snowflakes collecting on the branches outside the window.

"Your performance on board SMS Berlin has earned you holiday leave."

"Yes, sir," Gregor said, smiling. "Visiting my family for Christmas will be most enjoyable."

"You may depart tomorrow and return upon the New Year, 1913."

Gregor tried to suppress his surprise. "That is exceedingly generous..."

The commander nodded. "There is but a small requirement. It is my understanding you perform the classics well on the pianoforte. Is that correct?"

"Prior to my naval career, I played well enough. But that was—"

"I am informed your performance at a recent event left those in attendance widely impressed."

Gregor smiled shyly. "I did play some Brahms at a birthday fête—"

"I've received a request. The staff of the Chief of the Naval Cabinet has asked that you play the pianoforte this afternoon at the Stadtschloss."

"The staff of—the admiral . . . ?"

"It seems a high-level meeting has been called for 1100 hours. It will be followed by refreshments in the grand hall—with music."

"But respectfully . . . my lack of practice limits my—"

"I appreciate that, Steiner. But the short notice leaves me no choice." He smiled. "Do your best, we will be proud of you."

●   ●   ●

A line of uniformed servants preceded Gregor into the great hall. They carried platters of table settings, goblets and china, food and drink, all of which was soon arranged upon the linen-covered tables.

The grand piano featured carved and gilded elaborations facing the keys. Gregor sat rigid on its bench in his dress uniform until told he should begin. He played a Brahms Intermezzo. As he continued with works he knew by memory, the principals and their staffs arrived.

Admiral Georg von Müller led his entourage, followed by Admiral August von Heeringen, and then General Helmuth von Moltke. Once they were seated, Kaiser Wilhelm II in his formal attire strode the aisle and took his place at the head table. The room filled with the babble of talk and laughter mixed with the clink of silver. Gregor played on, glancing furtively at the splendor.

A few of von Heeringen's staff were seated near the grand piano. As Gregor played some of the many arpeggios, he overheard fragments of their conversations.

At one point, a Kapitän zur See leaned across the table, saying, "The Reichstag speech by the Chancellor did not settle well . . ." A high-ranked officer on the opposite side nodded.

"Note the absence of Tirpitz," one smirking officer said.

"He may not have been invited," a Kapitänleutnant across from him said, grinning. "Although I do agree with the widening of the Kiel Canal . . ."

"His Majesty agrees with Herr General Moltke that war cannot be avoided . . ." said a different Kapitän zur See.

"Herr General Moltke took not kindly to Tirpitz's advocacy for delay 'of the great fight' . . ." the Kapitänleutnant said, "despite His Majesty's reluctant 'yes' . . ."

Gregor was so stunned by the snippets of talk, the tempo of his play slowed.

One of the nearby officers swung around to stare at Gregor.

Gregor immediately resumed the correct tempo. Despite an increase in the loudness of his playing, he overheard one of the Kapitänleutnants say, "Speak more softly . . . in case the piano-playing Leutnant . . ."

PARIS

"Careful," Will said, as Adrienne turned abruptly and almost bumped one of the poles. "I would not want all this ornamental drapery to fall on you!" He smiled and pointed up at the colorful swag that hung from the numerous tall poles on the huge floor of the Grand Palais.

Adrienne smiled, her cheeks quivering. "These crowds! It is so difficult to navigate."

Will was enjoying this respite from École Polytechnique. "I must say I am glad for the break from L'X."

"Yet I will admit," Adrienne said, standing on one foot while resting the other. "I am foot-tired."

"Concours Lépine is such a huge event," Will said, enthused. "It will be unusual if we have visited even one-half of the inventions."

Adrienne frowned. "I prefer to leave. It seems the sponsors provide no opportunity for sitting."

Will nodded and began guiding her through the crowds clogging the aisles between many of the triangular display tables. Along the way, he glimpsed the model of an aeroplane on one of the tables and wanted to stop, but he kept walking.

Once outside the entrance, he said, "Follow me." He directed Adrienne across the esplanade to a wide park bench which faced away from Avenue Alexandre III. A single space remained unoccupied. "Oh," she said, sitting down, crossing her leg, and massaging the upper of her shoe, "please excuse me. I am not accustomed to being hours on my feet."

"Be as comfortable as you are able," Will said. "I have something to tell you."

The couple next to Adrienne looked at each other and rose to leave.

Adrienne said, "I do not mean to complain—I did enjoy the novelty—the latest creations of 1912."

The couple who had risen strolled away, and Will sat in the space they had vacated. Adrienne laughed and said, "I must say the 'dishwashing machine' shown by Madame Labrousse is an excellent idea. But what were you about to announce?"

"In a few days I will be leaving Paris."

"A trip? Where will you visit?"

"It is not a visit. My family is relocating to America. To New York." Will studied Adrienne's reaction. "My father's publisher has a new initiative which he is to lead. The move is a return to the country of my birth."

Adrienne frowned. "You speak French so well. You have never mentioned being—"

"I was but eight years of age when my father brought me here from the United States."

"Your mother did not . . . your mother was—"

"She died that year, 1902. A severe illness . . ."

"Oh." She frowned. "You have my lasting sympathy." She stared across the wide clearing, as if searching for an alternative to the topic of the moment. After a pause, she said, "But Will, you have completed only two years at École Polytechnique—you said—"

Will nodded. "I had every intention to take my degree at L'X." He raised his eyebrows and looked off across the Seine. "However, I am told I can enroll at MIT without a loss of credits. So that is—"

"MIT, what is that?"

"Massachusetts Institute of Technology. It is an excellent institution."

Adrienne uncrossed her leg and turned more toward Will. "So we shall part." She smiled and looked deeply into his eyes. "And I suppose you will be heartbroken."

"I will."

"But Will Marra, you must realize—it had to happen. This is an intervention that was certain in the future. It is better that it happens now . . ."

Will took Adrienne's hand. "It is not an intervention. And it is not better—at least for me."

"But Will, as I have so often told you—my life is dedicated to couture. We cannot—"

"I have your address, Adrienne. I will write to you often, wherever I am, from New York and from MIT, or somewhere else. Wherever I am. You know I cannot allow you out of my life."

Adrienne sat silent, seemingly composing her reply. She squeezed Will's hand. "Please understand. There is nothing bad in you. I don't wish you to think that. But I cannot, and will not, promise to reply to letters I receive from you. I am very determined to create beauty with my ideas—my life in couture is full to overrunning. Is that not understandable to you?"

Will squeezed her hands in return and searched her eyes. "What is understandable is not as I wish." He lowered his gaze to the ground. "Although I know you must act as you are impelled."

She rose from the bench and turned to Will with the open palms of her hands spread wide. "To add to it all, I have committed to exchanging letters with my dear cousin Gregor. He is in the Imperial Navy—a lonely occupation."

She turned toward the ornate decorations of the Alexandre III bridge over the Seine. She stared at them for a long moment, as though intimidated by the sunlit splendor of the winged horse sculptures atop the towers at the entrance. She turned back.

"There is really more to my life than I can ever accomplish, even allowing for only a few hours of sleep each night. You must understand."

•　　　•　　　•

Later, in November, Adrienne—in Paris—received a letter from Will Marra written in his looping, handwritten French:

Dear Adrienne,

The last time I was with you, we attended the Concours Lépine at the Grand Palais. I was very grateful to be with you as we shared good times and laughs at some of the pointless inventions. Although I did not disclose it at the time, I was busy and involved in a large task at our dwelling on Boulevard Montmartre. This task was aiding in the packing of all of our family's furniture, goods, and books.

Later, when all the matériel had been consigned to a shipper for transfer to New York, our family went by train to Le Havre, where we sailed aboard the French Line, reaching New York in five days. While we were in a hotel in New York, Father sought daily to secure a residence which would assist him in his new work— he will be writing books and articles there and entertaining important people.

We moved into the selected apartment the third week of August, after the arrival of our furnishings that had been shipped to America by freighter.

Following that, I left New York and am lodged in Boston where I have taken up studies at MIT. Classes here began the last Monday of September. All of this is by way of explaining why I have not been able to write until now.

After our attendance at the Grand Palais, I was saddened to tell you of my move to New York. I am now feeling really sad again because you are so far away. I know you are busy in your chosen career, but I sincerely ask you to write to me. I have written my postal address above in the hope you will answer.

My room here in Cambridge is on the second floor of what is known as a "walk-up." It has heating by steam which I am told will be of great comfort during the wintertime.

I have a window which faces onto the street. The traffic—a streetcar line runs on it—is noisy, but I am getting used to it. It is not far from the Copley Square neighborhood of Boston where the MIT buildings are situated. I attend classes in two buildings on Boylston Street and several on Trinity Place. The laboratories on Garrison Street are where hand work, measurement and experimentation are conducted.

The Institution of MIT is dedicated to the acquisition of understanding rather than simple knowledge. In that way it is similar to École Polytechnique (although all the instruction here is in English—I find this slightly strange at this moment). I have chosen to pursue the Mechanical Engineering curriculum. This is the curriculum nearest my true desire that is offered. Although the dean has granted me third-year status, I am required to take an extra course in mechanical drafting which was not required at L'X.

No classes in aerodynamics are given; this is less fortunate, as I am deeply interested in aeronautics. The school library contains a number of excellent works on aeronautical topics which I study during evenings when I have finished my class studies.

For a modest fee, I am able to take meals at the Technology Union, a building on Trinity Place for dining, student social activities, mail writing, and relaxation. This is good because my dwelling lacks facilities for cooking.

You will possibly find the following humorous: A couple of my fellow students have said that the English I speak sometimes has a French accent. I was unaware of this, but I suppose it is to be expected, considering that I have spent the last ten years and more in France, including two years at L'X!

I miss your beautiful smile and hope you will find time to reply to me.

Sincerely,
Will Marra

1913

PARIS

It was entirely unexpected, yet seemingly foreordained that Maison Paquin would, early in 1913, name Adrienne Boch "Le première d'Atelier de couture." The public announcement said Adrienne had from her very first days at the house demonstrated an unusual grasp of both the work and the managerial function. She and the Maison's hundreds of seamstresses "gave life to the famous couturier's ideas, with many contributions and complete dedication."

Adrienne was electrified with joy. But less than a month later, Adrienne was summoned to the office of Madame Paquin. "You are becoming slightly famous, Mlle Boch," the famous couturier said, fingering the page of a magazine on the expanse of her desk.

Adrienne glanced at the illustration on the page, but could not see the magazine's cover. "I do not understand."

Jeanne smiled. "Our evening costume has made one of the featured plates in the Gazette du Bon Ton."

Adrienne smiled. "Oh, that is wonderful." Then she had a second thought. "But . . ."

"I have just received a pre-publication copy. Here is what is said." Madame Paquin passed the magazine, open to the illustration, to Adrienne without added comment.

Adrienne saw that it was indeed Gazette du Bon Ton, the most elite of French fashion magazines. The dress illustrated, a blue silk charmeuse design, was familiar. It was a fancy gown incorporating embroidery of flowers with curlicue leaves. Adrienne's attention flew to the foot of the page, to the brief text where Paquin's design was praised. She glanced at the final sentence: "Especially endearing is the black silk chiffon drape and trim, reportedly added by Paquin's Adrienne Boch."

At first, Adrienne could not comprehend why her name was attached. Her mind raced back to the day when she'd been called to the showroom by the head of sales, Véronique.

"It is the Duchess of Arion," Véronique whispered to Adrienne. "She adores the dress, but there is a problem."

Adrienne approached and introduced herself to the Duchess, a tall woman with an impossibly-long neck and hazel eyes with flecks of gold. In French with a Spanish accent, she said her name was María de La Luz Mariátegui y Pérez de Barradas, but "please address me as María."

A short discussion ensued, during which the Duchess expressed strong interest in the blue silk charmeuse gown. "It is," she said, "exquisite, enchanting. However—" the Duchess smiled at Adrienne as she gestured below her waist—"I have a problem again—you understand."

Adrienne instantly understood that the Duchess was with child, and that the gown did not offer sufficient concealment. "I do understand. Let me show you an addition that will provide a very pretty distraction."

Upon that, Adrienne hurried into the atelier, retrieved some black silk chiffon, and returned to illustrate her addition.

"Oh, I am so pleased," the Duchess said.

And so the sale was consummated.

At this moment, however, in front of the desk of Madame Paquin, Adrienne had somehow to explain herself. "It is a mystery, Madame. I sought no credit, only to please the client. Perhaps the Duchess—"

"Indeed that is so," the older woman said, smiling. "I telephoned Lucien Vogel—the publisher of Gazette du Bon Ton. He confirmed that the Duchess of Arion was so pleased she contacted Monsieur Vogel and urged the coverage."

"I hope I have not overstepped—" began Adrienne.

"As I said, child, you are becoming slightly famous," Jeanne Paquin said, smiling. "Do try to remain humble."

•   •   •

On a spring afternoon, not long after the new issue of Gazette du Bon Ton came into wide circulation, the Crown Princess of Romania stepped from a carriage to Rue de la Paix and entered Maison Paquin. Almost unnoticed was the man accompanying her. Short, with a full beard, stiff collar, and freshly-pressed black suit, he swept behind her like a diminutive shadow.

Greeted by Véronique, the Crown Princess failed to introduce her companion. "I am here to view some shawls," she said in her English accent. "Meanwhile, this person wishes to speak with Mlle Adrienne Boch." Véronique noted the Princess's upward gaze and the emphasis placed on the word *person*. It seemed to signal at least reluctance, if not distaste.

"I'm not sure Mlle Boch is available," Véronique said to the man. "What is this about?"

"I am the bearer of a message for Mlle Boch. Beyond that I am unable to say."

Véronique said, "Please wait here." The man nodded, bowed slightly, and said, "Thank you."

Véronique directed the Princess to a display at the end of the elegant showroom. When they were beyond the companion's earshot, the Princess said, "He is an imposition—a favor on behalf of the Crown Prince. I am not privy to his concern, only that I am assured he is trustworthy. I hope you understand."

Véronique nodded, and after some added words about the shawls she left the Princess and went into the atelier.

"I can easily dismiss him," she said to Adrienne. "I told him you might not be available."

Adrienne dropped the paper pattern she was holding to her desk.

"Does he look dangerous?"

"He said he has a message for you. He is small. He is well-dressed. Beyond that I should not say."

"I will see him," Adrienne said, "when I am finished." After delivering some patterns to the seamstresses, she went to the front where the man stood, holding his derby. Upon presenting herself to him, she said, "I am Adrienne Boch. And you are?"

He bowed slightly and smiled. "You may know me as Monsieur Zêta, although my name is of no importance. I present myself through the courtesy of the Crown Prince so that you might have confidence I have no mission other than conveying a message to you."

Adrienne frowned slightly. ". . . And that message is?"

His lips formed a slim smile. "I should like to deliver the message, but it is not possible here, at this moment. From five on I will hold a table at Café Voisin this evening. You know the Café—on Rue St. Honoré?"

Adrienne continued her frown. "I know the Café Voisin, but . . ."

"It is a public place. Simply ask for Monsieur Zêta. If you so honor me, I will upon your arrival deliver the message. Whether you stay on for supper is completely your decision."

"It is impossible for me to say yes or no. I have many responsibilities."

"I understand," he said, bowing slightly. "You are 'Le première d'Atelier de couture.' Good afternoon, Mlle. Boch." He placed the derby on his head and left through the entrance doors. Adrienne watched as he stepped briskly toward the Place Vendôme.

•　　　•　　　•

Driven by curiosity, yet also reluctantly, Adrienne took the short walk to Café Voisin upon completion of her day at Maison Paquin. As she followed the maître d' to the gentleman's table in an isolated section, 'Zêta' rose. "Good afternoon, Mlle Boch, please join me."

When Adrienne was seated across the linen-draped table and the maître d' had retreated, she noticed the table was set for two. She said, "I must make myself explicit, Monsieur Zêta. I came only to receive the message you spoke of at Maison Paquin."

He nodded. "I understand." He coughed softly and laced his fingers together on top of the table linen. "But initially I must explain the source of the message. It comes from the leader of one of the finest houses of haute couture here in Paris."

With both hands, Adrienne gripped the linen below the table's edge. "And which house would that be?"

Zêta's gaze went to the vase of flowers at the center of the table, then rose to Adrienne. "Please understand. The identity of the house can only follow the message."

Adrienne's grip on the linen tightened. "I do not understand."

"The house wishes to convey its admiration for your talents. The leader of the house wishes to employ you, and, as an inducement, offers to pay you 50 percent above your current salary." He paused, smiled, and went on. "Employment is offered at 150 percent of your present salary—is that understood?"

"Yes, yes. I understand what you are saying." Adrienne frowned and her grip went to the edge of the table. "But . . . but—"

"That is most generous, don't you think?" Without waiting for an answer, Zêta continued. "I know this is unusual. Peculiar, even. But I assure you, the offer is genuine."

Adrienne raised her voice a bit. "What I do not understand, Monsieur Zêta, is the identity of the house making the offer."

Zêta's face became animated. "I was assigned to contact you so the house could refrain from revealing itself. That is, unless you—"

"Unless I blindly agree to the employment?"

His gaze turned icy. "That is so."

"But that is impossible." She pushed her chair back and stood. "Absurd."

Zêta began to rise from his chair. "Please, Mlle Boch . . ."

"Goodbye," she said. She turned, strode to the café's entrance, and walked out.

CAMBRIDGE, MASSACHUSETTS

L ate in the spring of 1913, Will entered the office of the dean in the Rogers Building.

"I am Will Marra. I received a note to report to this office." He noticed a tall, bearded gentleman in a suit seated next to the desk behind which the dean was seated. "I came as quick as I was able."

"That's fine, Will," the dean said. "Please take the chair there. This gentleman is Dr. Godfrey L. Cabot."

Cabot nodded and said, "I am pleased to meet you, Will."

The dean continued. "Dr. Cabot is a prominent member of the Aero Club of New England, and a friend of the Wright brothers. What brings him to MIT today is the thesis you submitted to your Mechanism of Machines class this semester. I'll let Dr. Cabot explain."

Cabot reached inside the valise beside him and removed a sheaf of papers. "Major Cole of the Military Science and Tactics Department was good enough to forward me your paper. I believe a copy was passed to him by your professor." He leaned forward. "You are about to complete your third year in Mechanical Engineering—is that correct?"

"Yes, sir. My preference would have been Aeronautical Engineering, which I understand will be offered starting next semester. My first two years of university, however, were completed at École Polytechnique in Paris."

"I noticed that your paper cites several French studies. But I am most interested in the claims your paper makes for the uses of aeroplanes by the military."

Will nodded and recalled from memory, "France's military, by the end of 1911, claimed 170 aeroplanes and forty rated military aviators.

It seems now obvious aeroplanes will have important application as machines of war." He studied the face of Cabot, then went on. "My thesis expands on these facts. I have studied developments in aeronautics since I first witnessed Wilbur Wright perform a 'figure eight' in his aeroplane at Le Mans in 1908. My thesis builds mainly upon recent advances in internal-combustion engines . . ." Will paused and smiled.

"The dean said you were a friend of the Wrights?"

"Yes," Cabot said, brightening. "I corresponded with the Wrights following their Kitty Hawk flight, and wrote to Senator Henry Cabot Lodge—a distant cousin of mine—recommending that the United States government take a stronger interest in heavier-than-air aeronautical machines. Unfortunately . . ."

"I believe that is extremely important. Did you have a specific question regarding my thesis?"

"I thought it a carefully-wrought inquiry. In particular, I found your idea that armadas of aeroplanes driven by multiple motors might drop explosives on enemy installations stimulating."

"That aspect is perhaps speculative," Will said, losing his smile. "On the one hand, basic calculation supports the idea that larger wings, with several gasoline motors driving propellers, can support increased weight and still leave the ground. On the other hand, new gasoline motor designs, with hundreds of horsepower, are currently in development. My calculations show that a fleet of multiple-motored aeroplanes carrying explosives thousands of feet above enemy territory would constitute a significant military threat."

"Yes," Cabot said, "and—"

"Excuse me, gentlemen," the dean said. "I apologize for interrupting, but I have an appointment very soon. Please take seats in the conference room across the hall, where you can continue your conversation . . ."

Dr. Cabot and Will moved into the conference room. After several minutes of intense discussion, Cabot said, "Will, I want you to address the Aero Club. You can possibly show the members how your analyses prove the importance of aeroplanes to the military. I will invite members of the Aero Club of New York as well. Will you do it?"

"Yes, I'll be happy to speak," Will said, smiling. "Only providing the date does not interfere with final exams. I believe they are scheduled for May 28 to June 10."

•   •   •

In the large room with its chandelier, brocaded walls, and framed photographs of Boston notables, Will stood at the speaker's table following his speech. He was surrounded by Aero Club officials and guests, several of whom came to the table to comment and praise his presentation.

A man with a large drooping mustache and pince-nez strode to the table and said, "I am Professor Frederick Miller. Your presentation was excellent. I hope you plan to complete your undergraduate degree at MIT . . . and stay on for graduate study."

"Thank you, Professor—I—well, I am not sure."

"I understand. There are sure to be scholarships and other financial aids available—if needed, of course."

"My concern, really, is with Aeronautical Engineering . . ." As Will spoke, another man in a tweed jacket pushed to the table. "Congratulations, Will. You spoke very well. I am Major Cole. I wanted to . . . oh, excuse me, Doctor Miller—I didn't realize you were—"

"It's quite all right," said the professor to the man in tweed. "I was simply encouraging Mr. Marra to stay on for a graduate degree here in Boston. I'm sure the Department of Military Science agrees that MIT needs men of his talent to secure advanced degrees."

"Yes, yes, of course," said the major. "There's not a doubt about that. And the MIT graduate curriculum in engineering is the finest in the country. I agree with Doctor Miller."

"Thank you both," Will said, gathering his notes for the talk and preparing to leave.

The professor nodded to both men and left. Major Cole said, "As I said, I wanted to talk to you . . ."

"Of course," Will replied, "although I need to leave. Finals, you know," he said as he folded his notes.

"I'll walk out with you, if you don't mind," the major said. "You see, I believe you are—let me rephrase that. I would be most interested in knowing—are you interested in flying?"

Will brightened and smiled. "Yes, absolutely. I've had the goal of learning to fly for some time." The two men made their way through the throng. When they reached the lobby, Major Cole said, "How about the military? Would you be willing to serve—as an officer-aviator?"

Will paused at the door leading onto Huntington Avenue. "Maybe." As he pushed on through, he said, "I'm unsure at the moment. Perhaps, you could advise me."

The major followed him. "Better than that," the major said. "I will put you in touch with a friend of mine, another Army major."

"This is someone to advise me?"

"No. This is a man who could place you in line for a commission. He is a leading Aero Club member as well as a Signal Corps officer. You may not know, but Brigadier General Allen supports the Aeronautical Division's close working relationship with the national arm of the Club."

"I did not . . ."

"I think the major would find your educational achievements— as well as speaking flawless French—a great match for the service. I believe he can secure you the opportunity to become an M.A.—a military aviator with the rank of Lieutenant. You would learn to fly at San Diego. What would you think of that?"

"Thanks for all you have said," Will said, grinning. "It sounds most intriguing."

"Goodbye, Will," the major said as they parted. "I'm sure you will do well on your examinations. I will talk to you when you're finished."

• • •

On the train to New York City, Will tried to decide the best approach to discussing the issue with his father. But now, arriving at the Manhattan apartment and receiving the hugs and cheery greetings from both his father and Marie, he realized he still had not envisioned a best scheme.

"I guess I should tell you my plans," he said, searching for words his father would expect. "I really am not pleased with the curriculum in Mechanical Engineering—it emphasizes steam power plants, drafting, tool design, and so forth."

They were seated in the Marras' luxury apartment just off Central Park. Marie, as always, was dressed in the very finest of fashions. Harlan, on the other hand, wore a shirt with his tie askew and rolled-up sleeves—Will assumed his father had been at his desk writing when he'd arrived home.

"You have made excellent progress in engineering at MIT," Harlan said. "Your grades, if I understood correctly, could not be better."

"Had an Aeronautical Engineering degree been offered last autumn, I would have jumped for it."

Harlan nodded. "That is natural. For the last few years, you've been highly enthused about aviation."

"What I'm trying to say to you is, I want to fly. I've been in contact with a US Army major—"

"Wait," Harlan said.

Marie's eyes focused on Harlan, whose face was now heavily lined.

Harlan leaned forward, eyes on Will. "I hope you aren't saying you are abandoning your pursuit of an undergraduate degree at MIT."

Will said, "This major, the one I spoke to, will sponsor me as a cadet at the Signal Corps' Aviation Training Center on North Island, outside San Diego, California."

"Go on," Harlan said.

Will saw that his father was upset by his remarks. "I will learn to fly. And if I succeed in passing the various tests, I will be awarded the status of Military Aviator and ranked as Lieutenant."

"But you will be without a university degree."

"Please understand. I am not interested in obtaining a degree that qualifies me to design furnaces and steam boilers. Those subjects bore me."

Harlan looked away, stroked his beard, and glanced at Marie.

Marie avoided his eyes and appeared to look at the bookcases that spanned the entire wall.

Will felt the ticking of the grandfather clock was annoying.

"Perhaps," Harlan said, in a resigned voice, "MIT was not the best choice for you." Then, in a slightly more cheery tone, he added, "Princeton, now—"

"I appreciate the support you have provided at both École Polytechnique and MIT." Will said, searching to engage his father's eyes. "But I hope you will also understand that I want to fly—that I have wanted it for a long time, probably ever since I watched Wilbur Wright fly years ago."

"Is it not possible that you might take flying lessons, perhaps near Boston, yet continue your education—at least for one more year?"

"I have already agreed to the Army's terms, Father."

Harlan pursed his lips and slumped back in his chair. "Well, I won't say I am pleased. I felt you had a brilliant career ahead, perhaps even as an academic professor. But . . ." He paused. "I'm sure you know the risks flying in these primitive machines."

"Yes sir. I believe I am prepared for the dangers."

"Well, then, you will just have to try it." Harlan turned to Marie. "We continue to wish you nothing but the best. Right, Marie?"

Will saw the reluctance in his father's face.

Marie nodded. "We wish you nothing but the best, Will."

NORTH ISLAND, SAN DIEGO, CALIFORNIA

It was quite dark when the boat docked at the pier. Will yawned, grasped his bag, and headed for the barn.

"Still sleepy, I see," Don Crippen said to Will as the men arrived from the pier.

"I guess," Will said, suppressing another yawn. "I am not yet adjusted to this early-morning class." He stowed his bag with the others in the tar-papered hangar. When he returned, he said, "What are we to expect today?"

"Turns and circles, I hope." Crippen glanced beyond the spruce rods and wires that formed the frame of the Curtiss aeroplane. He pointed, late, as one of the many island jackrabbits bounded across the sandy soil from under a fabric-covered wing. "There goes the fastest student on North Island," he said, to the applause and laughter of the group.

"I hope you are right," Will said. "About doing turns and circles, I mean."

Will thought about the past two weeks doing what the students called "grass cutting"—learning to guide the deliberately-underpowered Curtiss aeroplane in a straight line with just enough throttle to take off on a series of shallow flights a few feet off the ground. He felt he really had a feel for the machine. "I found it easy to control. But now, it—"

"It is boring," Crippen said, finishing Will's phrase. "Flying by fits and starts in a straight line is dull. I want to get more than a half-dozen feet off the ground. Seems to me the instructor is . . ." He did not finish as the figure of Instructor Callan rounded the corner of the barn.

"Okay, you guys," the instructor said. "Today we will continue the straight-line practice. I want everyone to be comfortable with the controls before we try turns and circles. Let's move the aeroplane to the starting line. Has the gas been freshened?"

"No," said one of the students. "I think Russell went to fetch the fuel can."

"Best have someone check," the instructor said. "We want to be on the line and ready before sunrise."

The sunrise start of the exercises, Will knew, was to allow as many runs as possible before the cross-island winds increased in the latter half of the day. A few of the students were skittish enough without adding the risk of brisk winds to their efforts to control the aeroplane on the thousand-yard run to the flag.

With a student grasping the control wheel and the propeller whirling, the rising sun cast long shadows across the starting line. The student onlookers standing behind him smelled the hot odor of the exhaust.

"All ready?" shouted the instructor from his position many yards down the course. "Go!"

The student advanced the throttle, and four other students grasping the tips of the lower wings released their hold. The lightweight craft leaped forward on its three wheels. As the craft approached him, the instructor shouted commands to the pilot through his megaphone. "That's right. Hold her level . . . "

Back at the starting line, Crippen said to Will, "Cross your fingers. This guy has not quite mastered the . . ." His sentence was swallowed up in the rush of air and dust that flew behind the craft. First, it bounded into the air, then returned to the sand. Then it bounded into the air again.

"He is having trouble keeping the nose level," Will said. "He's overcorrecting . . ."

The aircraft passed the instructor's station. The instructor whirled to face the tail of the aeroplane as it bounced toward the flag. He shouted into the megaphone, "No—no—no!"

Finally the propeller slowed, the craft wobbled, and its wheels thudded to earth. Now the instructor ran after the distant aeroplane.

Will, Crippen, and the group jogged down the sand toward the stationary aeroplane. They observed the instructor arrive, shouting at the pilot. Judging by his toss of the megaphone and the animated actions of his body, the instructor was delivering a decidedly negative lecture to his student.

"Hope that final bounce didn't bust the undercarriage," Crippen said.

"Yeah." Will cast his mind back to the prior week, when one of the students had dug the tip of a wing into the sand and ground-looped, resulting in broken attachment pins. "Not again."

The broken pins had taken two days to repair, during which this group of students did not fly. Sharing a single aeroplane among more than a dozen students meant waiting in line while praying the prior runs did not falter and break the craft before one had a chance to climb into the seat.

•   •   •

Will Marra sat in the fully-exposed seat in front of the wings, hands gripping the control wheel, as the motor behind him throbbed steadily. Although there was no way to determine his altitude, he reckoned he was about two thousand feet above North Island.

The motor's radiator was located behind Will's head, with the giant propeller behind the motor, providing thrust—this Curtiss craft was called a "pusher." The aeroplane was the latest model from Glenn Curtiss's manufacturing plant in Hammondsport, New York, one of three "D" models at the Curtiss School of Aviation on North Island.

Two years earlier, in 1911, the Signal Corps Aviation Section of the US Army had responded enthusiastically when aviator and inventor Glenn Curtiss had offered use of his facility without cost to the government for training fledgling pilots.

Model D had the wire-tensioned, spare wooden framework, fabric-covered wings, and three-wheeled undercarriage of previous models. Although the motor was large and heavy, it was not very powerful. The pusher weighed less than six hundred pounds ready for flight, and with urging could reach a speed of fifty miles per hour.

Will guided the craft easily, as the open framework afforded total visibility downward, outward, and upward. He completed the circle, retarded the throttle, and began his descent back to earth in a gentle spiral—what the instructors called "volplaning." (Being fluent in French, Will knew the term derived from *vol plané*, "gliding flight.")

When finally within a few feet of the ground, Will turned the motor off and by careful movement of the rudder wheel and shoulder yoke straightened his trajectory and brought the aeroplane to a gentle, rolling contact with the ground. Nearby students clapped as the craft halted and Will stepped from the seat to the ground.

Don Crippen was the first to arrive. "Good flight, Will. I hope I'll do as well when my chance comes."

Will removed his goggles and grinned. "It was fun! It is such a thrill to feel the air rushing by and—oh, I can't really say." He knew he couldn't find the right words to express how it felt to be at home in the air. "I'm sure you'll do well," he told Crippen.

The instructor approached the two students. "Will, your coordination of the rudder and the aileron yoke was excellent. Your volplaning was also good. But you need to baby the throttle better to meet the 'stopping at the mark' requirement."

The instructor referred to part of the test for a pilot's license that required five consecutive figure eights and a landing that stopped within fifty feet of a mark on the ground. The figure eights were to be flown around two ground-level pylons set a thousand feet apart. "Yeah," Will said, shaking his head. "I need to be smoother on the throttle lever."

As the students finished for the day, most of them looked to the south end of the field, where a Burgess J was flying. This pusher, No. 18, although made by Burgess, was identical to the Wright Model C. It was on a practice run incorporating figure eights.

After completing a right turn at about a thousand feet, No. 18 began volplaning. At about three hundred feet the student straightened the craft toward the landing area. He added power, and the angle of his glide steepened. He still continued on a straight line, but the downward angle grew steeper.

The onlooking students were initially confused by the aeroplane's attitude. But as the glide steepened, the onlookers murmured. The angle increased and became a dive. Several of the students gasped, "Oh no!"

The instructor yelled, "Pull up, pull up, you crazy . . ."

The Burgess J plummeted to the ground with a loud crunching sound at the south end of North Island.

Everyone began running toward the crash. When the fastest arrived at the crash, they realized the pilot was dead. His splayed body lay beneath splintered frame members. His right arm protruded grotesquely from beneath the smoking motor.

The aeroplane's central frames and the pilot had impacted the ground at speed. The spinning propeller then chewed its way through the wreckage, scattering spruce splinters, rudder and tail surfaces into a circular field of debris.

"Stay back," yelled the instructor, breathing heavily. "The gas tank may explode." He extended his arms as a barrier. "You cannot help the poor pilot. He's gone."

The date was Thursday, September 4, 1913. The student, Lieutenant Moss Love, age thirty-two, lost his life learning to fly. His death was the third that had occurred since Glenn Curtiss opened the North Island aviation school.

The students learned later that Lt. Love was known for his skill as a polo player. He, like most of the students, was single. The cause of the crash was never completely determined, despite the blame for other crashes that accrued to the Wright Model C over the next two years.

NORTH SEA

Gregor Steiner was pleased. Not only had he been promoted to Oberleutnant zur See, he had received his first command. And on this September Tuesday, he aimed to demonstrate the capability of his vessel and his crew. The binoculars hanging from his neck swung smartly in a short arc.

Gregor rebalanced himself on the conning platform. "What is the message, Komicht?"

Officer Komicht inquired of the speaking pipe in a voice loud enough to overcome the din of the North Sea breaking over the hull. When the reply came, he said, "Nothing, Kapitän, they are still decoding."

Helmsman Tauber wrestled with the wheel, first one way, then quickly reversing. Aiming the sixty-three-meter (207 ft) long torpedo boat was difficult.

Gregor scanned the sky. Jagged gray clouds ahead and the cooling of the air signaled possible rain. "Our maneuvers are in practice for actual warfare," he said. "But the 'enemy' today may be the weather."

"Yes, Kapitän," Leutnant Komicht said, listening at the voice pipe and reacquiring his balance.

Gregor squinted through the spray blowing to starboard. He saw only two plumes of black smoke, yet he sensed the positions of all the units in the flotilla. He and the flanking torpedo boats were maintaining twenty-two knots while progressing northeast of Heligoland Island.

In the far distance, a speck appeared. Gregor raised his binoculars to view the Zeppelin as it floated above the sea. At first, he thought he could make out the men in the two gondolas slung underneath. But in that moment he decided his imagination was stronger than his vision. Nevertheless, he held no envy for the airship's crew—they would be miserably cold, even at an assigned altitude of only 1,400 meters.

Officer Komicht straightened from the voice pipe. "Target has been located," he said. "Wireless is delivering to navigation."

"Understood," Gregor said. "Order 'combat stations.'"

"Combat stations," Komicht confirmed.

Gregor turned to Tauber. "Helmsman, stand by."

"Helm standing by," said Tauber.

Several minutes passed before Officer Komicht said, "Target twelve-thousand. Navigation recommends course two-seven-eight."

Gregor repeated the message: "Target twelve-thousand, Navigation recommends course two-seven-eight." He turned to helmsman Tauber. "All Ahead Full—two-seven-eight."

The helmsman spun the wheel and said, "All Ahead Full—two-seven-eight." He swung the handles on the engine-order-telegraphs to "Full." Shortly, bells sounded and the answer pointers swung to "Full."

"Engine room answers 'All Ahead Full,'" Tauber said.

Gregor said, "All Ahead Full."

A cloud of black smoke belched from the forward funnel.

Tauber's lips pressed hard together. Staring at the compass in the binnacle, he turned the wheel first one way, then reversed it, fighting the waves.

Rain began falling. Komicht pulled rain jackets from a locker and handed one to Gregor.

Tauber, blinking rain from his eyes, announced, "Steady on two-seven-eight."

Gregor said, "Steady…" but his attention was fixed on the Zeppelin. He now saw it distinctly without the aid of glasses. Printed on its side was "L-1." He squinted at it and turned to Komicht. "Look. It does not seem right."

"Yes. I see what you mean."

"Check wireless."

"Check wireless." Komicht spoke into his voice pipe.

The rain increased and was now very cold. The reconnaissance Zeppelin appeared to descend.

"The airship reports," Komicht said. "They signal distress—and that L-1 will land beyond Heligoland."

"They cannot land," Gregor said. "Heligoland is distant. There is only water."

Komicht continued to listen at the voice tube. "Now L-1 requests help."

Gregor turned to Tauber. "Helmsman, hard starboard, steer to the airship."

Tauber swung the wheel. "Hard starboard, steer to airship."

Komicht said, "On board they wire, 'Cast out all water'—what does that mean?"

"Unload the ballast—to lighten it . . . maybe the cold rain—" As Gregor spoke, the nose of L-1 dipped dangerously.

In an urgent voice, Gregor said, "Komicht—engine room, emergency steam!"

Komicht shouted into the voice pipe, "Engine room, emergency steam!"

Bells sounded on the engine-order-telegraphs as the answer pointers vibrated on "Full."

Copious black smoke streamed from the funnels. The torpedo boat sliced through the rain-churned waves as its speed increased.

Komicht said, "Engine room reports—three boilers fully stoked."

Gregor nodded. He could now see each of the two gondolas suspended below the airship, though they were several kilometers distant. He sensed each crew's anxiety as they flailed and the airship continued to descend, nose down, aimed toward the water.

Komicht said, "They will crash if they don't—" As he spoke, the forward gondola hit the water. The nose of the airship followed and struck with a giant splash. Ripples and then wrinkles deformed the upper part of the Zeppelin as its nose met the resistance of the water. Several men jumped clear from the rear gondola and fell into the sea. Next, the forward propeller pylon splashed and submerged. The giant airship folded near its middle and cracks opened, disclosing its interior.

"Bah!" Gregor said, noting the time of thirty minutes past 1800 hours. "It's going down! Wireless, alert the Kommandant!"

Komicht shouted into the voice pipe, "Wireless, alert Kommandant. L-1 is down! L-1 is down!"

"Curses," Komicht said to Gregor, "they will all drown."

Teeth clenched, Gregor lifted the binoculars to his eyes. "The airship is . . . folding into the water—how many are aboard?" Without waiting for an answer, he ordered, "Deck: Standby life rings. Rig dinghy for launch."

Komicht shouted into the voice pipe: "Deck, standby life rings. Rig dinghy for launch."

The buckled shape of L-1 lingered over the sea at the horizon, then slowly sank to the surface of the water. Within minutes only two rumpled mounds of structure protruded above the distant sea.

Although speeding at maximum steam, Gregor's ship took a dozen minutes to reach the disaster site. Both Gregor and Komicht scanned the sea with binoculars.

"Helmsman," Gregor said, "Full Back."

"Full Back," repeated Tauber. He swung the handles of the engine-order-telegraphs in almost a full circle. Bells sounded as the pointers whirled to "Full Back."

The torpedo boat slowed.

"Helmsman," Gregor said. "Stop."

Tauber repeated the order and swung the engine-order-telegraph handles to "Stop." Bells sounded. The screws halted. The boat moved slowly forward on its momentum alone.

"Look—look!" Komicht said, pointing off the port bow.

"I see him," Gregor said. "Helmsman, Ahead Slow, rudder to port."

Tauber repeated "Ahead Slow, rudder to port" and swung the

handles. Bells sounded. Some black smoke streamed from the rear funnel. The rain intensified.

Gregor said to Komicht, "Deck, standby life rings. Prepare to launch dinghy, port side."

Komicht repeated and spoke the order into the voice pipe.

Following the relayed order, two sailors went to the port rail with life rings. Sailors below the stern boom tugged lines that raised the boom. The dinghy lifted. Other men, using ropes, swung it toward the port side. Finally, it swayed erratically in the air over the port rail as the torpedo boat curved to the left.

"Helmsman," Gregor said. "Ahead Slow." He said to Komicht, "Do you see . . ."

"No, Kapitän—he is gone," Komicht said. "I do not know—"

Tauber said, "Ahead Slow." Bells sounded.

Immediately, Gregor ordered the helmsman, "Stop." Tauber repeated the Stop order, bells sounded, and the ship slowed.

With binoculars held to his eyes, Gregor said, "Deck, launch dinghy." Komicht relayed the order.

Sailors near the stern lowered the dinghy to the water. A petty officer and two sailors clambered into it. The sailors grasped the oars.

On the conning platform, Komicht found and lifted the megaphone. Gregor continued to scan with his binoculars, noting that only a single lump of L-1 wreckage now remained on the surface.

Dancing crazily on the waves and powered forward by the men's oars, the dinghy pulled quickly away from the torpedo boat's hull.

Gregor dropped the binoculars and turned to Komicht, pointing with his arm and hand. "Direct them that way."

Komicht, his arm outstretched and pointing, yelled the order through the megaphone.

The petty officer at the rear of the dinghy acknowledged the order by signaling. He turned the tiller and ordered the oarsmen to swing the dinghy in the direction Komicht had directed.

The big torpedo boat, denied the stability of forward motion, rocked from side to side in a widening angle as the rainstorm intensified.

Gregor again scanned with his binoculars. "There!" he yelled at Komicht. "You see?"

Komicht said, "Yes," and yelled, "Faster! Hurry!" through the megaphone. "There!" he shouted, waving his arm to signal where the dark, bobbing shape was located.

The petty officer at the tiller of the dinghy directed the rowing sailors. The dinghy approached the partly-submerged head of a man. The sailors threw their oars aside and joined at the gunnel, reaching into the water to grip the man's garments and body. The petty officer yelled encouragement while leaning far back on the opposite gunnel to prevent a capsize.

The two sailors, grasping, pulling, and yelling, hauled first the head and shoulders, then the soggy torso, clad in his oilskin, over and into the dinghy.

The petty officer directed the men back to their oars as he stumbled over them to the recovered man. He turned the torso to the side, threw the oilskin open, pulled and pressed the chest in an attempt to expel water from the man's lungs.

The rowers pulled strenuously on their oars. Deck Department sailors lined the torpedo boat's rail, urging and cheering their shipmates on.

By the time the dinghy reached the torpedo boat, the petty officer had rolled the torso onto its stomach. The form remained limp as he pummeled the man's back in an effort to expel water from his lungs. Then abruptly, the victim arched and, accompanied by great spasms, coughed and vomited.

Cheers erupted from the sailors on the torpedo boat's rail.

Once the rescued man was on board the vessel and warmed with several blankets, he seemed overwhelmed. He shivered, smiled thinly, and thanked the torpedo boat's sailors for his rescue. Haltingly, he explained, "The airship was completely soaked. The commander tried to escape, but . . . it was overloaded with twenty-one men and all the new devices. Most of the crew were trapped in the gondolas. I was simply lucky."

On the conning platform, Gregor continued to command a search for survivors. Later, his torpedo boat was joined by other members of the flotilla and a Dutch steam trawler named Orion.

The vessels searched all night and eventually returned to port with six survivors.

At a ceremony months later, Rear Admiral Hugo Kraft issued awards to Kapitän Steiner, officers, and crew of the torpedo boat for their exemplary performance during the unfortunate crash of Zeppelin L-1.

1914

PARIS

Although written in late December 1913 and mailed in California, this letter was not received by Adrienne—in Paris—until spring 1914.

Again, Will wrote in French:

Dear Adrienne,

As always, I am tardy in writing. Please forgive me. Also, I send best wishes to you at this Christmas time, although I do not know whether your gifts arrive from Père Noël or St. Nicholas.

Thank you sincerely for writing to me. It is very pleasing to visualize you sitting near and talking to me. I was thrilled for you being named Le première d'Atelier de couture at Maison Paquin. It proves what I have always believed—that you are a very intelligent, responsible, and talented woman!

Thank you also for saying you found my humor enjoyable.

It was also nice to learn of the appearance of your design in the publication Gazette du Bon Ton. I have tried to obtain this magazine here in California, but it is not available. Perhaps it is too soon for it to appear at this distance.

It seems strange to write to you in French because I have now been in the United States for a full year, and have become accustomed to speaking English, the language of America and my father, at all times.

Father and Marie have established themselves in New York City in an apartment near Central Park. It is very costly, but is regarded by Father as a necessity for his writing, including interviews with important people.

Many things have changed since I last wrote you. In June I completed the year three curriculum in Mechanical Engineering at the Massachusetts Institute of Technology (MIT) in Boston. As part of my studies, I wrote a paper on aeronautics which launched me onto a new path. After passing all my examinations in June, I went to San Diego, California, where I began flying lessons at the Curtiss School of Aviation. This is an advanced school headed by Glenn Curtiss, a genius aviator and constructor of aeroplanes. Training takes place on North Island, a small, barren, and uninhabited island about a kilometer off the coast of San Diego, a city south of Los Angeles. We take off, fly, and land on the island.

My family—especially my father—desired that I stay on at MIT for another year, to graduate with a degree in Mechanical Engineering, but I did not want to continue in a career that would lead to designing boilers and steam plants. I have now passed the pilot-license tests of the Aviation Section of the US Army, and am rated a Military Aviator (M.A.). Because of this and my technical knowledge gained at MIT and at École Polytechnique, I have been commissioned as an officer of the US Army with the rank of lieutenant.

I realize all of this will come as a surprise to you, although I believe I told you of my deep interest in aeronautics and flying. Flying these new aeroplanes is complicated, a little risky, but very satisfying.

Although I am flying frequently and helping with the training, I am awaiting an assignment for Army duty. It is quite a lonely life at the moment, and I do wish I could see and visit with you. I very much miss your beautiful smile.

Please write soon.

Sincerely,
Will Marra

•   •   •

Véronique rushed from the Paquin showroom into the atelier. "I do not understand. It is the Comtesse Cécile Sorel."

Adrienne said, "The actress? From Comédie-Française?"

"Yes. But she wishes not to view the costumes!"

Adrienne dropped her ledger to her worktable. She saw that Véronique was in high spirits. "But why is she here?"

"She wishes only to see *you*!"

Adrienne backed her chair away, stood, and faced Véronique. "Did she say why?"

"I asked, but she demurred."

"She refused to say?"

"Let me describe." Véronique gestured with both arms. "A big, polished machine pulled in front. A uniformed chauffeur swung our door open and a glowing phantasm whirled in, rows of pearls past her waist."

Adrienne smiled. "I can imagine."

"I said, 'Maison Paquin welcomes you.' She said nothing except, 'Direct me to Adrienne Boch.' I said I would be privileged to show her any costume in the house. She said, 'If I wished to see a gown, I would have said I wish to see a gown.'"

Both women laughed. Véronique continued, "I said, 'May I inquire the purpose?' She said, 'You may.' That is all she said."

Both women laughed again. Adrienne said, "That sounds exactly like Cécile Sorel."

Adrienne left Véronique and entered the showroom. Cécile Sorel was seated in a client chair. In her silken-gloved hand she held a platinum lorgnette.

"Good afternoon, Madame Sorel," Adrienne said, "I am Adrienne Boch."

Cécile raised the lorgnette. "Oh my. You *are* young."

"I hope that does not disqualify me from serving. You asked for me?"

"I did. But I assumed you would be—let us say—more from my era." Cécile smiled and Adrienne smiled in return.

Cécile lowered the lorgnette. "Never mind that. I should be less conscious of my wretched wrinkles." She smiled again. "I would be simply pleased if you would join me for tea—or perhaps an apéritif—at the Ritz. Say on Saturday at four?"

Adrienne lost the smile. "I, well . . . may I ask for what occasion—or purpose?"

"My dear, the occasion is, I wish to converse with you. The purpose is not at all mysterious or indecent. You simply arrive at the hotel and ask to be taken to the imperial suite where the crazy comedienne resides. May I depend on you?"

●　　　●　　　●

Adrienne stepped hesitantly down the seemingly endless carpet runner flanked by huge marble columns. In the vastness of the Ritz corridor, she felt akin to an insect on a mountain. At the concierge's station, she spied a poster for Chéruit—at 21 Place Vendôme. This reminder of the world of fashion somehow calmed her nerves.

"Mademoiselle?" the clerk said. "How may I assist?"

"I—I have an appointment—with Cécile Sorel. My name is

Adrienne—"

"Instant!" he said as he smashed the bell with his hand and nodded to a waiting bellboy. "Escort the lady to Madame Sorel!—instant!"

At the door to the imperial suite, Cécile greeted Adrienne, saying, "I hope the riffraff have not set your teeth on edge." She smiled. "The staff here is infinitely stuffy."

To Adrienne, the huge paintings, lacquered walls, and distant ceilings of the suite were not less intimidating than the trip inside. "Thank you for inviting me," Adrienne said. "I hope—"

"Tut-tut, my dear. Join me in the salon. I have already rung for tea."

"Oh, how cheering," Adrienne said as they passed embers crackling in the hearth below the ornamented silver emblems of the Ritz.

"Indeed," Cécile said, waving her arm full of bracelets toward the arched doorway. "It warms the toes as it charms the nose."

Once seated across from Adrienne with the silver tea set between them, Cécile became serious. "I regret drawing you away on the week's end, but your name has come to me from Maria, the Duchess of Arion. You know her, of course.

"Now please take one of these little cakes—they are too sweet for me." She paused. "Not to mention how they swell the ankles. Where was I? Oh, yes. Maria—the Spanish duchess—has relayed to me the genius with which you have so elegantly concealed—let us say—her predicament?" She laughed the booming, raucous laugh that was her trademark in the theater.

Adrienne, still slightly unsure of her own reaction, giggled.

"I, on the other hand, exhibit the intumescence that arises from age—and, did I say—those little cakes?"

Adrienne, with teacup in hand, was forced to rush the cup to her saucer before bursting into laughter.

"And still," Cécile continued, "'Auntie Cécile' is known offstage for her extravagant finery. Without the frills and furbelows, I cannot dare appear on the street. Do you perceive my difficulty?"

Adrienne, awkwardly suppressing her mirth, nodded.

"Therefore," Cécile said, "I beg of you to originate a small house of couture to serve my needs. I will contract for a space somewhere at your convenience, and equip it with the machinery needed for drawing, cutting, sewing—whatever it is you do so magically. You will be in charge, but at the beginning, it need not interfere with your position at Paquin—they need not be informed.

"You shall name the needed seamstresses—I will pay them the going wage. You will design my wardrobe, choose the fabrics, the furs, the ornamentation. Together, you and I will—at least this is the wish I cherish—upset the fashion apple cart." She smiled a wicked smile and paused. "You may name the house whatever you please. What do you say?"

Adrienne was wide-eyed. "I—I cannot know what to say . . ."

"As the business proceeds, you will expand to other clients. Then, independent of me, you will become the leading fashion house in Paris."

Tears flowed from Adrienne's eyes. "It is a dream—is it? I cannot be certain you are serious."

"When you decide a name for the house, I will fund for you an account with Monsieur Cox, president of the Bank of Paris. Will you find that convincing?"

PARAÍSO, PANAMA

The Leichenschmaus (funeral meal) had concluded, and although a few of the guests remained at the table enjoying the widow's Zuckerkuchen, Bruno Ackermann excused himself and went out onto the patio. Herr Lindoch followed and spoke quietly in German. "Your tribute to your father was most fitting. And thank you for your generous hospitality."

"I am pleased that you could attend," Bruno said, gazing out over the orchids. "The tribute is all tradition. The burial ceremony and Leichenschmaus as well. I presume it derives from our need for reminders." He paused. "Reminders of our debt." A slight smile came to his lips. "I found my sister's poem most touching."

Lindoch nodded. "Yes. Most touching."

Bruno turned to him. "You will stay overnight, Herr Lindoch. I can then accompany you on the return to Colón."

"Thank you, I will. It was fortunate I could attend the burial ceremony and all the rest."

An awkward silence followed.

Bruno turned and gestured. "Were it not for all the trees, you could see the Pedro Miguel locks from here, though it is distant several kilometers."

Lindoch nodded. "I am told the Canal will open soon."

"When they complete the digging at Culebra. And Panama will never be Panama again." He sighed and turned to Lindoch. "Where does your ship take you next?"

"Berlin is recalling."

"This is routine?"

"No. Not at all. I am uncertain why I am returning." Lindoch hesitated, then frowned. "I apologize for touching upon the matter during this time, but what will happen with the passing?"

Confused, Bruno faced Lindoch. "You mean here in Paraíso?"

"Yes," Lindoch said.

"The Telefunken facility will continue, without pause."

"Excuse me, but with the absence of your father . . ."

"Nothing will change. Mother will continue her supervision."

"Frau Ackermann, supervising?"

"Yes. She has been performing this all along—during Father's illness."

"I did not know. So the technical work, the tower . . ."

Bruno smiled at Lindoch. "Mother is a very capable woman."

"I see," Lindoch said, pausing. "That is why I heard no complaint during the—during your father's illness."

"There should be no worry," Bruno said. "She is very loyal."

•   •   •

The hoof-thuds of the mule and rumble of the wagon wheels clashed with the constant buzz of insects and the distant screech of birds in the jungle alongside the road.

Bruno turned to his seatmate. "You said your return to Berlin is not routine. What—"

"Yes. But—" Lindoch pointed at the driver seated in front of them. "I should not . . . in front of . . ."

Bruno laughed. "Oh, you mean Raúl? He understands not a single word of German. You may speak freely."

"To this moment I have refrained from a mention—on account of your bereavement, Bruno. You understand?"

Bruno nodded. "Thank you."

"Our tasks are soon to expand. I am told, and this is most secret, that we of this service should prepare for circumstances of warfare."

"Warfare?"

"I cannot name possible participants. But we must see to expanded servicing. In addition to other German vessels, our job now includes supplying submarines—the so-called U-boats."

"You are quite sure of this, Herr Lindoch? I mean of war?"

Lindoch waved a flying insect from his face. "This comes from qualified sources, that mobilization is underway."

Bruno shook his head slowly. "It is inevitable, I suppose, knowing our enemies. Yet . . ."

Lindoch's face became stern. "You must not speak of it, Bruno. But be prepared."

"I understand, Herr Lindoch." They rode on toward the Paraíso station without speaking for a time.

Bruno broke the silence. "How will servicing U-boats differ from that for other vessels?"

"Certainly food, water, lubricant, tools, and provisioning will be the same. I suppose it is only in the fueling—fuel oil rather than coal will be needed."

"The motors for the U-boats—they are diesel motors, like my boat in Colón. Is that correct?"

"Yes. Therefore they consume fuel oil rather than coal."

"I see. Perhaps many, many barrels of oil?"

"Yes. I suppose. But also, they have batteries." Lindoch's face took on a tense appearance. "Yes, yes. I remember now. When traveling under water, these U-boats are propelled by electricity. The electricity is supplied by batteries—lead-acid batteries, I believe. And these require—I think—sulfuric acid."

"Batteries. That is new. I shall have to look into that. Lead-acid batteries," he said with heavy emphasis, "lead-acid batteries."

PENSACOLA, FLORIDA

On April 17, 1914, Lt. Will Marra embarked on the strangest assignment of his Army career: He reported for duty at a United States Navy base.

The commander of Pensacola Naval Base, Lieutenant Commander Henry Mustin, sat with Marra's papers before him on his desk. He said, "I'm reading what this paper says, Lieutenant. But . . ."

Will, in uniform, stood stiffly at attention. "I'm following orders, sir."

"At ease, Lieutenant. We'll sort this out. First, tell me exactly what . . . uh, Captain Foulois said to you."

"Yes, sir." Will gestured. "He said I was 'detached.' That I should report to you here for temporary duty."

"Yes, that's what the paper says." LCDR Mustin gripped a pinch of lower lip with his left hand. He released it, dropped his hand, and stared at Will with a frown. "But I don't have any notification of this from the admiral. Your captain didn't say why you were 'detached' from your Army unit?"

"No sir . . ." Will paused to recall and backtracked. "Well, Captain Foulois did mention something about me being a certified aeroplane pilot."

"Uh-huh." Mustin stared at the paper and placed his finger on a line. "I see you have your license from the FAI."

Will nodded. "And he said something—something about there being a shortfall."

"Uh-huh." Mustin glanced upward to focus on Marra. "A shortfall in the Navy, eh?"

"Yes, sir."

"Well, he might have something there." Mustin smiled. "I happen to be 'Navy Air Pilot Number Three.'"

Will smiled. "Yes, sir!"

"Are you a Curtiss pilot or a Wright pilot?"

"I've flown Wright craft a couple of times, sir. But I trained with Curtiss controls."

"Good. You are aware, Lieutenant, that there might be a little dustup down in Mexico?"

"Yes, sir, but not the details."

"Uh-huh. I'm going to billet you with Lieutenant Patrick Bellinger. He's Curtiss-trained. He's in charge of the *Mississippi*'s aeroplane section."

"Mississippi, sir?"

Mustin grinned. "I keep forgetting, you're *Army*." His face relaxed. "The USS Mississippi is a battleship moored in our harbor. Bellinger's section includes three student-aviator officers and a crew of enlisted mechanicians."

Will nodded.

"Now, although you are an Army Lieutenant, you'll be subject to Bellinger's supervision. You can handle that?"

"Yes, sir."

"Okay, I'll forward your papers to the personnel clerk. Maybe he can figure out how to get you paid. Meanwhile, you go over there to the BOQ and introduce yourself to Bellinger. Tell him he can check with me if he doesn't understand—I'll be glad to tell him I don't understand either."

"Yes, sir, except, sir, I'm new here. Where are the BOQ, the officers' quarters?"

"Oh, yes. Well, with all the new construction, it may be hard to find—we've only been in operation here for a year. Just ask around—somebody will guide you."

•   •   •

Three days later, Will stood with Lieutenant Pat Bellinger on the Pensacola dock. They watched as the cruiser, black smoke billowing from two of its four funnels, was eased into the main channel by three tugboats.

Bellinger turned to Marra. "There goes our best stuff."

Will frowned. "What do you mean?"

"The cream. When the order for the Birmingham to sail came in, 'Rum' Mustin had to order the best of our aeroplanes, together with spares, supplies, and equipment on board. They expect action at Tampico."

"How will the aeroplane section operate down there?"

"I'm not sure," Bellinger said. "Depends on the situation. It's not what I'd call handy—they'll have to hoist the aeroplanes off the deck and into the water with that derrick. And that derrick was cobbled together from a boom stolen off the Mississippi."

"I watched them working on it yesterday. Do you think the aeroplanes will be assigned reconnaissance down there?"

"I suppose. If we end up down there, I've got a different slant, though."

Will grinned at Bellinger. "What's that?"

"I bought the latest camera put out by Eastman. I've experimented a little with it while flying."

"So you think you might take photographs from the air—that would sure be nifty."

"That's the idea—if we get involved."

•   •   •

Amidst the exiting crowd of ship's officers and some decorated Marines, Will Marra and Patrick Bellinger hurried from the base commander's building.

"Hells bells!" Bellinger said, "Things must be popping down there."

"I'll say." Will pulled his hat lower over his eyes. "Where they going to put all those Marines?"

Bellinger slowed to a comfortable jog. "More than five hundred Marines? No berths belowdecks—I suppose they'll all be sprawled on the main deck."

The two men resumed their pace. When they came to the first hangar, they stopped. Bellinger said, "You take one of the ensigns, Stoltz or LaMont, and four enlisteds. Stand by to get stuff aboard the Mississippi. I'll take Saufley, the other ensign, and the rest of the enlisteds. I'm going to have to scrounge up everything that didn't go onto the Birmingham. We'll round up everything we think we can use."

"Okay." Will thumbed to the west. "I think I saw LaMont talking to some enlisteds over by that dock. You have a preference?"

Bellinger grinned. "Nah. I'll be conferring with Caswell."

"Caswell?"

"Saufley. He goes by his middle name. Don't let his Kentucky drawl fool you—he may be West Point, but he knows where all the bones are buried."

"You think Mustin thinks we can get ready in time?"

"He's the captain. If 'Rum' says 'set a record, we sail before the forenoon watch,' he means it."

"I'll do my best."

"That's the word. And Will—let me know as soon as the bosun says the derrick's ready. Then you and I will see if we can motor those two seaplanes to portside and load them onto the ship." He turned and grinned over his shoulder. "Maybe without crashing them into the side of the hull."

• • •

Will mopped sweat from his forehead as he watched the gray smoke. The hazy gray filament rose, not from the stone bulwarks of the old fort that fronted the city, but inland, from among the pastel-painted buildings of Veracruz, Mexico.

"That's probably from the bombardment," Saufley said, pointing at the smoke. He peered from his crouch in the shadow of the A-3's lower wing. "I heard the Navy fired three-inch rounds during the battle. At Mexicans holed up in a building inside the city."

The A-3 was what Curtiss called a 'hydroaeroplane'—it was equipped with twin floats. It was a space-framed aeroplane, only slightly more advanced than those Will had trained in on North Island. It was powered by a Curtiss motor of limited horsepower driving a pusher propeller.

"Okay. Now you've got wheels," Will said, tossing his wrench to the canvas covering the sand under the aeroplane. "Too bad we arrived too late to join the fighting. That Mexican general should have known better than to tangle with the US."

"Yeah." Saufley bent backward, examining the connections of the frame to the undercarriage. "All that's left is scouting for lonesome cowboys." He gestured toward the undercarriage. "And thanks to getting rid of the floats."

Will stood up. "Did Mustin really say 'encampments or groups of five or more are regarded as enemy'?"

Saufley glanced at Will. "That's it. Bellinger said those are the words in the scouting orders. And also, we can't take revolvers with us in either aeroplane."

Will bent, gripped the tire of one of the wheels, and shook it. "This seems solid."

"Yeah." Saufley squinted at the axle. "It's tight, Will. I think everything's good. Bellinger will do his own inspection when he returns." He crawled out from under the wing and stood up. He arched his back and grunted.

Will looked through the spindly frame of the A-3 toward the sea inside the breakwater. He gestured toward where the C-3 flying boat was tied up. "I'm scheduled to scout at dawn tomorrow in the C-3. You want to be my observer?"

Saufley grinned. "Thought you'd never ask."

•   •   •

At an altitude of 2,200 feet, Will Marra steered the C-3 flying boat south, beyond Veracruz. In the seat at his right, Caswell Saufley squeezed a map, a pad and its leashed pencil between his legs. Both men wore life jackets in the cramped nose of the craft, the top of which was covered by fabric.

Powered by the motor behind them with its pusher-propeller at the rear of the motor, the seaplane moved at a reconnaissance speed of forty-five miles per hour, close to the maximum permitted by its seventy-five-horsepower motor. The roar of the Curtiss motor, however, made talking almost useless.

Enemy troops were reported north of Anón Lizardo, but Saufley had written nothing on his pad since their 4:00 a.m. takeoff. He tried to search the jungle below using field glasses, but buffeting caused by the lack of a wind screen meant steadying his aim became almost impossible.

At one point, Saufley held up his left hand to Will and pointed downward with his right.

Will eased the throttle back and lowered the nose. At the same time, he banked left so the machine made a gliding, sinking turn out over the water (volplaning at North Island came to mind).

Once the aeroplane completed a full circle, they arrived at the previous location over the jungle, but about four hundred feet lower.

Will leveled and straightened the aeroplane's flightpath.

Saufley seemed to have lost the target. He squirmed in the cockpit, sweeping his field glasses over the lush green foliage beneath them. After about a minute he lowered the glasses and shook his head.

Will lowered the nose again and began a second turn out over the water. When they arrived back over the jungle, Saufley shouted at Will and made frantic downward motions with his index finger.

Will leveled the aircraft. In his peripheral vision, he caught a fluttering movement below. Swinging his head left, he pushed his goggles up and noted a hole in the lower wing and a snippet of wing fabric flapping vigorously in the wind. Without pausing he let his goggles drop, increased throttle, raised the nose, and banked left.

Saufley lowered his field glasses, swung his head toward Will with his face contorted. He shouted, "What you doing?"

The aircraft was now over the water. In the middle of the turn Will took his right hand from the wheel and pointed to his left, toward the hole in the lower wing. At the same time he noticed a hole above, in the upper wing. He shouted at Saufley, "They hit us."

Saufley craned his neck to see around Will and grimaced.

Will shouted again, "Returning to base. Log what you saw."

Saufley slipped the pad and pencil from between his legs and scribbled.

Will nodded and straightened the craft to a northerly heading.

•   •   •

Will shut off the aeroplane's motor. The propeller behind the steaming engine slowed until he could see it twitch. The momentum of the hull drove it toward shore in the very modest wave action behind the breakwater. When the craft approached the piling, Saufley climbed out.

The water came to Saufley's knees. He pulled the hull to the piling with its tether and tied the tether around the timber. Then he retrieved his map and pad.

Will stood and leaned over to inspect the small hole in the fabric of the lower wing. Then he glanced up at the similar hole in the upper wing. As he climbed out, he looked at Saufley. "What'd you see back there?"

Saufley held up his pad. "Bright flashes. Wrote it all down."

"I can't believe it," Will said as he guided the tail of the aeroplane around toward the shore. "How many were there?"

"They were right there in that little clearing. But you pulled up so fast . . ."

"In uniform?"

Saufley tugged on the rope's knot. "They had rifles."

"But were they in uniform?"

"Hard to tell, Will. They wore big hats . . ."

"How many?"

"Three guys."

Will stopped and frowned. "Three?"

"I'm sure. Three. And I saw two flashes."

"Wow. What a lucky shot."

Saufley nodded. "One in a thousand."

Will chuckled as he tethered the aeroplane's tail into the prevailing wind. "And with just three we can't even claim they were the enemy."

CHARLEROI, BELGIUM

Dominique stood outside the entrance to the Boch home as her husband arrived.

Jean Boch stepped from the carriage and removed his hat. The driver drove off.

"I thought you would never come," she said as he passed her.

"Yes, yes. I understand." Jean turned and kissed his wife on the cheek.

"I hope you bring good news," she said, holding the previous edition of Le Soir with the headline, 'L'Allemagne Violé La Neutralité Belge.' (Germany Violates Belgian Neutrality.)

Jean mopped his brow with his kerchief and replaced his derby hat. "Let us get out of the sun," he said. "I am baking."

Dominique withdrew, closed the door, and said, "I have allowed the maid to leave early."

"One moment, if you please." He loosened his tie and his stiff collar. Sweat returned to his brow. "We suffered much commotion," he said, placing his derby on the hook.

They climbed the stairs. As they entered the library, Dominique said, "What was the commotion?"

"Clients swarming the tellers." He sat in the chair before the whirling electric fan. "Oh, that is better."

Dominique continued standing. "What does swarming mean?"

"They wished to withdraw their money."

"Because of the—"

"It was relayed to most that before dawn this morning, soldiers of the German Second Army began advancing on Liège."

Dominique sank into the opposing chair. Her eyes began to tear up. "Oh, no."

Jean frowned. "Do not be afraid. Liège is nearly a hundred kilometers by road."

"How can I be otherwise? Have not the Germans a big army?"

"Of course. But our defenses there, the ring of many fortified gun positions at Liège, they should protect the city. This afternoon—"

"Did any of the bank's clients withdraw all of their money?"

"As you know, I must refrain from discussing details of clients' banking. But several sought to convert to cash." Jean looked away. "We discussed—we dissuaded many of those from such drastic action. At least for now."

"Not all?"

Jean shook his head. "Not all."

"What about our money, Jean?" Small lines formed around her eyes. "Should we—"

"The bank is solvent. I think we should not worry."

"What is their object—the Germans?"

"It is reported they wish to punish France." Jean leaned his face into the breeze of the fan. "I myself think they have stupid, unrealistic notions."

"So they will come here, to Charleroi. On their way to France."

He turned to her. "The Germans? Not necessarily, my dear. This afternoon—"

"But we are between them and the border of France, are we not?"

"I know. But as I was saying, this afternoon we heard a firsthand account of the fighting. A client told us a man who had left Liège at midday said the Germans, in the darkness before dawn, marched foolishly toward the garrison at Liège by moonlight. They came steadily, he said, in 'thick lines' facing our machine guns, until they could no longer advance."

"Until they—what?"

"Until they could no longer surmount their dead and wounded, piled six or seven deep."

Dominique shut her eyes and turned away. "Oh, such horror."

Jean frowned. "You are feeling sorry—for the evil Huns?"

She turned back. "No. Of certainty I am not. Only for the death and the blood, the horror of humans killing humans."

Jean smiled. "The Huns will find it not easy to defeat our army."

Dominique dabbed at her wet cheek with the back of her hand. "But in the end they will defeat our army, will they not?"

Jean's face turned serious. "I suppose. If they are determined."

"And what shall we do, when they come?"

"We will be warned. I have spoken with a member of the Council. He assured me—"

"Yes, we will be warned." Dominique kneaded one hand with the other. "But the warning, will it be by days, or by hours, or by minutes?"

"Let us not overreact. In another day or two, we will learn more."

Dominique rose from her chair. "I think we should prepare, starting now. We should not wait. I will gather essentials and begin to pack. You should—"

"Dominique! You are overreacting."

"Name it as you will. I think we should prepare to seal the apartment and take the train. We have no knowledge for how long the trains will continue to run—"

"But there is no danger to the trains—"

"We can go to Paris—to Adrienne's apartment, Jean. Think about it."

"But that means I should have to resign my position and—"

"Adrienne is doing well. I am sure she would welcome us."

"Yes," Jean said, nodding. "Our daughter is more than a success."

"And France will defend Paris to the last man—on that we may be sure."

"Yes." Jean rose from his chair and went to the window. While gazing down to the courtyard, he stroked his chin. He turned and grinned at Dominique. "Yes. On that we are in complete agreement."

PARIS

Adrienne went to the telephone that, only a month earlier, had been replaced with the latest model. It was in the alcove off the showroom. Speaking into the small horn, she said, "Good day. This is Adrienne Boch speaking."

The voice at the other end was thin and reedy. "Adrienne—I apologize. I regret interfering at your employment—"

"Mother!" Adrienne said, recognizing the voice. "How worried I was—"

"I know it is not a good time, but your papa and I are here, at Gare du Nord, and—"

"Mother! With the war, I was desperate for you—I will come, immediately!"

Jumbled thoughts crowded Adrienne's mind as she made her excuse, flew from the door of Paquin, and hailed a taxi. She had half-expected the telephone call, considering the news that Von Bülow's German army was driving south along the valley of the Meuse toward her hometown of Charleroi.

As the motor of the taxi sputtered onto Rue Lafayette, she tried to order her thoughts. She had brought her identification papers with her—workers at Paquin advised that the authorities were checking, even though France was less than a month into the war. Her parents, she mused, would be considered part of the flood of fleeing Belgians, an influx that now crowded the Cirque de Paris. What had the Bochs brought with them? Records, mementos, and clothing, she was sure.

As for the streets, Paris seemed nearly deserted. Gone was the bustle of shoppers. Many of the shops along the boulevard bore papers on the door saying, "Closed on account of the mobilization." Only around banks and steamship offices did she see crowds. These people, she thought, represented foreigners in panic struggling to escape from Paris. But shortly her thoughts were vanquished by her arrival at Gare du Nord.

Inside, she found the din of crowds, steam exhausts, bells, and the shouts of luggage men unnerving. The arrivals consisted of every manner of persons, male and female, of all ages, differing widely in appearance and dress. The sound of their voices approached that of a roar.

On outgoing platforms, by contrast, somber crowds of men, not in uniform, but in everyday or even soiled clothing gathered. In tightly-wrapped cloth bundles, they clutched their few possessions. These men, Adrienne was sure, were Parisians leaving for the military.

Only after many minutes of frantic searching did Adrienne find her parents—near piles of canvas and leather grips, bags, cases, and satchels.

"Oh, dearest Adrienne—thank God," cried Dominique, and the three of them embraced.

"You are safe! You are safe!" Adrienne said through tears, smiling broadly.

Jean disengaged and grasped some of their luggage. "Dear Daughter," he said, "we shall have not a simple time with all this luggage—but I have inquired: help is simply not available."

"I know—the luggage men are all retained. But I shall make as many trips as are needed," Adrienne said, smiling. To her teary-eyed mother, she said, "Mother, you will please remain with the belongings as Papa and I transport some of the bags outside where I have a taxi waiting."

At Adrienne's apartment, the inverse action of transporting baggage from the taxi to the interior followed. When finally everything had been accounted for, the hot, relieved, and exhausted family sat in the tiny sitting room discussing the couple's journey. "It was utter chaos," Jean said. "We were only fortunate to obtain passage on the train. The bank refused for me to leave, but—"

"You are safe, now," Adrienne said. "That is the most important accomplishment. You shall stay here until I can locate larger quarters—although that may be not easy."

"I am certain Paris is flooded with visitors," Jean said, "or rather, refugees."

"Before we escaped, I learned that thousands were fleeing Belgium, even Brussels." Jean shook his head in dismay. "And the evil Germans—they boast of their intent to take Paris, as well as Brussels."

"Yes, Papa. We must pray that General Joseph Joffre, the commander of the French Army, will protect us to the end."

Jean nodded, but his face portrayed skepticism as he contemplated 'the end.'

"We simply closed and locked our door," Dominique said. "There was no other option." Her face was pale and strained. "I fear for those who failed—or chose not to—leave. The Germans show no mercy."

WILHELMSHAVEN, GERMANY

G regor tore into the brown envelope addressed to Oberleutnant Gregor Steiner. It had been forwarded several times, and because of the war, delivery was delayed by almost two months. The letter inside was from Adrienne, handwritten in French. It bore the date September 4, 1914.

Dearest Cousin Gregor,

I am answering your last letter which you wrote shortly before the war. I have used the address that you gave at that time. I hope this letter will reach you, although you may be on a ship at sea.

Your actions regarding the rescue of the man who survived the crash of the L-1 airship (Zeppelin) was most honorable and distinguished. I am pleased you did it. I was also sorry to learn of the loss of those who perished.

I am happy that you have gained another advancement, now to Oberleutnant. What does this new rank entail? Please explain in plain language, for I admit I do not easily understand military ratings, equipments, or all those special words.

As you know, I am living now in Paris for several years. Last year, I was named "Le première d'Atelier de couture" at Maison Paquin, one of the leading houses of couture in Paris. It is an honor, but great sadness has recently visited me. I refer to the fact my parents, your Uncle Jean and Aunt Dominique, are now here. The sadness is not that they are here, but rather that they were forced to flee from Charleroi by the invasion of the Imperial German Army. My parents could only escape with what they could carry of their possessions! They have no knowledge of what has happened to their home in Charleroi.

Neither your Aunt Dominique, Uncle Jean, nor I have received word from Grandmother Anne Boch now that Brussels has also been occupied by the German Army. As you know, Grandmother is ill and frail and cannot deserve to be ill-treated. We are all hoping and praying that she is safe and has not been harmed, and I know that you share our hope and prayers for our dear one.

I realize your last letter was dated before the war. However, from some of your words in that letter, I am uncertain of your position. I hope you oppose the invasion of Belgium by Germany. It has caused many deaths and much destruction, some of which has been described to me by my parents, who witnessed it. Your aunt and uncle were forced to abandon their home in Charleroi and were forced to take one of the last trains to Paris to escape, because the Germans did not exempt ordinary citizens like them from the cruelties of war. My dear father is now unemployed, although in Belgium he was a successful banker.

As I am given to understand, Belgium did nothing to deserve the German invasion. Your uncle Jean says King Albert only claimed Belgium was neutral, that Belgium's borders were sacred and that the Belgian government could not sanction free passage of the Imperial armies of Germany through Belgium territory in order for them to attack France. Yet the German armies simply marched in and attacked Belgium's citizens! And it seems that these same German armies now threaten to attack us here in Paris!

Please take care of yourself and write soon.

Your Cousin,
Adrienne Boch

NORTH SEA

Note to the Reader:
The Imperial German Navy was well aware that miscommunication on board a warship could result in catastrophe. They therefore required that every verbal command be followed by a subordinate's exact verbal repetition of that command. However, to avoid this repetition in the seagoing actions that follow, I omit most of the repeated commands. I also omit certain other details which are unimportant to understanding the actions.

O n patrol, Oberleutnant Gregor Steiner stood in the torpedo boat's conning bridge. Germany had been at war less than a month, yet the orders received from the High Seas Fleet directed the boat to hunt for "submarines or other activity."

He turned to his second in command. "Zimmermann. What is meant by 'other activity'?"

"I believe it to mean English ships."

Gregor again faced the North Sea fog. "A ship is not an activity."

"Yes. But we are patrolling for the English, are we not?"

"We are securing the German Bay. Suppose we encounter a fishing trawler of unknown origin."

"A fishing trawler would not be of significance."

Gregor smiled. "Might a fishing trawler conceal mines in its hold?"

Zimmermann smiled and squinted with his right eye. "You are laying a trap for me."

Gregor again faced the fog. "Well, what?"

"Yes. A trawler might conceal mines in its hold. An *English* trawler."

Gregor laughed. "So 'other activity' may mean almost anything, as long as it is English."

Zimmermann laughed.

Gregor's face went sober. "Wait . . . do you hear?"

Zimmermann faced an ear toward the barely audible sounds.

Gregor said, "That is not thunder. Order combat stations!"

Zimmermann confirmed, "Combat stations," and repeated the order into the speaking pipe.

Gregor turned toward the sounds and said, "Helmsman, hard to port—All Ahead Full."

The helmsman repeated the order, twirled the wheel, and swung the engine-order telegraph handles. The ship heeled. Bells sounded.

Black smoke issued from the ship's funnels. Crewmen appeared on the deck below them, hurrying to gun stations, turrets, and torpedo tubes.

"Zimmermann," Gregor said, "notify leader our position turning south toward gunfire."

Zimmermann confirmed and shouted into the speaking pipe, "Wireless: Send to Command: Position northwest Heligoland, two—" He stopped in response to a voice from below. He repeated the message wireless had received: "Wireless reports SMS Mainz attacked by enemy cruiser with several destroyers. Position west of Heligoland."

The sounds of gunfire grew louder as Zimmermann ordered wireless to relay the torpedo boat's position to Command.

Gregor reacted to the received message. "That's it, the gunfire we hear must be that of Mainz. Helmsman," he ordered, "steer to gunfire."

"Steer to gunfire," the helmsman confirmed.

"Damn the fog," Zimmerman said, upon completing his communication. "How will we make the range?"

Gregor said, "We should contact the Mainz or its attacker within a quarter-hour. Check Gunnery."

A moment later, a voice was heard on the voice pipe. Zimmermann said, "Gunnery reports guns loaded—ready for action."

The distant gunfire ceased. Yet nothing emerged in front of them except fog.

Gregor knew there was nothing to do but wait. The men on the conning tower tried to see beyond each layer of fog as the steel bow of the torpedo boat sliced through it.

The fog began to thin.

Gregor checked the time on the chronometer. "Helmsman, Ahead Slow."

The helmsman cranked the handles. Bells sounded, and the answer pointers rotated to 'Slow.' The ship began to slow.

Ahead, the fog dissipated. Black smoke appeared on the horizon. Below it Gregor saw a dark smudge, possibly a ship. "Standby," he said, raising binoculars to his eyes. "Three funnels—a cruiser." As the torpedo boat continued to slow, he tried to interpret the ship's profile. "Ah," he said after a long moment, "I think it is German. Hold fire!"

Gregor said, "Range?"

"I am trying," Zimmermann said.

Gregor said, "A Kolberg-class light cruiser, but . . ." As he continued to examine the cruiser, he saw illumination—a bright yellow illumination flashed behind the main mast. "There is damage—and fire."

"What?" Zimmermann stared at the distant ship and raised his binoculars. He stared for several seconds and said, "Wait—wait—I know this vessel . . . that is not Mainz—it is Cöln!"

Gregor said. "Helmsman, Ahead Half."

The helmsman confirmed and executed the order.

To Zimmermann, Gregor said, "You are sure it is Cöln?"

"Yes. I have a friend who is aboard it."

"Cöln moves very slow."

Zimmermann lowered his binoculars. "How do you judge?"

"The bow wake—note the small wake at the bow."

Zimmerman returned the binoculars to his eyes. "Yes, yes, it is little."

The torpedo boat continued its course toward Cöln.

A gun crewman emerged from the torpedo boat's forward turret and stared up at the conning tower with puzzlement on his face.

The two officers on the bridge continued to scan the horizon with their glasses.

"I see the attacker!" exclaimed Zimmermann.

"Yes," Gregor said. "Behind Cöln. There is black smoke."

"A flash!" Zimmerman shouted. "Another flash—it is firing! I think—"

"It is the English," Gregor said, "English firing on the Cöln. What do you make of the attacker, Zimmermann?"

"Not sure—three funnels—a light cruiser probably."

"No. Two turrets before the mast," Gregor said. "Two turrets make it a battle cruiser!"

"Oh no!" Zimmermann said. "Monster! The English dragon."

"Helmsman," Gregor said, "steer to starboard."

The helmsman affirmed the order and turned the wheel.

Zimmermann lowered his binoculars and stared at Gregor with wide eyes.

Gregor saw Zimmermann's questioning look but ignored it. "Helmsman, for now, I will instruct your steering. Do you see the nearest vessel, the Cöln?"

"Yes, Kapitän, I see it."

"When you see the other vessel beyond it, beyond Cöln, say it."

The helmsman squinted at the horizon. "Kapitän, I know there is a vessel beyond Cöln. But in reality what I see is its smoke."

"Yes. Now listen carefully. Steer to keep the smoke, and that English vessel, behind our Cöln. Do you understand?"

"Keep us in a line," the helmsman said, "the three vessels in a line?"

"Exactly!"

Zimmermann continued his quizzical stare. Gregor focused his binoculars on the attacker. "Zimmerman," he said. "We face a battle cruiser with eight thirty-five-centimeter guns . . ."

At that moment, multiple red flashes from the British battle cruiser lit the horizon. A few seconds later, multiple vertical columns of white water erupted near Cöln and two bright yellow flashes obscured it from view.

Seconds later, a huge roar reached the torpedo boat's conning bridge.

"Cöln is hit!" Zimmermann said. "Oh, no. Gun turrets are thrown from the deck! A funnel is crazy sideways!"

"Helmsman! Steer to port," Gregor said. "Keep Cöln between us and the attacker!"

"I am sorry," the helmsman said. He continued to correct his steering.

Gregor's torpedo boat now approached to a thousand meters from Cöln, whose frayed Imperial flag was now visible through glasses.

Zimmerman, eyes squinting into his binoculars, grimaced. "Oh no. Another salvo!"

Great geysers of white water erupted near Cöln, and more yellow flashes obscured the vessel for brief seconds. Although the British attacker remained hidden a long distance behind Cöln, the roar of its huge guns in salvo rattled the torpedo boat's conning tower.

Flames issued above Cöln's main deck, and from holes in its hull. Crewmen became visible dragging wounded to the stern, where officers and enlisted gathered.

Zimmermann dropped his binoculars to the strap hanging from his neck. He briefly closed his eyes, as if in pain. "Terrible . . ."

Gregor turned to the helmsman. "Excellent," he said, referring to the helmsman's performance. "The English cannot see us."

The helmsman nodded while keeping his vision focused on the Cöln and the British ship. He turned the wheel, first one way, then the other, maintaining the torpedo boat's position in line with the two other vessels.

A voice came from the speaking tube. Zimmermann leaned and listened. He said, "Wireless reports: High Seas Fleet Command issued an order: 'Facing an overwhelming enemy force, flotillas, and light cruisers shall immediately retire. Signed, High Seas Fleet Admiral Ingenohl.'"

White clouds of smoke rose high from Cöln, from both the fore-castle and the stern.

Gregor said, "This is impossible!"

Zimmermann said, "I am confused. I do not know what to think."

Gregor continued his view of the men of Cöln, many of whom began to jump from the deck into the sea. "They are like ants scattering—" he said. "What is the complement—how many on Cöln?"

"Two hundred or better, I am sure," Zimmermann said. "Also the admiral—Admiral Maas!"

"What the hell are those on the stern doing—" Gregor said, turning to Zimmermann in astonishment. "By God, they are singing, singing to the flag!"

"The order, Herr Steiner," Zimmermann said, "the Fleet Admiral's order—"

Gregor removed the binoculars from his eyes. "We cannot leave—Cöln is sinking! There are hundreds of men—"

"But Fleet Command's order—"

"What of the men in the water? I cannot—" Gregor stopped his statement. He abruptly realized his statement opposed an order by Fleet Command.

"The English," Zimmermann said, "they will surely rescue Cöln's crew. Take them aboard—as prisoners."

"Yes. I hope." Gregor, at this moment unsure, knew his duty. "Secure from combat stations," he said, shaking his head. "Helmsman, reverse course, All Ahead Full."

●   ●   ●

On the Sunday evening following their Friday experience, Gregor met with Zimmermann at a small second-story apartment off Gokerstrasse, in Wilhelmshaven.

Gregor looked uncomfortable. "It is all right to speak freely here?"

Zimmermann said, "My friend has no interest in naval activities."

He nodded toward the tiny kitchen that angled off the sitting room. "Janina—will you serve?" The slight woman in a beige gown, her hair in a bun, hurried off.

When she was gone, Zimmermann quietly said, smiling, "She does not seem even to know there is a war."

Gregor said, "I have today learned the numbers concerning the sinking of Cöln."

Zimmermann leaned forward on the couch. "I have heard rumors only."

"It is staggering: Four hundred ninety officers and men died."

Zimmermann sat upright. "You mean all those were killed by the bombardment of Cöln—or drowned afterward?"

"Yes. Today, a patrol picked a stoker—Adolf Neumann by name—from the sea, still alive."

"Today?"

"Today. All the others are gone. An hour in that cold sea is fatal."

"God—that is horrible." Zimmermann stared at the floor. "Thus my friend is lost, as well—"

"No one, not Neumann himself, knows how he survived."

Janina returned with a tray with two mugs and two bottles of beer. Each man silently poured beer into his mug. Janina took the bottles to the kitchen. The men lifted their mugs and took a swallow.

Gregor said, "It is reported—by the English press—that Lion, the battle cruiser, intended to rescue the men in the water. After they sank the Cöln."

Zimmermann paused with his mug in mid-air.

Gregor continued. "But the English news claims Lion's lookout sighted a periscope after Cöln sank. Thus the battle cruiser was forced to escape from what they believed was our submarine."

Zimmermann drank from his mug. "Ah, but who should believe the English press?"

Janina returned and sat across from the two men. She plucked a magazine from a table and began reading.

"It is likely all propaganda," Zimmermann said, shaking his head. "Has it affected you?"

"The deaths, you mean?"

"Our whole day."

"I try not to relive it." Gregor said. "I wish we could have saved— even one of the crew. But we were recalled. And no match for a battle cruiser."

After a minute of silence Zimmermann said, "I know. It is terrible."

Gregor stared at the floor, then looked at Zimmerman. "I feel guilt for leaving. It haunts me."

"But Gregor, you had to obey—"

"I could have disregarded Fleet Command's order. We might have rescued some of those men."

Zimmermann shook his head. "I think not. Not with that English battle cruiser present." He gestured with his arm. "You saw how quickly those big guns wrecked the Cöln. They blew one of its turrets right off its mount!"

Gregor did not speak. Grim-faced, he took a large swallow of beer.

Zimmerman watched Gregor's face, saying, "We could not have survived. That monster would have blasted us to scrap iron— in minutes."

"Those poor bastards," Gregor said, "killed firing their puny little guns against Lion's armor. Or drowning later. If we ever have the chance, I mean to show those English—"

"We should have been warned of English battle cruisers in the Bight."

"Perhaps." Gregor said, staring at his mug. "Perhaps they did not know."

Zimmermann took a big swallow of beer. "But the wireless—it is almost worthless—all static and slow. Decoding messages takes so much time. Meanwhile, our battle cruisers—they sit at anchor in the harbor at Wilhelmshaven." He paused. "Bah!"

Gregor drank some more beer and finally smiled. "When you

become Admiral, Zimmermann, I pray you will fix these difficulties."

"Ha," Zimmermann said, raising his mug. "By the time I make Admiral, you will command the High Seas Fleet. You can fix them yourself!"

•   •   •

Later, on 1 October, Gregor met with two other torpedo boat commanders in their quarters near the North Port in Wilhelmshaven.

Fischer sat on his desk, swinging his legs. "For six weeks, now, we are patrolling without contacts. It is very wearing."

"That is so," Weber said, leaning onto the wall and puffing on his meerschaum pipe. "Our vessels, not to admit crews—they are taking a flogging, I say."

"Without the patrols, however, our country will wither." Gregor rose from his chair and gestured. "Overall, we remain a thorn in the side of England, which attempts to strangle us."

Weber pulled his pipe from between his teeth. "The question was put, whether our big ships should come out from the estuary. In the battle of the Bight on 28 August, the visibility was so poor, they would have had no effect."

"Why do you say that?" Gregor said, evenly.

"All advantages are with the attacker. The English are unknown targets hidden by fog and mist. It is a useless exercise—and potentially risky—sending battle cruisers with big guns into the Bight in fog."

Fischer said, "It is not simply the possible imbalance of vessels under those conditions. We have not altered the security plan for Heligoland Bight since the twenty-eighth. Given another sortie by the enemy backed with battle cruisers, how might it conclude differently?"

Weber pointed at Gregor with his pipe. "And what of those who claim the Kaiser is protective—reluctant to commit the Imperial Fleet?"

"Gentlemen, I believe you fail to see the change that is with us." Gregor waved his arm. "Consider Weddigen! Three Royal Navy armored cruisers of twelve-thousand tons displacement—with twenty-three-centimeter guns: Are they to be feared? No! They now rest on the bottom of the North Sea."

"Oh, yes." Weber nodded. "You laud the feat of Kapitän Weddigen—in U-boat U9, last week."

Fischer's legs went still. "And yet I believe U9 is an outdated model," Fischer said. "Barely sixty meters in length, with but two torpedo tubes in bow and stern."

Weber nodded again. "Yes, that is so. I am told it is an older model."

Gregor grinned. "With the smallest of vessels, the greatest of effect." He went to the window and looked out.

"Three great ships sunk by one submarine," Fischer said, staring at the floor, "within a short time. How did he do that?"

Gregor turned and faced the two. "The three armored cruisers were patrolling south of Dogger Bank—the sea was so rough, their destroyers were forced to stay in harbor. And the cruisers could make only ten knots to the northeast, in parallel, a couple of kilometers apart.

"Weddigen fired first on Aboukir, the middle cruiser. His skilled aim produces a massive explosion. As Aboukir begins to sink, the flanking cruisers head toward it. Weddigen makes two turns and fires two torpedoes at the second cruiser, the Hogue. Hogue's guns fire at U9, but too late—the two torpedoes hit and both cruisers are now sinking."

Weber puffed on his pipe, and Fischer alighted from the desk.

Gregor continued, "But Weddigen is not finished—he has reloaded. He fires two at the third cruiser, Cressy. One torpedo misses, the other hits with slight damage. With only one torpedo remaining, he makes a direct hit, and Cressy begins to sink. And all of this within about one hour."

Gregor gestured with open hands. "So you see, this victory shows how the vaunted English fleet can be decimated. U-boats shall attack them under the sea, and I shall be there with them!"

Weber, wide-eyed, pulled the pipe from his teeth. Fischer said,

"What? You are—"

"Yes," Gregor said, "My application for transfer has been approved. I shall leave at the end of the month for the U-Boat School at Eckernforde where I will report to Commander Eschenburg for training on the firing of torpedoes in Kiel Bay under conditions of war."

"You must tell us more," Weber said, as Fischer looked on with a grin. "Although we shall miss you, I am much interested in what you expect!"

KIEL, GERMANY

A t the Kiel station, the train to Hamburg was unavailable. Was this because they'd been diverted for troop transport? The attendant did not know, or wouldn't say. Gregor stuffed his hands into the pockets of his uniform, attempting to keep them warm, and leaned against the station.

He watched a small boy at a distance. The boy, he estimated, was not more than eight. His hair needed a trim. He wore pants soiled at the knees and a jacket too thin for warmth. He walked among those waiting on the platform, thrusting a branch torn from a pine tree toward some of them. He smiled at a man in a derby and long over-coat, and spoke of Christmas. He announced the price for the twig, a few pennies. The prospective buyer turned and strolled away.

Forty minutes late, the train arrived. Gregor boarded and took a seat. He noticed a woman with a kerchief wrapped tightly around her graying hair seated near him. She stared intensely at him but he could not decide the reason. Was it his youth, his neatly-trimmed mustache, or the uniform? He nodded toward her, but her watery eyes seemed not to acknowledge.

As the train rumbled southwest, a few snowflakes swirled outside the windows. The car was unheated, and Gregor thought the woman sometimes shivered inside her knee-length coat. He smiled at her and for the first time, her mouth formed a slight smile.

It was good to be heading home—he'd not visited since the Heligoland battle. He wondered how his father would be feeling now, an older enlisted man of the Imperial Navy, trapped in the dingy supply office of the Naval Station at Cuxhaven.

The train stopped at Neumünster, where some passengers left and a few boarded.

Soon they arrived at the large train station at Hamburg. The platforms there held a few well-off families seemingly on holiday, knots of sailors he thought must be on leave, but only two uniformed Army men. A few of the sailors saluted. He left to find the Lower Elbe Railway. Once there, he found the tracks empty. And again the attendant could not tell him when the train might arrive.

Gregor tramped back through the interior of the hall, looking for sales of food. He found none and returned to the platform where he could only pace to keep warm.

It was dusk before a train arrived. He boarded, slumped into a seat, and shivered.

It was dark when the train arrived at Cuxhaven. As Gregor got up to leave, his stomach growled. He exited the car, entered the station, and quickly left to find his favorite food vendor. But the cart was not where he remembered it. He shrugged and hailed a cab.

Catherine answered the door and embarrassed him. "Ah, you are so beautiful in your uniform. We have been waiting and waiting." Behind her, Helmuth grinned broadly. "Happy Christmas, my son."

He hugged his mother. "Please Mother—do you have something to eat? I could locate no food on the train, in the stations, or on the street."

The mother's smile disappeared. "I know, I know. It is the war. Foods are rationed, yet it does not help. I have some soup—barley soup—that and some bread."

"Yes, Mother." He smiled. "That will be excellent."

Helmuth put his arm around Gregor's shoulder. "The trains, they were late, son?"

"Very late. I suppose—"

"It is the war." Helmuth shook his head. "The Imperial Army has taken priority for all trains. Throughout the country."

Catherine Steiner placed a pot of soup on the stove, propped her hands on her hips, and admired her tall son. "What is your—what does this signify," she said, pointing her finger at his sleeve.

"Oberleutnant zur See of the Imperial Navy. Finally—it has taken nearly ten years." He glanced at his mother's face. There were tiny wrinkles below the cheekbones he'd not noticed before.

Helmuth said, "Tomorrow is the eve of Christmas. I have secured a pine—not the best, but it is at least green. And what is the U-boat school like—there in Eckernforde?"

Gregor pulled the wooden chair from the table and sat down. "I have been there only a week, so I am just learning. The curriculum consists largely of lectures and classroom studies on construction and weight and balance of the boat, diesel and electric propulsion, firing of torpedoes, and much more. Hands-on practice with shore-based devices is scheduled later. It is very concentrated—there is much to know."

Catherine cut two slices from the bread and ladled soup into Gregor's bowl. Gregor drew himself to the table. He took a big bite of the bread. Chewing, he said, "Later on, we will drill in the training boat—an older boat which I think was built in '06 or '07. We sail in Eckernforde Bay."

Helmuth, now seated in the other chair, said, "Wilhelmshaven couldn't handle all the damage from the Heligoland battle. The T33 we received had a hole in the hull above the waterline and other damage."

Gregor stopped chewing and looked blankly at his father. He did not want to think about the sinking of the Cöln, especially during this Christmas season.

Helmuth continued: "There was a rumor that two of the crew died, but survivors could not confirm. I know you—"

"Please, Papa. I do not want to go into it." Gregor turned from his father and glared at his soup with spoon poised.

Catherine saw Gregor's face, stepped behind his chair, placed a hand on his shoulder. To Helmuth she said, "I think we should try to observe the spirit of Advent. 'Tis the season, and it is so joyful to have Gregor home with us."

Helmuth studied his feet. He said, "The spirit of Advent—yes. I was—"

"I know," Catherine said, smiling at Helmuth, "you were simply making conversation."

Gregor finished chewing, took a spoonful of soup into his mouth, and swallowed. "It's good soup, Mother."

•   •   •

The day after Christmas, Catherine returned to the Steiner house. Helmuth was at the Naval Station working, and Gregor was asleep in a chair near the hearth.

Gregor awoke at the sound of the door.

"It is good news I bring," Catherine said. "A woman at the market said a wonderful thing happened on the Eve of Christmas."

"We could all accept some good news," Gregor said.

"Along the trenches in Belgium, the woman explained, some snow fell on the eve of Christmas. Some of our soldiers heard English troops, across the wasted earth separating them, singing 'The First Noel.' Some of our soldiers began singing 'Silent Night.' Later, they heard from the enemy trenches shouts of 'German soldier, German soldier, happy Christmas.'

"And afterward, in the darkest of the night, our soldiers shouted, 'Come out, English, come out here to us.' The woman paused and added with a broad smile, 'And they came out and did not shoot at each other on into the day of Christmas.'"

Gregor smiled that his mother had heard words that cheered her. "Tell Papa, when he returns. It may cheer him. He seems so displeased—because the war is not progressing as he wishes, I suppose."

Catherine made a sour face. "Gregor, he is rather unhappy to be excluded from the fighting." She took up her needle and began darning one of Helmuth's socks. "But at his age . . ."

Gregor thought about his father's age and said, "At sea, Mother, age is not such a great hindrance."

Catherine glanced up from her darning. "On the water, perhaps. But those unfortunates in the trenches, there is no mercy." She continued darning, but interrupted to face Gregor. "I have so missed your music, Gregor. Please play something—like you used to."

Gregor frowned, but went to the piano and began to play his favorite Beethoven sonata.

Catherine smiled at the return of the familiar sounds.

Gregor abruptly removed his hands from the keys.

"What?" she said, resting her needle and looking at him with wrinkled forehead.

Her son shook his head in a small arc. "Sorry." He placed his hands on the thighs of his pants. "My fingers—they refuse."

"Maybe later," she said, resuming her darning.

Gregor went to the chair and slumped into it.

After a brief silence, she looked at him. "You were in the Heligoland battle, is that correct?"

He nodded.

She continued with the needle. "I saw you were annoyed—earlier, when Papa spoke of the deaths of the two sailors."

"Two men is nothing, Mother," he said, surprised by his own anger. "It's hundreds. Hundreds of men. Yet I . . ." He coughed to clear his voice.

"Yet you—what, my son?"

"I might have saved some, maybe many."

"You say 'I'—what does that mean?"

"I commanded a torpedo boat, but the Fleet Admiral ordered us to retire, immediately."

Her face displayed puzzlement. "I am not sure of your meaning."

"Our Navy's cruiser Cöln—a big warship—was destroyed. Its crew—the crew of the Cöln—was in the water. They were alive, some injured, but many there in the water."

"Yes. I understand now what you mean."

"My vessel was less a thousand meters from the men in the water. The English—"

"The English were attacking your ship?"

"No. I am told it was HMS Lion, an English battle cruiser with eight big guns. It shot and burned the Cöln, which later sank. It was terrible."

"You then should have rescued those—"

"You do not understand, Mother. We were ordered to withdraw, to return to Wilhelmshaven. Despite wishing otherwise, I obeyed the order."

"You did as your superior officer commanded—is that what you say?"

"Yes. I assumed the English—in the battle cruiser—would pick those hundreds from the water and take them prisoner. But they did not. They left the scene."

Gregor turned his gaze away from his mother. "Hundreds of men perished."

Catherine did not speak, but only nodded while continuing with her needle.

"They," he said in a firm voice, "the—the English—they are unworthy. I wish them nothing less than death."

1915

COLÓN, PANAMA

The message from Paraíso, when decoded, read: "Arriving Cristóbal 26-27 January on Norway freighter Fantoft. Provide secure indoor shelter in Colón for one motorcycle."

Bruno knew the message was from Herr Lindoch in Berlin. He also understood why Lindoch would arrive in Colón aboard a Norwegian vessel—arrivals from neutral nations aroused little suspicion among American port officials. But he wondered about the motorcycle. He had seen motorized trucks, and occasionally a motorcar, around Colón, but never a motorcycle. As he envisioned Herr Lindoch astride a motorcycle, a smile came to his lips—it seemed most bizarre.

Bruno entered the shop on Avenida Balboa and regarded the familiar face of the proprietor of Hung's Curios. "I am seeking to rent a small interior space," he said.

"Ah, Mr. Ackermann, I realize how small the rent must be." Hung's smile crimped his eyes to mere lines. "But you must inform me—how large must this small space be?"

Bruno spread his arms. "About this wide." He took two paces. "About that long."

Hung's face took on a sour look. "No one can possibly sleep in such a small room."

Bruno smiled. "It is not to sleep in. It is for storage, for a device."

Hung's right eye opened wide. "My son has such a space. Inside his room on Avenida Guerrero."

"No, no. The space must be separate, not inside another room. Available from the street. Closed and secure, with lock and key."

"Ah, Mr. Ackermann, so many necessities, so little notice." Wrinkles formed on Hung's forehead. "I shall have to think on that. How soon is your need?"

Bruno told him before the end of the month.

"Please re-enter my shop in three days," Hung said. "I should by then have an answer for you."

•　　　•　　　•

Rounding the anchored freighter's fantail, Bruno maneuvered his boat to the side of Fantoft's rusty hull and tied up at the access ladder. Shortly, Herr Lindoch climbed down the steep steps, followed by a young man with a full beard.

Lindoch briefly exchanged shouts with a crewman at the rail above, and a loaded cargo net was lowered over the side. Bruno and the young man transferred the wooden crates and heavy boxes from the net onto Bruno's boat. Finally, with all the cargo boarded and the net withdrawn, Bruno's boat left the freighter and headed east toward the dock at Colón.

"It is good to see you," Bruno said, shedding his work gloves while steering.

"The same for me." He gestured toward the young man who wore a short-billed fabric hat. "This is Hans Reinhart. Hans, this is Bruno Ackermann, the man I have told you about."

The two shook hands. Reinhart retreated to the stern where he sat gazing across the bay.

Bruno smiled at Lindoch. "I trust your visit at Berlin was useful."

Lindoch's face was shadowed by his wide-brimmed hat. "Yes. Meetings and more meetings. But it is cold, with snow. Norway was even worse." He gestured toward the swaying palm trees in the distance and smiled. "Berlin has its attractions, but I favor this."

Bruno grinned. "We have no snow, only rain. It seems this time of year there is rain every day." He glanced from Herr Reinhart to the labels on the crates. "I expected an assembled motorcycle. I did not expect motorcycle parts."

Lindoch smiled. "Do not allow the 'Motorradteile' lettering to mislead you. Those labels of Motorcycle Parts are meant only to misinform port and transfer authorities."

Bruno frowned. "So the message I received from Nauen was untrue . . . ?"

Lindoch nodded. "We must be very careful now, with the war. Although our telegraphic messages are coded, the true words may potentially become exposed. Our director, Commander Isendahl, stressed that Americans must not become aware of our espionage, or sabotage. So we take all measures to avoid exposure, including misleading you."

Bruno nodded toward the young man at the stern. "Does the presence of Herr Reinhart mean our activities are to increase?"

"Yes. Very important work lies ahead."

At the old timbered dock, Bruno and Hans Reinhart unloaded the boxes and crates. Bruno left the two and returned with a hired mule-drawn cart and driver. He, the driver, and Reinhart loaded the cargo onto the cart. They immediately set off for the rented space on Avenida Justo Arosemena.

●　　　●　　　●

After Lindoch and Hans Reinhart were settled into Hotel Washington for the day, Lindoch went alone to Bruno's apartment on Calle 7.

Once inside, he whispered, "It is safe to talk here?"

Bruno nodded. "Yes. The inquiring neighbor has moved. The new neighbor has gone off to his work."

"Good." He handed Bruno a clipping from the newspaper. "Our plan must include a larger boat. Here is an advertisement for one."

Bruno held the clipping to the light and read the Spanish: "Fifty-five feet steel riveted hull tugboat. Diesel engine. Large winch." He stared hard at Lindoch. "Fifty-five feet?"

"Well, I have figured it. Seventeen meters, that should be large enough."

Bruno read further. "This boat is docked at Portobelo."

"You can go there?"

"Yes. But . . ." He placed a finger on the price and held it out for Lindoch's view.

"The cost is not a problem. I will give you the money. Can you have it painted?"

Bruno frowned. "Painted. You have something in your mind?"

"Yes. We want it painted in our colors with a new name—La Fernanda."

"You want to have it painted with colors and the name La Fernanda—in Portobelo?"

"Yes. And equip it there with everything you think it needs. Can you take care of all that?"

Bruno lifted his eyebrows. "I believe I can. This is a large change, however. Perhaps you can explain."

"Yes. You will head a new business here in Colón. It will accomplish tasks assigned by Etappendienst. Hans Reinhart, as your employee, will assist. Papers for incorporation have been prepared by the office of Heinrich von Eckardt, the German ambassador. These are to be filed in Mexico. The business will be named the General Towing Company. I will cable von Eckardt the name."

"But you will want the name in Spanish, correct?"

"That would be best."

"Compania General de Remolque," Bruno said, nodding. "And what are to be the company colors?"

"Paint the boat gray with yellow trim—we wish to be seen as businesslike. Place large initials—that would be C.G.R., in yellow, on both sides of the boat."

Bruno paused to think. "Assuming it to be a sound and useful vessel, how will I pay—"

"You and I will attend the Bank of Tarapacá in Cristóbal. Perhaps this afternoon? I will tender a confirmed letter of credit to fund an account in the name of C.G.R. which you will draw on. Later, as required, the account will be refreshed from the homeland."

Bruno held up a hand. "I am not exactly familiar with how that..."

Lindoch smiled. "Do not worry. I will remain in Colón for a short period to help with the establishment of the business. In the interim, I will give you a key. The key will open a locked box of cash which you will use for expenses and to pay Reinhart. It can be replenished from the bank account when the account in the Bank of Tarapacá is funded."

"I look forward to the mission." Bruno smiled. "Perhaps you can—"

"Once you have secured and equipped a suitable boat, it will be equipped with a wireless station. The cargo stored in the rented space on Avenida Justo Arosemena—labeled 'motorcycle parts'—includes all the parts of a spark-gap transmitter and receiver. With the proper aerial, it has a range adequate to communicate with vessels in the Caribbean Sea. Hans Reinhart is a trained telegrapher and technician—he will install and operate the system while you command the boat."

ECKERNFÖRDE, GERMANY

G regor Steiner could not avoid comparing the U-boat with the torpedo boat he'd commanded before arriving at Eckernförde. Although both were the same length, the submarine was less than one-fourth the width of the surface vessel. Its interior seemed even more cramped because the steel of the U-boat's circular walls curved inward, limiting the space above and below one's waist. Only in a meter or so of space on the centerline of the hull could a crewmember stand easily upright. Even then, protruding structure, fittings, pipes, and valve wheels became hazards to easy movement.

Oberleutnant Manfred Vogel left off his quiet conversation with the wireless technician to tell Gregor, "We are about ten kilometers from the test area, Steiner. You will now take command. Take the vessel down and maintain this course."

"Aye." Gregor turned to the seaman behind him. "Leutnant Steiner in command. Switch to batteries. Submerge to periscope depth."

After the order was repeated into the control chamber's voice tube, the roar of the engines quit. Seamen tended valves and wheels controlling the diving planes at both ends of the U-boat. Soon whooshing and gurgles sounded as water filled the ballast tanks and the submarine slid beneath the surface of Eckernförde Bay.

Gregor was happy to be aboard UT-2. True, it was a training U-boat rather than a 'fleet' boat, and he was about to undergo a severe test of his ability. But being at sea, the element in which he was at ease, nevertheless came as a relief after six weeks of classroom studies. Although he welcomed learning details of torpedo design, how to manage electric propulsion, and the many other subjects a U-boat kapitän must master, the intense technical courses had proved daunting. In particular, using trigonometry to calculate a torpedo firing solution on paper was stressful and seemed to him artificial. It caused him serious difficulties.

Oberleutnant Manfred Vogel commanded UT-2, an older U-boat that had accidentally sunk off Kiel a year earlier. The refloated and refitted vessel had two bow torpedo tubes and two stern torpedo tubes and a complement of twenty-seven men. She carried seventy-seven tons of batteries that allowed an underwater maximum of eight knots compared to a surface speed of fourteen knots. She had begun this training journey eastbound on the surface at ten knots.

During this test in the Baltic Sea, UT-2 was temporarily under the command of Gregor Steiner, a candidate for elevation to commanding officer of a U-boat. Other candidates had preceded him and would follow him in the testing.

"All Ahead Standard," Gregor ordered, "bow planes zero." The U-boat settled into steady forward movement. "Raise," he ordered. The periscope motor hummed and the periscope rose to eye level. With his right eye on the eyepiece and left eye closed, Gregor completed a circle, scanning the entire horizon. He saw no smoke, no masts, no vessels. "Lower," he ordered, and the periscope moved down.

The school's test for commanding officers required each candidate to complete a successful torpedo attack against a target ship operated by the school. The torpedoes used were non-exploding torpedoes fitted with 'collision heads' that were later recovered and reused.

Gregor listened to the steady hum of the electric motors near the stern of the U-boat. "Keep her steady," he ordered. This was meant as an instruction for the crew: They should keep the underwater 'trim' of the submarine level, neither down at the bow nor down at the stern. The 'trim' was adjusted by rotating its fins ('planes') and by regulating the amount of water in tanks located toward the ends of the submarine that altered its balance.

Standing to one side, Oberleutnant Vogel, thirty-six, watched and assessed the twenty-seven-year-old student-commander's demeanor.

The humidity within the submarine increased, and drops of condensation dripped from the steel above to the shoulders of several of the control-room crew. They seemed not to notice.

Gregor, impatient, rubbed his fingers over the knuckles of his left hand.

Somewhere in the distance, Gregor knew, was the target ship, SMS Soligen. Its complement, he was told, included several skilled lookouts with excellent glasses.

If UT-2's periscope was sighted by Soligen during the simulated attack, marks would be deducted and a flag flown to signal the test must be repeated. Other than the name Soligen, Gregor was not informed of the target ship's characteristics—he had no idea what to expect. This lack of knowledge would test his ability to identify vital aspects of target vessels. He pushed the bill of his cap backward on his head. "Raise," he ordered.

The periscope came up and stopped. Gregor placed his eye on the eyepiece and began swinging the periscope around, scanning the horizon. He abruptly stopped and ordered, "Combat stations!"

The order was repeated, and noises of seamen scrambling about within the steel tube immediately followed.

Gregor saw nothing but black smoke on the far-distant horizon. He studied it for five seconds, but could discern nothing more. "Lower. Keep her steady." As the periscope slid down, he caught himself fingering the knuckles of his hand. He stopped.

Minutes ticked by. Gregor glanced at Vogel, who at that moment was tapping a depth gauge. Gregor glanced without smiling at each man in the chamber, one after the other. Most were sweating, despite the fetid 'refreshed' air that issued from the blower.

Finally, Gregor ordered, "Slow!" He paused to allow the U-boat to reduce speed. He then commanded, "Raise!" hoping the wake from the exposed head of the periscope would not be seen by lookouts on the target vessel. He stooped to meet the eyepiece with his eye before it halted. The vessel, although distant, was now exposed above the horizon. Concentrating on its image, he identified it as a merchant vessel.

Gregor said, "Cargo ship, mast height four zero." He estimated the mast height of forty meters by observing its configuration and from knowledge of similar vessels. This height would be used to determine the vessel's range.

Gregor nodded to Vogel and withdrew from the periscope. Vogel took Gregor's position and squinted into the eyepiece. He came away quickly and nodded to Gregor. He said, "Confirm target vessel."

Thus informed that the vessel Gregor had sighted was the SMS Soligen, Gregor commanded, "Lower!" and "Half Speed!" He peered once more quickly at the vessel's image, and ordered, "Lower!"

As the periscope descended, he said, "Bearing three-five. Target speed one two. Range three thousand."

After the commands and information were repeated, Gregor waited several minutes, during which he tightened his trouser belt. With all eyes in the control room now on him, he commanded, "Raise!"

He again met the eyepiece as it rose, observed the target vessel for about five seconds, and commanded, "Lower!" As the periscope slid home, he commanded, "Open stern caps! Flood stern tubes!"

Vogel frowned. Others in the chamber exchanged quizzical glances. Gregor ordered, "Helmsman, hard to port!"

The steersman whirled the rudder wheel counterclockwise to its maximum and repeated, "Hard to port!"

The men sensed a slight tipping to starboard as the U-boat began a sluggish turn to the left.

Gregor continued, "Bearing four-two, Angle on the bow: starboard one-five, Half Speed."

A seaman's voice reported, "Stern tubes flooded! Stern caps open!"

Gregor turned to address the steersman. "Helmsman, establish course three-one-five."

The steersman repeated, "Establish course three-one-five." He held the rudder wheel steady while staring intently at the binnacle that held the U-boat's gyro compass.

Gregor commanded, "Raise!" He again met the eyepiece before the periscope halted. The target vessel was now 'bow-on,' heading directly toward the turning U-boat.

Vogel gestured toward the periscope. To Gregor he said, "Let me—"

Gregor moved sideways to allow Vogel to view. Vogel said, "You know—"

"Yes," Gregor said, interrupting Vogel and resuming his station at the eyepiece. "I know." He then commanded, "Tube three! Standby!"

The steersman began whirling the rudder wheel back toward center. He announced, "Kapitän, turning to course three-one-five."

Gregor swung the periscope around as he followed the target vessel as it passed from left to right. He glanced from the eyepiece to the steersman. "Helmsman, give me a mark when on course three-one-five."

The steersman nodded and said, "Aye."

After some seconds staring at his compass binnacle, the helmsman announced, "Mark! On course three-one-five."

Gregor now faced the stern of the U-boat, squinting intently into the eyepiece. "Los!"

The order was repeated, the torpedo left stern tube three, and a seaman, watching the chronometer, began counting out, "One, two, three . . ."

Gregor commanded, "All Ahead Full!" and turned to Vogel, who was standing behind him. He gestured with his hand that Vogel should view the scene.

Vogel leaned in and brought his eye to the eyepiece. He watched as the torpedo sped away and the seaman continued his loud counting, "—twenty-six, twenty-seven . . ."

The torpedo slammed into Soligen's hull with a white splash of seawater.

Vogel smiled. "A hit," he announced. "Amidships."

Gregor ordered, "Lower!"

As the periscope slipped downward, Gregor's face broke into a wide grin.

The men in the chamber cheered. "I never saw such a shot!" cried one. Another said, "A beautiful stern shot."

Gregor quickly lost his smile and ordered the U-boat to surface and start engines.

Vogel conferred with the wireless technician, who wrote out a message to be encoded.

Once the U-boat assumed forward momentum for the return journey, the wireless man tapped the message into the spark-gap transmitter.

Later, a reply came to his receiver, which he quietly relayed to Vogel.

Vogel announced to those in the control room: "I'm pleased to report the wake of our periscope was never sighted by the target vessel's lookouts during the torpedo run."

The men cheered. Gregor smiled.

COLÓN, PANAMA

H ans Reinhart was unsure what awakened him. Immediately, he saw the flames.

He rushed to La Fernanda's side, dressed only in undershorts. The flames appeared to erupt just beyond the railway station, not more than three hundred meters away, across the anchorage. He heard the crackling sounds and thought he felt heat on his skin.

Once the fog of sleep cleared, Hans realized he'd been awakened by the tugboat's rocking motion, a result of the strong wind driving the flames through the town of Colón.

Hans hurried inside and pulled on his trousers, realizing the blaze approached Calle 7. He left the cabin, hopped over the bulwark to the dock, and ran down Calle 5.

On his right, tall orange tongues stabbed at inky smoke. He heard the cracking and snapping of the fire as it consumed the humble frames of the town's homes and buildings. The smell, strong and acrid, was mostly of burning wood.

He crossed Calle Bolivar, clogged with people fleeing the fire. Voices and shouts issued from them, and although Hans could not understand the Spanish, he understood the fear.

As he ran, the glowing furnace receded behind him and to his right. On the grassy median of Paseo del Centenario he paused to view its progress. The major blaze seemed to have raged beyond Calle 8 or 9, turning entire blocks of houses into glowing embers.

He angled south, walking a quick step. He turned east and continued on Calle 7.

In the distance a figure approached. The gait looked

familiar—indeed, it was familiar, it was Bruno. When Bruno came within hearing, Hans greeted him in German, "Hello, I was coming to see you. To see if your apartment was safe from the flames."

Bruno looked worried. "In all irony, I am on my way to see that the tugboat is not on fire." He stopped and both men gazed at the flames. Bruno swept his arm in an arc. "This is horrible. People will die." He shook his head. "Thousands will lose their miserable shanties and what few poor goods they possess."

Hans came closer to where Bruno was standing. The men faced the fire, which now looked to have progressed beyond Calle 10.

Hans said, "It seems as if the fire will continue on to Cristóbal, and the ships' piers—"

Abruptly, a bright yellow explosion occurred at exactly the location which commanded their attention. The ground shook as the sound, delayed by distance, arrived.

Debris and brown smoke filled the sky. A huge cloud arose and thousands of dark fragments fell from it. Only a veil of white haze occupied the space where the explosion had occurred.

Hans eyes widened. "What in the eternal hell was that?"

"Dynamite," Bruno said. "But there was no dynamite stored there—at least that I know."

●　　　●　　　●

Sweat rolled down Lieutenant Pritchen's forehead. He stuck his finger inside his standing collar to clear it from his neck. "What did they tell you?"

"They said the Army just came and took over." The Zone Police corporal stood with his campaign hat in one hand. "By orders of 'Colonel Cronk.'"

Pritchen slapped his desk. "You refer to Colonel Cronkhite, the commander of the Army troops."

"Yeah, Lieutenant, we all call him Cronk. Them Army guys must have figured they'd got everybody out. That's my guess."

"You mean before they set off the dynamite?" He assumed the answer and said, "And now Cristóbal's got two dead policemen." He shook his head. "Terrible. I can't believe it."

"For sure it stopped the fire." The corporal flipped the leather hatband of his hat. "Good thing, I guess. There's no way them fire brigades was going to stop the flames from coming here and burning Cristóbal to the ground."

"Yeah, I suppose." Pritchen glanced at the Station's booking sheet dated April 30, 1915. "How many looters has Sergeant Lawrence got now?"

"I don't know, Lieutenant. More than we got space for. Worse than that, all them people burned out are wandering the streets trying to figure what to do." The corporal grasped his hat by the roughrider dents and clapped it on his head. "I better go help Sergeant Lawrence."

"You do that," Pritchen said. "I'm trying to figure out how we're going to process all these damn bookings."

•   •   •

Bruno entered the crowded floor of the red-roofed station in Cristóbal. After standing in line while those before him were served, he spoke Spanish to the clerk behind the counter: "I understand you are holding Hans Reinhart. I want to see him."

The clerk said, "One moment." He lifted his mustache with his finger to wipe sweat from his lip, and raised his spectacles to examine the list in front of him. "Yes. You can check in with Lieutenant Pritchen."

Bruno glanced around the crowded room and saw no lieutenant. "Where do I find the lieutenant?"

The clerk pointed. "Through that door."

The door was open. Bruno entered and faced a second line of inquirers in front of Lieutenant Pritchen's desk. After several more minutes, Bruno stepped to the desk, and said in the local Spanish dialect, "I am Bruno Ackermann. I wish to see Hans Reinhart."

Pritchen frowned. "One moment." He ran his finger down a list of names on his desk, stopped at 'Reinhart,' and glared at Bruno. "What do you want?"

"I want to talk to Hans Reinhart."

"He is a foreigner. He does not speak the language."

"What has he done? Why are you holding him?"

"I am not aware of details—he was picked up by one of our policemen."

"I wish to talk to him. I speak his language."

Pritchen frowned at Bruno, but yanked the earpiece from his standing telephone. "Give me Desmond," he said into the mouthpiece. He waited and said, "Come here. Bring Hans Reinhart." He replaced the earpiece on its switch fork.

A colored policeman, dressed in the khaki, five-button, standing-collar uniform, showed up at the desk. Behind him was Hans Reinhart. The policeman glanced at Bruno before addressing Pritchen. "Yes, Lieutenant?"

Bruno glanced at Hans, who spread his hands outward and shrugged.

Pritchen gestured toward Bruno and said to Policeman Desmond, "This man speaks the language. He will translate. Proceed with your interrogation."

"Wait," Bruno said. "I did not volunteer to translate. I am here to—"

"Stop." Pritchen spoke firmly to Bruno: "Before you can visit Reinhart, I need to understand what happened. Because Reinhart does not speak the language, Desmond was unable to question him." He faced the policeman again and said, "Proceed with the interrogation."

Desmond looked at Bruno. "I encountered this man at Calle 7 and Avenida Balboa this morning, next to the smoldering remains of a house. He was westbound, carrying a satchel with silver buckles." He paused.

Reluctantly, Bruno translated the policeman's statement into

German for Hans.

Desmond looked at Reinhart and continued, with Bruno translating: "I inquired as to the satchel's contents. The man did not answer, but shrugged and set the satchel onto the road. I peered inside, at what appeared to be valuables. I asked the man if the contents belonged to him. He shook his head. I then told him I suspected he had taken them without permission. He continued to shake his head, speaking a foreign tongue."

As Bruno translated this, Reinhart protested angrily: "I was on my way back to the boat after meeting you." He went on to explain what had happened as he crossed Avenida Balboa.

Bruno said to the Lieutenant, "Hans Reinhart says the policemen was mistaken. The satchel was left on the side of the street. It was heavy and was probably abandoned by someone fleeing the fire. Hans Reinhart merely rescued it, hoping to return it to the owner."

Bruno turned to Desmond. "What was in the bag?"

"Goblets and trays and other serving pieces of silver."

Pritchen interrupted. He said to Bruno, "Are you willing to vouch for the honesty of Reinhart?"

"Indeed. He did nothing illegal."

"Ask him if he is willing to leave the satchel and contents with the police."

Bruno asked Hans, who nodded affirmatively.

Pritchen said to Desmond, "Get the address of this man and release Reinhart to him. That is all."

Desmond swept his hand sideways in a gesture allowing Bruno and Hans to precede him. The three men left the desk of Lieutenant Pritchen and returned to the lobby.

•　　　•　　　•

Hans turned to Bruno as they neared La Fernanda's dock. "Thank you for rescuing me from the police."

"You must try to learn the language. It will help you."

"Ah, it is useless. I have enough to work on with the wireless, and this boat. That policeman was stupid."

"It was confusing, with half the town on fire. And there was much looting. He was trying to do his job."

"He should not have accused me of looting."

"Mistakes happen in dire situations. Thousands have lost their shanties, their livelihood—even their family." He pointed toward the railroad. "Poor bastards are up there, living in boxcars."

"Boxcars?"

"That is all the authorities can identify for shelter. It is typical. The United States comes in, hires all these ignorant people from West Indies to build the canal. But now that they have their canal and the Zone, what the hell do they care for those people, the citizens of Panama?"

Hans looked vacantly at Bruno.

"You see them every day, the wretchedly miserable blacks, in Colón. You see their sad-eyed children padding about, oblivious. They are now of no more use to the United States than mosquitoes and buzzards. These children are the legacy granted by the gringos' power—the legacy left to the Republic of Panama." He shook his head in sadness. "We never should have given in."

KIEL, GERMANY

To Ludwig, Gustave Bachmann did not present the face of a successful Chief of Staff of the Admiralty. The fifty-five-year-old Admiral with the chin of skimpy gray whiskers appeared worried and weary. "Be at ease, Herr Geighoffer," he said. "I have called upon you on account of your knowledge."

Kapitän Ludwig Geighoffer, a member of the Admiral's staff, nodded and took a chair on the opposite side of the table. It was late in the day.

"I find all this as should be expected," Bachman continued. He grasped The New York Times from a pile of newspapers on the table and thrust it toward Ludwig.

Ludwig scanned the page one headlines and nodded. "We were yesterday informed of the sinking of the British liner Arabic. Kapitän Rudi Schneider and the crew of U-24 correctly performed their assignment—as is their duty. But surely you have not called upon me because of that information."

Bachmann frowned. "You are correct. You have studied the situation in America. What do you understand of this American, Robert Lansing?"

Ludwig placed the newspaper back on the table. "We were in a superior situation with William Jennings Bryan as Secretary of State in Washington. Following the sinking of Lusitania, he saw the situation correctly. You will recall he accused President Wilson of 'taking sides'—of favoring our enemy, despite the deliberate and obvious flaunting of the rules by the English, transporting munitions in supposedly 'clean' passenger vessels."

Ludwig now leaned forward with his forearm on the table, nearly toppling a precarious stack of manuals, reports, and torn envelopes. "But in June, after Wilson sent the offensive note directed to the Kaiser, Wilson excused Bryan. Now we have this Lansing as Secretary. He is very much influenced by the English. He, Wilson, and others, now say an American death from a U-boat action is to be regarded by the United States as 'deliberately unfriendly.'"

The Admiral pursed his lips, suggesting he saw it as did Ludwig.

Ludwig's eyes narrowed. "Perhaps I should not so assign it, but our Chancellor and Foreign Secretary seem not to disagree with Secretary Lansing." He shook his head. "Such is the lack of understanding of military necessities by our civilian leaders."

Bachmann's eyeballs, perhaps reddened by excessive reading, roved over Ludwig's pink face and stiffened collar. "What does your inside tell you?"

"There is some evidence of military success by our armies on the Eastern front. But the Western front is a stalemate. And the vaunted poison gas will not produce victory. Our espionage against the United States has been exposed by fires in munitions factories on the coast and the escapades of Eric Muenter and Werner Horn. These failures, joined to the sinking of passenger vessels and the shifting of Washington politics, are inciting fear in the populace of America."

Bachmann cast his eyes at the piles on the table, as though searching. "And so . . . ?"

"In time the United States will begin actions—actions against us."

Bachmann's gaze snapped toward Ludwig. "You believe they will enter—actively—into this conflict?"

Ludwig nodded. "I do not doubt. It may take time, but I believe it certain."

Bachmann leaned back in his chair. Only the flapping of the flag outside the window broke the silence for a short time. Finally Bachmann sat upright and spoke in a somber tone. "We then must defeat them."

"Yes," Ludwig said. "In the words of the recent U-boot Inspektion memorandum: 'The building up of U-boat fleets is even more urgent than the building of these other fleets.' We must abandon the idea of competing with dreadnoughts, of winning great battles with the Unites States Navy. The only way to defeat them is via the superior approach I have long advocated: stealth by sea.

"We must advance developments that promise to subvert the imagined military superiority of the United States, and do it while there remains time."

"Exactly," Bachmann said, smiling. "I want you to undertake this. I will see you are released from your current duties—Germany needs the advanced concepts you call 'stealth by sea.' Name it Project A-C, to outline in broad format, and promote the U-boat designs needed to secure our place as the superior world power. What do you say?"

"I say 'with enthusiasm.' But your confidence in me and the accommodations you suggest would be misplaced without the addition of shared time with Hans Techel, the genius engineer behind our present U-boat designs. He must be able to devote the time necessary to fully implement these advances."

"Indeed, you shall have it. I will secure access to Herr Techel and a small but adequate budget. I will designate an office in Kiel, where you can work isolated from the madness of Berlin. You will have access to the intelligence reports needed. You will report to me only—independently of Bethmann-Hollweg and those who offer little but distraction."

Ludwig rose from his chair. "God bless you, Admiral. Thank you for investing in me. I shall try to sleep small and imagine large." He saluted.

Bachmann returned the salute with a minor gesture. "Do not thank me, Herr Geighoffer. Only later, after much anguished labor, will you earn and I share the thanks of our nation."

•   •   •

Inside what is known as Germaniawerft, the Germania shipyard in Kiel, Ludwig Geighoffer was ushered into a large, high-ceilinged room. Long rows of workers bent over tilted tables covered in sheets of drafting linen. The workers paid him no notice as they measured, calculated, and drew precisely with their pens, using scales, protractors, and other implements.

Ludwig entered the nearby enclosure through a door labeled "H. Techel."

The forty-five-year-old behind the desk removed the wire-framed spectacles from his face and rose from his chair. "Ah, you must be Ludwig Geighoffer, from Admiral Bachmann's staff."

Ludwig bowed. "I am privileged to make your acquaintance. Thank you for allowing this meeting."

Techel invited Ludwig to be seated. "The Admiral spoke well of your project, Kapitän. I am sure it is worthy." He rested the spectacles on his desk, slowly and deliberately. "But I must inform you, we are behind schedule on all current submarine construction." He shook his head. "And still Uboot Inspektion wants to build new U-boats of the Project 31 type."

"You speak excellently of why Project A-C is so needed."

Techel paused and stared at Ludwig. "I am prepared to assist you, but I do not wholly understand."

Ludwig smiled. "The administrative body reacts—that is their function. When the war goes well, they are content with current U-boat models. When the war goes poorly, they immediately wish to change to new designs emphasizing the latest capabilities."

"What you say is true. It is also obviously inadequate."

"But design precedes construction, and the design of the complexities of a U-boat requires deliberation. The process cannot respond to changes occurring with the swiftness of battle results."

Ludwig paused to observe Techel's reception. He did not appear to react, so Ludwig continued. "What Admiral Bachmann envisions for Project A-C is design for the longer term: advanced concepts to foresee in broad format, and promote, requirements for U-boat dominance of the sea in the years ahead."

"That is as I understood from the Admiral." Techel narrowed his eyelids. "I presume you have arrived with a packet of those concepts in your valise."

"Not at all, Herr Techel. Not at all," Ludwig said. "What I bring now is an inference."

Techel directed a sidelong glance at Ludwig.

"And following the inference, the requirements that logic demands." Ludwig paused. "In the spring, Scheieger sank Lusitania, and Americans drowned. Then Schneider sank the British liner Arabic, more Americans died, and the US Secretary of State resigned. The American newspapers are aflame. President Wilson sends a note of outrage to the Kaiser. From these events I infer: Within a year, perhaps more, perhaps less, America will enter the war against us."

Techel nodded. "With that I agree."

"If you count those able to mobilize, America has a very small army, a tenth the size of European armies. The US military are unaware of new tactics, including trench and aerial warfare, new weapons such as tanks, poison gas, and aerial bombs. Their aeroplanes, mostly trainers, are at least five years behind current designs. They cannot possibly defend even the principal Atlantic coast harbors. The Atlantic fleet of the US Navy includes battleships, but of performance inferior to that of the English dreadnought.

"Most importantly, America's admirals are surface-fleet men. They prefer armadas, grand maneuvers of fleets on vast oceans, battleships, cruisers, and destroyers with the needed logistic supply fleets. They rarely think in terms of the undersea threat, the unique and deadly U-boats that I call 'stealth by sea.'

"Nevertheless, America as an enemy poses new, different, and difficult problems. U-boats designed to address some of those problems can be critical to our victory—if anticipated now," Ludwig said, emphasizing the last word.

"Even if England somehow survives to the time America declares against us, our path to enfeebling the US military is through preventing their ships—warships or troopships—from reaching Europe. To free our U-boats from dependence on either supply ports in the Caribbean area, or on vulnerable submarine-tender vessels, a fleet of longer-range U-boats of increased speed, both submerged and surfaced, is required. They must be capable of extended sorties into the Caribbean and the Atlantic coast of America, while preserving enough range to return home for resupply, repair, and provisioning.

"In addition, our 'stealth by sea' mission must delay reinforcement of the US Atlantic fleet from the great Pacific fleet at Pearl Harbor, Hawaii—by closing the Panama Canal."

With his thumb and forefinger, Techel pinched his lower lip. Then he said, "You conceive of this latter, closing of the Canal in Panama, as a task for a U-boat?"

Ludwig shrugged. "What else?"

IRISH SEA

At a longitude of six degrees, fifty-five minutes west, Gregor Steiner's westbound U-boat had passed the Isles of Scilly and turned to starboard. Hidden by the heavy mist, the diesel-driven submarine was now running on the surface, northbound at twelve knots outside Bristol Channel.

Gregor was glad for the moisture against his face, and for freedom from the incessant pounding noise of the two Krupp-M.A.N. diesels inside the submarine. Also welcome was the morning's chill on the bridge.

The mist lifted. The watch lookout dropped his glasses and pointed. "Smoke to starboard!"

Gregor raised his glasses to his eyes and found the smoke. "It's very black. Stop engines. Switch to batteries. Submerge to periscope depth!"

The horn sounded, and the men slipped down the hatch into the dim interior. "Probably a coal burner," Gregor said as he landed in the control room.

The pounding of the diesels ceased. The crew twirled valve wheels and tripped levers. Loud whooshing and liquid gurgles sounded. Despite changes in the U-boat's buoyancy caused by the venting of the ballast tanks, the crew kept the craft's fore-and-aft trim nearly steady.

A crewman finally reported, "All level."

"All Ahead Standard," Gregor ordered. "Raise!"

As the boat's forward momentum increased, Gregor peered into the periscope. The smoke was dense black and drifted left. He then completed a circle, scanning the entire horizon for evidence of other vessels' smoke. "Seems alone," he said.

"Hard starboard," he ordered, and paused to think. "Come to zero-six-five. Lower!"

As the helmsman repeated the order, the periscope hummed down. Following the helmsman's turning of the wheel, the indicator inside his binnacle started to rotate.

Within minutes the U-boat was on a course which Gregor estimated would intersect the future track of the distant ship—unless that vessel zigzagged, a tactic the British had recently initiated. Gregor pressed his lips tight. There was no way to know the outcome except to await it.

After a time, Gregor ordered, "Slow." When he sensed the submarine had slowed, he said, "Raise!"

The hull of the distant vessel was now visible above the far horizon. It became apparent that the steamer was an older, coal-burning cargo carrier. "Target vessel, turning. Mast height, thirty two. Lower!"

As the periscope descended, Gregor noted the target's bearing and approximate speed. It was several kilometers from the U-boat and turning to its starboard side.

After his commands and information were repeated, Gregor waited several minutes. With all eyes in the control room now upon him, he commanded, "Raise!"

The periscope view showed the target to be a two-masted, single-funnel cargo carrier flying a British flag. Gregor was unsure what the changing angle on the bow portended. "Lower!"

Again the men in the control room tensed as Gregor awaited more evidence of the target's track.

"Aha!" Gregor said under his breath on the next view through the raised periscope. It was now evident the target vessel had completed its turn and was heading more northward. Could its destination be Liverpool? He dismissed the mental question in favor of more important issues.

The size of the target troubled Gregor—was it large enough to merit a torpedo? He frowned, looked to the watch officer, and nodded toward the periscope. The officer tilted his head to the periscope's eyepiece and studied the image.

When the officer withdrew from the eyepiece, Gregor said, "Torpedo?"

The officer tilted his head to the opposite side and squinted. "A close call."

"Alert gun crew!" Gregor ordered. "Ahead Half Speed! Standby to surface! Lower!"

As the orders were repeated and relayed, activity by all crewmen increased. The rush of water past the hull was now louder. But Gregor could do nothing now except tighten the belt of his trousers—and wait.

After what seemed like a long time, but wasn't, Gregor said, "Raise!" When the periscope was up, he saw that his assessment of the size of the target was correct. He ordered, "Lower! Surface!"

The orders were repeated as the periscope hummed to its secure stops. Crewmen shouted and scrambled. Pumps began pulsing, hissing sounds issued, followed by the sounds of sloshing water.

The conning tower pierced the waves and sprouted upward, followed by the long steel of the hull as it shed foamy waves that glistened in the morning sun.

Inside, the watch officer climbed the ladder and unfastened the hatch that led topside. Gregor followed as the hatch was raised and sunlight streamed in.

First one Krupp-M.A.N. diesel, then the second, began to pound, with puffs of smoke issuing from the exhaust. The engineering crew would now be ready to supply a speed of fifteen knots, if needed.

A hatch popped open behind the conning tower on the still-awash deck. Crewmen scrambled up and out and splashed to the forward gun mount. They hurried to unpack shells, unlock the breech, and whirl the wheels that aimed the gun. Two other sailors scurried aft and began loosening the bindings that secured the submarine's small boat to the stern deck.

On the bridge, Gregor ordered, "All Ahead Full." The order was relayed into the voice pipe as Gregor gave the helmsman steering directions. Gregor then shouted down to the gun crew, "When in range, fire over the target's bow." The chief gunner shouted confirmation back to Kapitän Steiner and raised the elevation of the gun barrel to a slight angle.

Gregor turned to the navigator and said, "Feodor, when they are within distance, you do the English." Feodor nodded. "Aye, Kapitän."

Gregor turned to the chief petty officer. "Prepare a boarding party." The chief saluted, descended the external ladder, and headed toward the open deck hatch.

The rusty hull of the British vessel now approached off the starboard bow of the U-boat. Its progress showed no sign of recognizing danger. When its approach narrowed enough, the chief gunner announced and triggered the 8.8-centimeter cannon. It roared, flame flew from the muzzle, and the submarine rocked slightly sideways. Shortly, a tall geyser of seawater erupted on the far side of the British vessel.

Both the target vessel and the U-boat continued on what appeared to be courses toward a collision. The gun crew continued to track the vessel with a lowered gun barrel.

Gregor shouted to the gunnery chief, "Hold your fire!"

Feodor readied his conical speaking trumpet.

The wave at the waterline of the British vessel's bow diminished.

Gregor ordered, "All Ahead Slow!" He turned to Feodor. "When a crewman appears, order the vessel to stop."

Both vessels continued forward, although the cargo vessel's bow wave appeared to subside. A crewman in working clothes and suspenders appeared at the ship's bow rail.

In English, Feodor shouted through the speaking trumpet, "Kapitänleutnant Gregor Steiner of the Imperial German Navy orders your vessel to immediately halt for inspection!"

The crewman waved in a dispirited manner and disappeared from the bow rail.

Gregor told the U-boat's helmsman to take the submarine along-side the cargo vessel. He turned toward the stern and conferred with the chief petty officer, who had come forward to the base of the conning tower. Afterward, the chief petty officer returned to the stern, where the boarding party was readying the dinghy for launch.

The U-boat slowed to a stop ten meters from the now-halted hull of the cargo vessel, and Feodor shouted instructions about boarding to the crewmen at its rail.

Shortly, the boarding party launched the U-boat's dinghy from the submarine, and Feodor accompanied them as a crewman rowed them to the hull of the cargo ship. He and the chief petty officer climbed the pilot's ladder that was lowered from the cargo vessel's deck, and disappeared.

After the boarding party returned to the U-boat, Feodor climbed to the bridge and reported to Gregor: "Kapitän, here are the master's official papers. The vessel flies the British flag and carries five thousand tons of coal destined for Liverpool. I informed the ship's master, on Kapitän's order, to evacuate his vessel within ten minutes. The crew is presently lowering two boats for their escape. The dingy has taken our crew with the bomb and returned to the English vessel."

"Well done," Gregor said. He watched as the small lifeboats splashed to the stern of the ship, and crewmen lowered themselves into the boats. When the last man was aboard, the crews began to row away. One of the boats held the ship's master, who wore his captain's hat. Gregor faced that boat and saluted the ship's master. The master returned the salute without enthusiasm.

Within a short time, the fuse was lighted and the boarding party returned to the U-boat. The dingy was retrieved and secured.

With a loud roar, the bomb exploded inside the cargo vessel, and the hull rocked in the water. Within minutes it took a slight list. Black smoke began to pour from the holds. The odor of burning coal filled the air. Soon, flames became visible as the ship's hull began to settle lower in the water.

Gregor said, "All Ahead Standard." As the order was repeated, cheers from the U-boat's crew rang out. Feodor said, "Congratulations, Kapitän. This makes four sinkings in three days."

Gregor said, "It is my duty. All the same, the demise of a commerce vessel which no longer contributes to our enemy is not as personally satisfying as a victory over a military adversary."

•　　•　　•

Gregor ordered, "Raise!" He peered into the periscope. The smoke on the far horizon was dense black. "Another coal-burner," he said quietly. He completed the circle, scanning the entire horizon. He saw no other smoke. The western sky was a brilliant pink.

"Hard to port," he ordered, and paused to think. "Come to three-one-zero. Lower!"

As the helmsman repeated the order, the periscope hummed down. Gregor turned to the navigator. "How long before sunset?

The navigator consulted his charts and the U-boat's chronometer before answering. "Thirty-three minutes to sunset."

"How long between sunset and darkness?"

The navigator frowned. "For darkness, do you seek the end of astronomical twilight?"

Gregor chuckled at the navigator's question. "No. How long after sunset until I cannot see to attack?"

The navigator paused. "I—I cannot predict with precision, Kapitän."

"Dare an estimate."

The navigator paused for several more seconds. "One-half hour—less, or perhaps more."

"Thank you."

After some minutes, Gregor ordered another five-second periscope viewing.

Finally, on the next peek, Gregor identified the target as a single-funnel cargo vessel. "Funnel markings suggest English." He noted its bearing, size, and estimated speed.

"Alert gun crew!" Gregor ordered. "Ahead Half Speed! Standby to surface!"

After what seemed like a long time, he took another periscope view and ordered, "Surface!"

Upon clambering to the foamy bridge, Gregor ordered the gun crew to their stations.

The U-boat's hull came awash, the aft hatch popped open, and crewmen scrambled out and loped toward the forward gun mount.

Gregor raised the glasses to his eyes and quickly lowered them. "Alarm! Alarm!" Gregor ordered. He next shouted to the crewmen on deck, "Quick, below! Emergency! Go below!"

The crewmen, confused, initially paused, then scurried to the open hatch and entered, one after the other.

A loud explosion sounded. Gregor glanced at the target ship but saw nothing. Within a second, a huge splash of seawater erupted a few meters to the portside of the U-boat. "Damn!" he said.

Meanwhile, as the second Krupp-M.A.N. diesel sputtered to a halt, seawater whooshed into the vented tanks, the U-boat's bow dipped, and waves rushed across it.

"Hard to starboard! All Ahead Full!" Gregor ordered as his feet hit the deck of the control room and he let go of the ladder.

Above him, the navigator slammed the hatch closed and latched it. Gregor ordered, "Report!"

"Engine room awash," came the reply. "Hatch now closed!"

Gregor demanded, "How much water?"

Confused voices followed. A single voice said, "Ankle deep."

"Gas?"

Gregor couldn't hear the reply to his question on chlorine gas because a crewman in the control room was loudly counting out the meters of depth achieved: "Twelve . . . thirteen . . . fourteen . . ."

Gregor quietly ordered, "Helmsman, steady on course."

The helmsman repeated the order and centered the rudder wheel. The U-boat continued to dive.

"Quiet!" Gregor said.

From outside the U-boat came the unnerving scream of propellers. Faint at first, it grew louder and louder. Gregor followed the source with his eyes as it approached from the portside.

"Sixteen . . . seventeen . . ." the crewman said, quietly announcing the depth.

The screech of propeller noise grew ever louder. It now seemed to originate slightly above the U-boat.

Gregor turned his head to follow the propeller noise as it moved toward the U-boat's stern.

Finally, the propeller noise diminished. Everyone in the room issued sighs of relief.

The navigator faced Gregor, "What was . . . ?"

In a soft voice, Gregor said, "The vessel I thought a merchantman was not. It was armed. It increased speed and aimed for us."

"To ram?"

"To ram." Gregor tilted his head to listen and ordered, "Stop battery power! Thirty!"

The helmsman repeated. The U-boat slowed but continued downward.

"Trim to depth!" ordered Gregor.

Crewmen spun wheels on valves and cycled pumps to trim and balance the craft at thirty meters of depth.

"Silence," Gregor said. "We wait." Beads of sweat formed on his forehead.

Moisture condensed and ran down on the interior surfaces of the cold hull.

The sound of the target vessel's propellers continued to diminish as it mingled with the diminishing water sounds outside the hull. After a time, the sounds abated and there was only silence.

Later, when Gregor was convinced the Irish Sea was in complete darkness, he commanded a rise to periscope depth. Upon observing no lights, he ordered the U-boat to surface for the charging of batteries.

NORTH ISLAND, SAN DIEGO, CALIFORNIA

The letter from Adrienne Bock was written and mailed in May of 1915. But because of worker shortages, shipping restrictions, and interruptions caused by the war in Europe, Will Marra did not receive it until late in 1915. Nevertheless, he was thrilled to receive her letter. It was handwritten in French:

Dear Will,

I am writing to your last address in the United States. I hope my letter reaches you, although you may have changed location, and there is now this horrible war.

It is a year nearly since I received your letter. It is difficult for me to know you are now flying an aeroplane. I must admit I fear for you, although I believe I understand why you decided against completing the University degree.

Your letter is here on my desk as I write. I find myself choking a little, considering you may have taken the opinion that my delay in writing intends I no longer wish to relate with you. Although I am understanding of this, please know our relationship is changed. Please allow me to explain.

As your letter acknowledges, I have now lived in Paris for years, and have experienced advancement in my aspect of couture. What you could not know is that I now have my own business. With humility for the patronage of the wonderful Comtesse Cécile Sorel, I maintain the house on rue du Faubourg Saint-Honoré (8 Arr.). It is named "Atelier Adrienne."

This is well and good, but the war has changed everything. Paris is pinched, there are many new faces, women have taken slots surrendered by men gone to fight, even to the driving of taxis. During this last winter, coal was scarce and wool clothing valued. Still, I am thankful that women of aristocracy and wealth continue to desire haute couture, for that maintains my life.

You will have difficulty seeing the Paris where hotels become hospitals, soldiers are everywhere in the town, uniforms on crutches, uniforms limping, uniforms with an empty sleeve—how my heart hurts for them!

Last year when the war came, my parents were forced to flee from Charleroi by the invading German army. Mother and Father only escaped with what they could carry of their possessions. They have no knowledge of what has happened to their home, which may be destroyed. They arrived on one of the last trains to Paris to escape Belgium, because the Germans did not exempt ordinary persons from the cruelties they inflicted. It is merciful that they arrived safely, and that I was able to provide for them here in Paris.

My father, Jean Boch, is not robust, and he climbs our steps only slowly. He often seems lost, absent the friendship of his Belgian confidants. He has gained fortunately employment as a records-keeper for a drink company, despite the fact that in Belgium, he was a successful banker.

To be sure, it is good to have my parents safe and

in Paris with me. My mother is a mainstay. As you may envision, however, my residence was not large enough for their comfort nor for my frequent coming and going. I therefore rented a larger residence in an inconvenient sector, where the three of us now reside (the address is found on the cover of this letter). This old dwelling is not satisfactory, owing to the two flights of stairs needed to enter, and certain other deficiencies, but in the Paris of year 1915, we must find it acceptable.

I have received no word from my dearest Grandmother Anne Boch now that Brussels is occupied by the German Army. Grandmother is ill and frail and cannot sustain to be ill-treated. We remain hoping she is safe and is not harmed. But after months of absence and no word from her, it is not without effort to remain hopeful.

One of my seamstresses, a very simple and sincere woman, has received word that her husband-to-be— they were to be married but he was overnight taken to the front—was killed at the Marne. By what instrument she is not told. She cannot think of Alain but to bring on tears. I have done whatever I could to help her, but her sadness does not abate.

These events I write of have produced in me a leaning toward deeper thoughts of life, and how I should importantly regard it. I return many times in my mind to the circumstances we shared together—even when there was but a short walk to the Place Vendôme.

I now think my actions were then partly misplaced, for I did not accept your friendship with the grace you displayed—my attitude was often bound up in achievements rather than in acceptance of your warmth and sincerity. Please know that this has changed. I hope you will understand that I now know I was unfair and that I wish my starry sky to return.

I have no method to know where in America you are. Nevertheless, I hope this letter reaches you, that you are safe, and that you are well. You will by then see I wish to reject my former attitude and repair our relationship.

With warmest regards,
Adrienne

KIEL, GERMANY

G ustave Bachmann's eyes glowed with enthusiasm, despite his replacement in September as Chief of Staff of the Admiralty by Admiral von Holtzendorff. Although he no longer had the ear of the Kaiser, the fifty-six-year-old remained a fervent advocate of the U-boat war as the key to German supremacy.

"Be assured," he told both Hans Techel and Kapitän Geighoffer at the beginning of the current meeting in Kiel, "our path to victory passes underneath the sea. And this project embodies the means to that end."

At the end of his presentation on the results of their study, Ludwig Geighoffer said, "These are, by their nature, general features. Herr Techel has listed detailed specifications for each of the proposed U-boats. Perhaps there are comments?"

"This is all as I should have expected," Bachmann said, leafing through the papers. "But perhaps Herr Techel might enlighten us concerning the technical advances that are included in the designs."

Techel smiled. "I am more than pleased to outline the approach. Although I will endeavor to avoid entangling my remarks with technical phrases like Reynolds numbers or thermal efficiency, I must, however, emphasize the importance we placed in integrating science into the design of these machines." His smile faded. He focused on Bachmann. "As you know, this approach has not always dominated past designs."

Bachmann met Techel's gaze, but remained silent.

"In a conflict with the Americans, distance becomes the key," Techel said. "For example, New York Harbor is 6,700 kilometers by sea from Bremerhaven—by the most direct route. To give a sense of this, fifteen days of travel at ten knots speed are required to achieve this distance—what we call the 'transit.'

"The transit to, and return from, the east coast of America would use more than 80 percent of the fuel on our advanced Type 31 U-boat, leaving little fuel for operations. The predicament is worse for operations in the Caribbean or at the Panama Canal—the Type 31 is unable, with a single load of fuel, to even execute the transit and return. This explains the dilemma that must be solved.

"Three possibilities exist: one, refuel at neutral ports; two, refuel by vessels at sea; and three, increase the amount of fuel placed on board the U-boat.

"Neutral ports for refueling are ill-positioned, unfriendly, and illegal. Refueling by vessels at sea is possible, but requires contacts by wireless, excellent timing, superb coordination, good weather, and superior nautical skills.

"There is little doubt the optimum solution is an increase in the amount of fuel oil on board the U-boat. It must afford transit, return, and adequate operational time. We think the range of the A-C should be at least double the range of the Type 31."

"And how is that to be accomplished?" said Bachmann.

"We envision a double-hull design similar to Type 31, but with a pressure hull of five meters diameter versus the Type 31's four meters. This results in a beam of eight meters, not quite two meters wider than the Type 31. Because of a larger hull, an increase in diesel power is required to propel it. The latest propeller design will produce improved propulsive efficiency, meaning each kilogram of fuel yields a greater distance at nominal speeds."

"I am not sure I fully understand all those terms," Bachmann said, "but the boat you describe is larger—what is its overall length?"

"Our preliminary design calls for no increase in length."

"And armament?"

"Two fifteen-centimeter guns, fore and aft. Two bow torpedo

tubes, twelve torpedoes."

"No stern tubes?"

"The larger diesel engines, electric motors, provisioning space, and oil bunkers consume all the hull, so there are no stern tubes."

"What about the attack on the Panama Canal?"

"The Canal is a special issue. That operation has yet to be planned."

"Yes, I realize. But for such a long distance . . ."

"The Atlantic entrance is about five thousand nautical miles—that would be about 9,300 kilometers by the most direct route. This calls for an altered design, which Kapitän Geighoffer is working on." Techel gestured toward Ludwig. "Perchance . . ."

"Understand, this is a work in progress," Ludwig said. "We refer to the Panama unit as S-3. We believe the planned quantity of fuel oil in the A-C project boats will be entirely adequate to power its diesels and charge the batteries. The increased space for provisioning the crew is also adequate. Nevertheless, the great distance requires modifying the basic design.

"The transatlantic and Caribbean transit may take three weeks. During such a transit, it is likely S-3 will encounter vessels requiring it to submerge, to maintain stealth. Also on its return. As you may also understand, speed is heavily compromised when submerged due to the resistance of the entire form to the propulsive thrust provided by electrically-driven propellers.

"Let me explain. A U-boat's hull and conning tower, or fairweather, are smoothly shaped for low resistance to the flow of water when submerged. But large caliber guns are blunt objects that provide severe obstacles to the flow of the water. Other blunt objects on the U-boat's external surface, such as a dinghy, also contribute as obstacles. These items slow the forward momentum and thus contribute to reducing the underwater speed.

"Although operational planning will clarify the issue, we think guns will not be useful during a Canal operation. We therefore propose to eliminate the guns, the dinghy, and certain other blunt objects on this U-boat in an effort to improve its propulsive speed underwater." Ludwig glanced at Techel, then back to Bachmann.

Bachmann nodded. "It appears you and Herr Techel have produced creditable designs. What do you estimate for production time, Herr Techel?"

"The time to produce the basic A-C design depends heavily upon the priority that is assigned, Admiral. If it were allotted adequate priorities—and absent some of the shortages we are currently experiencing—we could build such a design within five months."

"That is very encouraging. I shall begin a campaign, aided by von Tirpitz's contacts, to gain the needed support."

"I understand," Techel said. He paused, closed his notebook, and looked straight at Bachmann. "You will, sir, note the five-month period does not include launch, testing, and fitting out for service. Also, we must have access to the needed machinery—especially the larger diesel motors—which are critical to achieving the needed thrust for these larger boats."

NORTH ISLAND, SAN DIEGO, CALIFORNIA

Two newspapers, a borrowed atlas, and a handwritten letter lay on the table before Will. Next to the letter was the tattered envelope that had held it.

Will read the letter from Adrienne Boch several times in an attempt to embed it in his mind before replying. Finally, he took pen to paper. He discovered that writing in French no longer came without effort. He found he had forgotten when to apply some of the accent marks. Worse, he struggled with his emotions. He'd already torn up and discarded two attempts. He began a third.

Dear Adrienne,

I have searched the newspapers for news of Paris, because I am worried about you. I could find nothing about Paris, and only one mention of the fighting in France. It was entitled "Intense Artillery Actions in the West." The French War Office reported "the enemy directed a violent bombardment against our positions at Tahure." After a time, I located Tahure on a map. This appears close to Riems, a city distant from Paris. I very much hope this means you are safe.

Your letter which you dated May 19 is before me. Because of delays (war limitations, I suppose), the letter arrived only days ago. I have great sorrow for what has happened to your family and more generally to Paris, as you describe it. Although the United States has not decided to enter the European conflict,

I believe the German invasion of Belgium and France is morally wrong.

I recently saw a report on the fighting at Vimy Ridge which said the French casualties were near 100,000 men. This level of violence is horrible. Not only am I worried about you and your family, I fear for friends of my French years—some boys I know may have already perished in those murderous trenches.

However, it was with great pleasure that I learned of your successful house of couture on rue du Faubourg Saint-Honoré. That is wonderful. As you will recall, I have always said you were so expert and knowledgeable at couture—now it is apparent to others. Please write more about this comtesse, Cécile Sorel.

Contrariwise, I have sympathy for your difficulties with obtaining larger living quarters, and the stairs-climbing needed to obtain the floor. Thank you for your new address. I strongly hope my letter arrives, even if there are delays.

I do remember your writings of your beloved Grandmother Boch, and I too hope she withstands the occupation of Brussels. Your story of the seamstress who lost her husband-to-be at the Marne was very sad. Perhaps you could write of others of our acquaintance next time, of happier adventures I hope.

My heart goes out to you on what you termed your "leaning toward deeper thoughts of life." You said you have returned many times to our times together. I can assure you, have I as well! You said you wish to "repair our relationship." I am thrilled that you are taking this attitude toward me. I care so deeply for you. I now know I am very much in love with you.

I sincerely wish I could be in Paris to see you, to

tell you these thoughts while we walk along the Seine or pause on one of the bridges. Instead, I am here at North Island, near San Diego, California. Whereas I learned to fly on this island as a student of the Curtiss School, the U.S. Army has now taken over and established an Aviation School with an officer staff of about thirty, including me. I am now instructing recruits on how to fly Army aeroplanes.

However, as a Lieutenant of the Army, I am subject to military orders and can never know where I shall be in the future. If the United States enters the war—an action that has been talked about following the German sinking of HMS Lusitania in May—I will take an opportunity to volunteer for service in or near France. This might enable me to visit you!

I hope my letter reaches you in good health and that you are safe. Please also convey to your family that I hope they will remain safely in your care. You said you thought your previous actions were partly misplaced—well, I believe mine were too, because I never took the opportunity to kiss you.

Please write soon.

Warm regards,
Will

PARIS

Cécile Sorel burst from the cold into the modest showroom on rue du Faubourg Saint-Honoré.

Although involved with a client, Adrienne excused herself to greet her friend and patron-comedienne. "Cécile! How wonderful—it has been many weeks. Please shed your wraps."

"Pay me no attention," Cécile said, gesturing for Adrienne to return to her client. "I bring only news of a two-gram loss from my waistline."

After Adrienne's business with the client was concluded, she invited Cécile into her small office. "What—other than your diminishing waist," she said, smiling, "brings you here today?"

"I have most glorious news." She withdrew a newspaper from under her arm. "I can read only to you what has appeared in Sunday's New York Times. Although I must apologize—it is in English."

She unfolded the paper and began reading. "The 'Fête Parisienne' in New York in November has brought a new epoch. One onlooker was so affected she said, 'I see I have never been dressed—I have only been covered.'"

Adrienne laughed, and was joined by Cécile, who continued: "'Despite certain deviations, skirts continue voluminous and full of inches at the hem. Shown are pointed ruffles or overskirts edged with gold or silver ribbon or braid. Purple, in its many shades, violet, heliotrope, orchid, all will be accented this winter.

"'Wind and wide skirts join forces to produce ludicrous sights. During the first windy days of the month, the new skirts showed of what malicious evil they were capable. They swirled in the air like prize ribbons at a county fair. The legs of passersby became involved as well, wrapped in several yards of material such that entire strangers were sometimes held in a tight grip, their double embarrassment preventing a graceful release. If women wearing them do so with pleasure, much can be said for the control of fashion over mind.

"'But the women who have believed that the wide skirt was the only skirt in existence for fashion superiority should modify their verdict, as little by little a narrower skirt is creeping into the picture. It may not be advocated by the most popular Paris houses at present, but you see fashionable women wearing them at all hours, not only in the street, where they are gratefully received, but in the evening, to the opera, and to the dances.

"'Shown at the Paris Fashion extravaganza was a remarkably beautiful gown made by Adrienne in amber and gold brocade, with straight lines from the décolletage to the knees, with very little suggestion of a waistline; the sides turn out into the train just as they leave the ankle, and the back width joins them. There is a glimmer of amber tulle, a flash of gold on the shoulders to finish it in magnificent style. Atelier Adrienne is one to keep watching.'"

Cécile lowered the paper and studied the woman seated behind the desk.

"I—I don't know what to—" Adrienne began, as her eyes began to reflect tiny sparkles.

"Drat!" Cécile said, in clown-like seriousness, "I came here expecting sympathy for my wrinkles. Instead, I'm met with confused bluster."

Adrienne laughed through her tears. "Oh, bless you. I did not know of the Times' mention. I had almost forgotten that the gown was consigned to the committee—the Syndicat de Defense de la Couture Parisienne—weeks ago."

"You surely have earned the praise, my dear," the comedienne said.

"My parents—they will be joyous. Especially Papa. As I have said before, he is not robust. He is unhappy here and blames it all on the war. But he has always supported my desire to succeed in couture."

"None of us are happy about the war," Cécile said, suddenly serious. "Except perhaps the manufacturers of munitions." She paused, furrowed her brow, and as an afterthought said, "And the purveyors of absinthe."

1916

NORTH ISLAND, SAN DIEGO, CALIFORNIA

T he base commander said, "As I understand it, you flew missions on the Veracruz operation a couple of years ago."

"Yes, sir," Will Marra said. "Very unusual. I was on temporary duty with the Navy . . ."

The commander narrowed his eyes, lowered the paper in his hand to his desk, and remained silent.

Will continued, "Operating an A2 and a C-3 seaplane for 'Rum' Mustin. It was uneventful—nothing but recon duty."

"This assignment might not be as routine. You have flown Jennies?"

"Yes, both JN-2 and JN-3. The JN-2 is not a successful aeroplane—in my opinion."

"You're aware the 1st Aero Squadron was tapped to support General Pershing's hunt for Pancho Villa in Mexico?"

Will nodded.

"The squadron flew south on March 19 from Columbus, New Mexico. They flew eight JN-3s and headed for Pershing's base." The commander lowered his gaze to his paper, and began reading, "'Limited in fuel and heavily loaded, they encountered darkness before reaching the objective. One aeroplane turned back, one cracked up in a forced landing, and the other six landed short, two of which were only located a day later. Difficulties have continued to increase. There are altitude, cargo weight, and airfield limitations—'"

"If I may say so, sir, some of the First's pilots are new and inexperienced. I think I've instructed one or two. And the JN-3 has problems . . ."

The commander looked up. "You've been flying the 'three'?"

"Almost every day. The aeroplane has some deficiencies, but the main problem is the motor. It's—"

"Well, that's why you were selected—you know the technical aspects. The War Department wants you to go down there and help them out. You are ordered to join the 1st Aero Squadron's operation, not as a pilot, but as a mechanician. The idea is to help them with all these problems—to straighten out their logistics and reduce their technical faults. Right now, Pershing seems to think 1st Aero are only useful for carrying mail to the troops. And not much of that, thanks to their ships' load limitations."

"That means I won't be flying there. How am I to travel?"

"You'll be on your own mode of travel. The Mexico North-Western Railroad out of Ciudad Juárez runs to Colonia Dublán and Chihuahua. That's your best bet. The Juárez depot is just across the border from El Paso, Texas. You speak French fluently, right?"

"Sure. I grew up in Paris, lived there for more than ten years."

"Of course, we'll get you to El Paso. And see to your needs for iden-tification, travel money, and expenses."

Will's face showed his puzzlement. "Why the question about me speaking French?"

"Well, this is sort of delicate. When President Wilson sent Pershing to Mexico with the 7th Cavalry to run down Pancho Villa, he didn't reckon that Mexican citizens would see it as an outright invasion. But I should warn you there's no love lost between many Mexicans and United States Army 'gringos.'

"The War Department's thinking is that your travel to Colonia Dublán will be expedited if you travel as a French civilian, rather than as an officer of the United States Army."

"So I'll be traveling on my own, in civilian clothes. How soon should I—"

"That's an issue with the Department. Can you pack up right away? We'd like to get you to El Paso before April 1."

•   •   •

Will Marra, dressed in an open-collar white shirt, black trousers, a wool coat, and a wide-brimmed gray hat, crossed Calle Ferrocarril. Although it was near noon, the sky was choked gray with coal smoke from the many chimneys and from steam engines in the nearby switchyard.

Mexicans awaiting the train stood outside the depot on the dirt beside the tracks. An official of some sort in a broad hat lingered nearby on horseback.

Will entered the depot, and after checking with Mexican customs, bought a first-class ticket—second-class tickets allowed only fifteen kilograms for baggage.

It wasn't much of a train—three passenger cars with open plat-forms at either end. Its stubby steam locomotive's bell clanked loud enough for it to lead a 20-car passenger train. All the cars had a dusty, well-used look, and were adorned with lettering reading 'Nor-Oeste de México.'

After climbing onto the last car, Will saw it was divided into three sections: an eight-seat smoking section at the rear, general seating in the middle, and a short, padlocked baggage compartment at the front end. Although he didn't smoke, he chose a seat in the smoking section because he thought it might be absent bawling children. He hoisted his bag up and onto the iron rack over an arched window.

By the time the train shook to a start, two passengers had joined him in the section: an old man with a white beard carrying a shoebox tied with string, and to Will's surprise, a United States Army corporal in uniform carrying a regulation duffel bag. The old man puffed on a pipe as he selected the seat across the aisle from Will. The corporal chose a seat nearest the end of the car.

Will dug out the latest newspaper he'd bought in El Paso and began reading. Under the page one headline, 'American Cavalry Pressing

Villa Hard,' was the following report:

March 29, 4 P.M.—FIELD HEADQUARTERS UNITED STATES PUNITIVE EXPEDITION, COLONIA DUBLAN, Mexico (by Army aeroplane to Columbus, N.M.) It is officially confirmed by aeroplane that the southernmost American cavalry forces are pressing Francisco Villa hard. But he may slip through, officers said to this correspondent today. Villa is reported fleeing toward the headwaters of the Santa Maria River.

Mexican President Venustiano Carranza has denied the use of railways to our troops, despite President Woodrow Wilson's authorization for the U.S. Expedition in response to Pancho Villa's raid on Columbus, New Mexico during which 18 Americans were killed. Thus the Expedition's current transport capability requires four wagon train companies; each company has 27 escort wagons drawn by four mules. This totals to a combined resupply capacity of 162 tons of stores, rations, fuel, and forage.

General Pershing reported, after Villa's fight with the Carranza soldiers at the edge of the mountainous district south of Namiquipa, that Villa was making his way south. The U.S. Cavalry resumed its unrelenting ride on his trail, notwithstanding it might lead them into the dangerous mountain passes of the region.

"Villa is like a coyote," Gen. Pershing says, "and you know how hard a coyote is to catch."

Aeroplanes are now regularly patrolling our lines between here and Columbus, scouting and acting as aerial postmen. Below this headquarters are infantry units who only last week marched all the way from the border through the sand, but notwithstanding, consider themselves lucky in being here. Near freezing at dawn, near ninety at noon, and near freezing again as the sun sets, bugles are sounding, lights are beginning to show in the tents.

It is said there is typhus in Casas Grandes nearby. The command remains free of any disease, but as a precaution every man and officer was told today to drink no more river water. Wells have been sunk in the silt a hundred yards from the river, and pumps have been installed. While there is no contagion, hospital tents continue to treat the small hurts, infected limbs and feet, countless ailments to which men everywhere are heir.

As the train chugged its way southwest from Juárez, the landscape flattened to a high plateau devoid of people. Sparse vegetation, cacti and mesquite, dotted the tan hills. The old man attempted to talk to Will, but returned to puffing on his pipe when he received a reply in French. The tobacco smoke mixed with cool air from the open door at the rear, contriving an agreeable odor.

About an hour later, the train spluttered to a stop at a village. Will stood and left the train via the rear platform, greeting the corporal as he passed, "Bonjour, Monsieur." The corporal, surprised, issued a delayed, "Hello" in reply.

Will stood outside for a few minutes, squinting at some horses and the adobe huts and houses in the sunlit village. He returned to the railcar as vendors exited who had boarded with jewelry and food items for sale. Inside, he faced a woman hawking uncooked chicken eggs at ten cents apiece. He declined, saying, "Beautiful eggs, Madame!" as she left the car.

The train hissed on, spewing plentiful black smoke and coal dust. Almost an hour after a stop at Barreal, the train pulled into Guzman. Prominently visible and scanning the passenger cars was a man in a sombrero on horseback. He wore crisscrossed bandoliers filled with cartridges. A rifle in a scabbard was strapped below his saddle.

At the last moment before leaving Guzman, a heavyset woman with her head in a ragged kerchief followed by a boy of about sixteen climbed the rear platform and entered the car.

Breathing heavily, the woman plopped onto the seat across from the corporal. The heavy-built boy sat next to her on the aisle. The car shook, and the train chugged forward. As the track curved south, Will glanced out the window and saw there were mountains to the south-west. He realized three more hours or more would be needed to reach his destination.

The train moved slowly on the curve. The cars wobbled.

The boy screamed at the corporal, "¿Qué diablos estás haciendo aquí?" What the hell are you doing here?

The corporal, not understanding, said, "What?"

"Gringo sucio!" the boy said. "Gringo sucio!" Dirty Gringo!

The boy's anger was now apparent to the corporal. He relaxed into his seat with an expression of resignation.

The heavyset woman spoke something into her son's ear. The boy lunged across the aisle, clutched the corporal's collar, and punched him in the face.

The corporal, stunned, rubbed his cheek. "Why'd you do that?"

The boy stood up and swung his fist again, hitting the corporal. Will came to his feet.

The woman screamed, "Pedro!"

The corporal, now on his feet, evaded the boy's fist. He grasped an invading arm. The two wrestled. The boy was more powerful than the corporal, and flung the corporal into the seat back. The corporal bounced up and rushed the boy as the boy turned toward his mother.

The mother's foot shot into the corporal's shin. He bent in pain, and the boy pounded the corporal's body with both fists.

Will moved quickly to the fight. He pulled the sagging corporal from the boy.

The boy punched Will's side, hard. Will answered with a swift fist to the boy's jaw.

Lips bloody, the boy swung wildly with both fists. Will blocked each, and thrust a quick left fist to the boy's right eye.

The boy yelped and staggered onto the rear platform. Will struck him with a left to the stomach and a right to the jaw. The boy staggered and fell off the platform. He landed in a heap on the gravel beside the track. After tumbling forward, his body stopped moving.

The mother screamed, rushed out, and jumped off the platform. Her heavy body splayed onto the gravel, then rolled. But she immediately rose and headed for the prostrate boy, whose legs began treading air.

Will rubbed the throbbing knuckles of his right hand with his left. The corporal picked his hat from the floor.

The corporal felt his left cheek. "Thanks. I wasn't expecting that. I mean the way he came—"

Will said in English, "Americans are not welcome here. I suggest you ditch the hat. Where you headed?"

"Colonia Dublán—the encampment."

"Forget I spoke to you. I'm Army—undercover." With that, Will returned to his seat across from the old man.

The train rumbled on across trackless valleys, past Sabinal, Ochoa, and the junction at San Pedro. A few more Mexicans boarded and chose the smoking section, but no other incidents occurred.

Finally, after more than six hours, the train stopped at Colonia Dublán, a small settlement among a number of eroded and tumble-down adobe dwellings. Will and the hatless corporal hefted their luggage and left the car.

•　　　•　　　•

Inside the pyramid tent, Will sat on a wooden crate. Across from him, with his pipe in his left hand, sat the commander of the 1st Aero Squadron, Captain B. D. Foulois. "In addition to talking to the pilots," Foulois said, "I recommend you speak with our mechanicians, especially M.S.E. Idzorek. His men have temporarily set up the mobile machine shop east of the Aerodrome."

Will rose. "Yes, sir. And thanks for your support." He turned to leave.

Foulois smiled. "I know tent living is not your choice. The chow is not the greatest, either. But at least we're not being shelled by giant artillery."

"For that I'm grateful, sir."

"And Marra. See me before you return to the States."

"Yes, sir, I will." He lifted the flap and exited.

•   •   •

Two days later, Captain Foulois listened as Lieutenant Will Marra summarized what he'd determined.

"Although the Jennies you have remaining are worn, the crews have done well in maintaining them. Master Signal Electrician Idzorek is a whiz at keeping machines running, including those Jeffery Quad trucks.

"The propeller problem is serious. The glue used to laminate the wood does not hold in this dry environment. Keeping them covered helps, but the humidor they've installed at Camp Furlong seems only a temporary fix. I recommended having someone visit that huge lumber mill up at Pearson—the people there know wood and may know of a solution to these propeller failures.

"Your pilots have also done well, despite the situation. The lack of decent landing fields, the logistic snarl of long truck trains from the United States border, and the rather primitive conditions here make both flying and maintenance difficult.

"The pilots don't like being limited to carrying mail and messages, but it's not their fault these aeroplanes are unsuited for reconnaissance. Threes—and your JN-2s have been turned into JN-3s—have inherent problems: high drag, low power, sensitive rudders, weak undercarriages, and narrow wheels.

"The worst of the problems is the motor. Jennies lack adequate horsepower even at sea level. The service ceiling for the JN-3 quoted by the Curtiss factory is 6,400 feet. Here in Dublán, where the elevation is over 5,000 and the mountains are around 10,000, the thinner air reduces power by 15 to 20 percent. Longer takeoff runs are required to become airborne, and landing speeds are too fast for safety, especially on sandy, uneven soil. Winds, unpredictable downdrafts, and dust storms complicate everything.

"Controlling these aeroplanes when near their maximum altitude is almost impossible, and flying over the Sierra Madre mountains should not even be attempted.

"The mission given me by the War Department was to help the First with logistics and technical support. I've done what I could, including some flight instruction. But there is little I can do about the aeroplanes. Unsatisfactory aeroplanes will remain unsatisfactory."

Foulois gestured with his pipe. "My reports to General Pershing," he said in urgent tones, "demonstrate—absolutely, and finally—the limited military usefulness of the present Squadron equipment for military service in high altitudes and in a mountainous country."

"Yes, sir. General Pershing has his hands full. A deeper problem exists. The United States' aircraft industry barely exists. There are some small companies with good people, but they produce only a few aeroplanes a year. Military spending has not encouraged development of improved designs, despite the European war. It's almost as if we've stayed where we were ten years ago with regard to aviation innovation.

"When I get back, I'll submit my report to the War Department recommending more powerful aircraft, maybe Thomas or Sturtevant, as replacements. With both General Pershing and the War Department pushing, maybe the situation will improve."

"Good luck, Marra. I wish you every success."

"And you, sir, the same."

PARIS

U pon reaching the apartment, Adrienne placed her two bulging bags on the floor of the landing. After two heavy breaths and a sigh, she entered.

Dominique met her at the door. "Oh—let me help." She took one of the string bags from Adrienne and bore it toward the kitchen. Adrienne followed with the other bag.

In the kitchen, Dominique glanced at Adrienne. "Bless you, your face is white. Perhaps you—"

"It is the stairs, Mother." She hoisted the bag onto the pastry table. "I count every step." She began removing the purchased items. "Or perhaps it is the funeral."

"The funeral?"

"Yes. Today they gather—at Notre-Dame de la Croix—to honor those killed by the bombs."

"Oh, the bombs from the cursed Zeppelin." Dominique shook her head. "We pray to heaven."

Only the rustle of packages and tins filled the room. When Dominique spied a particular item among the contents of the bags, she exclaimed, "Wonders! Rice! In what location did you find it?"

"Les Halles. And only by standing in a queue for many minutes among the baskets and the litter. And there—I must tell you—"

"—and cheese!" Dominique pointed at the small package and raised her hands in joy. "We shall have a good supper tonight."

Adrienne did not react to her mother's cheer. "Mother, what I saw was distressing. A man, a French soldier—I suppose he was on convalescent leave—stood with an older woman, probably his mother. One arm was stiff, bandaged in a sling. He spoke to her of 'Verdun,' the fight we hear of only in rumors."

"Verdun. Yes, I have heard the rumors," Dominique said.

Adrienne halted her task. Her voice broke a little as she spoke. "I tried to not listen, I did not wish to overhear, so anguished was he about his ordeal. He said, 'It is impossible.' He said it was 'nothing but mass slaughter.'"

Dominique's smile vanished. "This is most difficult, my child. Yet we must carry on." The older woman paused and turned away from her daughter. "I suppose the prices—I suppose you had to pay more for everything?"

Adrienne returned to sorting the groceries. "Yes, Mother, for certain. Everything costs more, yet there is less and less of everything. We now approach two years of war. When will it end?"

"My child, it is all so . . . so sad." Dominique looked intently at Adrienne. "Is there a deficiency of money?"

"No, Mother, I am fortunate. Even without what Papa adds, we need not fear poverty." She held up a small box labeled 'Comprimés de Bouillon' and smiled: "This will have to substitute for braised beef."

Dominique laughed as if she applauded Adrienne's joke. "It is magnificent!"

Adrienne opened a cupboard door and placed the bouillon cubes inside. "Papa—he has returned from work?"

"He is asleep in the chair, or as I saw him he was. He works too long there, and did not return until a half hour before you came home."

Jean appeared at the doorway. "What do you mean, Dear Wife?"

"Oh, I thought you were asleep."

"Papa!" Adrienne said, turning toward him. "I have a question. A business question. Excuse me while I find the message." She closed the cupboard door, found her purse among the groceries, and dug inside. She withdrew and unfolded a paper. "Today I received this cablegram. Please advise me what I should do."

TO: ADRIENNE BOCH, ATELIER
ADRIENNE, PARIS
ADMIRED AMBER AND GOLD BROCADE
GOWN AT FETE PARISIENNE NEW YORK
NOVEMBER 1915 (STOP) WISH TO EXHIBIT AT
I MAGNIN STORE SAN FRANCISCO (STOP)
FULL SECURITY GUARANTEED (STOP) ADVISE
LOCATION OF GOWN AND TERMS FOR
EXHIBITING (STOP)
GROVER A MAGNIN FOR MARY ANN MAGNIN
I MAGNIN CO

Jean looked up from the paper. "The gown that you sent to the New York show. You have it?"

"It was returned to me after the exhibition. But it no longer exists. We used the brocade and tulle for another garment."

Jean returned the paper to Adrienne. "I. Magnin is a large apparel merchant in America. I believe it was founded by Mary Ann Magnin well before the century turned. She wished to pay you to exhibit the gown in the I. Magnin store in San Francisco."

"Really!" Adrienne said. She stared at the groceries for a moment, thinking. What must she do now?

Jean spoke to the silence. "It is a genuine compliment. You must inform her that the gown is not available."

"Yes, but . . ."

"Perhaps another gown?"

Adrienne shook her head. "That would not do. But I do have something." Adrienne glanced at her mother. "Mother—I should remain to help here in the kitchen—"

"No, Daughter." She waved her hand. "Go with your father—he knows business."

Adrienne left the kitchen, followed by her father. "I have not done a cablegram, Papa. How do I proceed?"

"You should prepare the wording beforehand. Remember that the telegraph office charges for each word."

"You mean the cost increases with every word?"

"Exactly. I will help you."

•   •   •

Adrienne rose from the desk and contemplated the message she'd struggled to write for several minutes. "Tell me, Papa, if this is an appropriate reply."

Jean read what Adrienne had written. "The 'colored drawing' you cite. You would have I. Magnin display a drawing?"

"Yes. It is part of my planning. Before we sew, I draw the concept on the figure."

"Excellent. But notice all the words in your message—the telegraph office will charge you a small fortune!"

"But Papa . . ."

"You must learn to convey your thoughts in fewer words. Look at how the message you received was constructed. Instead of saying, 'The fullest security will be guaranteed,' Mr. Magnin wrote, 'Full security guaranteed,' using three words rather than six. Yet the meaning is clear."

"Yes, I see." She took the paper from her father's hand. "It does seem unnatural." She returned to the desk and began revising the message. After several more minutes, she presented her father with what she considered an improvement:

TO: GROVER A MAGNIN I MAGNIN CO
GRATEFUL FOR APPROVAL (STOP) NEW YORK
GOWN NOT AVAILABLE (STOP) ORIGINAL
COLOR DRAWING AVAILABLE (STOP) ADVISE
IF INTERESTED (STOP)

Jean studied it and said, "This is better, but I believe it can be improved: Substitute 'NY' for New York. Eliminate 'ORIGINAL,' and 'IF INTERESTED.' I think that will save four words, yet convey the message."

"You are wonderful, Papa. I will change the message and take it to the telegraph office as soon as we finish in the kitchen."

KIEL, GERMANY

Damning the stinging sensation in his eyes, Kapitän Ludwig Geighoffer hurried toward the huge gray building and over-hanging steel superstructure near the estuary. "It must be the coal smoke," he told himself.

His path lay between the rail sidings and tall cranes of the Kiel shipyard. Now that he concentrated on them, he noticed that the tops of the taller smokestacks were only visible as silhouettes in the gray gloom.

He entered the ground level door, checked through the guard, and climbed the stairs to the overlook. Herr Techel would be there before him, he mused, perhaps the only civilian attendee allowed.

"Ah, you are early," Hans Techel said. "Anxious to see it, I suppose."

Ludwig felt stiff in his dress uniform and high cap. "Not so much to see it as to see the performance," he said, smiling. He looked down at the workers climbing about on the maze of girders, ladders, and wooden scaffolding. He then glanced to the side along the handrail, hoping he might identify someone. He leaned closer to Hans and said in a low voice, "I do not see the Admiral."

Hans nodded, but quickly looked away.

Ludwig said, "Perhaps he is ill. Then again . . ." He let the thought go. He again looked down at the gray steel hulk on the slipway. "It is clean, as we specified. But we will not know—"

"Indeed. We will not know its performance before the trials." Techel paused and glanced from the workers to Ludwig. "On the other hand," he said sardonically, "it is only three months behind schedule."

Ludwig nodded. "I know. The coal situation—and the shortage

of workers."

"The powerhouse had outages—we had a complete blackout." He gestured at Ludwig's uniform. "Why can we not demand coal?"

"Demand, yes. We demand." Ludwig shook his head soberly. "Our demands do not equal coal."

The launchmaster's shouts distracted both Ludwig and Hans. He appeared to direct his megaphone toward the workers lower on the slanted spillway, shouting commands observers on the overlook above could not hear. The workers reacted to the launchmaster, altering the position of chains, cables, ladders, and wooden scaffolding.

"Those crewmen now on board," Ludwig asked Hans, "they will complete the fitting out?"

Techel pushed his spectacles upward on his remarkably straight nose. "No. There is only a skeleton crew on board. Final installation and many tests follow in the estuary. Only then will a full crew take to the vessel for the trials."

Ludwig said, "What is your information on the diesels?"

Hans continued watching the launchmaster. "M.A.N.— Maschinenfabrik Augsburg-Nürnberg—have guaranteed a maximum of three-thousand horsepower in these six-cylinder models. This may be enough, with the new propellers, to achieve seventeen knots, surfaced." Hans turned to face Ludwig. "But much depends upon the worthiness of M.A.N.'s guarantee, eh?"

Ludwig nodded and frowned. "You understand I am most concerned about the speed submerged."

Techel seemed not to hear. "Has a captain been named?"

"I know of none." Ludwig resumed watching the activity on the slanted slipway. "I hear only rumors about changes in organization . . ."

"I do not know." Techel looked across the slipway and pointed at the control office. He raised his voice above the noise from the workers and the attendees. "I know only that I have not seen Admiral Bachman for some time."

Ludwig shook his head slowly. "I am uncertain. What do you—"

Hans opened his mouth to reply when the launchmaster signaled to the control office and a klaxon began sounding. It was so loud it overcame whatever Hans replied.

Both men scanned the activities on the slanted ways as the klaxon blared. Workmen at the lowest level, next to the cradle at the U-boat's stern, used big hammers to knock chocks from the ways. The big gray body and its cradles began to slide downward on the angled ways.

The klaxon continued as the U-boat, stern first, moved faster and faster toward the water. The propellers, planes, and stern splashed into the estuary, creating a tall crest of water that rolled outward in an expanding circle which slowly diminished in height. The sound now became that of a large displacement of water, as the rounded middle slid into the surface.

The angle of the U-boat began to flatten as the hull floated into the water at the foot of the ways.

The initial wave burst against the nearby quay, showering spray on a few onlookers who had gathered there.

The stern of the U-boat surfaced, creating a secondary wave with foamy crest. Hawsers and cables tightened, slowing the movement of the U-boat. The gray form flattened to near horizontal and floated free. Finally the U-boat was reefed in by its crew as applause and cheers echoed off the metal walls of the big gray building.

Ludwig could not avoid smiling. He glanced at Hans Techel, who squinted toward the floating gray form with an unchanged set to his jaw.

NORTH ISLAND, SAN DIEGO, CALIFORNIA

The commander shook his head. "Either you've got H. L. Menken working publicity for you or you're the luckiest lieutenant in this man's army. Now it's the Army Chief of Staff issuing your orders."

Will Marra frowned. "General Scott?"

"Uh-huh." The commander narrowed his eyes and read from the paper in his hand. "Captain B. D. Foulois, Commander of the 1st Aero Squadron, reported that propellers made from Pearson's wood performed very well."

Will remained silent and expressionless.

The commander looked up from the paper. "So your trip to Mexico has been rated a success, despite Pancho Villa's ability to hide out in the mountains."

"Commander Foulois reported to General Pershing that the aeroplanes of the 1st Aero were unable to fly high enough even to pass through the local mountain passes. Also, that one or two of the original propellers made of laminated wood slabs came apart in the air.

"My report to the War Department on my duty in Mexico recommended new aeroplanes able to fly higher. Also that propellers made from a single piece of wood native to the local area might work." Will paused. "Did you say General Scott issued an order for me?"

"Yes. He's ordered you farther south—all the way to the Panama Canal. You'll be reporting to Governor Goethals and to General Edwards at Fort Sherman."

"Goethals." Will grinned. "You mean George Washington Goethals, the man who built the canal?"

"That's him. But reporting to him seemed unusual to me, so I asked for clarification. It seems before he was assigned to build the Canal, General Goethals served as an expert on coastal defense. This may have contributed when he persuaded the Chief of Staff that the Army's harbor defenses of Cristóbal-Colón are inadequate."

"Cristóbal-Colón?" Will squinted. "I'm not sure I—"

"I'll help. That's the harbor at the Atlantic entrance, the harbor that fronts the Gatun Locks that allow entry into the Canal itself."

"I'm confused. I don't know anything about the harbor, the Canal, or its defenses."

"A number of artillery batteries are emplaced there—big guns, including twelve-inchers, I'm informed. But General Goethals is concerned. Although he admits those guns might repel an attempted invasion, he also thinks the British Royal Navy has the German Imperial Fleet bottled up and unable to mount an invasion.

"He thinks, however, the Kaiser might send a submarine intent on blowing up the locks of the Canal. You know—one of those so-called U-boats."

Will considered this and said, "Yeah, I suppose that's possible . . ."

"I read part of what Goethals wrote to General Scott. He says a German merchant submarine named Deutschland sailed from Bremen, Germany and docked in July at Baltimore, Maryland. There it discharged 163 tons of aniline dyestuffs worth $6 million. He claims that's evidence German submarines have long-range capability, allowing an armed submarine with sufficient range to reach as far as the Canal, with disastrous results.

"Therefore, the Chief of Staff concluded the Army should supply the capability of aerial surveillance of the ocean near the Atlantic entrance." He handed a paper to Will. "Here's what the order says."

Will read the dispatch:

1. Chief of Staff, U.S. Army designates Lt. Will Marra to head a patrol force under the control of Panama Canal Zone Governor G. W. Goethals and the U.S. Army in

the Canal Zone (C.Z.), Brig. Gen Clarence R. Edwards, Commanding. The patrol force shall consist of one or more R-3 or R-4 aeroplanes, supported by mechanicians and riggers. Additional pilots and aeroplanes may be ordered as the patrol becomes operational.

2. The patrol force will organize daily aerial surveillance for the purpose of identifying and tracking foreign submarine activity in the Cristóbal-Colón harbor area of the C.Z. and the Caribbean Sea beyond the breakwaters. The intelligence gained is to be shared and cooperation is to be afforded with both the U.S. Army's land-based defense of the C.Z. and with the U.S. Navy's submarine force operating in the C.Z. from the U.S. Navy tenders Ozark, Severn, Tallahassee, and Charleston.

3. The patrol force will billet and operate from Fort Sherman, which has no airfield. The force will therefore utilize Fort Sherman Lagoon or Limon Bay for takeoff and landing. Dockage, fuel, and lubricants will be supplied by the Fort Sherman quartermaster. Necessary Signal Corps personnel will be ordered as required.

4. Officers and enlisted men are reminded that the patrol force will operate within the boundaries of a country whose peaceful inhabitants are to be treated with every consideration. It is also desirable to maintain the most cordial relations, and cooperate as far as feasible, with the de facto government of the isthmus.

By command of Maj. Gen Hugh L. Scott: R.C. Dennis, Lt. Col., Staff.

Will looked from the dispatch to the commander. "I hope the Chief of Staff clarifies item one. The Curtiss aeroplane—either R-3 or R-4—has to be equipped with twin floats. Also longer wings. Longer wings are required to support the weight of the floats. Sending a standard-winged model down there would be useless, even with floats."

The commander pursed his lips. After a moment he said, "I see. I'm not informed on the design of these aeroplanes. I'll transmit your suggestion."

"What I'd really like to see is the new R-6, with its bigger V-2-3 motor. That would reduce the takeoff run, which might be important."

"Okay. I'll add that you prefer an R-6 aeroplane," the commander said, scribbling a notation onto his notes. "Anything else?"

"Well, 'identifying and tracking a submarine' is fine and useful. But if we were at war, wouldn't it be better if our aeroplane carried a bomb to drop on the invader?"

The commander closed an eye while staring at Will. "That's a question far above my pay grade. I'll pretend you didn't ask it."

Will nodded. "When do I sail for Panama?"

"We'll get you on board a steamer shortly."

•   •   •

Will Marra studied the man across from him. They were sitting in Will's temporary quarters at Ft. Sherman. The man, rated as a Master Signal Electrician, was older than he. "The cargo ship is the SS Chasehill. You're sure of the sailing date?"

M.S.E. James Oakley, assigned as Will's crew chief, said, "I'm sorry, Lieutenant. I can't be positive. The eighteenth is what the quartermaster sergeant told me." He glanced at his puttees.

"So the vessel will dock at Cristobál. Is that your understanding?"

"The sergeant said the quartermaster corps would handle the transfer of all shipments."

"So they'll deliver the shipment here—from the ship to Fort Sherman?"

"I think that's what he meant." He gestured with both hands. "I'm not privy to the bill of lading."

"Why can't we get a positive—oh, I know, it's 'the rattle and roar of Freedom's battle.'" Will sighed, chuckled, and glanced out the window toward the lagoon. "But you believe the aeroplane is the R-9 from the factory."

"That's what the sergeant says the Curtiss factory said." Oakley used the edge of his hand to wipe sweat from his forehead.

"The R-9 is a version of the R-6 that I requested. I assume it will arrive in crates. Probably we'll get a fuselage, engine, wings, in separate crates, a pair of floats, plus a tail section partly assembled. What do you think?"

"I have no experience with the Curtiss R series, sir."

"How do you see the process of assembling the aeroplane?"

"As I said, I participated in the assembly of the Jennies for the Punitive Expedition in Columbus. And I had some air time as observer. But I expect the assembly would go about the same."

"Okay. Do you have the people you need for assembling the aeroplane as well as what you will need for operations?"

"I think so. I've got five men, one of who I worked with in Mexico. He's pretty handy with motors."

"He may not have much experience with this motor—it's a V-8. In the meantime, we need facilities in the lagoon for servicing the aeroplane. I've written out a list for you. Although we'll have to live temporarily with beaching the aeroplane for service, we should submit a construction order right away for a concrete ramp—with tie-downs—and some kind of nearby shed for tools and equipment."

"Yes, sir. Maybe south of the Engineers Dock?"

"If the water depth permits it there. When assembly of the aeroplane is finished, we'll need a pier with cleats where deckhands can operate. And a fueling capability—"

"The quartermaster says fueling will not be a problem. They service tugs and other types of boats there all the time, so—"

"We need to guarantee we can pump aeroplane gas—filtered to remove contaminants and water. I'm not going to fly this aeroplane with any sort of questionable fuel. Also on the list is a service boat for towing the aeroplane, and a wind sock." Will glanced at Oakley. "And you'll need to find some hand pumps to pump out the floats."

"Yes, sir."

". . . and I want you to see what you can find out about a wireless."

"Wireless? You mean a wireless set for the aeroplane?"

"Yes. Our mission is searching from the air for a submarine." Will paused. "But suppose we sight one, what do we do then? We need to notify the command on land—right away! My idea is to place a wireless transmitter on the aeroplane, so a signal can be sent to the defense on land. That way, they'll have the information and we can stay with the submarine we've sighted."

"I see what you mean. But operating the transmitter . . ."

"The observer operates the transmitter while the pilot flies the aeroplane."

"Oh, so I guess I will be operating the wireless." Oakley smiled at the prospect, but quickly lost it. "But I don't know Morse code."

"You can learn, right?"

"Sure. Yes, sir."

"Until then, we'll just send some kind of simple signal meaning we've sighted a submarine. I'll be speaking to General Edwards about setting up codes and a receiver here at Fort Sherman. They'll need someone to operate the set, monitoring for our signals, as well."

Oakley nodded, then was silent for a moment. "I haven't heard of any wireless installations on an aeroplane, sir. The sets I know of are darned heavy."

"That might be a problem. We may have to carry less fuel to compensate."

"And I think they require an aerial. Plus, electrical power."

"Yes. That's what I want you to look into, Oakley. You'll have to dig a bit, find out what the Signal Corps' technical people know about wireless transmitters in aeroplanes. Good luck."

FT. SHERMAN, ISTHMUS OF PANAMA

The wind was from the northwest, which Will Marra estimated at about five knots. They passed over the east breakwater and then over the city of Colón. But Will wasn't on a sightseeing flight—he was testing out the newly-assembled Curtiss R-9 aeroplane.

The noise in the leading cockpit of the craft's two tandem cockpits was deafening. He poked his left arm outside the open cockpit where it was buffeted by the slipstream. He turned the back of his hand to the sixty-five-mile-per-hour wind and signaled to Oakley in the observer's cockpit with his finger pointing downward. He then began a descending turn to the right.

The left upper wing fluttered and rattled on the outside of the turn. He'd have to tell Oakley to tighten some turnbuckles.

The craft dropped too quickly, causing Will to nudge the throttle and ease the descent.

The surface of Limón Bay on the landward side of the west breakwater looked calm enough. Despite the roar and flame from the V-8 motor's exhaust pipes, the one-ton aircraft reacted only sluggishly to Will's input to the controls. And he discovered that working the ailerons was a source of excellent morning exercise. He heard himself say, "This machine flies exactly like a brick."

Will decided the performance of the R-9 was being limited by the weight and resistance of the floats and the structure attaching them below the fuselage. Each of the massive twin floats was twenty feet long, attached to the fuselage by six three-foot-long struts. Of course the floats were needed for water operations, but could something be done to reduce the performance deficit?

Halfway through the '180,' Will tried to figure out where he ought to splash. There were two ships at anchor on the west part of the Bay, one of which lay on the ideal line into the wind. Will decided he would aim his final landing run to the left of that vessel.

He straightened the aeroplane's path and reduced power. Slowing for a safe splashdown was essential, but every few seconds he glanced at the airspeed dial to assure his speed was above the R-9's stall speed. The aeroplane dropped easily toward the water—too easily! He added a little more power, slowing the descent. They passed the ship at twenty feet. Slightly nose-up to prevent the floats from dipping into the water, causing the aeroplane to flip upside down, he warily dropped to the surface of the Bay.

The slight crabbing of the approach needed to avoid the ship resulted in a jarring, hooking splash. Gallons of seawater fell on both men, and Will knew his first landing in the R-9 was not just wet—it was clumsy. The craft complained loudly, but its wooden frame, the slender struts, and its steel wires held, so he and Oakley were safe for now.

As he taxied, he observed the aeroplane slowing very quickly. The floats offered high resistance to the water. He recognized he'd finished his landing run too far from the lagoon.

As he cruised across part of the Bay that converged to the lagoon entrance, Will considered the aerial reconnaissance mission. How might he plan to assure the aircraft was ready for regular daily flights? It would require a high level of reliability—yet all he could currently rely upon was a hastily-selected crew of five enlisted under M.S.E. Jim Oakley that had only worked together intensely for the two weeks assembling the aeroplane.

He turned his head to view Oakley. The older man grinned beneath his outsized goggles and gave Will a thumbs-up.

Will rounded the jut of land, entered the lagoon, and carefully steered the craft through the narrow passage into the main basin. Several ground crewmen awaited the arrival of the aeroplane on the just-constructed pier.

He slowed the motor more and allowed the breeze to push the aircraft, tail first, toward the pier. Oakley clambered out and stood on a float while hanging on with one arm. He shouted directions to the men on the pier. As Will attempted to cushion the docking using the throttle, the port float made hard contact with a piling. Crewmen on the pier quickly attached lines to the aircraft, securing it.

Will turned the motor off and climbed out of the cockpit, shaking his head. Once on the pier, he threw off his goggles and leather helmet. "We will have to do better tomorrow," he said. "My flying was pretty shaky, but this crate flew fairly well—at least we made it.

"Oakley, have one of your men get in the water and check the float. It hit something—I'm pretty sure it's damaged. We better order replacement floats. And see what you can do to tighten the turnbuckles on the upper wing. I didn't like all that shaking." He paused. "How are the enlisted barracks coming?"

"Our guys are happy to be inside. There's still trim and painting to be done, but it's coming along."

"What's the latest on wireless equipment?"

"That Marconi 'cat's whisker' receiver you signed off on—the brass does not seem to think it's useful unless we have a transmitter, so they've denied it."

Will's lower jaw quivered. "Our folks are making a big mistake. If we don't get this equipment, we'll be stuck with transmitting our 'recon' messages to the shore batteries by weighted drop bags. I'll speak to the commander about it . . . again."

Oakley directed the crew with his arm and hand as he said to Will, "Rumor has it that the Navy is writing up purchase specs for a wireless transmitter light and small enough to be fitted into an aeroplane. But I can't seem to find out what companies they're going to sound out."

"The Navy, eh?" Will shook his head. "Keep on it. I'm heading over now to see how the ramp is coming along. Has the carpenter's shop started making the float dollies yet?"

"Haven't been there today. They had not when I last

talked to them—"

"Check it."

"Yes, sir."

PARIS

"It is very important that I tell you what has happened," Adrienne said.

Cécile Sorel, curls piled high under an outsized hat, smiled at her protégée and fingered a pearl on her generously-long necklace.

Adrienne continued, "First, you will recall I sent my sketch to I. Magnin in San Francisco?"

Cécile approached a pink floral shawl on display in the salon and took the fabric in her hands. "Yes, I remember."

"I, on the other hand, had completely forgotten." Adrienne paused and smiled at her failure. "Then, three days ago, a well-dressed gentleman came in an elegant coach."

Cécile whirled from the shawl to Adrienne with an arched eyebrow. "Handsome, I hope." She smiled a comedienne's smile. "You have taken a lover?"

"No, no." Adrienne laughed. "Oh Cécile—you must take me seriously!"

"Very well," Cécile said, fingering her necklace again. "But you really must try to be more romantic. And sensual."

"He wore glasses, a black tie on his stiff collar. He was very businesslike."

"A shame."

"You don't understand. This was Grover Magnin—the president of I. Magnin Company—here in my humble shop."

Cécile was suddenly serious. "My dear Adrienne, your atelier is not to be diminished." She rearranged ribbons on her bodice. "The gentleman was here to pay his respects, I am sure."

"Partly, I would say, but later he made an offer—an extraordinary offer!" Adrienne clasped her hand over her mouth and quickly removed it. "He said the firm, I. Magnin Company, wishes to employ me."

Cécile's eyes went to the ceiling, and she smiled. "Of course. Your atelier is the pinnacle of Parisienne couture!"

"No—you misunderstand. Not the atelier. The gentleman wishes me to establish and head a line of high fashion within the I. Magnin Company—in America."

Cécile waved her hand. "Impossible!"

"I realize it sounds . . . well, I know it does not make sense." Adrienne paused, wishing that Cécile would not disbelieve what Grover Magnin had said.

Cécile waited a moment for Adrienne to continue, and said, "One moment, Adrienne. You mean this person wishes to employ you, as a person?"

"Yes."

"But you—you are Parisian. For how many years has it been that you have been absent from Belgium?"

Adrienne nodded. "More than five years—it seems a lifetime." She turned away from Cécile to think. She walked around a showroom chair that was upholstered in needlepoint and gripped the back with both hands. "The war, Cécile. It is so terrible." She frowned with utmost seriousness. "And my family—"

"Your family, indeed." Cécile's face retained its serious mien. "You cannot think of leaving them. You must disregard how much filthy money is offered by this Magnin."

Adrienne's grip on the back tightened. At this moment, she wished to abandon the conversation. Instead, she threw the palms of both hands outward toward Cécile. "I don't know how to tell you. Mr. Magnin insists I bring Father and Mother with me—to America. The company, I. Magnin, will see to all the costs."

Cécile's lips quivered slightly, but quickly became a smile. Her voice turned theatrical. "Ha! As I expected! A purloiner! What Americans cannot provide, they steal!"

Adrienne turned and faced the small window fronting her fashionable street. "Yet you, my friend and patron, express only love and generosity. Through you, I have enjoyed such success—success I cannot begin to measure."

Adrienne renewed her soulful gaze at Cécile. "Yet Guillaume Apollinaire lies in hospital, shrapnel in his temple. My dear mother has shrunk, though she denies it is the fault of the rations. The war has worn on for two years, Paris is exhausted, and still we cannot predict—"

"Stop!" Cécile said, gesturing with both hands. "I cannot bear more thoughts of Paris and the war. Comédie-Française has accepted Lenéru's new play—yet the troupe cannot perform it. Such is the lack of performers. Misery! What are we to do?"

Adrienne returned to gripping the chair. "I have no acceptable answer. Were I alone here, I could press on, even with Paris occupied by Germans. But my dear family—"

"Without a doubt, you must accept. Mr. Magnin is most generous, and America is a safe place. You will thrive wherever fashion remains alive." Abruptly she looked puzzled. "But how—how will you travel to America?"

Adrienne was relieved at Cécile's approval, and pleased for her concern. "There is much remaining to plan." With one hand Adrienne swept an arc. "I must first see to the termination of this atelier and the dear seamstresses. And if you permit, I will see that the lease is fully paid."

Cécile waved her index finger side to side. "Do not concern yourself with the lease. I shall find a use for this space—perhaps a speaking room for poetry, to train the untrainable in diction or how to suppress one's nasal tonality."

Despite her natural reserve, Adrienne laughed.

"But I must inquire," Cécile said. "How will you travel? You and your family—"

"Mr. Magnin advised we should seek out an agent of his trust in Lisbon. He informed me how to contact this man—José Mendez Dias. He will secure passage for us on a steamship liner from that port to America."

"I think I understand," Cécile said before pausing. "Portugal is neutral regarding the war. That is good. And the help of this agent, Mendez Dias, that also is good." She frowned and placed a finger on her lower lip. "But Lisbon is a long way. How will you travel to Lisbon?"

"It will require a land journey across Spain. We are inquiring into that, and talking to friends. Perhaps you—"

"Spain takes no side in the war." Cécile fingered her necklace again. "At least you will not be in danger of meeting handsome, military Spaniards of the masculine species." She smiled. "I believe I visited Andorra in my youth, but I recall little of it. Spain is a land of mountains and revolutions. I favor neither."

"This," Adrienne said, looking away. "is the most anguished decision I have made in my twenty-six years." Wetness came to her eyes. "I fear I do not know how to manage it. Most devastating of all, I shall miss you. From that day of our first encounter at the Ritz, I have so benefitted from your confidence—and rejoiced in our friendship." The younger woman embraced Cécile. "I love you."

Cécile could not fully reciprocate. She broke away.

Adrienne noted the tears on Cécile's cheeks as she retreated out the door and walked swiftly toward the intersection with Rue de Penthièvre.

WILHELMSHAVEN, GERMANY

As he closed the heavy door behind him, Gregor wondered why he was told to come to the room marked "016." The small chamber was located in the basement of a supply building inside the Imperial dockyard at Wilhelmshaven. Its walls were of bare concrete, lit only by two overhead electric lamps.

Seated facing him at a wooden table was a Kapitän zur See, a man of about forty with a yellow mustache. He seemed to have read Gregor's mind. "You are without doubt wondering why you were directed here. That will be answered shortly. I am Heinrich von Kupwurzer." He pointed at the other chair. "You may take that."

Gregor sat uneasily in the straight-backed wooden chair. The room, which smelled of mildew, was unfurnished except for the table, two chairs, and a steamer trunk on the floor against a wall.

"As you know, Grand Admiral von Tirpitz, the most trustworthy as leader of the Navy, has resigned," Kupwurzer said. "However, Admiral Scheer, commander of the High Seas Fleet, supports our aggressive U-boat strategy, and he has named squadron commander Andreas Michelsen as Commander of all U-boats. Commander Michelsen has assigned you to lead a mission of highest importance." Kupwurzer paused to glance at the paper in front of him on the table.

Gregor considered Kupwurzer's behavior strange but said nothing.

"I represent Commander Andreas Michelsen, who is away." Kupwurzer paused and smiled at Gregor. "You are to report to Kapitän Ludwig Geighoffer at the naval facility in Kiel. He will explain your mission. Needless to say, your mission is secret. When you return to Wilhelmshaven, you will use this room."

When Kupwurzer did not say anything further, Gregor said, "Kiel is a big facility. Where am I to contact this kapitän?—Kapitän Geighoffer."

"My understanding is he is on Admiral Bachman's staff." Kupwurzer thrust a key toward Gregor, who accepted it.

Gregor raised his hand with the key. "And this key . . . ?"

"It is the only key that fits the lock on the door to this room. When you and I leave, you will lock the door and keep the key. The key has no marking, and I was told you should not reveal your use of this room. You should not take anything out of this room. It is only for your study."

Gregor frowned and gestured toward the steamer trunk. "So the trunk contains materials I am to study—for the mission?"

Kupwurzer nodded. "I believe so. It was delivered to this room by Naval Intelligence. The trunk is locked, and I do not have a key."

"So I should request the key to the trunk from Kapitän Geighoffer?"

"Perhaps. I was not told." He paused. "It is probably good that I was not told more than I have told you just now—absent intention I cannot reveal what I do not know."

Gregor nodded. "So there are no orders—no document, no papers?"

"That is correct. The paper I have here contains only the name of Kapitän Ludwig Geighoffer. The commander suggested I write only the name on it."

"So that is all?" Gregor squinted at the Kapitän zur See.

"That is all," Kupwurzer said, then, after a smile, "shall we go?"

Gregor nodded and opened the door. Kupwurzer turned out the lights and they left the room. Gregor locked the door marked '016' and slid the key into the pocket of his jacket.

•   •   •

Gregor entered the office of Kapitän Ludwig Geighoffer in Kiel.

"Close the door, please," Geighoffer said.

It was a small cubicle with a single window facing the parade ground. Its walls were faced with bookcases with large and thin books, packets of research papers, envelopes and cloth satchels, poorly-folded maps, and stacks of writing tablets. Ludwig's single desk was similarly overloaded.

"You may have to clear that chair to be seated," Ludwig said, "I never have enough space to work."

Gregor picked up the materials, glanced around, but could find no place for them. "Where should I—"

"On the floor," Geighoffer said, waving his hand. He paused for several seconds, searching Gregor's face. "Your record in U-boats is meritorious, Leutnant. It is a pleasure to meet you."

"Thank you, sir."

Geighoffer leaned back in his chair. "I am sure you find this meeting somewhat unusual."

"A Kapitän zur See by the name of Kupwurzer in Wilhelmshaven spoke on behalf of Commander Andreas Michelsen. He said you—"

"Yes, yes. I am given to understand you do not know anything of the mission to which you have been assigned. Is that so?"

"It is all quite irregular—there is a room '016' at the shipyard in Wilhelmshaven—"

"I will get to the room in a moment. But first I must explain that this mission is highly secret. It is of the highest classification." He leaned forward, over the jumble on his desk, and lowered his voice. "Part of the reason for your unusual treatment is security: Division of the information between different offices is meant to ensure no one person has a complete understanding."

"Oh," Gregor said, narrowing his eyes and frowning.

"You realize that you cannot reveal the mission to anyone, including the crew of the new U-boat which you will command, until you and they have reached the destination."

"I understand," Gregor said, although there was little he understood.

"Your mission is to render the locks of the Panama Canal useless to the United States Navy."

"The Panama Canal?"

"Yes. That is the canal in Central America which connects the Atlantic and Pacific oceans."

"I did not mean to question the Canal's location. But a U-boat—"

"Yes." Ludwig drew back in his chair. "You were about to suggest a U-boat is unsuited to attacking locks?"

"I spoke out of turn." Gregor made a weak effort at a smile. "Forgive my interruption."

"The Gatun locks at the Canal entrance are thirty-three-meter-wide chambers more than twenty meters deep." Geighoffer splayed his hands, illustrating the geometry. "They are long enough to accommodate a vessel half-again as long as our huge battleship Bayern!

"The locks are constructed of concrete eighteen meters thick. Each pair of gates that opens and encloses each lock is two meters thick, built of heavy riveted steel, braced like the hull of a ship."

Gregor noticed that Geighoffer spoke easily, the details rolling without hesitation from beneath the wavering of his neatly-trimmed mustache.

"Our latest torpedo," the kapitän said, "with 160 kilograms of explosive Hexanite, likely would produce a hole in a gate and damage the concrete but would not likely shut the canal for long. That is why your task is to observe a large ship entering or leaving the lock, and to torpedo it while the gates are open. The wreckage of the sunken ship within the lock will incapacitate it for a long period of time, perhaps months." Ludwig leaned forward again and stared intently at Gregor. "Do you understand?"

"The Canal is American, correct?" Gregor did not pause for an answer. "Yet Germany is not at war with America. I find this a little confusing."

"Admiral Scheer, commander of the High Seas Fleet, foresees the return of unrestricted U-boat activity soon. He believes, as do we, it is the sure way to defeat the English, by sinking the ships that supply the isles. Disabling the Canal will unbalance and discourage the American Navy from aiding the English, yet is less provoking than a direct attack on an American shore."

"I see the logic of the plan," Gregor said, glancing at the framed photograph of the uniformed Grand Admiral Tirpitz on the wall. "I certainly agree that the key to victory is unrestricted U-boat sinkings."

Geighoffer smiled. "As you have a right to." He cleared his voice. "Additionally, the intent of the Panama attack is to convince Wilson that the oceans belong to Germany."

"And perhaps the mission will be as rewarding," Gregor said, attempting to hide the bitterness in his voice, "as sinking numerous warships of the English."

The kapitän slapped his hand on the cover of a thick book on his desk. "It will be more glorious—completely unanticipated! An attack far distant from the fatherland."

"Yes," Gregor said, nodding. "The transatlantic and Caribbean transit from Wilhelmshaven, unless I am mistaken, should be approximately ten thousand kilometers."

"Indeed." Geighoffer quickly turned grave. "This is exactly where engineer Hans Techel and I have concentrated our efforts. You will take the command of a vessel that has been designed from the keel upward as an extreme-range U-boat. With 248 tons of fuel oil, it should have a range of 16,200 nautical miles at 9.5 knots on the surface. Its undersea speed is as yet unknown, but we expect it to be fast."

"I eagerly await viewing it," Gregor said.

"I have set aside tomorrow for a full tour, beginning at seven. The next day, you shall meet your officers and crew. On Monday there will be a brief ceremony installing you in command. Then you will be free to set a date for sailing to Wilhelmshaven, where you can begin the sea trials." Ludwig searched Gregor's face. "I believe this concludes—"

"Thank you," Gregor said, raising his index finger, "but you did not explain 'room 016.'"

"Ah, yes," the kapitän said, squeezing his chin with his right hand.

"I can tell you the room was established by Etappendienst, but not much else. They instructed me there is a trunk inside containing materials you will need on the Panama Canal." With that, Geighoffer removed a key from the upper drawer of his desk and handed it to Gregor. "This opens the trunk. It is the only key, and is unmarked. You are instructed to study the materials inside the room and to remove none of them from the room."

Gregor rose from his chair and saluted. "Thank you, Kapitän. This briefing has been most useful. I shall be at the shipyard at seven."

NORTH SEA

G regor ordered, "Ahead One Half. Standby to surface."
The orders were repeated and relayed, and activity by all crewmen increased. The rush of water past the hull grew louder.

Gregor tightened the belt of his trousers while noting that the pretrial hull integrity, steering, and astern running tests were complete and satisfactory. He addressed the second officer, Oberleutnant Max Krauss: "We should prepare the full speed trial, northbound."

Krauss consulted the 'trials' sheet. "What of the alarms test?"

"That can be delayed. We need to verify the running speed and fuel consumption Geighoffer seemed sure of." Gregor saw beads of condensation forming on the steel overhead. "Then we'll need a second run—southbound."

Gregor noted Krauss's reaction and ordered, "Raise." When the periscope was at its up-stops, he swung it in a complete circle to scan the entire horizon. "Lower."

Meanwhile, second officer Krauss explained the speed trial to the control room crew.

"Surface!" Gregor said. Krauss repeated the order; crewmen shouted numbers and scrambled as the periscope hummed to its down-stops. Hissing sounds issued from the tangle of pipes and valves. The sound of sloshing water diminished as the 'blow' continued. The conning tower pierced the surface of the North Sea and sprouted out, followed by the sleek steel bow as it shed foamy waves into the chop.

"Even trim," Gregor ordered. Pumps hummed, crewmen eyed dials and turned valve wheels. The interior deck began to level.

After a short time, the watch officer climbed the ladder and opened the hatch. Gregor followed as the hatch disappeared and sunlight streamed in. He climbed and took a standing position on the bridge. He raised his field glasses to his eyes.

Inside and below, in the sweat-filled engine room, the chief engineer commanded first one M.A.N. diesel, then the second, to start. Engulfed by the loud pounding from the diesel cylinders, a crewman stripped to the waist rechecked the battery switches. Another secured the air freshener.

Once the diesels were running, Gregor said, "All Ahead Full." The second officer relayed the order into the voice pipe as Gregor issued steering directions. The pitch of the engines increased and the U-boat sliced through the waves with increasing velocity.

Second officer Krauss turned to face the petty officer behind him. "Note the start time on my mark."

"Aye," said the petty officer, his hand hovering over the writing pad.

Gregor smiled at Krauss. "Better, eh?"

Krauss nodded. "Excellent."

Gregor noted the speed and nodded to the second officer. Krauss turned to the petty officer and said, "Mark!"

Half the pounding died. As if snagged on an unseen hulk, the U-boat's momentum collapsed. The craft swerved into a sloshing starboard turn while the helmsman desperately tried to correct.

Gregor felt the veer and shouted, "Stop engines!" Krauss repeated the command.

The pounding ceased. The port propeller stopped. Sluggishly, the U-boat slowed. Within a short time, the boat wallowed uneasily in a slimy sea. Krauss ordered a report. A hollowed-out voice growled from the voice pipe. "Starboard diesel broken."

Gregor hammered the rim of the fairwater with his fist, and cursed.

Krauss demanded details. A calmer voice echoed from the voice pipe. "Engineering chief, Kapitän. Something broke on the starboard diesel—I shut it. Maybe an exhaust valve. I'm not sure. Port engine remains good." He paused. "Standing by."

Krauss inquired, "Can the diesel be repaired?"

The echoing reply came from the pipe, "Aye, possibly. If it is an exhaust valve, it will take at least a day."

Gregor said, "What speed can we make on one engine?"

The chief engineer said, "Eight or ten knots—estimating."

Krauss frowned and spoke to the voice pipe, "Charging?"

"Eight or ten knots, no battery charging."

Gregor gritted his teeth and to Krauss he said, "We shall transit to port. For repairs."

Krauss nodded and consulted his navigation charts. Gregor ordered the helmsman to proceed on one engine.

●　　　●　　　●

At Wilhelmshaven, inside the control room of the docked U-boat, Kapitänleutnant Gregor Steiner answered the man in greasy overalls. "Yes, we began the speed run test immediately."

The man in charge of the repair facility wiped his hands with a dirty rag. "I thought that. This is a Germania boat, right?"

"Yes. Launched from the shipyard. Why?"

"The boat is new in the water, am I correct?"

"Yes." Gregor's voice turned assertive. "But I do not understand so many questions."

"There is a pattern, Kapitän. The shortages and the crews."

"My crew was in error?"

"No. No. I refer to crews in the shipyard; those at the M.A.N. factory."

"What do you mean?"

"The fourteen-hour workdays, the conscripts—all of that."

Gregor frowned. "Oh. You speak to the workers' long hours. Meaning—"

"There are so many errors." The repair man shook his head. "Rush, rush, rush. Shortages. Substitutes. Miswiring. All the—"

Gregor nodded.

The repair man continued. "People who are pushed. People who sometimes do not know what they are doing."

Gregor nodded, but refused to engage. "I know what you mean." He paused. "What about our diesel engine?"

"I would recommend replacing all exhaust valves."

Gregor was bewildered. "What?"

"I have a supply. It is completely in your hands, of course. But I suspect the new steel."

"This is not acceptable." Gregor gestured with both hands. "Why bad steel?"

"Two years of war, Kapitän. Vital ingredients are absent. Strikes. Conscripted workers, even prisoners. And bread that is unfit to be eaten."

"Yes, yes." Gregor pinched his jaw. "How much time—to replace the exhaust valves?"

"You are not first in line. Allow me a week or more."

"Today is Wednesday." Gregor kept his glare. "Wednesday, a week. I must count upon it."

•　　　•　　　•

Gregor Steiner spent most of the day in Room 016. He was leaving the shipyard on foot at about 4:00 p.m. when he encountered Max Krauss. Krauss stood at the intersection of the shipyard entry road and the road that led inside the Naval facility.

"Hello, Krauss," Gregor said. "What are you doing over here?"

"I was out for a walk." Krauss said, smiling. "I might ask you a similar question, as well."

"Yes, but I suspect your walk had a secondary purpose." He smiled. "Besides that of exercise, I mean. Did you expect to engage me?"

Krauss laughed, glanced at his shoe, and knocked a piece of gravel aside with his foot. "I did."

"Well, then," Gregor said, "shall we walk together to the dormitories?"

The two officers, of nearly the same height, began to walk, side by side, along the road.

Krauss said, "I noticed, while our vessel has been docked, you have each day come this direction and disappeared for many hours. It seems habitual. May I enquire as to—"

"I have a requirement within the shipyard," Gregor said, his view never straying from straight ahead. "It is related to our future on board the U-boat S-3. That is about as much as I can tell you at this time."

"Thank you, Kapitän. I presume you mean your daily activity is to remain secret."

"That's correct. The most I can say is that I am preparing for our mission."

"I must admit, I have been quite curious as to why, over the past several weeks, you have not explained to me or ship's complement, the mission of S-3, once the sea trials are complete. My prior experience onboard U-boats leads me to consider deck guns as essential to the mission of an undersea marauder. Yet this vessel, S-3, lacks deck guns. It is as if it were designed for an activity other than sinking ships."

Gregor continued walking, but turned his head to view Krauss. "You are perceptive, Krauss. I'm very fortunate to have you as second-in-command. However, I have sworn an oath not to reveal our coming mission—the mission we shall begin when we complete the sea trials."

Krauss shook his head slowly. "It is too bad. Men like to know their mission. And many of your complement, including me, will speculate. As, I'm sure, many who have seen the vessel, with its deck devoid of so much as a handrail."

"As I explained in my briefing, Krauss, a single steel cable rigged on the vessel's centerline will serve as a crewman's handhold during surface operations."

"Yes," Krauss said with a trace of bitterness, "you explained that.

But you are aware that a handhold on a cable is less secure—especially in a rough sea."

Gregor continued to look at Krauss as he spoke. "Yes. It will render our mission slightly more dangerous than it would otherwise be. You will always stress the importance of hanging tightly to that cable whenever a sailor is on deck." The two men approached the dormitories.

Gregor said, "Do you have other comments for me at this time?"

Krauss engaged Gregor's eyes. "Just one. I look forward to serving with you on S-3. I predict it will be the most successful mission undertaken by our flotilla."

"Thank you, Krauss."

FORT SHERMAN, PANAMA

Originally, the meeting at Fort Sherman was called to discuss targeting. Coast Artillery Corps officers representing the big guns at Fort Randolph and Fort DeLesseps, as well as sponsoring officers from Fort Sherman, were present. Because he was now part of the targeting system for the Coast Artillery, Panama Canal Defense, Army Lieutenant Will Marra was also invited.

Will paid attention as the men discussed the 'horizontal-base system' using azimuth-reading telescopes to direct the big guns. Later, when the subject turned to spotting, he was called on to explain his views on the method for communicating corrections.

"There's not much controversy over using the clock code system for conveying artillery corrections to gun batteries," he said. "The more difficult problem arises in the method used for communicating those corrections.

"I've recommended equipping the Curtiss aeroplane with wireless, both a receiver and a transmitter. These, together with matching equipments on the ground, will allow transmission of firing information and corrections to and from the aircraft while the aeroplane remains in the target area. This is especially important when targets are located far offshore, let's say twenty miles or more, yielding much more time for accurate targeting to occur.

"Unfortunately, these wireless instruments are bulky and heavy and are in an early stage of development. They require electrical power and an antenna. So far, neither the Signal Corps nor the War Department has been able to supply wireless equipment that can be mounted in the Curtiss aeroplane, powered up, and operated by a trained observer riding in the second seat of the R-9."

Will's comments were applauded. Unfortunately, those present were Coast Artillery officers who held no power to persuade "the brass" to expedite the development and equipping of the R-9 aeroplane with the needed wireless devices.

As the meeting wore on, some officers had started discussions of complicated issues of fire control, including the shift from 'Case Three Pointing' to 'Case Two Pointing.' At this juncture, Will considered that the meeting had gone on far too long.

Finally, the lead artillery officer from Fort Sherman read a letter, dated Nov. 5, 1916, from the office of George W. Goethals, Canal Zone Governor. "Memo to the C.A.C.: The German (unarmed) merchant U-boat Deutschland, under the direction of Paul Konig, docked Nov. 1 at State Pier, New London, Connecticut. This is the second time this vessel has visited the United States. It previously traveled from Germany to the United States and returned to Germany. Although this vessel is not armed, attention should be paid to the long-range capability of Germany's U-boats insofar as the defense of our Canal is concerned." The message was signed by Goethals' staff officer.

This reading caused discussion amongst the participants. Will observed that many of the officers present seemed less concerned about a German U-boat than they were about the German High Fleet, with its huge dreadnoughts equipped with large-caliber guns capable of lobbing big shells into the Panama Canal.

●   ●   ●

Will now felt more confident piloting the R-9 in the air. In particular, he became accustomed to the sluggish aerial response as well as the swift braking action the floats produced upon contact with the water. But his lack of float-plane schooling placed him at a disadvantage in maneuvering once the craft was settled upon the water. It was vastly different than taxiing a wheeled aeroplane on land.

Water conditions (waves, tide, currents), wind conditions (speed, direction, gusts), combined with the shape of the lagoon, the narrow entrance, dock and ramp positions, and ships anchored in Limon Bay, resulted in extreme day-to-day and hour-by-hour changes. He found that an attitude of constant vigilance was essential to safe takeoffs, landings, and taxiing in the area. Occasionally he viewed the dockside windsock and saw that high winds and rough water required him to cancel a mission.

Will understood that much practice was required to master the art of guiding the aeroplane on the surface and avoiding obstacles. He began a regimen of spending hours driving the R-9 within the lagoon, through the narrow entrance and around Limon Bay, without taking off. It was a regimen that occasionally produced minor damage or a tear in a wingtip, but he regarded the self-teaching as essential. He had attached handling ropes to the floats and equipped the aeroplane with a stubby paddle that was useful in freeing the aircraft from an occasional unintended beaching.

For straight-ahead taxiing, he applied power with up-elevator to force the nose to rise, then eased the nose downward. Reducing the power slightly allowed the plane to level out and maintain speed while taxiing.

With increasing breeze, he saw that the aircraft would tend to nose into the wind, or weathercock, even at increased throttle. Thus steering, if it meant turning downwind, demanded an artful combination of adjustments.

One solution, he found, was a maneuver he learned by diligent practice. The maneuver involved a modest increase in power, a slight right turn, followed by full left rudder, and added power with a nose-up attitude. If held, this combination resulted in a left skidding turn toward the downwind direction. Once the desired direction was achieved, controls were eased or neutralized. He called this a "question-mark turn."

The question-mark turn could also permit a downwind takeoff

in light winds—less than about ten knots—although Will generally sought to avoid the longer run a downwind takeoff required.

Will also practiced allowing the weathercocked aeroplane to be pushed backward by the wind as would be sometimes required to position it for docking, ramping, or takeoff.

Occasionally he found that a more drastic version of the 'question mark' operation was required to avoid a collision or beaching. In such an emergency he would apply full power, rudder, ailerons, and full up-elevator to achieve a vigorous nose-up turn that resulted in much spray and noise. In this maneuver, the craft tended to tip, so intense concentration on keeping the wings level was essential. Sometimes the spray of this severe action obscured his forward vision. Risks, including motor overheating and spray damage to the propeller, meant this drastic maneuver was to be avoided except for emergencies.

Despite Will's dedication to improving his handling of the aircraft on water, ground crew members made jokes about his sometimes-awkward mistakes.

"Aha!" cried a crewman on one occasion, "our leader would rather sail the aeroplane onto the sand than spend time flying it!"

But Will persisted, recognizing that some of his practice would inevitably either end with embarrassment—or worse—end with hilarity.

1917

OFF PUNTA COCAL, PANAMA

The old steel tugboat rocked uneasily in the swells. The rumble of its idling diesel yielded a comforting vibration. Bruno Ackermann turned from the helm and asked, "Are you sure—absolutely—that we are to wait here?"

"Yes," Hans said, referring to the paper in his hand. "I decoded it carefully. The decoded message was exactly, 'Must meet Estrella Segura two kilometers west of Point Cocal, January 13, 1917, two hours post dawn.' I believe this message was relayed by Nauen."

Bruno did not reply, but the furrows on his brow deepened. It was now nearly five hours since the local dawn.

Scanning the horizon with his binoculars, Bruno saw something on the horizon, north of their location. Within minutes he identified it as smoke. "Wait," he said, "perhaps . . ."

Hans aimed his glasses in the same direction. "Yes, I see it. Black smoke. Two masts. A single funnel."

"So it is not another fishing boat," Bruno said, lowering his binoculars and sighing. "Thank heaven. I do not enjoy these peculiar demands thrust upon us."

Hans continued viewing the vessel. "It is the war, Bruno."

"Yes, yes, I understand." Bruno slumped back against the captain's chair. "But what are we to do?"

Hans shrugged, said nothing, and continued squinting into his binoculars.

"You'd better go below," Bruno said. "Check the bilges. I don't like sitting here hour upon hour like a duck."

Hans lowered his binoculars, stowed them in the surround atop the wood cabinet, and left the wheelhouse.

Minutes passed, and soon the vessel of interest became visible to Bruno's naked eye. It appeared as a tan-colored smudge in the bright sunshine beneath a cloud of dark gray smoke. How was he supposed to know the name of a vessel until it was upon them? He heard thumps from below as Hans entered the engine-mechanical room below decks.

Bruno studied the approaching vessel through the side window. It seemed to be on a course southwest. It was a low-slung tramp steamer, with a central funnel flanked by goosenecked ventilators. The navigating bridge straddled the fore part of the central house. Besides the two masts, it carried auxiliary cargo derricks fore and aft.

A few minutes later, Bruno again raised his binoculars to his eyes. The faint outlines of a portion of the name on the bow became visible. He identified the letter 'E' followed by 's' followed by a 't' and 'r.' His anxiety eased some. "I think it is the Estrella," he announced.

Hans, who had returned to the wheelhouse, nodded.

"I suppose we should try to hail it," Bruno said. "I'll take an intersecting course." He threw the gear lever. Puffs of black flew from the stack and the tug splashed to life.

After a few minutes, Bruno nodded toward the steamer a hundred meters off the starboard bow and said, "What the hell?" The steamer seemed oblivious to their presence. "You would think they would slow. But no, they just plow ahead on course."

"Try to pull alongside," Hans said. "I'll go on deck and shout at them with the megaphone."

"What language?"

Hans frowned. "German, what else?"

"They might speak Spanish."

"Yes, I suppose." He shrugged. "What can we do?"

"Go ahead," Bruno said, nudging the throttle to drive the tug closer to the steamer.

The C.G.R. tug moved slowly toward the portside of the steamer. Bruno noticed barnacles above the waterline catching the sun, so the steamer had to be lightly loaded. No crew were visible on its poop deck, but Bruno could now read the name Estrella Segura in black, painted on the bow.

Hans stood on the tug's rear deck with the megaphone aimed at Estrella. He yelled something in German that Bruno could not hear. There was no response, although the steamer was now closer than thirty meters to the tug.

Hans threw his hands into the air in frustration while hanging onto the megaphone.

Bruno mashed the boat's horn button with the palm of his hand. The horn issued a low, loud blast.

Bruno struck the button again, for a second blast, and waited.

A man with red suspenders over his bare dark-skinned chest appeared at the rail of the Estrella. He waved a hand and arm at Hans and disappeared beyond the rail.

Bruno maintained the C.G.R. tug about ten meters outside of Estrella's bow wake as more minutes ticked by without any apparent action.

Bruno noticed the bow wake of Estrella finally subside. He retarded the throttle to match his speed to that of the slowing ship.

On deck, Hans shouted through the megaphone in German, "This is the C.G.R. tugboat La Fernanda."

No one appeared at the rail of Estrella.

Both vessels slowed almost to a stop, which pleased Bruno. He struck the horn button with the palm of his hand, causing two short blasts of greeting.

No one appeared at the rail of Estrella.

Finally, two crewmembers became barely visible on the weather deck, busy near one of the portside derricks. Shortly, the man in red suspenders appeared at the rail and shouted something in Spanish that Hans did not understand. Hans shrugged and turned toward the wheelhouse.

Bruno clutched the diesel out of gear, and left the wheelhouse to join Hans on the starboard deck.

At this moment, Herr Lindoch appeared at the rail of Estrella. Upon sighting Bruno, he shouted between his hands in German, "Hello, Friends! Greetings from the Imperial Navy!"

Bruno took the megaphone from Hans and shouted through it, "Greetings to you, also, Herr Lindoch." He lowered the megaphone and said to Hans, "This is a most peculiar vessel of the Imperial Navy."

Herr Lindoch pointed toward the derrick and shouted, "They will furnish a net. Send Hans to me."

Within minutes, the crewmen on Estrella tended the auxiliary derrick. A cargo net descended over the portside of Estrella's hull. It was suspended from a line on the derrick.

Bruno entered the wheelhouse, engaged the diesel, and deftly steered the tug under the net. The net plopped onto the tug's deck and Hans sat in the middle of the netting, knees bent. As the crew on Estrella hauled away with the derrick, Hans was curled inside with his hands gripping the net. Shortly he was hauled up, inward and disappeared behind the vessel's rail.

Bruno maintained his position next to the Estrella, waiting. The black tire fenders on the starboard of the tug bounced gently against Estrella's hull in response to wave action.

Minutes passed.

The net, with Hans again curled inside, appeared over Estrella's rail, and descended. The crew slowed its arrival to the deck so Hans could untangle himself. He stood up with a package in his hands, and said to Bruno, "Herr Lindoch apologizes."

"Apologize? For what?"

"He apologizes for the lateness of his arrival. He said he also apologizes for 'the mode of his transportation.' He explained that he sailed from a port in South America. He said he was forced to take this tramp steamer because he has been called urgently to Mexico."

The empty cargo net was now raised to the deck of Estrella.

Bruno pointed at the package in Hans's hand. "What did Herr

Lindoch give you?"

Hans shrugged and handed the pack to Bruno. "I don't know. Herr Lindoch says you must receive it. He says you are accountable for its safety."

Bruno unwrapped the package and saw what it was. He handed it back to Hans. "Here. This is for your use."

Hans read the title printed in German. "Oh—a new codebook." He paused and grinned. "Now I understand."

Estrella began to pull away from the side of the C.G.R. tug.

Bruno halted his trip to the pilot house. "What is it that you now understand?"

Hans smiled. "Now I understand why Herr Lindoch insisted I tell you, 'Burn the old, burn the old.'"

CUXHAVEN, GERMANY

Catherine flung open the door facing Wiesen Strasse. "Ernestine!" she cried. "What happened to you?"

"I am unsure," the blood-spattered woman said. Obviously dazed, she stared at Catherine, dark shadows around her eyes. "Please—may I . . ."

"Helmuth!" Catherine shouted. "Come help!"

Helmuth strode into the room from the narrow hallway. "What is it—oh, no."

He went to Ernestine, crouched, lifted her good arm over his neck, and helped her into the sole upholstered chair. "Catherine," he said to his wife. "Quickly. Some linens. And boil some water."

As Catherine hurried into the kitchen, Helmuth lifted Ernestine's blood-soaked coat sleeve to inspect the injury.

Ernestine cried out.

"My razor!" Helmuth shouted. "From the washstand!"

Catherine entered with some large scarves and handed them to Helmuth. Ernestine's eyelids drooped. "The kettle is on the stove," Catherine said as she circled from the room into the hall.

"I am sorry to hurt you," Helmuth said, staring at Ernestine's sleeve. "But we shall have to see . . ."

Catherine reentered and handed Helmuth his razor. He swiftly but deftly sliced Ernestine's left coat sleeve, from above the elbow to her wrist. She moaned.

Helmuth examined the distorted arm. A bloody bone protruded. "We need a doctor. Did you fall?"

"No," Ernestine said. Then weakly, "The police, they came.

And then—"

Catherine said to Helmuth, "Cover Ernestine with your heavy coat. We must take her to the clinic."

"No—no, please," Ernestine said, shaking her head. "They will arrest me."

"But your arm is broken," Helmuth said, lowering his Navy coat from the hall hook. "Maybe twice. And those bruises—"

Ernestine sobbed. "Please, no. Keep me here."

Helmuth shrugged and covered Ernestine's torso with the coat. He glanced at Catherine. "I don't see how we can take care of this."

"If you will get a board, I will set the bones," Catherine said.

Helmuth squinted and moved away. "A board. Yes—but you are not—"

"It is like pork bones I have butchered." She gestured. "Get a board. And brandy."

•   •   •

Ernestine was flat on the blanket with her head on a pillow. Helmuth's uniform coat covered her torso. On the floor next to the black iron bed sat the kettle, wisps of steam still rising from it. Piled next on the floor were bloodstained scarves.

"I was gone," Ernestine said, "I must have done a dream."

"The brandy," Helmuth said, smiling. "It was the brandy."

Holding Ernestine's right hand in hers, Catherine gave Helmuth a negative look. She said to Ernestine, "How do you feel?"

Ernestine raised her head with a look of dread. "My ration cards. Where are they?"

"Have not a worry," Helmuth said, "your cards and DMs are safe—on the cabinet."

Ernestine turned her head to view her arm. It was bandaged and banded with rags tightened around a bed slat. "What have you done?" she said.

"I have done the best I could," Catherine said. "Both bones above the wrist were broken—one twice. What happened?"

"It was the demonstration. You did not attend—"

"Helmuth is Cuxhaven Navy," Catherine said, shaking her head. "The admiral would have Helmuth's head."

"I forgot," Ernestine quickly said, skin sagging into the hollow under her cheekbones. "There were many hundreds, women and children. We walked down the Strasse in peace, the children all bones, wishing to face the Burgomaster.

"We wished him to see what no meat and no potatoes—what sickness, even the absence of turnips—has made of the citizens."

Helmuth said, "But your injuries, the blood, how did that happen?"

"The socialists," Ernestine said, "not more than twenty, they saw the opportunity."

Helmuth burst out, "Ah, led by the Parvus, probably. He always takes advantage of the poverty."

"I do not know," answered Ernestine. "Those people shouted slogans of revolution, they swarmed into the crowd, all rough. I hoped they were to go on away. But in minutes there was disarray. Some attacked the shops. There was smashing, there was looting." She paused to sweep a tear from her eye with her good wrist.

"It all fell apart. The police came, they tried to return order to our demonstration. But disorder became the rule. I was very fearful."

Catherine frowned. "You were attacked by the looters, the socialists?"

"No. No. I fell once, but got up all right. No, it was not until the soldiers came. I tried to tell the policeman, 'It is all so unfair.' Do you not know? Food may be bought on the black market, and from some farmers.

"But those who buy some flour, or peas, even the 'substitute' foods—then the inspectors at the railway station, they await the return to Cuxhaven. They then confiscate every gram. 'It is illegal,' they declare."

Ernestine tried to turn, to adjust her frail body, but abandoned the action, grimacing in pain and crying out.

Her voice became weaker. "Neither the soldiers nor the police, they know not what we know. They never see what we see. They only try to stop the disorder. They thus swing their clubs or sticks, or rifle ends, in all stupidity. It becomes a battle. That is all I remember—until I came upon your house."

"Disgusting," Helmuth said, spittle spraying from his mouth. "I shall contact my friend Müller—"

"You dare not," Catherine said, glaring at him.

"What of your son, Gregor?" Ernestine said in strained attention. "He too is part of the Imperial Navy. What do you know of him?"

Catherine swallowed and swallowed again, seeming to swallow her emotions. "We have not seen him for a long time. We know only what he writes, in the letters that reach us."

"He is alive, good," Ernestine said, calm smoothing her features. "Our neighbors are not so blessed. Their Cramer was shipped home from the trenches in a coffin."

"Gregor is now a Kapitänleutnant," Helmuth said, a sparkle in his eyes. "He has commanded a ship."

Catherine shook her head through a small angle. "I fear for him—all this winter there has been no letter from him. He has abandoned the piano. And now we understand sailors' rations also are shorted." She glanced at Helmuth. "Did you say fifty grams?"

Helmuth stared at the items on the floor. "We need to clear away the linens, Catherine. I do not remember the amount."

"I will tend to them. But now, we must allow Ernestine to rest." Catherine nudged Helmuth and turned away from the bed.

"Yes," Helmuth said. "She must be allowed to rest." He grasped the kettle by its swivel wire and lifted it to his side.

Catherine stooped and gathered the scarves into a bundle. As she straightened, she saw that Ernestine seemed asleep. "We shall speak to no one of her," she whispered, "conceding that the police may seek her whereabouts."

"I do not wish to foster anything illegal," Helmuth said, passing through the doorway with the kettle.

"Yes, I agree," Catherine said, carrying the bundle of scarves and following behind Helmuth. "We should at all times behave legally in every way." She grasped the knob and pulled the door to a soft close behind her. "It may be several days before Ernestine has recovered sufficiently to leave."

FORT SHERMAN, PANAMA

T he aeroplane, floats now resting on dollies, was anchored with tie-downs on the sloping ramp. Supported a couple of feet above the floats were two planks. Two sweating crewmen stood on the planks working on the R-9's motor.

Standing on the ramp, Will Marra watched the activity for a time. He turned to the crew chief and said, "What do you think?"

"Larry says the broken valve spring will be replaced, once they get the rocker off," Oakley said. "But I got to tell you, sir, we're really short of parts for this motor. Can't you light a fire under somebody up the line?"

"That's not the problem, Jim. The problem isn't with the line. As I understand it, it's a factory problem."

"You mean the Curtiss factory—in New York?"

"No. It's other factories. Other factories across the United States make different parts for the motor."

The furrow between Oakley's eyebrows deepened. "They can't make the parts—or what?"

Will pressed his lips in a dismissive manner and shook his head. "It's the holders of the basic Wright patents. It seems they've driven a number of the small aviation shops in the States out of business. Maybe—"

"You mean like the shops that make valves, or—"

"Yeah. Now maybe things will change. As General Edwards announced yesterday, President Wilson broke off relations with the German government on Saturday. I'm sure that means we're close to war. But it also means he's pressing the Secretary of War to get more factories up and running."

The mechanic without a shirt interrupted and pointed. "Hey, Jim. Get me that clamp there, will you?"

Oakley bent over the big toolbox, found the clamp, and handed it up. He turned back to Lt. Marra. "Boy, I sure hope they do something for us down here. It's pulling teeth to get parts. Not to mention the shipping time. And why don't they understand? We need a wireless set that we can fit in the rear cockpit of the aeroplane."

"Yeah," Will said, nodding. Slowly, he shook his head. "I've explained the wireless problem till I'm blue in the face. You'd think the War Department would give us some priority, now that the Atlantic fleet has been charged with 'covering' the Panama Canal. That sure includes our mission of offshore surveillance."

Oakley continued his comments as he climbed up on the plank to assist the mechanics. "What good is spotting an enemy ship from the air if we can't let the shore guns know right away?"

Will didn't answer. As he mulled Oakley's remark, a recurring issue of his own filled his mind: Why wasn't he flying a bomber—an aeroplane that could instantly bomb the enemy's ship or submarine at sea? The answer, as he well knew, was that no U.S. bombers existed. None existed because the Army Signal Corps brass consistently avoided expanding the Aviation Section's equipment or capabilities.

Oakley grinned down at Will. "So you think we're going to get into the war?"

"Listen," Will said, absent a smile. "I need this aeroplane. We've skipped a full day of reconnaissance with this misfire. Let me know when you've got it cranking."

"Yes, sir."

Will turned to leave, then halted. "And, as for your question on war, Germany announced three days ago they started unrestricted submarine warfare. Their U-boats are out there sinking every damned ship they can find, including those of the United States. That should answer your question."

NORTH ATLANTIC OCEAN

Kapitän Gregor Steiner ordered all lights extinguished in the control room for a third of an hour. This had the surprising effect of suppressing the informal chatter of the control room crew. Only an occasional comment broke the gurgle of water and the hum of the electric motors from the engine room far to the rear.

Time seemed to drag. Finally, confident that his vision had sufficiently adapted to the dark, Gregor ordered the periscope raised. He swung it in a complete circle. Although the moon was partly obscured by scattered clouds, dim rays of light glinted from the crests of the Atlantic's swells. The sea conditions were moderate, he concluded.

Upon completing the 360-degree scan, he saw that the area was clear of traffic. "Lower," he ordered, and then, "Surface."

Oberleutnant Krauss repeated the order; crewmen shouted numbers and scrambled as the periscope hummed to its down-stops. Whooshing sounds issued from the tangle of pipes and valves as the 'blow' continued. The conning tower pierced the surface of the Atlantic and sprouted out. Crewmen tended wheels and valves that regulated the U-boat's fore-and-aft balance. Once the U-boat was stable, the diesels were started and Gregor ordered, "Full Ahead."

To the second-in-command Gregor said, "Note the speed and enter it."

When the conning tower hatch was opened, Gregor, Krauss, and a petty officer climbed to the bridge. There, the men faced a chilling wind.

"What do you think?" Gregor said, noting that his breath turned to a cloud.

Krauss surveyed the sky. "Yes," he said, "there are stars enough." He accepted the sextant tendered by the petty officer, brought its eyepiece to his eye, and began aiming. As Krauss called out the readings, the petty officer wrote the time from the 'hack watch' and the associated numbers under each star name.

When Krauss's sightings were complete, he and the petty officer returned below to complete the navigational calculus. Gregor remained on the bridge until relieved by the lookout.

Krauss referred to the U-boat chronometer, then to his watch. He made notations and, with the petty officer, completed the mathematics. The petty officer filed the books of tables into the holder while Krauss transferred the celestial results to the navigational chart.

"Here is our location," Krauss said, holding his pencil point where he had marked the chart. Gregor nodded. Krauss glanced at his watch. "Or rather where we were, seventeen minutes ago."

Gregor studied the mark. "I see. About eight miles from my dead-reckoned location."

Krauss said, "I have also logged the current speed—a little over twenty knots."

"Thank you, Krauss," Gregor said. "I hope you are happy with the sea-chronometer. It was produced by GmbH Hamburg. It passed the palladium special examination by Deutsche Seewarte."

"Indeed it seems an excellent timepiece, Kapitän." He squinted at the gyro compass card. "Present heading: two-one-nine." He glanced back at the chart, and smiled at Gregor. "What shall I set for our destination?"

Gregor said, "Aim for Ponta Delgada."

"Ah, the Azores," Krauss said. He chuckled. "And those pleasant subtropical breezes."

Murmurs of approval filled the control room.

"Be not deceived," Gregor announced to the control room crew. "The Azores is not an ally of Germany. Ponta Delgada is an interim aim point—we shall not go there.

"As I told you in Wilhelmshaven, our destination will only be revealed when we have arrived. And as I also told you, we will hold daily, all-hands torpedo drills during this voyage. Those begin tomorrow, at zero-eight-hundred hours."

PARIS

The family had consigned their heavy luggage to a baggage man. Adrienne carried the wicker basket with their food for the journey, while Dominique gripped a cloth bag of personal items and a canvas tote of miscellany.

Jean Boch straddled his suitcase resting on the cobbles. He paid the cabbie and the Unic taxicab chugged off toward the line of waiting cabs. Jean turned to Adrienne. "Have you the tickets?"

"Yes, Papa."

"And you are very sure that all is set with Grover Magnin."

Adrienne patted her coat pocket. "Yes, Papa, his confirming cablegram is in my wallet."

"We are off then." Jean hefted the suitcase and the trio trudged into the stone entrance of Gare d'Austerlitz. They passed a quartet of men in khaki uniforms with duffel bags queued at one of the windows—a reminder of the trench war raging in the north.

Inside the noisy train shed, they made their way to the assigned platform. The Sud-Express train consisted of steam locomotive and tender, four passenger cars and a baggage car. While the two women boarded the teakwood coach, Jean idly glanced toward the front of the train. Twisting clouds of steam rose high to the overhead canopy. The sky visible through its lattice of iron and glass showed a brilliant blue hue. "I think I shall miss Paris," he said in a soft voice, shaking his head.

The carriage filled quickly. Adrienne and Dominique sat together facing Jean, whose seatmate was a gaunt woman wearing a hand-knit shawl. Adrienne set the wicker basket at her feet.

"Oh, this is cheery," Dominique said, stuffing her bags next to the window. "A bit of a chill," she admitted, tightly folding her arms until her hands were hidden in her coat sleeves.

"There is a muff in the canvas bag," Adrienne said.

"I know . . . perhaps later."

Jean consulted his watch. "It is near time."

A French Army officer appeared at the open door to the vestibule. He glanced about, as though counting the passengers. He approached the Boch family and tipped his blue cap by its visor toward the women. "Pardon the intrusion, but I make a request for kindness. Thanks to the grace of the conductor, my Poilu rides free, but he cannot sit. He will depart the train in Poitiers. Will you guide him?"

"Oh yes!" Adrienne said.

Jean raised a hand and frowned. "Indeed, sir, we wish to help. But what is this soldier's condition?"

The officer shook his head slowly. "He was wounded in the head retaking Fort Vaux. He claims to see, but I do not trust his opinion."

As Jean was about to speak, a tall man in a wrinkled trench coat emerged from the vestibule. He moved slowly toward them.

Jean spoke out of earshot of the soldier. "So we are to substitute our eyes for his?"

"Your kindness will be much esteemed."

The soldier in the trench coat halted before the officer and saluted. "Thank you, sir."

The officer returned the salute. "I hear the call now." He bowed to the passengers and said, "I must hurry."

The coach jerked and began to move. The palm of Adrienne's hand flew to her lips as the soldier's hand gripped the back of Jean's cushion and the officer disappeared into the vestibule.

As the train accelerated alongside the platform, Adrienne sighted the officer. "He made it off the train. Despite the movement."

Dominique said, "But with such caring."

The soldier nodded toward the women. "Pay him no attention,

ladies—the colonel does not understand."

Adrienne scrutinized the soldier's smiling face. Although his blue eyes appeared perfect, an indentation in the left temple seemed connected to a horizontal scar beneath his eyebrows.

Dominique addressed the soldier. "He was inquiring after your health."

Jean turned toward the standing soldier. "He said you were wounded during the freeing of Fort Vaux. I offer you my seat."

"No, no, I cannot accept. The controller of this train has granted me passage to Poitiers absent a ticket. In exchange, I must not sit."

"That is not comfortable for us." Jean shook his head. "You have fought for France's freedom."

The soldier pursed his lips and said, "Poitiers, it is not distant. We shall be there soon."

"The ladies and I," Jean said, "we are from Belgium—Charleroi, to be exact. We are headed for Lisbon."

"I was at Verdun. That is not too far from Belgium, I think. The concrete of the Fort was very thick. Much more than a meter. Forty-centimeter artillery could only chip it." He smiled at Adrienne, then at Jean. "But it was very loud."

Dominique said, "But your health—it is good?"

The soldier laughed. "Do you perceive a disability?"

The rumble of the train, now at speed, became louder as it crossed some rails.

Jean said, "The colonel asked that we—that we aid you to your destination."

"Yes, to my home in Poitiers, France. But you are not destined for Poitiers. You said you are aiming for Lisbon."

"Exactly," Adrienne said, followed by a smile. "We are sailing—to establish a new life in America."

"That requires a great quantity of money." The soldier gave a short laugh. "My last franc was on the cards I held." He gave another short laugh. "And then the lights went out."

Jean looked inquiringly at him. "You were playing cards, and . . ."

"I am telling what happened inside the Fort as the German shells fell. The electricity failed."

After a short silence, Jean said, "The electricity failed. And thereafter, what happened?"

The soldier smiled and said, "I cannot say."

Dominique glanced out the window and said, "We are slowing—this must be a stop." The car shuddered, and squeals came from wheels and rails. Shortly, the conductor appeared in the doorway to the vestibule, shouted, "St. Pierre-des-Corps!" and disappeared into the vestibule.

The train stopped inside a long iron shed, and a few passengers departed and boarded the car.

The train resumed its journey, and Jean turned to the soldier and smiled. "I should inform you that I am Jean Boch. This is Madame Boch, and my daughter, Adrienne."

"I am very pleased to know you. My name is Emile, Emile Ligier. My family—father, mother, and aunt—lives on the fringes of Poitiers." He laughed, again the short laugh. "In the poorest neighborhood, I should add. We raise chickens and a few rabbits. But cheese is scarce, now, eh?"

Dominique nodded. "Yes, although it flourishes on the black market."

The conversation with Ligier lengthened, until finally the conductor appeared again and announced, "Poitiers!"

The train stopped, and some passengers began to depart the car. Emile Ligier said, "Ah, it is sad, but I must leave of this pleasantry. Au revoir, M. Jean, Mme Dominique, and Mlle Adrienne."

The Bochs returned the parting phrase. Ligier bowed, turned, and followed the departing passengers out of the car.

Adrienne said, "That was most interesting—a benefit to the passage of time on the train." She stood to view the people outside, on the platform. "There he is—M. Ligier."

The palm of Adrienne's hand flew to her lips. "Oh. No!"

"What?" Jean said, rising from his seat.

"M. Ligier has walked right into a lamp post!"

Jean stared out the window. "Yes. But he seems all right. He has straightened and signaled to those attending him that he is not injured."

"But Papa! It is as the colonel said—M. Ligier cannot see!"

Dominique stood and said, "He is blind?"

"I would not have believed it." Jean said, shaking his head. "But yes, the Poilu cannot see."

The Bochs slowly resumed their seats. "Now I understand," Jean said. "Ligier must have been struck by debris during the German bombardment. That would explain the scar under his eyebrows. And that is why he could not tell me what happened after the electricity failed."

Adrienne frowned. "Perhaps there was no failure of the electricity, Papa. Perhaps M. Ligier simply recalled what was for him the onset of permanent darkness."

IRÚN, SPAIN

As the train slowed, Adrienne's father rose from his seat. "Spain, like Portugal, is neutral in the war. My bank experience suggests there will be questioning at customs, but I think we should proceed with calm."

Adrienne whisked some crumbs from the lap of her dress and closed the lid of the food wicker. "My printed timetable says Irún is the station where we change trains."

"Yes," Jean said, "although we have already crossed the river into Spain."

Dominique said, "We are now in Spain? I don't understand." A loud hiss sounded outside their carriage.

"We change tracks here," Jean said.

The train slowed more. Sunlight turned to flickering shade as the carriage passed into a train shed. "Spanish railway tracks are wider than French railway tracks," he said. "The two widths of track exist in parallel between here and Hendaye, France. Thus we must transfer at this station to the Lisbon-bound train, which is situated on Spanish rails."

Dominique squinted at Jean. "Why in the world would the Spanish invent such a difficulty?"

Jean merely wrinkled his brow and grasped his suitcase. "Gare Irún is but a short distance into Spain from the border of France." He rested the suitcase on the floor. "The Civil Guard of Spain will likely be in charge of entry and customs. We do not speak their language, but we must try to show due respect."

The door to the car's vestibule slid open and the conductor shouted, in French, "End of the line! All passengers depart!" He disappeared from view.

The train jerked to a stop and the Boch family gathered their belongings.

In the vestibule, Dominique prepared to descend the stairs. "Ah, it is warmer here," she said, gripping the handrail with her free hand. Adrienne followed her mother, handing the wicker basket below to Jean before descending.

Inside the station, they stood in a line of passengers next to a sign, "Puerto de Entrada," and studied the interaction of passengers with an officer of the Civil Guard. Most of the passengers either spoke Spanish or simply signed an offered form and quickly passed on with their luggage unopened.

The officer they faced was dressed in a green uniform. Adrienne and Dominique seemed fascinated with his polished leather hat.

"Welcome to Spain," the officer said in Spanish. The thumb of his left hand stretched the breast of his tunic outward against the restraint of six shiny brass buttons.

"Thank you," Jean said, depositing his identity papers into the Civil Guard's outstretched hand. Dominique and Adrienne followed with their papers. The officer examined the papers briefly, then produced a pad of forms. He pointed and seemed to explain that they should sign on a line at the bottom of the form. He dipped a pen in an oversized bottle and handed it to Jean.

Jean glanced through the wording. "I don't know Spanish," he said.

The officer continued to point at the line. "Firma," he said, and more forcefully, "¡firma esto!"

Jean showed the form to Adrienne, who set the wicker basket on the Civil Guard table. "I'm not sure—but the other passengers signed," she said.

Jean decided he would sign. "Go ahead," he said to the two women as he signed the form.

The officer said something else while pointing at the wicker basket.

Adrienne smiled at the officer and said, "Some food for the journey." She opened the lid.

The officer removed his left hand from the tunic, placed two fingers on the edge of the basket, and peered inside. Next to a nearly-empty wine bottle and three spoons was a container that had held potted cheese. An open tin held several dried fruits. Protruding from a wrapped towel was the end of a baguette. The officer lifted the towel, which revealed not only the remains of the baguette, but a small jar of red currant jelly. The officer smiled.

Dominique said, "We have only a few rationed foods for our—"

Adrienne interrupted, saying, "—but you are welcome to verify their quality."

Adrienne noted the officer's attention. She smiled, deftly opened the lid of the prewar jar of jelly, tore a small piece from the baguette, and scooped some jelly onto the bread. She offered it to the officer.

The officer grinned, accepted the bread, and thrust it into his mouth. He chewed it with obvious pleasure.

With a smile, Adrienne repeated the action. The officer accepted the second donation, chewed, and grinned at Adrienne. He lifted the leather tricorne from his head and held it on his chest over the brass buttons, still chewing. He bowed slightly and said, in perfect French, "Thank you. I shall not forget your kindness."

Adrienne smiled. "We wish you a very good day." She replaced the cap of the jelly jar and closed the lid of the wicker.

The officer replaced his tricorne on his head, assumed a military bearing, and thrust his tunic forward with his left thumb. With his right hand, he waved the Boch trio through the port of entry and pointed them toward the Spanish train.

OFF THE AZORES

Although Oberleutnant Krauss's navigation had placed them off the sea-lane southwest of the Azores, the S-3 U-boat had been forced to submerge by the sighting of a distant armed British merchant ship.

Cruising at periscope depth, the crew discovered that the air-cleaning system could not keep up with the crew's breathing. And the ventilation blower simply moved hot, oily air from one end of the submarine to the other.

Condensation of crewmen's sweat dripped everywhere from the cold hull. The hot, humid air was so thick watchstanders felt as though each breath was their drowning last. Hungry men refused to eat. The putrid smell of soggy bodies and their toilet was unbearable.

Every surface was wet. Wooden drawers swelled closed and cabinetry doors swelled shut.

In the engine room, men dressed only in undershorts and oily shoes tied soggy rags across their heads to prevent being partly blinded by sweat trickling into their eyes.

Off-watch sailors lay naked on berths in an effort to avoid the brutal heat—sleep was nigh impossible.

As soon as safety allowed the U-boat to surface, Gregor ordered all hatches opened. Officers came to the conning bridge, and off-watch crewmen lolled on deck enjoying the fresh air and breeze. But the temporary relief came to a sudden halt when another ship was sighted.

Gregor ordered, "Alarm!" and scrambled down the conning hatch to the control room.

Crewmen on deck jogged to the hatches and disappeared into the hull. Once the hatches were secure and the U-boat sank below the surface, Gregor ordered, "Periscope depth."

Before Krauss could repeat the order, the interior became upset. Men grasped at pipes, wheels—any handhold—to stop from tumbling toward the stern. The upward angle of the boat continued to increase until the prow pierced the surface with a swell and splash.

Almost immediately, that action ceased. The hull fell to horizontal, then the bow plunged downward. The crew now braced to prevent a lurch forward.

Gregor grasped the effect—the boat was porpoising.

"Surface!" he commanded.

Several seconds passed as crewmen struggled to execute the command. They turned valve wheels and shouted gauge readings, but nothing prevented the bow from dipping back into the sea. As the downward angle increased, the stern lifted out of the water. The boat slowed as its propellers came out of the water, flinging swirls of spray into the air.

In the control room, Gregor commanded, "Stop motors!" Whooshing sounds issued from the tangle of pipes and valves as air filled the tanks and water was forced out.

The stern plunged back into the water. Crewmen steadied themselves. The conning tower burst upward and cleared the surface. The boat gradually slowed to a wobbly stop.

"Start diesels. Ahead One Third," Gregor said. The boat settled, slowly rocking fore and aft, and began to move forward. The chief boatswain clambered up the ladder, opened the tower hatch, and disappeared from view. In a moment he reappeared and shouted toward those below, "No vessel in sight, Kapitän."

Gregor nodded and spoke to Krauss, "Establish a lookout. Engineer, report to control."

Krauss commanded into the voice pipe, "Engineer report to control," and signaled for a crewman to take to the conning tower as a lookout.

Crewmen tended wheels and valves that regulated the U-boat's fore-and-aft balance. The boat finally moved forward in a stable manner, its deck awash as a wake formed at the bow.

The chief engineer appeared at the hatchway that led aft from the control room. "Kapitän Steiner?"

"Engineer Vogel—there is a fault with the hydroplanes," Gregor said. "Investigate and report."

Vogel gave a half-salute with his right hand, turned, and disappeared aft toward the engine room.

•   •   •

Vogel appeared at the passageway leading forward from the control room. He was frowning. He thumbed behind him.

Gregor stared at him. "What is it, Vogel?"

"It is the motor, the motor that drives the forward hydroplanes, Kapitän." In his left hand he held pliers and a screwdriver. "It is kaput."

Krauss looked up from his chart. "Burned out?"

"The windings, they are cooked," Vogel said, switching the pliers to his right hand.

"That is why we lost control," Gregor said, maintaining his stare. "You can repair the damage?"

Vogel swung his head side to side. "No. The wires have arced. The windings are cooked. The motor cannot be repaired."

Krauss asked, "Have you a replacement motor?"

"We carry no replacement motors," Vogel said. "These motors, sir, they—"

"Never mind," Gregor said.

Krauss stared at Gregor. Gregor gazed downward, thinking. Krauss said, "We must return—"

"A moment, Krauss," Gregor said, beckoning him forward with a tilt of his head. To Vogel he said, "Excuse us, Vogel." The two officers passed by Vogel as they left the control room. They disappeared into a doorway off the forward passageway.

Vogel shrugged his shoulders and made his way aft, squeezing his way past a chattering crew in the control room.

Inside the tiny forward cabin, Krauss said, "Without the forward diving planes, we cannot submerge. We have no choice but to return to Wilhelmshaven."

Gregor looked away from Krauss. "You forget that there are three identical motors onboard. We shall have to replace the faulty hydroplane motor with the rudder motor." His gaze returned to Krauss. "I shall so order Vogel upon our return to the control room."

Krauss's eyes went wide. He shook his head side to side. "Remove the rudder motor? How can you wish that?" He gestured with both hands. "The helmsman would be severely restricted! How—"

"Be not hasty, Krauss. It is true the helmsman's muscle will be tested to turn the rudder by his hands alone. At least to make abrupt corrections. But we must have both bow and stern diving planes fully active to enable submerging."

Krauss continued shaking his head. "At highest speed, with the absence of a rudder motor, the helmsman will find it impossible to move the rudder more than a few degrees from dead center." With the side of his hand, Krauss wiped drops of spittle from his lips.

With deliberate slowness, Gregor nodded. "You are correct. At the higher speeds, our turns will be heavily restricted. At slower speeds, our helmsman can probably get the rudder to better than ten degrees. But as I said—"

"But suppose," Krauss said, interrupting, "—and only you know what situation we may face—but suppose we are fully in battle. Without a rudder motor, we will be so slow to maneuver . . ."

"Correct," Gregor said, nodding again. "That is the risk."

"Perhaps we should call for help. There may be an Imperial supply ship somewhere . . ."

Gregor shook his head in slow, negative arcs. "Our wireless is forbidden to break silence."

Krauss's intense gaze fixed on Gregor's seeming lack of expression. "Perhaps a port . . ."

"We are in the middle of the Atlantic Ocean," Gregor said, now smiling. "What port?"

Krauss fell silent. He stared at his boots for a long moment. "Removing the rudder motor is a very risky decision. I do not like the choice."

"Understand—I do not favor it, myself," Gregor said. With teeth bared he turned toward the door and unlatched it. "But we must press on—the war will not wait."

LISBON, PORTUGAL

Dominique straightened her dress and rose to leave the train. "Oh," she exclaimed. "I think my legs have gone asleep."

Adrienne's father stood nearby, looking skeptically at his watch. "We are late. I am concerned that this fellow Mendez Dias may have abandoned waiting. And we have yet some time to claim luggage." He extended his free hand to help Dominique to her feet.

"Papa, please do not worry," Adrienne said, heading toward the vestibule with the wicker in her grasp. "Mendez assured me on the telephone that he would meet us in the station here without fail."

Jean Boch replaced the watch in his vest pocket and picked his suitcase from the floor of the car. "But we do not know him. And that was at that station, Entron . . ."

"Entroncamento," Dominique said, smiling at Jean. "I promised myself I should not forget that peculiar name."

"Be careful with your step, Dominique," Jean said, "it is quite dark outside."

The platform inside Estação Ferroviária de Lisboa, Santa Apolónia, was long, wide, and crowded with passengers leaving the Sud Express. The train shed was huge, in keeping with being the railway's end of the line alongside the estuary of the Tagus River at Lisbon, Portugal.

Adrienne led the couple along the tall station wall, which was punctuated by series of arched entrances. Because the high lamps on the underside of the shed roof threw only pale light, she was forced to squint at the face of each man she came to. Then she saw him, in a black hat, with the black eye patch on a band across his forehead.

Adrienne slowed, faced him, and said, in French, "I am Adrienne

Boch. I believe you are meeting us. You are José?"

He smiled, exposing a mass of malformed teeth. In perfect French he said, "Good day. I am José Mendez. Welcome to Lisbon."

Jean Boch extended his hand to Mendez tentatively, because the eye patch did not cover either of Mendez's eyes. Rather, the patch was affixed high on his forehead.

After greeting Jean and Dominique, Mendez said, "We must not tarry—follow me." He began walking.

"I have made the arrangements with La Trasatlántica," he said. "But the lateness means you shall not have a day to rest." He turned toward a nearby arched entrance. "We must now see to your luggage."

Adrienne stepped faster, next to Mendez. "José, please. I must send a cable . . ."

"We do not have much time," he said, slowing as they approached the CP—Comboios de Portugal—luggage stand. "The telegraph likely will be closed at this hour."

"May we confirm that?"

Mendez pointed at an arched entrance a considerable distance along the platform. "The telegraph is there, do you see the sign? Your family and I will see to your luggage and await your return." He began conferring, in halting Portuguese, with the CP agent.

Adrienne hurried toward the telegraph office.

•   •   •

Upon Adrienne's return to the CP stand, Mendez said, "We must go now to the Compañía Transatlántica office." The three Bochs followed him.

Adrienne said to her father, "José was correct, the telegraph was closed. But I must cable Will. What shall I do?"

Jean frowned. "Dear Adrienne—is it essential that you—"

"I must, Papa—I must." She gave her father an imploring look.

Jean sighed. "Have you prepared a message?"

"Yes. I have written it out," Adrienne said, removing a folded paper from her wallet.

"With an address?"

"Yes, Papa. It is all here."

Jean accepted the paper and slipped it into his jacket pocket. "I shall see what I can do."

•　　•　　•

Several passengers were ahead of the Bochs in a line at the Compañía Transatlántica window. Mendez said to Adrienne, "Were you able to sleep on the train?"

"Some," she said. "But fitfully. The noise and the movement—you understand."

"I have not slept in two days," Jean said. "It was impossible."

Mendez smiled, showing his teeth again. "Ah, but you will sleep as a child once you are on the ocean. You are so fortunate to have Senhor Grover Magnin as a benefactor."

The Bochs stood by as Mendez consigned their luggage to the agent at the Compañía Transatlántica window. Once the forms were stamped and their tickets to San Francisco dispensed, they followed other passengers to a small crowd on the embarkation platform.

The Alfonzo XIV sat tied at the quay, a two-masted passenger liner with one funnel. It was small by Titanic standards, with but two decks above the weather deck.

Spots of rust showed through the hull's black paint. A tugboat puffing dirty smoke appeared poised to assist the liner's departure.

Jean Boch glared at the ship. He faced Mendez. "This is the Alfonso XIV?"

Mendez nodded. "The Alfonso XIV is not a great liner like the Mauritania, but—"

"I understand—there is the war, yet this vessel is smaller than I envisioned." He turned to Adrienne. "Are you satisfied with this

Spanish vessel?"

"Yes, Papa. It is our chance for a new life—away from the war. We have gone over this before. The choices were severely limited."

Dominique smiled at Jean. "I do not understand. It is long, it is iron, steam issues from its chimney. What more do you wish?"

Jean said nothing, only tilted his head and looked away.

The Bochs sighted their luggage being loaded into an opening in the bulwark. Transatlántica officials went to the gangway and passengers ahead of the Bochs approached the officials.

Mendez said, "You will soon be on board and on your way. I wish you a peaceful and speedy voyage. It has been a pleasure serving you."

Adrienne smiled. "Thank you. On behalf of my family, we are grateful for your assistance."

Jean nodded to Mendez and took a position between Mendez and the women. The two men conferred in lowered voices, and Jean passed a paper and a sheaf of francs to Mendez.

Mendez bowed and retreated. The Bochs identified themselves to the officials at the gangway, tendered their tickets and identification papers. The officials marked their lists, assigned passenger numbers, and welcomed the Bochs. The three of them grasped their bags and suitcase and began the climb up the gangway.

Partway up the gangway, Adrienne paused to allow her father to replenish his breath. "You paid José to send my cablegram?"

Breathing heavily, Jean said, "Yes. I overpaid him. I only hope he completes the task and sends the message."

Adrienne slowly turned and began climbing again. "Yes, Papa." A small wrinkle formed on her brow. "I concur earnestly with your wish."

CARIBBEAN SEA

Following Gregor Steiner's order, First Watch Officer Krauss had arranged S-3's trek across the Caribbean Sea so that the U-boat could arrive in the middle of the night.

The lookout on the bridge of the conning tower peered into the inky night. He saw two lights and shouted his sighting down the hatch.

Max Krauss, on watch in the control room below, ordered the diesels to neutral. He sent a seaman to wake the Kapitän while climbing quickly to join the lookout on the bridge.

"What do you see?" Krauss said to the lookout while raising his binoculars to his eyes.

The lookout lowered his binoculars. "Dead ahead may be a light tower. A second, weaker light, four points off the starboard bow. Also winking lights—probable buoys."

Below, Gregor wiped the sleep from his eyes and grasped his binoculars. He climbed to the bridge and joined Krauss and the lookout peering into the darkness.

After a moment, Gregor ordered, "Ahead One Third." He turned toward the two men. "We must approach in order to make a positive identification." To Krauss he said, "Get some sleep—I will awaken you when a watch is warranted."

As Krauss descended through the hatch, Gregor leaned on the fairwater and squinted straight ahead into his binoculars. The wind had died, so wave action did not strongly disturb observation. The air was warmly humid, and he felt sweat beginning to form under his oilskin.

The position of the two bright lights matched those on the navigation chart of the Isthmus. Still, the shore was but a blur. Three points off the starboard bow were two separated blinking buoys. Neither Gregor nor the lookout could see any breakwaters.

Gregor knew from his examination of photographs in the shipyard room at Kiel that identification of the big hotel on the northwest shore of the peninsula was critical to identifying the town of Colón. He also knew two riprap breakwaters were angled more than two kilometers seaward from the town. He expected to see acetylene-powered buoys at the entrance between the breakwaters. The two blinking lights to starboard might be—he thought—those buoys.

Gregor spoke into the voice pipe, "Ahead Very Slow." Although he now saw a proliferation of tall palm trees onshore, he was unable to discern any structures. The U-boat slowed, making only a slight wake.

Low clouds helped visibility by reflecting lights from habitation back down onto the shore. But except for some twinkles of electric lights, nothing prominent appeared in the shadowy outline of the coast.

Gregor and the lookout sighted the silhouette of a single tall smokestack at the same time. "Not an identifier," Gregor said to the lookout. "It is not included in the identification protocol for our destination."

Gregor next perceived the outlines of buildings. "Stop engines," Gregor ordered. "There is a town."

"Buildings, yes," the lookout confirmed.

Lacking propulsion, the U-boat glided forward on its own momentum. On shore was a large structure with three levels of windows. Gregor said, "You see the big building?"

"Confirm, Kapitän. Three stories of height."

Focusing acutely, Gregor saw that the porticoes on the ground floor were punctuated by large arched openings.

"Destination confirmed," he said to the lookout, smiling while lowering his glasses. He immediately ordered, "Astern Full." The diesels coughed as they drove the propellers in reverse. The craft's momentum propelled it forward, but at ever slower speed.

"Rocks ahead!" the lookout said.

A low row of riprap—a breakwater—became visible, a few hundred meters ahead. It angled off to port, where it disappeared from sight.

With the diesels furiously driving the propellers in reverse, the U-boat came to a wobbly stop. From a standstill, it began immediately to move backward. Because of the location and angle, Gregor identified the obstacle ahead as the shorter, east breakwater. He ordered, "Astern One Third," to slow the retreat.

He lowered the binoculars from his eyes. He had positively confirmed the identity of Hotel Washington—the critical item signaling that U-boat S-3 had arrived at its intended destination, the Atlantic entrance to the United States Panama Canal.

Now it was time to hide.

•　　•　　•

Gazing at his watch, Gregor mentally calculated how far seaward the U-boat was moving from the east breakwater. At 1.5 kilometers, he ordered an engine stop.

"Begin sending code fourteen at quarter-past," he told the wireless operator. "Send it every quarter hour until answered. Until one hour before dawn we will station here, decks awash, to charge batteries. We will then submerge."

With S-3 paused seaward of the east breakwater, the chief boatswain announced a meeting with Kapitän Steiner. As they gathered inside the cramped pressure hull, Gregor noted the apparent weariness of many crewmembers.

"I am aware that our journey has been long and arduous," he began. "Nevertheless, your performance has been as expected of Imperial seamen, and I am pleased to announce a brief period of rest. Except for the tower lookout, you all may relax.

"As I said I would when we left Wilhelmshaven, I can now explain our mission, as assigned by Tactical Order one-two-seven.

"We are now outside the north entrance to the United States'

Panama Canal. We will torpedo a large ship in the first level of the Gatun Locks, blocking the Canal. The selected target will be a minimum of one hundred meters in length, thus blocking the Canal. If the United States decides to enter this conflict on the side of the English, this attack will deal a crippling blow to the United States naval fleet." He noted the smiles on many of the crew.

"It is necessary to remind crew of the absolute importance to remain hidden during all maneuvers—our success depends upon our stealth.

"One hour before dawn, we will submerge. We will remain submerged from one hour before dawn until one hour after sunset each day unless you are instructed differently. Obviously, use of any lamps or light sources outside while surfaced is forbidden. For you smokers, that includes all flames.

"When a suitable target vessel is awaiting entry to the Canal, we shall enter Limon Bay, inside the breakwaters. We will wait there, submerged, until the target vessel enters the channel that leads from Limon Bay to the Gatun Locks.

"We will follow the target to the Locks, a distance of about eleven kilometers. When the gates of the Gatun Lock are opened and the target vessel enters the Lock, we will launch one or more torpedoes, sinking the target inside the Lock.

"The exact attack sequence will be explained to you prior to the attack. I look forward to sharing this formidable victory with each crewmember of U-boat S-3."

●　　　●　　　●

Bruno Ackermann was awakened by the ringing of his telephone. It was Hans Reinhart, who spoke anxiously. "Come quickly to the boat."

Bruno pulled on trousers and a shirt and left the apartment. At the Colón dock, no lights were showing on the C.G.R. tugboat, although he heard the generator running. As he approached, he saw that Hans was pacing the aft deck of La Fernanda.

"Yes?" he said upon boarding the boat. "What is it?"

Hans waved Bruno to follow him inside, to where a dim lamp lit the wireless. "I received the code fourteen transmission. I replied with our code. The S-3 unit is offshore, Bruno, just a couple of kilometers beyond the east breakwater. This is outstanding! Can we go now?"

Bruno consulted his pocket watch. "We could go now, but there is much to discuss with the crew of S-3. There is not enough time to talk and return to the dock before dawn. To protect the security of the operation, we must therefore delay. Tell S-3 we will meet them at that location at ten o'clock tonight, Colón time."

Hans frowned and said, "Are you definite? I thought this meeting was—"

"Hans, wire them exactly as I said." Bruno squinted at the younger man. "We will meet S-3 at that location at ten o'clock Colón time, tonight."

"Alright, alright," Hans said as he seated himself at the fold-down table. He picked a pencil from a cubbyhole and began writing on a paper pad.

Bruno took the code book from its hiding place. "I'll help you encode the message," he said.

When they finished the encrypting, Hans slapped earphones on his head, adjusted the spark-gap, and tuned the transmitter. Without looking at Bruno, he began tapping the telegraph key.

●　　　●　　　●

Adrienne grinned from the rail of the side deck. "Look—I see land!"

Dominique stared. "Are you not imagining? I see only a great expanse of water."

"I am sure of it. A sliver of green." Adrienne turned to her father, who sat reading in one of the Alfonso XIV deck chairs. "Papa—can you see land?"

Jean Boch laid the book aside and rose from the chair. "My," he said, "it is becoming warm." He went to the rail beside Adrienne and shielded his eyes from the sun. "Yes, I think we approach the coast."

"Then we will soon sail aboard this vessel through the Panama Canal," Adrienne said. "That will be so exciting!"

"Yes," Jean said. "I hope there will be nothing beyond the usual delay."

Adrienne turned to her father with a somber face. "The 'usual delay'?"

"Usually there is but a day or two at anchor before entering the Canal. That is, if the Canal experiences no landslide. You see, in the very year you were born, my dear Adrienne, the French abandoned digging a canal across the isthmus, largely because of landslides."

"The day of my birth seems so long ago," Adrienne said, shaking her head. "But please continue with your tale of the French canal."

"The French had endured more than eight years of trying. Some two decades later, the United States was successful in constructing a canal, the one we are approaching." Jean looked from the distance toward Adrienne. "But landslides are a fact. They have blocked the U.S. Canal each year since it opened, three years ago."

Dominique frowned at her husband. "Do you mean a landslide might block the Canal and prevent our use of it?"

"It is unlikely," Jean said to her, "but not impossible."

Adrienne looked soberly at her father. "Though I have become a French citizen, I am deficient in French history. Why was France unable to complete the canal?"

Jean chuckled. "The answer is very complicated. I shall only try to tell you my impression. To the French at the time, in the 1880 period, it became La Grande Entreprise. The canal was promoted by Ferdinand de Lesseps, a most clever man, a man of unshakeable faith, yes, perhaps of unshakeable faith—in himself."

The women laughed.

"Do not laugh. De Lesseps was an ingenious and successful hero. He was the builder of the 170-kilometer-long Suez Canal."

"That surely is magnificent!" Adrienne said. "That certainly recommended him."

"Indeed," Jean said. "I seem to recall learning that he was addressed as 'The Great Engineer'—a miracle man to whom failure was impossible. Although, as I later learned, he was uneducated as an engineer and knew little of technical importance."

"But Papa—I do not understand. What went wrong in the effort to span from the Atlantic to the Pacific Ocean?"

"As I recall, the construction of the French canal was made impossible by two faults. First, the canal was planned to cross the continental divide from the Atlantic Ocean to the Pacific Ocean—at sea level. Second, it was to be financed by the people of France, led by de Lesseps."

Adrienne said, "I see nothing wrong with either instance."

"A sea-level canal was a dream only. After five years of effort, only a small fraction of the earth had been dug. Yet both the loss of workers' lives and the expense grew enormous. Finally, around 1889, the French company, known as Compagnie Universelle du Canal Interocéanique, became bankrupt."

Adrienne peered landward and seemed to identify some habitation. She turned to Jean. "Yet the United States overcame the obstacles you name. They were able to complete a canal. Why?"

"The U.S. came to Panama later, with improved equipment. And, as you might think, the U.S. government's treasury was equal to the huge expense. The U.S. planners rejected France's concept of a canal at sea level." Jean smiled. "Instead, they built a big dam on the Chagres River. This created a giant lake that spanned much of the path between oceans. At either end, they built locks that first raise ships to the level of the lake and then lower them at the opposite end. It was necessary, it was clever, it was successful."

"Aha!" Dominique said, "It seems the United States learned from the mistakes of the French."

Jean smiled at his wife and said, "You may interpret it in

that manner."

Dominique glanced and waved her hand toward the distant coast. "But then as you say, there today remain the hazard of landslides that can halt use of the Canal."

Adrienne raised both hands, palms outward, toward her mother. "Please, Mama, let us at this moment think of something less worrisome—and much more pleasant: a safe, direct, and interesting journey through the Canal to the Pacific Ocean."

SEAWARD OF COLÓN

The thrum of the diesel was like a friend to Bruno, especially now, in the dark. He liked the feel of power with his fingertips curled around the throttle handle.

As always, night navigation was a challenge that never failed to provide a chill. Ahead was the blinking buoy at the west end of the east breakwater. Standing at the helm, Bruno feathered the throttle and turned the tug to starboard. How was the sea outside the breakwaters? Would there be swells, or just a chop? He squinted hard into the shower of rain in an effort to verify.

Hans, seated behind Bruno and silent since they'd left the dock, finally spoke. "With no lights, how will you find it?"

"Shouldn't be too difficult," Bruno said, completing the turn around the buoy. "It is big. It is at least sixty meters long." He glanced at the compass and set a course of twenty-five degrees.

Bruno turned briefly to Hans. "You might as well get into your oilskin—the submarine will show soon enough." Bruno's concentration heightened as, without mention, he reached and switched the tugboat's running lights off.

With the tug now barely creeping forward, his right hand hovered nervously between the throttle and the gear lever.

Abruptly, a gray shape appeared out of the gray rain. "Get out there!" Bruno ordered, as his hand went first to the gear lever, clutching the gear changer into reverse. He then increased the throttle while quickly turning the helm with his left hand. The conning tower of the U-boat emerged from the rain.

The tugboat turned to port and slowed nearly to a stop. Outside,

Hans snatched the coiled line from the bow deck and swung it in preparation.

Shouts issued from the U-boat's lookout. Shortly, two crewmen in oilskins appeared on its deck. Hans tossed the weighted end of the line toward them, but it fell short. He retrieved it, coiled, and again tossed it. A crewman caught the line and secured it. Hand over hand, Hans drew the line to him. The tug's rubber fenders bumped against the steel hull of the U-boat. Shouted German greetings flew between the two vessels.

Hans secured the bow line and hurried to the side deck, where he grasped another coiled line and tossed it to the waiting crew on the U-boat.

Within a short interval, the tug was secured to the starboard side of the U-boat, and Bruno prepared to board it. He stopped the diesel and glanced at the chronometer above the instrument panel. He had arrived early, ten minutes before ten.

When Hans reentered the pilot house, Bruno said, "Keep a sharp eye topside. If you see something, shout out 'danger.' Get down quick, throw all lines but one, and start the diesel."

"You mean if a vessel approaches?"

Bruno nodded. "In such an emergency, S-3 will order a dive. I will get back to the tug as quick as I am able."

●   ●   ●

Hans caught himself as his head sagged to one side. He had gone asleep and almost fallen off his perch. He started to stand but, realizing his oilskin hat was missing, he stooped to retrieve it. He took a handhold on the flag mast that sprouted from the top of the aft cabin and quickly glanced at the U-boat's conning tower. The lookout on its bridge seemed to be staring off toward the breakwater and likely had not noticed his misadventure.

Hans stood, grasped the railing, and swung around onto the

starboard ladder. The rain had quit. In two lunges he was down to the weather deck, where he circled aft and around to the cabin door.

Inside, Hans stomped his boots and glanced at the chronometer. He returned to the foredeck of La Fernanda in time to see Bruno climb down from the bridge of the U-boat's conning tower. A Navy crewman followed Bruno. Bruno grasped the guide line for stability, trod the deck, and hoisted himself from the U-boat onto the tugboat.

"You were gone two hours," Hans said, reaching for one of the mooring lines. "What took such time?"

"Forget it," Bruno said, hurrying into the cabin. "I must start the diesel. We are casting off."

Hans shrugged, and waited for the crewman on the U-boat to detach the mooring lines. As he retrieved loose line, two loud blasts issued from the S-3's horn.

Whooshes of air shot from vents below the U-boat's waterline, causing big burbles and spray. The crewman scrambled up the exterior conning ladder and disappeared from view. The metallic clank of its hatch followed.

With the tug's diesel chugging, Bruno eased the boat away. Swinging the helm with one hand and increasing the throttle with the other, he guided La Fernanda into modest swells to the southwest. He glanced back at the U-boat as its conning tower slowly sank into a foaming sea. He shook his head slowly and set a course of two-zero-five degrees.

His deck chores completed, Hans entered the cabin and threw off his oilskin. "So. How went it?"

Bruno craned his neck, seeking the lights of the buoys at the entrance between breakwaters. "That Captain Steiner, he is a dogged sailor. He has good knowledge of the layout of the Canal and the entrance, but little knowledge of how a vessel traverses the Canal." He turned the tug's running lights back on.

"You mean he does not understand how the locks work?"

"He understands that the Gatun Locks raise vessels twenty-six meters up to Gatun Lake." Bruno's intensity eased as he identified the blinking light of the nearest buoy. "But he knew nothing of how a vessel proceeds in reality. I was forced to spend much time explaining."

Hans leaned against the cabin bulkhead. "I am unsure what you mean."

"One moment, Hans," Bruno said, as he reduced throttle in advance of turning around the west end of the breakwater. After completing the turn, he set course for the dock and said, "I needed to explain that the vessel must register and pay in advance for Canal passage, that the assigned Panama Canal pilot must board while the vessel is anchored in Limon Bay, that this pilot takes control of the vessel when passage is scheduled . . ."

"Kapitän Steiner did not know of the Panama Canal pilot?"

Bruno shook his head. "Poor fellow, he has not seen the operation. He did not know of the electric locomotives—the "mules"—on each side that guide the vessel in the lock, so he did not know the piloted vessel must stop outside the lock entrance to allow line handlers to get the cables to the mules . . ."

"Bah!" Hans said, shaking his head. "How can the German Imperial Navy dispatch a kapitän on this mission with such ignorance of his target?"

"Ah, Hans," Bruno said, seeing the La Fernanda dock ahead, "you are too harsh toward the Imperial Navy." He pulled gently on the throttle and the diesel went to idle speed. "Who did the leaders of the Imperial Navy send to instruct the young U-boat commander?"

Hans started to speak. Instead he smiled. He looked at Bruno and laughed.

Bruno chuckled, and prepared to dock La Fernanda at Colón Harbor.

COLÓN HARBOR

Hans sat at the fold-down desk, lit only by a shuttered lamp. Despite sweat that turned his tan shirt brown, he said, "The temperature is narrowly less than it was this afternoon."

Bruno stood behind La Fernanda's helm at the Colón dock. He grimaced. "It is the moisture—the moisture that makes the heat unbearable. I wish for a stronger wind." He grasped his binoculars, raised them, and aimed westward through the open door. "The electric illumination has been switched on for some time." He lowered the binoculars. "At this time they must be sipping their after-dinner Grand Marnier."

Hans grinned. "While the dance orchestra is tuning—to the key of G."

"The key of G?" Bruno lowered the binoculars and looked at Hans. "You know music?"

Hans curled his lips. "Poorly. I was raised to sing—in the choir of boys. You understand."

Bruno glanced up, at the chronometer. "No. I would not have guessed. It is time to encode the message. Read to me what you have."

"Bird: – Spanish liner Alfonso XIV – arrived March 28 – anchored merchant ship anchorage west of dredged channel – signal if qualified."

Bruno narrowed his eyes to encounter Hans. "Can we give the L.O.A. of the liner?"

"It is longer than the other anchored vessel. But I am not able to state its length."

"It is perhaps 140 meters. Not as big as the Pennsylvania, which was here some time in the past." He raised his index finger. "You have monitored wireless signals from the Canal saying a pilot and inspectors will board the liner Alfonso XIV at sunrise?"

"Correct."

"You must append that information to the message."

Hans took up his pencil and began writing.

Bruno raised his binoculars and peered again out the door. "Kapitän Steiner most assuredly has the published listings for Alfonso XIV. He will take the decision." Bruno lowered his binoculars. "If he selects the liner, stealth requires that he use the remainder of the night to enter Limon Bay and submerge."

Hans nodded and reached for the secret compartment that held the code book.

•   •   •

In the aft cabin, Bruno squinted against the electric light and said, "Read to me what you have decoded."

"S-3 at 2320 March 28: – will begin entry to Limon Bay surfaced 0230 March 29 – send alert (CODE 6) by lamp if danger threatens – will sleep on bottom south of west breakwater – Alfonso XIV qualifies."

Bruno's idle glance went to the bulkhead facing him. "So the attack begins."

Hans looked up from his seat that faced the wireless set. "Why does the U-boat not submerge?"

"Perhaps it is too difficult." Bruno began rubbing his chin with his hand. "Navigating in the dark through the entrance, looking only through a periscope may be very risky."

"How does the U-boat intend to torpedo the passenger liner?"

Bruno held up his hand. "A moment, Hans." He began to pace, but the small space restricted his movement. With his thoughts formed, he halted, facing Hans. "We shall have to stay here, keeping a careful watch, until S-3 passes through the breakwaters and submerges. You should be poised to send a CODE 6 by lamp if S-3 is threatened. This will allow them to dive."

"But it is not yet midnight," Hans said. "The U-boat does not appear until after 2:30 in the morning. I do not cherish the lack of sleep you propose."

"It is as you said earlier, Hans—it is the war." Bruno grasped the handle of the door to the main cabin. "Switch off the interior lamp. Bring the signaling lamp. We must compose a reply to S-3."

Inside the main cabin, Bruno turned to Hans. "Begin the message with this: 'Bird: Limon Bay traffic normally increases following daylight.'"

Hans began writing.

Mostly to himself, Bruno said, "There is no way to predict the time required by the quarantine inspector and customs officer. We should warn Kapitän Steiner of the risk of premature discovery."

Bruno shut his eyes and spoke slowly to Hans. "Add this to the message: 'Avoid risk of discovery – remain on bottom until minimum 0645 March 29 – only when cleared by pilot and inspectors can target begin transit of eleven-kilometer channel to locks.'"

FORT SHERMAN, PANAMA

The windsock at the entrance of the Fort Sherman lagoon drooped enough to convince Will Marra that the breeze out of the northeast was less than five miles per hour. He centered the controls and pushed the throttle forward. The propeller of the R-9 floatplane chopped the air as the two airmen adjusted their goggles. Will taxied the aeroplane slowly out the narrow lagoon entrance into Limon Bay.

On Will's left was the breakwater that angled more than two miles into the Caribbean Sea. It was named the 'west' breakwater to distinguish it from the much-shorter 'east' breakwater. The half-mile opening between the two breakwaters constituted the entrance used by vessels aiming to transit the Panama Canal to the Pacific Ocean.

Consisting of rubble covered with rock, the west breakwater was topped by railway tracks that the railroad used to build the breakwater. Rubble was plentiful—a consequence of the thirty thousand tons of dynamite that had been exploded in digging the Canal.

Directly across Limon Bay was the town of Colón, mostly a home to poor blacks who had been recruited to dig the Canal. Also across the Bay were the Canal's administrative buildings and piers of Cristóbal. Between Will's aeroplane and Colón was the almost seven-mile-long dredged channel that split Limon Bay and led directly to the first level of the Gatun Locks.

As was now his habit, Will left the lagoon, swung the Curtiss aeroplane sharply around Shelter Point, and increased the throttle. The usual wind direction this time of year required him to taxi a distance toward the Gatun Locks—paralleling the dredged channel—then turning around to achieve an upwind takeoff run. Will first lifted the nose, then dropped it slightly. The aircraft gained speed, its floats leaving double wakes that collapsed into a broad single wake in the distance behind the aircraft.

Will listened to the roar of the exhausts, studied the tachometer and the oil pressure gauge, then glanced to his left, toward the merchant ship anchorage adjacent to the dredged channel. A single small freighter sat low amongst the glittering reflections of the morning sun.

Limon Bay's water displayed only a slight chop, so the ride was fairly smooth. Will's thoughts turned to the cablegram he had—finally—received at the beginning of the week. It had been re-routed from San Diego and delayed, presumably while the Army searched its records for his current duty station. The message, datelined Lisbon, said: "SAILING ALFONSO XIV TO USA STOP NEW JOB STOP SEE YOU SOON STOP LOVE ADRIENNE STOP." He found this message extraordinarily puzzling because the last letter he'd received from Adrienne Boch had described her as happily guiding Atelier Adrienne to success and acclaim in Paris.

Will glanced behind him, where Oakley's goggled head was visible over the tiny windscreen.

Oakley responded with hand gestures that indicated, "What's up?"

At the takeoff point, Will swung the craft into the wind. After a quick scan of instruments he gave Oakley a thumbs-up with his left hand, advanced the throttle, and began the takeoff run. When the Curtiss regained a position opposite the small anchored freighter, the aeroplane lifted sluggishly into the air. Will adjusted the manifold pressure and banked left, over Fort Sherman. The ground crew waved as the aircraft flew over them.

Thursday's 'recon' sortie over the seaward approaches to the Panama Canal by the U.S. Army's sole aeroplane had now begun.

●   ●   ●

On their return flight at two thousand feet, with Fort Sherman on his right hand, Will flew over the breakwaters, and on over Limon Bay. He aligned the heading of the floatplane with the dredged channel in anticipation of turning back toward the breakwaters for an upwind landing.

He began a slow descent. He squinted and was surprised to see, in the far distance, a large, single-funnel vessel near the entrance to the Locks.

How had he missed such a large vessel during his pre-flight taxi? He guessed that, concentrated as he was upon his preparations for take-off, he had simply not peered far down the dredged channel toward the Locks.

Will reduced throttle and dipped the R-9's nose. The floatplane glided lower along the channel towards the vessel. He now saw she was a single-funnel, two-mast liner with two enclosed decks and a bridge deck above the weather deck. He estimated her length at slightly less than five hundred feet.

Will banked steeply to his left and dropped to an altitude of eight hundred feet.

Oakley, in the rear cockpit, yelled toward him, "What're you doing?" Will heard the outburst but could not interpret Oakley's words over the roar of the motor.

•   •   •

Adrienne and her father hurried forward on the second covered deck of Alfonzo XIV. "The ship has stopped," Adrienne said to her father as they rounded to the foredeck. Seeing that a large crowd of passengers had lined the forward rail to gaze over the ship's bow, the couple returned to the side deck and settled for leaning over the rail.

"Look, Papa," Adrienne said, gazing down toward the water, "two men in a rowboat."

"I see them. Workers, I suppose."

"The man in the rear of the boat, he is dragging something in the water."

"Yes, I see." Jean studied the action below. "He holds ropes—or something like that."

"Yes, Papa, but—"

The line-handlers' boat moved in toward the vessel's hull, and Adrienne said, "Now the lower deck is in the way. I cannot see the boat."

"Well, I think those ropes—or cords—connect to the little loco-motive on shore." Jean turned to his daughter and gestured, "Do you see them?"

"No," Adrienne said, abruptly looking upward. "Now there is an aeroplane overhead!"

•   •   •

Will banked the aircraft to the right as he passed over the liner. He aligned the aeroplane with the channel below and headed back toward Limon Bay and Fort Sherman.

At that instant he saw another vessel in the channel. It was about two miles behind the liner, a wisp of black smoke trailing from it. Although its bulk was barely visible on the surface, its central tower stood tall. A bulky tower atop a long, thin, and barely visible hull was what Will and his Army observer had trained themselves to recog-nize—a possible hostile submarine.

Will quickly thrust his left arm out of the cockpit and signaled to Oakley with a downturned thumb. He cut the throttle, banked steeply, and made another three-quarter turn, descending toward the submarine the entire time.

He leveled the aircraft. At fifty knots, skimming a hundred feet above ground at right angles to the vessel, Will was intent on identify-ing the vessel.

The gleaming gray steel of its hull was unmarked. As he passed over the riveted conning tower, he saw a uniformed officer standing on its bridge. The uniform, the cap, the shape of the insignia—he was sure—the man was a German Naval officer.

•   •   •

Gregor Steiner glanced at the aeroplane overhead. He immediately recognized the insignia on the underside of its wings as denoting a U.S. military aeroplane. But its flight was lumbering and it was equipped with large floats—obviously a reconnaissance aircraft that he could ignore as an immediate threat.

Gregor spoke to the voice tube, "All Ahead Slow." He raised his binoculars and aimed toward the Alfonso XIV. "Helm, steady. Open bow tube doors."

Below, Max Krauss repeated the orders and added to them, "Report."

The engine order telegraph bell rang. Krauss glanced at it and nodded. "Ahead Slow," he confirmed to the C.T. voice pipe.

One minute later, a voice from the bow torpedo room reported. Again, Krauss repeated the report to the C.T. voice pipe, "Doors open, tubes flooded."

Gregor acknowledged the 'doors' confirmation while studying the scene ahead at the entrance to the Gatun Locks. The entry gates stood ajar, and the liner Alfonso XIV appeared stationary in the waiting area in front of the gates. A slight haze of gray smoke rose from the ship's funnel.

Had the 'mules'—the electric towing locomotives on the sides of the lock canal—moved? Although they were difficult to discern because of their small size relative to Alfonso XIV, Gregor strained to see them while adjusting the glasses' focus knob.

The mules appeared frozen to their rails.

"All Ahead Very Slow," he commanded, lowering his binoculars.

• • •

Intense and confused thoughts raced through Will Marra's mind. He needed to stop the U-boat, but he also needed to gain both speed and altitude. He pushed the throttle forward and raised the nose. The low-powered craft answered his input lazily.

He banked steeply into a turn toward the Locks. The fabric of the wings fluttered. He glanced at the airspeed indicator. Its needle dropped—forty-five, then forty-one knots. "Damn!" he said. He quickly lowered the nose to prevent a stall.

As the aeroplane regained speed, Will shouted back toward Oakley, "No guns—no guns!"

Oakley understood Will's words, but not their meaning. "What?" he yelled.

Will only shook his head.

The aeroplane had gained a little and was nearing one thousand feet above the water. "Never mind," Will shouted at Oakley.

It did not matter that Oakley didn't understand. What was crucial was that the lack of deck guns on the U-boat meant it would launch torpedoes from its bow, torpedoes aimed to sink the passenger liner in the first lock, disabling the Canal.

• • •

Adrienne Boch glanced forward from the side deck toward the wall of concrete that towered above, forming one side of the lock. "It looks as if those ropes . . . are they ropes, Papa?"

"Those seem heavier than rope," Jean said. He squinted at the several cables that swung over the water between a lower deck of Alfonso XIV and two of the locomotives above—on the wall of the lock. "They may be cables—or—I'm unsure."

"It looks to me as if they are becoming straighter." Adrienne swept her hand sideways. "It sounds silly, but they appear to sag less and less."

"Yes, I see what you have observed." He continued to stare at the lines. After a short time he turned to her. Brightly, he said, "I think we are moving."

Adrienne scanned forward, then towards the wall of the lock. "Yes, Papa, the ship is moving! Can it be that those cables, and the little gray locomotives to which they appear attached, are tugging us into the lock?"

GATUN LOCKS, PANAMA CANAL

G regor squinted into his binoculars. The two mules that Alfonso XIV's hull did not block from view had definitely moved. "Ah," Gregor said in a low voice to himself, "the target moves." He lowered the binoculars, and into the voice pipe said, "Range, three thousand. All Ahead One Third."

He then noticed that the military floatplane was flying toward the Alfonso XIV. Although his concentration remained on the target, he watched as the aeroplane passed the ship and disappeared behind it. Probably it was off to report its discovery of the U-boat.

The U-boat's steel prow now produced a small bow wake as it moved toward the Gatun Locks and the target steamship.

"Torpedoes, standby," Gregor said into the voice pipe. "We will shoot number one at range one thousand. Number two, we will wait for a range of five hundred meters—or less—to assure finality."

He returned the binoculars to his eyes, and was surprised to see the military biplane passing near the Alfonso XIV while flying toward him.

•   •   •

Will glanced downward into the ship's funnel, smelled its coal smoke, and guided the R-9 directly along the dredged channel toward the U-boat.

Quickly losing altitude, the aircraft passed over the rounded fantail of the vessel. Will was vaguely aware that some passengers at the stern rail waved at the plane. He maintained the descent and gave Oakley the thumbs-down landing signal.

Oakley shook his head in disbelief. He yelled at Will, "What the hell you doing?"

Will kept the biplane's nose down while trimming throttle to maximize the angle of descent. He turned and shouted at Oakley, "Gotta stop the sub."

Less than a dozen feet from the surface of the channel, Will angled the nose upward and trimmed the power to slightly above that of a stall. The aeroplane sank quickly toward the surface.

The floats struck with giant splashes. The sudden resistance chopped their speed, slamming both aviators forward with jarring effect.

Will immediately pushed the throttle to maximum.

•　　　•　　　•

Gregor saw the splash ahead, and realized the biplane had landed between him and the locks. He momentarily wondered if it had suffered a mechanical failure. But he immediately banished the incident from consideration. At that moment, the aiming of U-boat S-3 and the targeting of its torpedoes was his ultimate and sole intent.

Was the forward speed of one-third adequate? Gregor knew the response of S-3's rudder. A lower speed lessened the rudder's influence and thus his targeting ability. A higher speed would improve the U-boat's response and improve his aim.

Gregor spoke loudly into the voice pipe, "Ahead Half."

•　　　•　　　•

Adrienne glanced skyward as the aeroplane flew above, making a loud clatter. She followed its path as it flew away, paralleling the channel. She also sighted the dim image of a submarine beyond it.

"Look, Papa," she said, straining her eyes to the rear along the ship's hull and noting the unexpected. "The aeroplane landed on the water. Why did he do that?"

•   •   •

At maximum throttle, the motor roared to high speed. Will eased the aeroplane's nose up slightly. This caused the aircraft to both rock backward and surge forward, though at a slow speed.

The ten-foot propeller pulled giant quantities of seawater into a huge fan of spray that showered over and around the aeroplane. Both Will and Oakley were instantly soaked. The spray was so thick and wide Will could see only a silhouette of the conning tower in the distance ahead.

Oakley instantly recognized the maneuver. Will had practiced and used it in the past when learning the intricacies of taxiing. Will called it "plowing"—an emergency measure that allowed the aircraft to turn quickly to avoid obstacles. But Will said continued use of the "plow" threatened to erode the propeller and cause engine overheating.

The aeroplane was now skittish. Will whipped the controls back and forth, countering the aircraft's tendency to tip, douse a wing, and turn over.

•   •   •

The huge fan of spray around the aeroplane troubled Gregor. He had never seen such a display and did not understand it. He nevertheless forced himself to concentrate on the aiming of the U-boat. The view forward was not affected by the distant fan of spray.

Squinting, he aligned his sight along the centerline of the hull, using the tip of the prow as a guide to where—in the distance—his torpedo would strike.

He spoke into the voice pipe, "Range, two thousand. Standby to fire one."

Gregor perceived the leading quarter of the liner had passed into the concrete entrance of the Gatun Lock. The U-boat's alignment was now perfectly aimed at the Alfonso XIV and the final thousand meters to the firing distance were quickly shrinking.

●　　　●　　　●

Amid the downpour of seawater from the spray, Oakley gripped the cockpit surround attempting to keep the aeroplane from overturning. "Easy, skipper—easy!" he yelled, "damned if I want to swim for it!"

The motor noise overrode Oakley's outburst. Will strained forward to peer through the spray, but could barely see. He yanked the goggles from his helmet and tossed them to the cockpit floor.

The U-boat loomed ever larger as the R-9 approached. Will squinted and swiped water from his brow.

He swiveled in the cockpit to view the Gatun Locks behind, then quickly alternated between looking forward and looking aft. Flipping the rudder left and right in quick succession, he maintained the aircraft's position and stability on a line between the U-boat and the locks.

●　　　●　　　●

Gregor faced the aeroplane's fan of spray as it headed directly toward him. He could no longer see the Alfonso XIV. In fact, he saw nothing but a gray sheet of seawater. He leaned right, then left—but neither action improved his view.

In frustration he shouted into the voice pipe, "Rudder, hard to port!"

Below, Krauss repeated the order. The helmsman gripped the wheel and grimaced. The wheel turned only a fraction. The helmsman grunted, muscles tensed, sweat beading on his forehead. "It won't move more!"

Krauss motioned to the nearest crewman. "Help him—help him!"

The crewman grasped the rim of the wheel over the helmsman's shoulders and pushed, then pulled. The wheel rotated a small increment.

On the bridge, Gregor saw the boat angle left. Fearing the drift toward the limit of the channel's dredging, he shouted into the voice pipe, "Rudder, hard starboard!"

•   •   •

Although his vision forward was heavily obscured, the U-boat appeared to move to Will's right.

He glanced behind to judge the relative bearing to the locks, and swung his rudder. The aeroplane crabbed a short distance rightward as the distance to the U-boat shrank.

Vibration shook the airframe. Oakley gripped the edges of the cockpit.

Will envisioned the propeller flying apart, ending the fan of spray.

The U-boat was only yards away.

Will glanced at the oil pressure gauge. Its needle swung towards zero.

•   •   •

The U-boat angled slightly to port. A loud scraping sound startled Gregor. The vessel shuddered and slithered to a halt. Gregor lost his footing, flew forward, and crumpled into the steel fairwater. He heard a thud and a snap as he hit.

Below in the hull, crewmen tripped and tumbled. They smashed into bulkheads and equipment. Tools and parts collided with the men and other obstacles.

Chaos ensued.

Gregor instantly knew his left arm was broken. He cursed.

•   •   •

Dimly through the spray, Will saw the U-boat stop. Although the action was initially confusing, he surmised it had run aground.

The aeroplane now headed directly at the bow and conning tower of the U-boat.

Will applied maximum rudder to swing the aircraft left.

Will turned and shouted to Oakley, "Look out!"

Will slid the throttle to idle a second before impact.

The center of the lower right wing of the R-9 smashed into the fairwater of the conning tower. Wood splintered, fabric ripped, debris flew and the upper wing twisted downward.

Momentum forced the craft into a fast, swinging loop around the U-boat's conning tower. This thrust Will and Oakley outward like passengers on a merry-go-round.

The right-side float struck the steel hull in front of the tower. Its struts broke and the fuselage slumped. The aviators bounced forward in their cockpits and Oakley's face hit the front edge.

Although slowing, the aeroplane's engine continued to run, its big propeller slinging giant swaths of seawater into the air.

Will fumbled at the controls and turned the motor off. He turned to view Oakley, whose nose shed a stream of blood.

DREDGED CHANNEL

K apitän Gregor Steiner cradled his left forearm in his other arm and tried to regain his feet. He failed.

On his knees and soaking wet, he shouted down the open hatchway, "Krauss—are you there? Krauss?"

There was no answer.

Gregor winced and allowed his broken arm to sag. Using his right arm and hand, he clawed himself to his feet. He shook his head in pain, and again cradled the forearm in his other arm. He peered dazedly at the crashed aeroplane, the upper wing of which dangled over his head. A few meters away, the aeroplane's unpowered propeller continued thrashing. Seawater gushed from every part of the airframe, inundating the area.

The smell of hot oil and burnt insulation filled the air.

Gregor spoke into the voice pipe, "All Astern Full." Hearing no confirmation, he shouted, "All Astern Full."

Krauss's voice replied weakly, "All Astern—Full."

After a delay of minutes, the diesels loudly sped to maximum and black smoke shot from the aft compartment.

Underwater at the stern, the propellers spun energetically in reverse, raising big, agitated mounds of water over them.

The U-boat, however, did not move.

•   •   •

Dripping seawater from his soaked tunic, Will Marra unfastened his lap belt.

The fuselage creaked. Bubbling sounds rose from water around the crumpled right float.

Will sniffed the acrid air and thought about fire. He rose partly out of the cockpit and turned around. "You okay, Oakley?"

Oakley nodded, holding a bloody rag to his nose. He fumbled, unlatching his lap belt.

Will climbed from the cockpit onto the left, undamaged lower wing.

He half-smiled at the German officer less than twenty feet away on the conning tower. Sweeping his arm in a dramatic semicircle, he said, "Doesn't look good, Captain."

•　　　•　　　•

Adrienne Boch squinted, still peering backward along the hull. "Oh-oh—something bad happened. It appears the aeroplane and the submarine have crashed together."

Jean followed Adrienne's line of sight. "Unfortunate. One hopes no one was injured."

The morning sun cast deep shadow on the starboard side of Alfonso XIV as the ship moved into the concrete cavern of the lower Gatun Lock. Jean pointed. "But look, we are almost entirely inside this enormous lock." He glanced upward. "The locomotives are slowing us. Fascinating! I believe they will soon close those gates behind us and—"

Adrienne continued squinting rearward. "I think I see movement of men. Perhaps the injuries are not serious." She faced her father. "I do not understand why that aeroplane swooped to the water and crashed into the submarine—there was much room elsewhere."

She glanced back and pointed. "Now, there is a boat, a powered boat, racing from behind us toward the crash. Do you see it?"

"That must be rescuers—officials going to investigate the collision." He glanced around. "But we are—our ship has now stopped."

He glanced to the rear. "The gates—the big iron gates are swinging closed. How fascinating!"

•   •   •

Bruno Ackermann hurried across Colón's timbered pier and scrambled onto the side deck of La Fernanda. Hans Reinhart met him when Bruno opened the cabin door.

"I was about to summon you," Hans said. "I have received a wireless from the U-boat."

"Is it decoded?"

"Yes. There are three words only: 'Crashed-stuck-come.' Although the distance is short, I am fairly sure they have rigged a temporary antenna."

"Let me see," Bruno said.

Hans handed Bruno the paper.

Bruno's view remained on the paper as he sat down. He took the code book from the fold-down desk and studied the paper. After several minutes, he said, "I believe it is correctly decoded."

"What does it mean?"

Bruno looked gravely at Hans. "I came here because I received a telephone call from a man at Gatun Locks Operations. He said there has been a collision blocking the Atlantic-side approach channel. He said on behalf of—"

"Oh—no! Our U-boat—"

"Stop!" Bruno said, "and listen. He said on behalf of the lockmaster, our company, Compania General de Remolque, is authorized to send the tugboat to the site to help clear the channel."

"Did he say what occurred?"

"He did not say, only that there was a submarine and an aeroplane involved. And that payment was guaranteed."

"You believe the submarine is our U-boat?"

Bruno's face frowned. "If I put the wireless message together with the telephone message, I conclude our U-boat is stopped in the channel following a crash with an aeroplane."

"Then we must go there—immediately."

Bruno shook his head. "I think we should be thoughtful, Hans. The wireless asks help for Kapitän Steiner. The telephone message asks help for Canal Operations. These messages represent conflicting loyalties. We must proceed with caution."

●   ●   ●

Water dripping from their flight suits, Will and Oakley stood on the Cristóbal dock, facing the two policemen in khaki uniforms and campaign hats.

"Look," Will said, "you've got this all wrong. This man next to me is Sergeant James Oakley, and I'm Lieutenant Will Marra, United States Army." He swung his arm and hand toward the channel. "What happened out there—"

"I'm not arguing, sir," the police sergeant said. The two policemen stood stiffly at attention, eyes forward.

The police sergeant said, "My lieutenant says the Port Captain has issued the order."

Will stared at the silver badges clipped on the left chest above the pocket flap, then at the puttee leggings and tan shoes. "Who the heck is the Port Captain?"

The police sergeant glanced at the corporal beside him. "I don't know his name, sir. He's a U.S. Navy officer. As I get it, he's in charge of all of the Atlantic ports."

Will frowned. "Well, that's fine. So he's in charge here, the dock where we're standing." He swept his arm toward the dredged channel. "But out there, there was a German submarine. A U-boat on attack. It was about to torpedo a big ship and the Gatun Locks. We stopped it. We saved the ship—and probably thousands of lives."

The police sergeant shrugged. "If you say so, sir. I'm not arguing. But we got orders, orders to escort you two gentlemen—"

"Yeah, I see your badge. I see it says, 'Canal Zone Police.' I'm not questioning your authority here. I know we don't look like it, we're soaked, dirty, we've just been through a hell of an action. But we were flying a United States' Army aeroplane on reconnaissance orders issued by the United States Army, probably Colonel Cronkhite."

Will frowned. "You know who Colonel Cronkhite is? Does that mean anything to you?"

"Sir, I don't mean to argue. We got orders to take you to the station. There, you can tell your story to Lieutenant Pritchen. He'll be able to sort through everything."

●　　　●　　　●

The splintered lower right wing of the floatplane remained impaled on the conning tower of the U-boat. The damaged upper wing collapsed on top. Twisted wires and broken struts of the two wings served to keep the wreckage attached to the U-boat. The balance of the aircraft angled precariously alongside the riveted hull, wobbling with the action of the waves in the channel.

Tethered to the stern of the U-boat was a motor launch, "Canal Operations" printed on its side. A worker in a drooping hat stood at the transom of the launch. He signaled to the approaching La Fernanda to tie up.

Bruno Ackermann slowed the tugboat and steered it alongside the motor launch. When La Fernanda stopped at the side of the launch, Hans threw lines which the worker in the drooping hat secured.

A second, hatless, man on the launch shouted in Spanish that he was trying to save the aircraft. "It is an Army aeroplane," he said, pointing at its insignia. "One of the floats is damaged, maybe leaking. Maybe that is why the aeroplane tips. Can you tow it?"

Bruno squinted at the aircraft. "We can possibly pull it loose. If the main chamber of the float is not damaged, we can tow it. What happened to the aviator?

"There were two men in it. I took them to shore—to Cristóbal."

"And where should I take the aeroplane?"

"Operations says it belongs to the Army at Fort Sherman. Can you take it there?"

"Probably—if I can squeeze it into the lagoon. I should at least be able to get it to Toro Point."

While noting the temporary antenna rigged on its deck, Bruno pointed at the U-boat. "What about this vessel?"

"They say it is a German submarine. But it is not moving—it must have run aground. The crew remain on board. They speak a foreign language. We ordered a larger boat to take them ashore. There are more than twenty men inside."

Bruno nodded. "The captain—he is also on the submarine?"

"He was injured. But the men are caring for him."

"All right. My mate will go over there, inspect the float, and attach lines." Bruno swept his arm toward the U-boat. "What happens to the submarine?"

"It must be pulled back into the dredged channel. Did they contact you about it?"

"Yes. That is going to be a tough job—it appears solid as a rock."

●   ●   ●

After more than an hour's wait, Lieutenant Marra and Sergeant Oakley, escorted by the two Canal Zone Police, stood in front of the desk of Lieutenant Pritchen, telling their story.

"As you can tell," Will concluded, "ever since we arrived at Cristóbal, we've been treated as though we've done something wrong, whereas actually—"

"I see your view," Pritchen said. "but I have no report with which to compare. I have only the word from the Port Captain that the two of you were involved in blocking the Canal, a violation of Canal Navigation Law. And now you have related to me that you were there, where the blockage is. And that you purposely drove your aeroplane into a collision with a foreign vessel, in the middle of the channel leading to Gatun Locks."

Will glared for a few seconds at the high ceiling of the Cristóbal police station. "Yes, of course. We did our duty. We stopped a foreign threat to a passenger liner and the Gatun Locks. As I explained."

Pritchen shook his head, slowly. "I don't know what to tell you. There will be a hearing tomorrow on the Port Captain's complaint. That will offer you an opportunity to explain. In the meantime, I must hold you overnight."

"Wait a minute." Will bent forward toward Pritchen. "You're going to arrest us?"

"Now, sir," Pritchen said, stiffening, "let me straighten you out. I did not say you were to be arrested. Get this straight, there's no arrest here. You'll just be held overnight for the hearing tomorrow."

"You mean in a jail?"

"Yes, sir. In the jail here. But you're not arrested—you haven't been charged."

"That's wrong, Lieutenant. And what the hell happened with the Germans? The German crew of the submarine?"

Pritchen paused and glanced at his paperwork. "Well, it says here they're to be held, also. All of them, including a Captain Gregor Steiner. They couldn't hold them here, we don't have room. They're supposed to go to the penitentiary at Culebra. They'll ride the train."

Will turned to Oakley. "Well, this is all haywire." He smiled sardonically. "But at least the Germans will be behind bars, too."

•　　　•　　　•

The chief mechanic stood in water to his thighs, directing the ground crew. The crew removed the lines that tethered the aircraft to La Fernanda. Then the crew pushed and pulled the aircraft through the water toward the concrete ramp.

"Get the dollies under the floats," the chief ordered.

Once the dollies were in place, the chief mechanic waved at the tugboat. He shouted, "Thanks, fellas," then tried his weak Spanish. "Gracias por—rescatar—avión—gracias!"

Hans continued pulling lines aboard La Fernanda, coiling them neatly on deck. Bruno turned and went inside the cabin. He changed the gear and backed the tug. He then pulled forward, turning the boat toward the narrow entrance of the lagoon.

"Huh," the chief mechanic said, shaking his head, "those guys are not very friendly."

The crew in the water was busily maneuvering the battered aeroplane onto the ramp. "Goldies, probably," one of the crew said. "They're in it for the money."

Once the aeroplane was out of the water with lines securing it to tie-downs, the crew gathered around the damaged wings. "What happened?" said one. Another said, "Was Oakley—or the lieutenant—injured?" A third said, "I see bloodstains on the rear cockpit."

"I don't know any more than you guys," the chief said. "Let's hope they're okay. In the meantime, we've got to figure out how to get this thing repaired. Pete—get in the cockpit and work the right ailerons. Let's see if the control cables are busted."

CRISTÓBAL, CANAL ZONE

The interior of the courtroom smelled of mildew—and human sweat. The overhead fan blades whirled, but the resulting cooling seemed negligible.

Lieutenant Will Marra stood facing the magistrate's desk. He was almost finished explaining the events of Thursday: "I tried to avoid hitting the submarine, but I was too close. The right wing struck the conning tower and whirled us around, where we smacked a float on the hull. I shut the motor off. My observer, Sergeant Oakley, suffered a wound to the face. That's about all, except for getting picked up later by the Canal Operations launch.

"I'd like to conclude by saying there was no need to hold Sergeant Oakley and myself in this jail here in Cristóbal. We didn't do anything but our duty—which saved at least a thousand lives."

Will turned to sit down next to Oakley when a vocal hubbub erupted. The magistrate rapped for quiet, and said, "Now this is a hearing, not an adjudication. But just the same, we will observe some decorum. We are attempting to determine what happened in the channel yesterday, March 29, 1917.

"I suppose there are questions from those who requested to be here." He nodded toward the people in front of his dais, then addressed Marra, who had returned to his chair. "I would ask the lieutenant if he is willing to answer—although I caution, he's not required, and he's not under oath."

Will looked at the magistrate. "Sure. I'll answer questions. About what I know, that is, and what happened."

The magistrate smiled. "I see. According to my list of people requesting attendance, we have a lady reporter from the Star of Panama, a representative of Canal Operations, two officers from the U.S. Army, and of course, Lieutenant Pritchen of the Canal Zone Police." He looked up. "Do I have that correct?" He paused and surveyed the requesters, who sat in a row of chairs at the foot of the dais. Seeing nods, he said, "Why don't you start us off, Lieutenant Pritchen."

The policeman stood and faced Marra. "You said you were on a 'recon' mission yesterday, Lieutenant. What is that, and who authorized it?"

"As I understand it, the recent Governor of the Canal, General George W. Goethals, believed the Canal was vulnerable to attack by submarine. He spoke to the Secretary of War about it, and I ended up here with the Curtiss R-9 aeroplane to fulfill the need.

"Yesterday's mission, like our regular schedule, was authorized by the U.S. Army—specifically the U.S. Coastal Artillery at Fort Sherman, to conduct aerial surveillance of the Atlantic Ocean near the entrance of the Canal. Our objective is to locate any hostile submarine that might threaten the security of the Canal."

The policeman bit off his words. "But crashing your aeroplane into the approach channel to the Gatun Locks was not part of that directive, is that correct?"

One of the two U.S. Army officers rose from his chair and interrupted. "That's impertinent, sir. You are attempting to—"

The magistrate rapped for silence and glared at the men. "Gentlemen, please!" After a moment, he said, "Let us hear from the Army . . . you go ahead, please, but refrain from any recrimination."

The Army officer who'd interrupted stood and faced the magistrate. "I represent the U.S. Army Coast Artillery. What Lieutenant Marra said is correct. He flew a reconnaissance flight authorized by the Coast Artillery from Fort Sherman on Thursday, March 29, 1917. As he said, he spotted a German submarine, determined its hostile intent, and by clever means, foiled a torpedo attack on a vessel legitimately scheduled through the Panama Canal." He sat back in his chair.

The female reporter, whose dark hair was closely bobbed, stood and looked at Will. "I am a reporter for La Estrella de Panama, the daily newspaper in Panama." She spoke with a lilting Spanish accent. "You said you thought the submarine in the channel was foreign. Why did you think the vessel was foreign?"

Will stood and looked at the magistrate, who nodded and said, "Go ahead, Lieutenant."

Will glanced at the woman and said, "Didn't I read in your newspaper under a Norfolk, Virginia dateline, about reports brought in by foreign merchant ships—that German submarines were observed in the Atlantic Ocean?"

"I—I could not confirm that," she said. "But why would you think the submarine you saw was not one of the local submarines—those of the United States Navy?"

"The submarine was not marked, but there was black smoke coming from it."

"And what is the significance of smoke which is black?"

"The subs at our base here—at Coco Solo—are all gasoline-powered. This was a diesel-powered submarine." He paused and smiled at the reporter. "Diesel smoke is black." He glanced at the magistrate. "The submarine was big, too—twice as long as the C-class submarines at Coco Solo. It also had a tall conning tower, much larger than what the U.S. Navy calls their 'sail.'"

"Are there other, larger U.S. submarines than those you call C-class?"

"Yes, there are the H-class submarines. But only a few. And the only one it could have been is H-2, operating in the Caribbean Sea. However, I know H-2, and this sub looked nothing like H-2."

The reporter grasped a notebook from her chair and wrote something in it. She again faced Will. "You said you identified the submarine as German. How did you determine that?"

"I flew very low—about a hundred feet above the water—and slow, directly over the submarine. An officer was on the bridge. He wore a visor cap that I identified as a cap of the Imperial Navy."

"Can you say how you knew it was a German cap?"

"Sure. It had a black visor, a black hatband, with a white top. The U.S. Navy 'service whites' cap is similar in appearance, but its gold-colored emblem features an eagle and anchor. The German cap's gold-colored emblem is all feathers, with a red dot in the center. There are other differences, too."

"You have made a study of the uniforms of foreign navies?"

Will paused, looked up toward a ceiling fan, and said, "Yeah, I guess I have."

The reporter made another notation in her notebook and frowned at Will. "You said the German submarine was preparing to torpedo the passenger liner in Gatun Locks. What evidence do you have for that?"

"The German had trailed the passenger liner in the channel for five miles. He was commanding from the bridge, intent on attack. But his boat lacked guns—the artillery used to sink ships. That U-boat's deck was clean as a whistle." Will stopped and smiled at the reporter.

For several seconds the reporter looked blankly at Will.

Will lost the smile. "Well—with no guns, it was obvious why the German was aiming his U-boat. He was closing in, to improve his range. He intended to fire bow torpedoes and destroy the passenger liner in the Lock. That would shut the Canal."

The Army officer with all the ribbons stood, raised his hand to belt level, and stared at the magistrate. "May I interrupt? There's a need to clarify what has been said so far at this hearing."

The magistrate frowned at the officer, whose tunic featured a chest-full of campaign ribbons. "You've already interrupted. So, all right, go ahead, but make it short."

"I represent Brigadier General Clarence Edwards, commander of all U.S. forces in the Panama Canal Zone." He paused for effect. "Although Lieutenant Marra is correct in saying he flew an authorized reconnaissance flight, he was not authorized to land in the dredged channel near the Gatun Locks. Also not authorized was his attack on a vessel of the Imperial Navy of Germany." He paused again. "I must emphasize that landing and striking a vessel of the Imperial German Navy was not authorized. The United States was not yesterday, and is not today, at war with Germany."

The other Army officer glared at the speaker with widened eyes.

A murmur rose from some of the sparse audience sitting at the back, in the rows of mostly-unoccupied spectator chairs. Included among the few spectators was Bruno Ackermann.

The magistrate rapped for silence.

The final requester, a partly-bald, well-tanned man in white shirt and tie, stood and said, "I'm here from Canal Operations, or, if you prefer, from the Port Captain, who asked me to read from the regulations." He lifted a sheaf in his hand and started reading. "'Regulations relating to the navigation of the canal, the terminal ports, and the waters adjacent thereto and of harbor dockage—'"

The magistrate interrupted in a firm voice. "If you please, sir. This is not a legal proceeding and we're not marine attorneys. We're here to understand what occurred in the channel and what's to be done about it. Confine yourself to whatever the Port Captain wishes us to know."

The man lowered his sheaf and glanced nervously at the magistrate. "Yes, sir. The Port Captain says this blockage of the Canal is a clear violation of the navigation regulations for the Canal. He intends to hold those responsible to account for whatever damages are caused."

"Thank you," the magistrate said. "Thanks to all of you. I believe that concludes this hearing." He stood, walked off the dais and entered his office.

The requesters stood. A shuffle of feet and excited babble followed. The requesters broke into separate verbal wrangles accompanied by occasional whispers.

Within minutes, Will Marra and Sergeant Oakley were whisked from the room in the company of the two Army officers. Lieutenant Pritchen's eyes followed them. He shrugged and sauntered toward an interior doorway.

• • •

On his way to the dock on Saturday morning, Bruno Ackermann bought a newspaper at Hung's on Balboa. He boarded La Fernanda and climbed the three steps to the wheelhouse.

Hans Reinhart, alerted by the footfalls, lifted the earphones from his head, left the wireless compartment, and entered the portside door. "You have snored long," he said to Bruno.

"Not long enough," Bruno said, searching the news.

Hans put a foot on the first step. "What happened at yesterday's hearing?"

"Nothing of importance."

Hans climbed the steps. "I have been listening. There is nothing from Nauen on our mission."

Bruno grimaced at the newspaper and stomped his boot. "This is ugly. Bad."

"What?"

"I will translate. Here is the headline on Thursday's crash: 'Aviator's Risky Action: Heroic?'"

"Referring to the flyer who crashed the aeroplane? What does it say?"

"I will not translate all the story, but here is part: 'The collision came dangerously close to seriously injuring Army Lieutenant Marra, who commanded the aeroplane from the front cockpit. But if the German submarine was truly on a mission to sink the passenger liner Alfonso XIV, his action saved an estimated 1,500 lives of passengers and crew.'"

Hans shook his head. "The newspaper fails to recognize the existence of war."

"Worse. In the same place, the newspaper says 'The Zimmermann telegram attempted to array Japan and Mexico in war against the United States. With the United States drawn into the war through no desire of its own, Americans are convinced that the war is a war of self-protection and self-preservation. There is growing favor for sending immediately after the declaration of war an American force to join the Allies in France.'"

"So the United States intends to declare war," Hans said. "They entirely neglect the fact that Germany was forced, by England, into the U-boat war."

Bruno read further. Abruptly, with emphatic force, he crushed the newspaper. "Outrageous! It is ridiculous how this newspaper fails to understand that closing the Canal will finally begin reunification to the people of Panama—ridding them of the elephant who relentlessly treads upon them like so many beetles."

"Wait," Hans said, raising a finger, "before you destroy the newspaper—what of the crew of the U-boat? Does it not inform of their whereabouts?"

"Well, perhaps." Bruno tempered his emotions and smoothed some creases in the paper as he searched. "Oh, here," he said, and began to read, silently. After moments, he laughed and placed the newspaper to the side. "Canal Zone Governor Harding's authorities claim the U-boat violated United States neutrality. Ha! As if the Americans have ever been neutral in this war!"

"Indeed," Hans said. "Does it say the crew remains on the U-boat?"

"No," Bruno said. "They have been imprisoned in the penitentiary at Culebra." He again translated as he read from the newspaper, "They are charged with 'breaking navigation rules and regulations regarding the use of radio instruments in waters under American jurisdiction, and are therefore subject to seizure of the submarine.'"

"Is there any mention of the Kapitän?"

"Let me see." Bruno continued to read. Finally he said, "Yes, there is a brief mention. 'Gregor Steiner, the commander of the U-boat, was taken to the hospital at Ancon, where he was treated for a broken arm and released back to the penitentiary.'"

FORT SHERMAN, PANAMA

When Will Marra opened his door, he faced a short, nearly bald man wearing wire-rimmed glasses.

The man smiled. "Hello. I'm Kellogg 'Cog' McCrorie, United States Representative. It's been a devil of a time getting to see you. May I—"

"Representative? You mean the U.S. Congress?" Will swung the door wider.

"Yes, but never mind that. I finally got to see you. May I come in?"

"Well, I'm sure." Will closed the door behind the man. "Kellogg McCrorie, you say?"

"It's 'Cog'—short for 'Kellogg.'" He smiled. "I claim to be the 'cog' that keeps the foreign affairs committee on track." He walked past Will to the opened window, loosened his tie, and glanced around the room. "I've been to Ancón, Balboa, Colón, Cristóbal, and now to Fort Sherman—but the Army brass, they haven't made it easy for me to see you."

"That's because I've been confined to quarters"—Will yanked the chair from under his wood writing desk and offered it to McCrorie— "waiting for a court martial." Will pulled the blanket up on his bunk and sat down.

"That's one of the reasons I'm here." McCrorie gestured toward the floor. "I debarked the Alfonso XIV—the passenger liner you saved— at Balboa Harbor. But it took all this time to locate you, and then bucking a lot of defensive runaround before they okayed me to—"

"Wait. You were on the—the Alfonso XIV—the ship?"

McCrorie nodded. "You bet. Headed to San Francisco from Portugal. What's the matter?"

Will's hands went to his face, which abruptly turned pale. He stared at McCrorie. "You're sure it was named Alfonso XIV?"

McCrorie frowned. "Of course I'm sure. Why?"

"A young lady—a dear, dear lady—Adrienne Boch, is on that ship."

McCrorie smiled. "Oh. I see. A girlfriend?"

Will sheepishly nodded and smiled. "Yeah—a lovely lady from Paris, and Belgium."

"Well, all I have to say is, you were one smart, brave flier—I saw what you did. Yesterday I talked to news reporters in Cristóbal. They're still piecing the story together. I helped them out, telling them how you aimed your aeroplane right at that U-boat, defeating its attack. I couldn't believe my eyes!"

Will shook his head. "Top brass doesn't think it was so great. I violated all different rules, and busted up the aeroplane."

"That's one of the things I wanted to talk to you about." McCrorie removed his glasses. "I figured the brass might not understand." He shook the spectacles for emphasis. "What are they charging you with? Exactly."

"All I've heard is that the main charge is Article Sixty-Two, 'conduct to the prejudice of good order and military discipline.' I don't think they're going to charge 'conduct unbecoming an officer.'"

McCrorie frowned and nodded. "Sixty-Two, Articles of War. But no specification?"

Will shrugged. "They haven't come up with any—yet."

"That's because they know the charges won't stick. They know you're a hero, but they're hidebound by their confounded regulations." McCrorie lifted and fitted his glasses over his ears. "I'll defend you. I'll call the Coast Artillery boss—whoever he is—to testify you were absolutely doing your duty. I'll call the captain of the liner as a witness for the defense."

Will's eyes went wide. "Holy mackerel, Cog! I didn't—"

McCrorie forced his index finger into the palm of his left hand. "Was your aeroplane the only aeroplane on reconnaissance for hostile submarines?"

"Uh-huh, that's right. The one and only."

"And at the same time, the German Reichstag is issuing more threats of U-boat attacks, the British steamship Alnwick Castle was torpedoed last week in the Atlantic, the Times says warnings were sent out a week ago of U-boats in the Atlantic. And the Congress of the United States focuses to one point—the center of motion for a vigorous prosecution of war with Germany.

"You'll be assigned an Army defense lawyer before any court-martial. He'll be of help. But you can add me for free—pro bono. How does that sound to you?"

Will spread his hands. "That's very generous of you, Cog."

"Thanks to you, Lieutenant, I'm alive." McCrorie smiled and tilted his head. "Frankly, I'll be the one they'll fear—a defense attorney who knows the law inside out. Hell, I'll call all 1,375 passengers on that ship as defense witnesses if I have to. I'll subpoena Canal Operations, everything the Army issues, the Port Captain's reports, Canal Governor Chester Harding, if I need to."

"So you think charges of 'reckless disregard for injury and/or damage'—that's the rumor I hear they'll use—won't sway the court?"

"Even the President—and surely the Secretary of the Army—by now knows you acted correctly. I have heard that Secretary of State Robert Lansing has fired off a cable to the German government charging the Imperial Navy's U-boat with violating United States neutrality as well as other breaches of international law."

"Wow. Didn't know any of that—I haven't been able to get much news."

"I'll keep you informed from here on. Right now, I'm going to take the harbor boat back to Colón."

McCrorie stood up, smiled, and offered his hand for a handshake. "I'll be staying at the Hotel Washington. Believe me, we're not going to let the military railroad you."

•   •   •

Tuesday morning, April 3, 1917, the tug La Fernanda was tied to the grounded U-boat in the channel. Hans Reinhart tended lines on the side deck.

A United States Navy Chief Machinist's Mate tended lines on the deck of the U-boat.

Navy Lieutenant Hazlett stood on the aft deck of La Fernanda, nervously performing the mandatory introductions. He began in English, "Master Ackermann, this is Gregor Steiner. He is—well . . ." Hazlett thumbed toward the U-boat. "He's the captain of the submarine. And Master Steiner, this is Bruno Ackermann, master of the tugboat." He followed by repeating the introductions in his inadequate Spanish.

Bruno glanced quickly at Gregor, but endeavored to avoid Gregor's steady gaze. Instead, he stared at the snipped shirt sleeve, the sling, and the splint on Gregor's left forearm.

Gregor's blue eyes glittered over a slight smile.

Hazlett attempted to explain in Spanish: "Me and other U.S. lieutenant be aboard submarine while Captain Steiner—"

Bruno interrupted. "I speak some German, Lieutenant. Why don't I explain to Captain Steiner how we're going to proceed with this task?"

"Oh, really." Hazlett smiled. "That sounds great. Go ahead."

Bruno maintained a stoic look while speaking German to Gregor. "Sorry to observe your situation. I have been retained to help pull your U-boat off the sand and into the dredged channel."

Gregor's gaze went from Bruno to the water. "I failed. I was too close to the limit of dredging. There is no other way to explain what occurred."

Bruno saw that Hazlett did not understand anything Gregor said. "Nevertheless," Bruno said with a hint of sadness, "I wish you the best." He paused and pointed toward Hans, who was uncoiling a two-inch hawser. "We will attach a bridle to your stern and a hawser to our H-bitt. When you signal we will combine thrusts, you motoring astern, us motoring forward. If the U-boat comes off, I will pause to retrieve the bridle and hawser. Otherwise we will continue to work. Is that satisfactory?"

With a sigh, Gregor said, "I will be on the bridge. I have protested, but my crew and I are indefinitely detained. The captors have given me no choice: I have agreed to sail U-boat S-3 to Cristóbal Harbor and abandon it there. This is my final command. It is ignominy of the worst kind."

Bruno squinted toward Gregor for seconds, pursed his lips, and spoke Spanish to Hazlett. "Captain Steiner and I agree on the procedure for towing. We will begin when you and the machinist's mate are aboard the submarine, the tow is arranged, and Captain Steiner signals me to start."

•　　　•　　　•

U-boat S-3 sat empty at the U.S. pier at Cristóbal. The German captain and his skeleton crew were absent, having been led away to a waiting autobus. A knot of U.S. Navy officers stood on the high wharf adjacent to the U-boat's conning tower listening to Lieutenant Hazlett.

Hazlett said, "Of course, we haven't much experience coming the six or seven miles from the dredged channel to the dock. But it's a much larger machine, twice the size of our C-class boats.

"It took three tries to move the beast off the sand. Very complicated to operate—much depends on the captain's commands because each crewman has a small but intricate function. The skeleton crew was hard-pressed during the removal and docking to keep up with the skipper's commands.

"The insides stink. The filth and garbage accumulated during the long voyage from Germany to Panama are terrible.

"This submarine is not very maneuverable—the helmsman had a terrible time steering. Of course, it's a long boat, but our inspection revealed the cause—the steering motor had been removed—we don't know why."

Hazlett turned to the petty officer. "What would you say about the propulsion, Chief?"

The machinist's mate said, "Both the M.A.N. diesels and the electric motors are new to us. The gears work well, and the revolutions seem proper. I haven't had a chance to judge what speed she would make. We only came surfaced and slow, using the diesels."

"Thanks, Chief," Hazlett said. "As far as torpedoes are concerned: Two torpedoes were in their tubes, armed. They are G-type with wet-heater propulsion. They are now disarmed. Two more torpedoes of identical type were in guides, ready to be loaded. The torpedo doors on the bow were open; they are now closed."

One of the Navy officers, a submariner, spoke. "So you're saying the Germans were preparing to fire both torpedoes at the passenger liner?"

"Without a doubt," Hazlett said. "Why else would they open both doors and flood the tubes?"

FORT SHERMAN LAGOON

L arry wiped sweat from his temple and pointed to the propeller lying on the floor of the machine shack. "Look, Sarge, how the wood is gouged."

The chief mechanic knelt near the hub of the ten-foot, two-blade propeller. He ran his fingers over the edges where the wood and the steel hub joined. "Yeah, I hear what you're saying. It's like the blades were rocking. I don't know how we're going to fix that." He pushed himself up with both hands, stood and shook his head. "We really need a new propeller."

Larry turned from his workbench, holding the end fitting of a strut. "A new prop has been on order for five weeks."

"I know. You'd think the suppliers would have priority for an aeroplane actually in the field over those sitting on the production line. They aren't even flyable, yet—why do they need propellers?"

Larry pursed his lips while trying to bend the corner of the fitting. "Not the way the quartermaster sergeant tells it. He says there's such a push on for aeroplanes for 'war preparation,' the shops are overwhelmed. He said the Curtiss plant has orders for more than six hundred R-6s, as well as half that for R-4s. And they're building another big plant in Buffalo." He placed the fitting on the bench. "What we going to do about control cable?"

The chief shook his head. "I don't know. We really need the seven strand. It has to be strong, but really flexible to bend around the pulleys. We can't just—"

"I can't use that stuff he sent over yesterday," Larry said. "It's too big in diameter and too stiff. How come those quartermaster guys don't get it—that this is an aeroplane, not a damned steam shovel?"

The chief went to the door. "I'm on my way to talk to the Navy's supply officer at Cristóbal. Maybe he can help us out. I at least expect he knows the difference between a hoist and the aileron of an aeroplane."

•   •   •

Cog McCrorie thumbed toward the Bay as he crossed Will's room. "I saw that German submarine on the way over here this morning. It was parked at those piers over by Cristóbal. It sure is big," McCrorie stepped inside as Will closed the door behind him. "Biggest sub I ever saw. It's in all the papers. The U.S. Navy has taken it over—they're trying to learn all the Germans' tricks." McCrorie sat on the edge of the bunk. "I thought I'd come over and bring you the latest news."

Will smiled. "Thanks. It sure seems peculiar, not to be out there—wait! Yesterday, a guy shows up here around ten. Johnston by name. He says, 'I'm your defense lawyer.' Young guy, yellow hair—but sharp."

McCrorie nodded. "A lieutenant from Army Reserves, I'll bet."

Will chuckled. "You named it. How'd you figure that?"

"Probably hasn't been out of law school very long. He'll be good at knowing the stuff a fresh lawyer needs to know for the bar exam. You told him about me?"

"Yeah. He seemed awed, said he looked forward to working with a 'distinguished' member of Congress."

"I'm sure we'll do fine." McCrorie leaned forward and yanked a rolled newspaper from the rear pocket of his trousers. "Meantime, the sub's captain, Steiner, claims the submarine was in the channel 'by accident.' He denies any intent to torpedo the liner. But a U.S. Navy lieutenant who inspected the German sub is quoted as saying the setup inside the sub 'proves' it was about to attack."

McCrorie unrolled the paper and said, "Listen to this." He placed a finger under the headline 'Official Cable from Government of Germany,' and read aloud, "'Regarding the accusation by Secretary of

State Lansing on 30 March, 1917: As far as I am aware, no breach of neutrality of any kind has been committed by a vessel of the Imperial German Navy. Germany never had the slightest intention of attacking the United States of America, nor any attack upon a passenger liner of the La Trasatlántica line, nor any attack upon the Locks of the Panama Canal.

"'Our information is that the crew of the German submarine sought refuge from dangerous waves off the coast of Panama and entered the Panama estuary for safety. Most unfortunately, the vessel became the object of an attack by a United States military aeroplane. Attempting to avoid the attack, Kapitän G. Steiner drove his vessel onto shoals.

"'Detaining the submarine and its crew, as has occurred, violates accepted law and freedom of nautical passage. The German government demands release of the crew and vessel for unhindered return to the German nation.'"

Will, although facing McCrorie attentively, found himself thinking again about Adrienne on the Alfonso XIV—might she have been thinking about him? And now that she was on her way to the United States, where was she at this moment?

McCrorie continued reading: "'If the American nation considers this a cause for which to declare war against the German nation, with which it has lived in peace for more than one hundred years; if this action warrants an increase in bloodshed, Germany shall not have to bear any burden of responsibility for it. –Signed, Johann Heinrich von Bernstorff, German ambassador, in absentia.'"

"In absentia?" Will said, "What's that about?"

"The United States broke diplomatic relations with Germany back in February."

"Oh, yeah, now I remember." Will shook his head. "Hard to believe they can lie so easily."

McCrorie laughed. "It's called diplomacy, Will."

FT. SHERMAN QUARTERS

"I came as soon as a morning boat was available," Cog McCrorie said, breathing heavily. "It's official—Congress voted a declaration of war—at three o'clock this morning!"

Will, in his bathrobe, said, "I just finished shaving." He wiped his jaw with a towel. "So this means—"

"This means everything is scrambled. Before I left the hotel, the desk told me Western Union has cables for me—probably notifications of the House vote. On the boat over here the skipper said Harbor Operations announced that the Canal will close tonight, April 6, at sunset. Cristóbal and Balboa ports will close to navigation and all lights will be put out. No vessels will be allowed passage through the Canal until after sunrise—from now on."

Will shoved the towel into his laundry bag. "So the United States is at full-scale war with Germany, now?"

"Apparently. The President will sign the bill today."

"I woke early, wondering what was going on," Will said, slipping his arm into his uniform shirt. "There was a lot of noise and hubbub at the barracks down the row—I'll bet they were alerting the troops."

"I saw infantry—with rifles—hurrying toward the parade ground as I walked over here."

A knock sounded, and Will, his shirt still unbuttoned, went to the door and opened it. An Army lieutenant in uniform entered. "Hello, Will," he said. "Sorry to roust you, but I—oh." He noticed the civilian standing near Will's desk. He faced him and extended his hand. "I'm Charlie Johnston, Will's attorney. And you are—?"

"Glad to meet you," McCrorie said, introducing himself and

shaking hands. "I'm Will's civilian defense, although I doubt he'll be needing us, now."

"That's what I came to tell you," Johnston said to Will. "My commander says it's unlikely the court-martial will be called. War with Germany means the prosecutor will be very reluctant to charge you with crashing a German submarine and preventing a torpedoing. I think your confinement will be lifted."

Will turned to McCrorie. "You think that's right?"

McCrorie nodded. "I think Johnston's right. We'll have to wait and see, but yeah, most likely, the charges will be dropped—quietly, I suppose. I'd be surprised if they don't simply vanish."

•   •   •

At eleven o'clock on Saturday, April 7, five reporters gathered in a corner of the spacious lobby of Hotel Washington, in Colón. Their presence attracted onlookers, who stood near the grand marble staircase, gawking.

In suit and tie, Cog addressed the reporters. "I am U.S. Representative Kellogg McCrorie. I was returning from a fact-finding trip to Portugal when the ship I was on, the Alfonso XIV, was attacked by a German submarine with the intent of torpedoing it. This attack might have blocked or seriously hampered the operations of the Panama Canal.

"My ship was entering the lower level of the Gatun Locks when an Army floatplane swooped low and landed on the water between my ship and the submarine. The aeroplane aimed at the submarine, causing a huge fountain of spray. It then crashed into the tower of the submarine, which injured the submarine's captain.

"The heroic actions of the Army pilot of that aeroplane saved the lives of everyone on the Alfonso XIV by causing the submarine to become grounded before it could launch its torpedoes.

"As you all now know, war has been declared and the Army has announced that armed guards will now board all vessels transiting the Canal to assure its safety and integrity. Also, that the captain and crew of the German submarine are being detained as the first prisoners of war in this great struggle for democracy. And finally, that Lieutenant Will Marra is no longer confined to his quarters at Fort Sherman.

"I want you to meet the heroic pilot of that Army aeroplane, but first I must thank him." Cog turned toward Will, who stood behind him. "Thanks, Lieutenant, for saving my life—and 1,375 other passengers." McCrorie faced the reporters and gestured toward Will. "Lieutenant Will Marra. Lieutenant?"

Murmurs arose from the onlookers, followed by their brief applause. A reporter said to Will, "How did you know the U-boat was going to attack the liner?"

"I identified the U-boat as a hostile submarine. It had no deck guns. Thus its only possible purpose for following the passenger liner into the Gatun Locks was to torpedo it, blocking the Lock."

A reporter with a heavy mustache waved his hand. "Dan Carbonif, Reuters Limited. The date of your attack," he said to Will, "was March 29, right?"

"I think that's right—it was the Thursday recon flight."

"That's more than a week ago," Carbonif said, "and war with Germany had not been declared. Did your action not exceed your bounds of duty by attacking and colliding with a vessel of a foreign nation during peacetime?"

Murmurs arose from the onlookers. One of the other reporters spoke loudly. "That's not the issue."

Will smiled at the reporters. "I've been assigned the duty of aerial reconnaissance for the Coastal Artillery Defense Force for several months now. My aeroplane, the Curtiss R-9, is unarmed—it has no guns, it carries no bombs. There was no other means available to me for stopping the attack of this U-boat."

Questions and answers continued for another ten minutes. At that point, Cog stepped ahead of Marra and addressed the reporters.

"Thanks—thanks to all of you for coming . . ."

The onlookers applauded. The reporters turned to leave. McCrorie held up his hand. "There's one thing the lieutenant didn't tell you."

The reporters halted.

McCrorie continued. "He didn't know it when he attacked the U-boat, but there was a young refugee aboard that passenger liner Alfonso XIV—a Belgian lady by the name of Adrienne Boch—someone very special to the Lieutenant." He turned toward Will. "That's true, isn't it, Will?"

Will grinned, but didn't speak. After a few seconds he nodded, still grinning broadly.

Four of the reporters laughed and turned to leave. The fifth reporter said, "Wait just a minute, okay?" The reporter fumbled in the pockets of his trousers and withdrew a folded piece of newsprint. He gestured with the paper. "You said this lady by the name of Boch was a refugee, right?"

McCrorie glanced at Will, who nodded. "Right," McCrorie said.

The reporter unfolded the newsprint and ran his finger down its list. "This is newsprint of refugees listed on the Alfonso XIV's manifest. It says here," he said, pointing, "'Jean Charles Boch, wife Dominique Boch, and daughter, Adrienne Boch.'" He looked at Will. "That's Miss Adrienne Boch's parents, right?"

Will's eyes widened. "I-I didn't—may I see your paper?"

The reporter handed the paper to Will.

McCrorie craned his neck to see the listing. "There it is!" he said, pointing.

Will swallowed, his Adam's apple wobbling. "I didn't know. I'm surprised. This means her family not only escaped the German invasion of Belgium, they are with Adrienne. The family is on their way to the United States. That's wonderful!"

McCrorie said to the reporter, "Thanks, friend, for bringing that to the Lieutenant's attention. I think you've done him a great favor."

The reporter nodded and with the others headed toward the exit.

•   •   •

The following Tuesday, Will received this cable:

ARRIVED SATURDAY SAN FRANCISCO (STOP)
FAMILY SAFE THANKS MY HERO (STOP)
AWAITING KISS (STOP) ADRIENNE

•   •   •

After visiting his mother on the outskirts of Paraíso, Bruno Ackermann journeyed the few miles across the Canal to Culebra.

He climbed the hill toward the three-story framed building, sweating generously in the June heat. This, and the other smaller buildings of the penitentiary, was surrounded by a twelve-foot-high wire fence braced by a multitude of wood poles painted white.

Bruno entered through the guarded gate and checked in at the District of Emperador No. 2's headquarters. After explaining his mission, he was assigned to one of the smartly-uniformed, brown-skinned guards in canvas puttees and British-style pith helmets.

The guard searched Bruno to assure he carried no weapons.

"What is this?" the guard said in Spanish, frowning and pulling a folded newspaper from Bruno's rear pocket.

"A German newspaper. My mother, a German, subscribes. It comes by ship, so it is always out of date. You read German?"

The guard narrowed his eyes and shook his head.

"I brought it for my young friend. He does not read Spanish."

The guard said, "That is permitted, I will give it to him."

"This way," the guard said as he turned and marched down the hallway carrying the folded newspaper. Bruno followed him into a small alcove.

"Sit here," the guard said, indicating a stool. He withdrew.

A few minutes after Bruno sat on the wooden stool, a different guard brought Gregor Steiner to the other side of an enclosure made of wire lattice. The guard stood at attention behind him.

Gregor sat on a wooden chair, facing Bruno, and smiled.

Bruno noted he was pale and his uniform was highly wrinkled.

"Hello," Gregor said in German, "it is good to see you." He gestured at the newspaper on his lap. "Thanks for bringing the news."

"Are they treating you well? Is the food tolerable?"

Gregor shrugged. "I am not starving. We keep to our discipline."

Bruno pointed to the newspaper. "I brought that because it is about the incident in the channel."

"Oh." Gregor unfolded the paper and scanned its headlines. He laughed. "They describe me as a victim of fate. How odd." He smoothed the fold, scanned down and read rapidly.

Bruno smiled. "Are you allowed to exercise?"

"Wait—wait," Gregor said, his voice rising. "This list—oh my God!"

"What?"

Gregor's eyes went wider. "Here on this list—the manifest! It cannot be!" He tossed the newspaper to the floor, and covered his face with both hands.

"I do not understand," Bruno said. "What is wrong?"

Gregor lowered his hands. Overcome, he stared at Bruno. "Under 'B.' It must be mistaken! The list of passengers on that vessel—it includes Uncle Jean, Aunt Dominique, and my dearest cousin, Adrienne."

Bruno could only watch as Gregor's body curled, his head bent to his chest, and he convulsed. His feet angled painfully under the chair.

The guard behind Gregor stared at the prisoner without understanding. After a few moments, he grasped Gregor's shoulder and demanded that he stand.

Gregor did not respond, but repeated, "No, no, it cannot be."

The guard who had led Bruno to the enclosure appeared and motioned to Bruno to leave. Reluctantly, Bruno rose from the stool and followed the guard.

As he left, Bruno glimpsed Gregor, still convulsing.

FT. SHERMAN LAGOON

Will Marra stood on the portside float next to the fuselage of the damaged Curtiss R-9. He was speaking to the floatplane crew, who were spread out in the shade cast by the machine shack.

Will squinted into the morning sun and said, "It won't mean anything to you guys, but I've been promoted to 1st Lieutenant."

The men yelled congratulations and applauded wildly.

Will held up his hand. "But that's not why I asked you here. Adjutant General McCain has cut new orders for us."

The men fell silent.

"Captain Henry H. Arnold has formed a new reconnaissance group for Panama Canal defense. It's called the 'Seventh Aero Squadron.' They're nearly ten times our size, about sixty strong. Right now, they're based at Empire. There's no airfield at Empire, but they don't need one—they haven't got any aeroplanes, yet."

The men laughed.

"Eventually, they'll move here, to Fort Sherman, replacing us. They'll be equipped with brand new R-4s and R-6s, maybe even some better aircraft."

With his left arm, Will patted the engine compartment of the R-9. "This bird—the bird with a crippled wing—is done flying. But it's been a terrific bird, able and willing—though not very powerful—thanks to the industry and ingenious care you guys, and M.S.E. Oakley, have consistently provided.

"Some of you will be reassigned to the Seventh Aero. You won't be surprised to learn that, despite my promotion, they haven't let me in on who, yet."

The men laughed again.

"There's a war on, so the remainder of you will go wherever the Signal Corps needs crackerjack mechanics and riggers—maybe France. Before you say hurrah, remember that there's shooting going on over there.

"In the meantime, all I want to say is 'thanks.' You men have been a marvel at keeping Oakley and me from kissing dirt—or worse, kissing Neptune."

Sergeant Oakley stood up. "Wait, sir. Didn't you say we all got orders? What about you?"

"As of the fourteenth of June, I'm sailing from Balboa aboard a Panama Railroad steamer back to the States, back to North Island at San Diego. They've decided in their infinite wisdom that I should teach kids who want to fly. Teach them what I know.

"What I know isn't all what it's cracked up to be, of course. But Uncle needs lots of pilots to win this war, so I'm willing." He paused and smiled. "And of course, there's a side benefit I can't disparage— Miss Adrienne Boch is just a few hundred miles north—at San Francisco."

The men laughed.

"Okay," Will said, stepping off the float to the ramp. "That's all."

END

ACKNOWLEDGMENTS

THANKS, as always, to Anya Carlson for her loving support and maintaining order in the research files for this project.

I'm grateful to Dwight R. Messimer, whose books kept my story grounded in reality.

Thanks also to the crew at JKS Communications who caught my errors and shaped the final book.

AUTHOR J.B. RIVARD

J.B. writes deeply-researched fiction and nonfiction. His writing bene-fits from a widely-varied working life, four years in the military, and a multiyear career on the technical staff of a U.S. National Laboratory. A graduate of The University of Florida, he lives in Mesa, Arizona.
www.illusionsofmagic.com